ARNOLD BENNETT'S UNCOLLECTED SHORT STORIES

1892-1932

From the Potteries to Penzance

Edited and with an Introduction by John Shapcott

www.arnoldbennettsociety.org.uk

To Martin Laux, the inspiration behind this collection.
His document searches and transcriptions were selflessly undertaken,making editing a pleasure.

The cover is a painting by Sally Richardson
from a railway poster of the 1930s -
Bennett's final story takes him to Penzance.

CHURNET VALLEY BOOKS
1 King Street, Leek, Staffordshire ST13 5NW 01538 399033

ISBN 9781904546740

Printed by Cromwell Press Group, Trowbridge, Wiltshire

CONTENTS

PART III LATE VICTORIAN YEARS

PART IV EDWARDIAN YEARS

PART V WAR-TIME

PART VI POST-WAR

INTRODUCTION

"I came to London at the age of twenty-one, with no definite ambition, and no immediate object save to escape from an intellectual and artistic environment which had long been excessively irksome to me" (p. 43). This is Arnold Bennett's mundane description in *The Truth About An Author* of his life-changing escape from the Potteries in March 1889. There is no hint of the successful journalistic and literary career that is to follow, no obvious precedent for the imminent flood of short stories with which he was to establish his literary credentials. Bennett came to London to continue the legal career chosen for him by his father, working as a shorthand clerk in the law offices of Le Brasseur and Oakley. There was perhaps a clue to Bennett's future in the brief and anonymous contributions to local papers, the *Staffordshire Daily Sentinel* and the *Staffordshire Knot*, although all thirteen of these articles dealt with parochial matters, ranging from a paragraph about the North Staffordshire Steam Tramways in April 1887 to the deterioration of footpaths in the "Knotty Notes" of February 1889. But for Bennett "provincial journalism, without meed in coin .... had already lost the charm of novelty, and I had been doing it in a perfunctory manner. I made no attempt to storm Fleet Street" (*The Truth*, p. 43).

For two and a half years Bennett worked diligently at the law office, soon earning £200 a year, whilst devoting much of his spare time to book collecting. It was at the urging of his artistic friends that he was persuaded to enter a competition in the weekly magazine *Tit-Bits* offering a twenty-guinea prize for the best parody of Grant Allen's popular novel *What's Bred in the Bone*. Bennett won and the appearance of his parody in *Tit-Bits* on 19th December 1891 represented the tentative beginning of his career as a writer. Between February 1892 and January 1893 Bennett wrote three short articles on legal matters for which *Tit-Bits* paid ten shillings each. Bennett's biographers pay scant attention to these minor pieces of just a few hundred words apiece, but more crucially fail to mention the appearance in print of his very first short story, pre-dating the legal articles, and which also appeared in *Tit-Bits*, on 20th February 1892. Re-printed for the first time in this collection, "He Needn't Have Troubled How He Looked" is a short story of some six hundred words introducing us to the Bennett of the romance of the everyday, the gap between desire and reality, the hopeful presentation of self and the failure to make an impact. There is an echo here of Bennett's recollection of the first childhood story to make an impact on him. "I was six or so when *The Ugly Duckling* aroused in me the melancholy of life, gave me to see the deep sadness which pervades all romance, beauty, and adventure" (*The Truth*, p. 13). Many of the short stories that were to follow also ask "And the girl?" and often with an undercurrent of "deep sadness".

Whatever its perceived literary merits, Bennett's first paid free-lance work as a London journalist was no small achievement. To put it in context, it is worth noting Peter Keating's observation that "Conrad, Woolf and Joyce all submitted work to, and had it turned down by *Tit-Bits*" (p. 38).

Its appearance in this volume is thanks to Anita Miller's *Arnold Bennett. An Annotated Bibliography 1887-1932* (1977) which is an invaluable detailed guide to locating the originals of the great majority of the stories re-printed here for the first time since their ephemeral appearance in the popular magazines of the day. There is, however, one notable exception, the beautifully crafted 1904 Christmas story "The Railway Station" published in the *Staffordshire Sentinel* and which Martin Laux discovered in the Hanley Library Archive.

Bennett's early magazine work appeared either anonymously or under a variety of signatures and female pseudonyms, such as "Cecile", "Barbara" and "Sarah Volatile". I have indicated these signatures in the Notes to the stories. The validity and ascription of these is important for the future quality of Bennett research and criticism since there exists a longstanding carelessness in ascribing and assessing his early work, dating back to Georges Lafourcade's 1939 book *Arnold Bennett: A Study*. Lafourcade created a non-existent "Gwendoline" as one of Bennett's signatures, wrongly ascribed various contributions and clearly failed to read and examine the stories themselves. Unfortunately the previous lack of ready access to Bennett's early work in Victorian periodicals appears to have encouraged the majority of later biographers and critics to follow the route mapped by Lafourcade's misdirections. Whilst it would be instructive from the viewpoint of literary, social and cultural criticism to have most of Bennett's journalistic work in published collections - his book reviews and theatre criticism of the 1890s are particularly astute and proleptically accurate - the publication of the uncollected stories is an important first step in making available the full range of the work in this genre of one of Britain's major literary figures.

It would be premature to claim that this collection is the definitive complete uncollected short stories; "The Railway Station" came to light only recently and the British publication of "The White Feather" was first identified in May 2009. It is a reasonable assumption, therefore, that other stories remain to be discovered. I have made an editorial decision on the exclusion of borderline items such as Bennett's prize-winning parody "What's Bred in the Bone" and such entries as "Restaurant Spooks" and "How Percy Goes to the Office" which read more as advice or opinion columns, cleverly camouflaged as stories. All these omissions are listed along with publication details in the "Notes on the Text".

Bennett's second free-lance published story "The Artist's Model" may be read both for its inherent pleasure and for the opportunity offered to refute the misinformation previously accorded it. Reginald Pound's generally sympathetic 1952 study, *Arnold Bennett*, maligns the tale as "tailored for the trade, down to the old *rat-tat* cliché for the postman's knock. It showed deft appreciation of the importance of money and luxury as fiction ingredients appealing to readers not intimately connected with either. A certain facility is obvious and the story reads much like the work of an amateur ..." (p. 84) whereas, in fact, there is no postman and precious little luxury. Dudley Barker's 1966 *Writer By Trade: A View of Arnold Bennett* compounded the error and, seemingly without reading the story, condescendingly dismissed it as having "no artistic value": "He wrote a short story about an artist's model (all that reading in French fiction!), and *Tit-Bits* gave him a guinea for it" (p. 57). Little wonder then that there has been no enthusiasm to read the original and examine its merits. These are largely formulaic but they do unveil a portrait of a writer who, from the outset of his professional career, understands and adheres to the principles of magazine short story construction, later codified in his 1903 guide *How to Become an Author*:

> .... however slight a plot is, it must have a central idea; it must have a "point"; it must raise an issue and settle that issue; the interest of the reader having been excited must be fully satisfied. In other words, the plot must be complete; it cannot be a mere slice cut from something longer.... the [writer] should err on the side of melodrama and ingenuity, rather than on the side of quietude and simplicity. What he wants is a tale "that tells itself", a striking situation, a novel climax.... the story may or may not relate to love; but it must not end unhappily - this is essential. (pp. 96-97)

Whilst "The Artist's Model" can undoubtedly be defined in the craft terms Bennett outlines it also stands on the threshold of the debate between aestheticism, art for art's sake, and the needs of commercialism. Bennett's early stories about ambitious artists—"Rejected", "My First Book"—tap into a popular reading public's demand for Romantic images of the unworldly artists depicted in, for instance, George du Maurier's *Trilby* (1894) and Puccini's *La Bohème* (1896). Read in this context Bennett's story becomes an early contribution to an important literary debate. It is intriguing to reflect that it may also have played its own small part in subconsciously influencing a young Virginia Woolf who was writing at the time for the Stephen family's newsletter: "The *Hyde Park Gate News* [1891-1895].... is a mixture, like the children's favourite paper *Tit-Bits*, of announcements, stories and a correspondence column" (Lee, p. 108).

Several of Bennett's stories, beginning with "The Heavenly Twins On The Revolt Of The Daughters", refer to Sarah Grand's 1893 novel *The Heavenly Twins*. When it first appeared it was seen by many as dangerous and perverting with its uninhibited portrayal of venereal diseases and its presentation of a cross-dressing heroine determined to escape the constraints of her sex. Bennett saw it as making "a fearful breach in the walls of the Home.... The book was eagerly and gratefully accepted by women, who perceived in it not only the bold utterance of their timid aspirations, but also a distant hope of release from the somewhat Ottoman codes of men" (*Fame and Fiction*, p. 73). Bennett criticised its literary stylistics whilst praising its polemic. It is fascinating, then, to read the numerous intertextual references to Grand in Bennett's Victorian stories, printed in mass circulation periodicals and aimed, as in the case of *Woman*, at a predominantly female readership. Stories such as "The Heavenly Twins On The Revolt Of The Daughters", "Five O'Clock at the Heroines' Club" and the "Strange Stories of the Occult", are an under-researched part of the late-Victorian debate around deep-seated patriarchal agendas. It is worth noting that Bennett's intertextual references serve to smuggle this debate into the heart of a largely traditional and market-driven format: "Where twentieth-century women are induced to go to heroic lengths (and expense) to meet a physical ideal disseminated by clothing manufacturers and fiction magazines, these Victorian women are induced to go to heroic lengths to keep their minds 'pure'" (Ermarth, p. 209).

Andrea L. Broomfield's essay "Eliza Lynn Linton, Sarah Grand and the Spectacle of the Victorian Woman Question: Catch Phrases, Buzz Words and Sound Bites" provides the background enabling us to position Bennett's early stories within a general context of periodicals as covert educators, albeit with significant surrounding advertisements and articles antithetical to the Women's Rights movement. Although the periodicals to which Bennett contributed adopted a relatively apolitical approach to divisive socio-political topics, Broomfield provides for a reappraisal of his cultural poetics and politics in the 1890s, that would place him alongside those "Victorian women's rights activists [who] were realizing many of their objectives with help from periodicals that disseminated their ideas" (p. 269).

Bennett's fictional New Women, however, tread a very careful path between the traditional values of domestic femininity and public activism aimed at appropriating masculine privileges. Their tentative appearance in "Five O'Clock at the Heroines' Club" in *Woman*, soon after Bennett became Assistant Editor, avoids controversy by distancing them from contemporary realities, and channelling their energies into such non-incendiary subjects as the current game laws, and their risqué behaviour into seeing "who could smoke a cigarette quickest". Not only do they appear as fictional characters—Jane Eyre, for example—but the novels they appear in have been safely absorbed into the cultural mainstream. Bennett's Heroines' Club is also organisationally neutered by the obfuscation of a procedural dispute over gender and membership, concluding with sub-committees and delay.

In real time, the feminist club movement was actively pursuing a far more radical and socially disruptive progressive programme than anything envisioned at the Heroines' Club. For example, the Pioneer Club's badge was an axe, signalling a blow against gender prejudice. By way of contrast, Bennett's *Woman*'s mast-head motto was "Forward!

But Not Too Fast", a sentiment incompatible with the more radical socio-cultural and political challenges to the hegemony of the late-Victorian patriarchal narrative. Reflecting on his editorial days at *Woman* Bennett conceded that the Board was

> .... so determined to offend the feelings of nobody that our columns almost never indicated in what direction progress ought to be made. No downright opinion upon any controversial topic affecting the relations of the sexes was ever expressed.... Nevertheless *Woman* did mysteriously acquire a reputation for being in the van of progressive movements, though nobody who now examined its files could possibly conceive why.
>
> (*Savour*, pp. 143-144)

Certainly Bennett's version of the New Woman in "Fenella: A Manx Idyll" was unlikely to cause flutters of nervous apprehension in her readers. She is something of a male fantasy figure able to combine an outdoor life of physical prowess with an intellectual grasp of current literary debates. In any case, Bennett quarantines her threat to gender stability by locating her safely offshore in the Isle of Man and making it clear that for all her brave ventures into the masculine world of the cruel sea she remains a safely and happily domesticated married woman. There is an interesting, if unconscious, parallel here with the line taken by Grand, much admired by Bennett who interviewed her at length for *Woman* (2nd May 1894). Ann Heilmann describes this policy as

> promoting the New Woman as a feminine superstar, whilst advising aspiring feminists to refine their seduction skills, Grand constructed femininity at one and the same time as an innate quality *and* a performative act.... Her articles.... were aimed at seducing female middle-class readers to feminist ideas (however diluted), while offering an object lesson to feminists on how to best market the cause. (p. 19)

Published two months prior to "Fenella", Bennett's "An Academy Work" in the *Sun* constructed another type of heroine who fits Grand's blueprint. Kitty Cartwright is a New Woman devoted to her art—again, at a safe overseas distance—who chooses to retain her independence and to pursue her professional career at the expense of a financially rewarding marriage with a cotton magnate who has succumbed to her feminine "seductive skills". The resourceful, spirited and independently-minded heroine who eventually opts for domestic married bliss and her counterpart who resists conventional endings for as long as possible are two classic Bennett types encountered in these late-Victorian stories. Their continuing centrality in the study of femininity in Bennett's fiction can be gauged by the fact that they are still debating many of the old New Woman arguments in the binary persona of Gracie Savott and Violet Powler in his final novel, *Imperial Palace*, published in 1930.

It was one thing to parody the New Woman safely confined within her Club or to depict her as a muscular avatar of Grace Darling with literary interests policed by marriage, but something altogether more risqué to picture the world of the dandified male aesthete and to hint at an emergent homosexual identity. Yet Bennett's story "The Repentance of Ronald Primula" is a subtle outing of fictional/factual characters within the context of a seemingly light-hearted and playful narrative that neatly skips between issues of aestheticism and decadent sexual ambience. It takes on a noteworthy prescience by appearing in a popular women's paper in January 1895 at the start of a year that was to witness the trial and subsequent disgrace of Oscar Wilde. It was also the year that signalled Bennett's entry into the cultural avant-garde with the publication in July of his short story "A Letter Home" in John Lane's experimental and literary quarterly *The Yellow Book*, alongside a story by Henry James.

"The Repentance of Ronald Primula" revolves around a diary carelessly left on a park bench by Primula, and picked up by the story's journalist narrator. Readers were alerted early to a possible coded dandified text when Bennett describes the diary as "daintily written, with wide margins, on hand-made paper". But it is the diary's contents that link Primula with Wilde, and in such a manner as to suggest a level of silenced homosexual representation that may have eluded many of *Woman*'s contemporary readers but which, in the light of our knowledge of Wilde's trial and public humiliation, gives it both piquancy and literary-historical interest. The narcissistically inclined—"The Moorish lamp.... threw a wan, seaweed-coloured light on my face and the seductive page of the *Figaro*, and altogether I was the centre of a gracious and pleasing picture"—and epigrammatically inventive—"[Novels] are like income-tax notices, they make excellent pipe-lights"—representation of Primula makes him Wilde's fictional doppelganger. Likewise, his friend Lord Cecil Dover, or Cessy, is a lightly disguised version of Lord Alfred Douglas. The physical closeness of their relationship is apparent from Primula's remarking, "I pictured you asleep, one pale hand outside the coverlet and your mouth open". Lord Cecil alerts Primula to the impending danger of public exposure with the publication of a novel, *The Cream Chrysanthemum*, by the punningly named Willie Rash.

Rash's real-life counterpart was Robert Hichens (1864-1950), best remembered for his sub-Wildean novel *The Green Carnation*, published in September 1894, and of which Bennett would have been aware. Based on notes made by Hichens during a Nile cruise with E.F. Benson, Reggie Turner, Frank Lawson, and in the company of Lord Douglas, the fictional creations of Lord Reggie and Mr. Amarinth bear an obvious resemblance to Douglas and Wilde. In the novel Amarinth/Wilde is the mentor and controller of Reggie/Douglas as they pursue a life devoted to elevating triviality and frivolity into an epigrammatic celebrity life-style. In Bennett's story, publication of *The Cream Chrysanthemum* prompts Primula to retire gracefully from the London literary scene, whereas for Wilde *The Green Carnation* added to the ground swell of public disfavour that he was encountering in early 1895. It did not help matters that Hichens was a known homosexual and that his literary representations might therefore be accorded a degree of authenticity.

If *The Cream Chrysanthemum* was not itself a clear enough clue to the identities behind the masks of Primula and Dover, Bennett interjects a number of other clues pointing to Wilde and the various cultural avant-garde currents swirling around the world of *The Yellow Book*, the New Woman, male aesthetics, dandies, and decadence. Primula declares that his "successive ideals were false ideals .... They were like a woman with golden hair and big feet", following closely in the footsteps of George Egerton's lampooning of the male aesthete in her story "A Lost Masterpiece", published in *The Yellow Book* in April 1894, where the narrator exclaims "Blame her, woman of the great feet and dominating gait" (p. 196). The ambiguities of sexual identification and desire explored in such *Yellow Book* stories as Victoria Cross's cross-dressing tale "Theodora: A Fragment" (January 1895) are echoed in Primula's conjecturing whether the heroine of Rash's novel is "masculine, or new, or neuter, or only feminine?" Perhaps the most uncanny Wildean moment in Bennett's story occurs when Primula's female working-class cook appropriates "Bunburying" a mere two weeks before the opening of Wilde's *The Importance of Being Earnest*: "Whenever she wanted a holiday she would say that her sister was down with indigestion of the lungs, or her niece was suffering from ulcers. Always one or the other. Of course it was merely an excuse." Whilst I am sensitive to the danger of Bennett's story sinking under a weight of critical exegesis it surely needs to be rehabilitated for its contribution to the jigsaw picturing the cultural politics of the *fin-de-siècle* and, in particular to the commentary surrounding Wilde's 1895 *annus horribilis*.

Like Wilde, Bennett was an ardent Francophile, frequently

looking to France as a source of literary inspiration. He was fortunate in his early choice of lodgings, moving to Chelsea in 1891 to stay with Frederick Marriott's artistically inclined family. Mrs Marriott was fluent in French and helped Bennett improve his French conversation, whilst his rapidly increasing skill in reading French novels in the vernacular was assisted by his taking a daily French newspaper. From his earliest journalistic days Bennett was reviewing and encouraging the reading of French novels in translation. It is, perhaps, not altogether surprising then to find that one of his earliest stories is his own translation of a fantasy by Remy de Gourmont, "The Silken Serpent".

De Gourmont's original story, "Mains de reine", appeared in the volume *D'un pays lointain* in 1898. It was the seventh story in "Livre I—Miracles", the first part of a three-part collection. All the thirty-two stories were very short and were previously published in the French daily newspaper *Le Journal* between 1892 and 1894. Bennett certainly found "Mains de reine" in this newspaper where it appeared on Wednesday 14th February 1894, a mere fifteen days before his translated version in *Woman*. The translation is certainly a very creditable performance, maintaining the sense and rhythm of Gourmont's style. Whilst not strictly an original story, its appearance in this collection is important not only as evidence of Bennett's aesthetic credentials linked to a sophisticated cosmopolitan literary poetics, but also as an early example of his speed of composition once imbued with an idea.[1]

Bennett wrote two other stories in genres to which he never subsequently returned. The first of these was a fairytale for adults, "The Adamless Eden. A New Fairy Tale", published in *Woman* in October 1895. It opens promisingly enough with the concept of a successfully functioning all-female utopia, which he then, however, disappointingly fails to develop. Yet

1. Bennett's only other French translation appears to be "Little Popow", published a month later in *Woman* (21st March 1894). This story by George D'Esparbés is an ven darker tale, in which a father throws his son to a pack of wolves in order to e his own life.

the notion of man as the disruptive serpent had the potential to tempt Bennett into areas of sexual politics later explored in Charlotte Perkins Gilman's 1915 novel *Herland*. Bennett, however, appears to have stuck rigidly to his own precepts—reviewing a collection of contemporary fairytales, he wrote that they "are too ingenious, too clever, too complicated", further remarking that "[w]it .... is utterly out of place in a fairy tale" (*Woman*, 22nd December 1897, page 9). These are precisely the qualities that "The Adamless Eden"'s opening premise demanded, and lacking them it has to be considered a failed literary experiment.

Bennett's sole venture into writing for children was his 1898 Christmas story, "The Great Fire at Santa Claus' House". He confessed himself to be rather pleased with the result.

> I also wrote a Children's story for Xmas Number of *Woman*. It came to me all of a sudden, & I (quite literally) jammed it down as quick as I could shift the pen. Regarded not only from the popular but from the artistic standpoint, I think this a very good tale.... Tertia [Bennett's sister] was enthusiastic about it, & she knows a thing or two. (*Letters II*, p. 116)

He would also have had a good reason to be pleased with the ten lavish illustrations, including a near full-page depiction of the fire-crew rescuing Santa Claus from the attic. Bennett freely admits to the speed and ease of composition, a facility to write to order that would never desert him. Today, the story is noteworthy as a child-orientated example of the plethora of fire rescue narratives aimed at an adult audience in the late 1890s. Their popularity can be attested to by the frequency with which they occur in song, on stage, as part of magic lantern slide shows and, increasingly important, on film from 1894 onwards. Indeed, the first issue of the *Strand* magazine in 1891 featured a fire rescue story. Bennett the magazine editor clearly recognised the demands of the market.

Also very much an integral part of the late-Victorian

cultural scene was the interest in the occult and the paranormal, as illustrated by such works as *Dr Jekyll and Mr Hyde* (1886), *The Picture of Dorian Gray* (1891) and *Trilby* (1894). George Bernard Shaw captured the pervasiveness of the spirit of the occult zeitgeist in his Preface to *Heartbreak House*, describing those who were " .... superstitious, and addicted to table rapping, materialization séances, clairvoyance, palmistry, crystal-gazing and the like.... it may be doubted whether ever in the history of the world did sooth-sayers, astrologers, and unregistered therapeutic specialists of all sorts flourish as they did during the half-century [before World War I]" (p. xiv). It was to this level of public demand for occult sensationalist stories that Bennett the pragmatic editor responded:

> But happening to mention to my Editor that I thought 'Occult' stories would go down well just now, & that I had a lot of material for them in hand, I was a little surprised to see him jump at the suggestion, & offer to buy the serial rights of eight stories at once. So, deeming eight stories sold in advance to be better than a novel perhaps on my hands, I have shelved [A Man From The North] for a time, & am to be seen daily reading a vast tome *Mystères des Sciences Occultes*. I tremble to consider the bad art which will be compressed into those stories! (*Letters II*, pages 12-13)

Bennett's concluding self-deprecating remark is somewhat at odds with his admitted background reading and serves to disguise the considerable amount of research that went into his "Strange Stories of the Occult". Certainly he would have been aware of the debates emanating from the Society for Psychical Research, founded in 1882, and his own stories may be re-evaluated in the light of their pioneering role in popularising the Society's publications on psychical phenomena. They also merit attention as the forerunners to Bennett's novels *The Ghost* (1907) and *The Glimpse* (1909) and their echoes at the end of his literary career, with the short story "Dream" in *The Night Visitor and Other Stories* (1931) and the unfinished novel *Dream of Destiny* (1932), demonstrating a continued interest in psychic phenomena and a later reading of Einstein and chronological aberrations. George M. Johnson's recent study *Dynamic Psychology in Modernist British Fiction* (2006) challenges Virginia Woolf's identification of psychological realism as the dividing point between modernists and the Edwardians and the late-Victorians, and in the process directs a critical light towards the important role of dynamic psychology in Bennett's fiction.

Bennett's "Strange Stories of the Occult" explore, albeit at a popular and relatively superficial level, the psychological interaction between apparition and human, raising the possibility of the survival of personality beyond death. This is central to the story line of a crystal-gazing induced vision in "The Phantasm of My Grandmother", although interestingly the narrative extends to issues surrounding the New Woman. The latter concern is also embedded in the feminised text "Dr Anna Jekyll and Miss Hyde" where Miss Hyde is seen with a "smoke wreath uncurling from her lips". The heroine-narrator's split personality is mirrored and negated by the magazine's surrounding contents. Alongside psychic visions of emancipated women we find columns with hints on home-dressmaking in the French style and articles directing readers to sources of more socially acceptable oral satisfaction: "After all, eating innocuous caramels is a preferable habit for a woman to that of opium or tobacco smoking" (*Woman*, 27th March 1895, p. 14). Such a juxtaposition of advanced and traditional notions of behaviour, many of the latter antithetical to female emancipation, suggests a number of qualifications when interpreting the contemporary impact of Bennett's introduction of a feminist dimension in the "Strange Stories of the Occult" onto the pages of *Woman*. The commercial packaging and consumption of the New Woman phenomenon in Bennett's 1890 stories is a part of the dynamics of late-

Victorian journalism deserving further investigation.

Whilst patriarchal domestic authority might feel threatened by the New Woman, the wider political economy faced a potentially greater threat from anarchist groups. Although few in number, and mostly made up of foreign refugees, in the wake of the judicially rigged execution of the Chicago Anarchists in 1890 they brought the possibility of Continental European acts of terrorism and political assassination to the streets of London. It is against this background that "Dragons of the Night", in which murder and kidnap are justified as necessary acts in the "war on society", asks to be read.

Bennett's plot deals with potentially explosive material, with danger and (ultimate) safety standing in erotic counterpoint. Despite the near certainty of the genre's carrying a guarantee of solution, it would be a mistake to underestimate its impact on the intended audience of the day. It would have made uncomfortable reading for the ladies of *Hearth and Home* to find the heart of London—"a tributary of Tottenham Court Road"—represented as a site of social anarchy, an urban heart of darkness on their doorstep. Indeed, Bennett had chosen his location well, for the French anarchist Martial Bourdin, who botched an attempt to blow up the Greenwich Observatory in 1894, was a well-known habitué of the Autonomie Club, an anarchist meeting place in Windmill Street, itself "a tributary of Tottenham Court Road". Bennett's formulaic mastery of amateur detective adventure fiction allows the readers of *Hearth and Home*—advertised in 1898 as "The Daintiest Ladies' Paper"—to enjoy the vicarious thrill of political unrest without fear of personal contamination. By way of additional reassurance of the story's sure progression from confusion to solution Bennett's hero bears the patriotic name of Paul English!

Shifting notions of patriotism underline the first of three uncollected stories published during World War I. Prior to its appearance in this volume "The White Feather" had been known only in its American version. In fact, the English version, published on 19th September 1914, pre-dated the American one by four weeks. Not only is it Bennett's first piece of First World War fiction but also it lays claim to being the first "White Feather" story of the conflict. Neglected by biographical and critical studies—with the exception of Kinley E. Roby's 1972 *A Writer at War*, which dismissed it as "a very slight story" (p. 56)—the tale's interesting features include an insight into the psychological pressures faced by young men fit for military service, an exposure of the hypocrisy of industrial war profiteers, the shallowness of an ill-informed public opinion and a politically validating intertextual link to H. G. Wells's early war journalism.

Bennett himself was perplexed about his conflicted feelings on volunteering: "When one sees young men idling in the lanes on Sunday, one thinks: 'Why are they not at war?' All one's pacific ideas have been rudely disturbed. One is becoming militant" (*Journal II*, p. 98). Written as early in hostilities as 10th August 1914, Bennett's distancing technique of substituting "one" for his usual confident journalistic "I" offers evidence of his discomfort. At the same time he was anxious to assure his friends that he was not a "Kiplingian patriot, but rather the reverse...." (*Letters II*, page 35). The jingoistic "Kiplingian" messages posted by the Imperial Blank Manufacturing Company were duplicated in the newspapers of the day. Laux's article "Damned if you do, damned if you don't" cites a message in *The Town Crier* (Deal, Kent) from September 1914, as a factual equivalent of Bennett's fictional "messages to 'shirkers'": "Oyez! Oyez! The White Feather Brigade. Ladies wanted to present to young men of Deal who have no-one dependent on them the Order of the White Feather for shirking their duty in not offering their services to uphold the Union Jack of Old England" (p. 28). The verisimilitude of Bennett's satire is afforded additional weight by the intertextual and metaphorical connotations of the Imperial Blank's director's name, Hawker Maffick. Maffick is a "bachelor of fifty-eight, [who] was perhaps (though Wells may disagree with me) the greatest of all the Mafficks". When an employee, Cedric Rollinson, with a young family to support, decides to enlist at considerable financial sacrifice, Maffick reneges on his promise of monetary support in favour of maintaining the firm's profitability. Bennett's choice of name, and reference to Wells, would have alerted readers to the disreputable nature of the family as war profiteers. In *The War That Will End War* (1914) Wells describes the Mafficks as "the most pampered and least public spirited of any stratum in the community" and, recalling the Boer War, the most likely to "maffick at the victories it has done its best to spoil" (p. 22).[2] Read against this background Bennett's story becomes a valuable, and early, addition to the fiction of World War I that examines the social tensions generated by military hostilities.

"The Life of Nash Nicklin" is a welcome addition to Bennett's Five Towns tales. It is an unsentimental history of a man who never recovers from being crossed in love and nurtures an enduring obsessive dislike for his rival. The story reads as a condensed gazetteer of familiar Bursley landmarks, with the added attraction of filling in a little of Denry Machin's (*The Card*) back-story. Traversing this nostalgic terrain might have given readers experiencing the first Christmas of the War a comforting, if misplaced, belief in the unshakeable solidity of provincial social structures. Prior to publication in *Pears' Christmas Annual* in December 1914 the magazine's editor wrote to Bennett's agent, J. B. Pinker, expressing his opinion that "The story is excellent & quite in the author's special vein" (quoted in *Letters I*, p. 223), and Bennett seconded his view: "All that I have to remark is that I think [it] is one of my best short stories...." (*Letters I*, p. 219). Bennett was perhaps

2. Bennett would have been familiar with Wells's articles before they were published in book form. The eleven articles appeared variously in *The Daily Chronicle, The Nation, The Daily News,* and *The War Illustrated* between 7th and 29th August 1914.

understandably annoyed with Henry James Whigham, editor of the American *Metropolitan Magazine*, when he was less than enthusiastic about the story's quality and, doubting its popular appeal, delayed its American publication until September 1915. When it did finally appear in America Bennett had the satisfaction of seeing his estimate of his story's worth critically confirmed. Roby is the only scholar to have examined the forgotten Five Towns tale and to give an account of its American reception.

> [Bennett] noted its publication and remarked that there was also a 'eulogistic' article about him in the same issue [of *Metropolitan*]. The article, signed J.E.H., was a piece of unqualified praise of Bennett's success in rendering life through the people and setting of the Five Towns. In the Five Towns, according to the writer, Bennett had "tasted the true salt and savor of life itself". Praise was also given to Bennett's ability to draw for his readers the lighter side of life, but the writer concluded that Bennett's greatest strength was his awareness of the drama of existence and that it was his powerful rendering of it which 'takes us by the throat and makes us gasp'. (p. 154)

Bennett would no doubt have appreciated the irony implied in this complete reversal of critical judgement appearing in the very magazine that declined to publish his story the previous year. Now readers again have the opportunity to assess the merits of "The Life of Nash Nicklin" for themselves.

"The Muscovy Ducks" is also a Five Towns tale, featuring as it does Stephen and Vera Cheswardine, whose youthful marital adventures are chronicled in two short stories in the collection *The Grim Smile of the Five Towns* (1907). English readers were never afforded the opportunity to follow the middle-aged and financially secure Cheswardines's move from the Potteries to the surrounding countryside, nor to frown at their increasingly acrimonious relationship, as the story never appeared outside America. Perhaps not altogether surprisingly, then, America has provided the only critical commentary on the story. Roby's insightful two-page appreciation of the story's biographical significance in *A Writer at War* remains the only mention of it. This is regrettable because, quite apart from any literary value, the story throws a biographical light upon the fractious nature of the relationship between Bennett and his wife Marguerite during the War years at their Essex home, Comarques. As Roby helpfully points out:

> Their house is clearly Comarques. Vera is Marguerite; Stephen is Bennett; Ingestre is Lockyer, Bennett's head gardener; and the Muscovy ducks are a pair from Marguerite's flock of ducks which she kept on the ornamental pond at Comarques.
>
> The story involves an episode in the continuing battle between Vera and Ingestre, who are described as enemies, a term that characterises the relationship that existed between Marguerite and Lockyer. (p. 61)

Bennett clearly bore a grudge against both Marguerite and her ducks: "I had already had them taken away from the lake because they kept me awake .... But we had to go through it all over again. One duck, then two, then several. And again I can't sleep because of them .... I give definite orders. Straight away, *without anyone saying a word to me,* my orders are cancelled" (*Letters IV*, p. 129). And all this domestic disharmony was being played out against a background of a war that was laying claim to much of Bennett's time and energy.

This fictional/factual domestic warfare clearly left Bennett with a damaging, and possibly distorted view of sexual/marital relationships, and we find him returning to this most distressing period of his married life in the plaintively titled *Our Women: Chapters on the Sex-Discord* (1920), his highly personal take on the relationship between the sexes. The seemingly trivial argument about who has authority over the gardener's duties becomes the battleground for the sexes in the book's final two chapters. *Our Women* asks to be read in the light of the war years at Comarques and their fictional representation in "The Muscovy Ducks". The story offers a revealing insight into that ambiguous part of Bennett's mind that, whilst able to depict an often insightful fictional analysis of female psychology, was never quite able to reach a similar level of understanding in real life.

Despite its essential Englishness, this collection's concluding post-war stories were all published in American magazines. When Eric Pinker succeeded his father as Bennett's agent in 1922 he was in tune with the increasing economic dominance of America and he considerably expanded the American side of the business, opening a second office in New York and moving into the West Coast film business. Both these developments are reflected in Bennett's 12th December 1930 letter to Pinker, mentioning "The Flight" and floating the possibility of filming his most recent novel. "I thought it very probable that 'The Flight' would sell easily. It seemed to me the sort of story which does sell easily.... And what about the talkie rights to Imperial Palace?"(*Letters I*, p. 409).

Published posthumously in 1932, "The Flight" was written in Lamorna, Cornwall, during Bennett's 1930 six-week summer holiday in an area he had never previously visited. The references to the rail journey from Paddington to St. Erth, Penzance harbour and the steamer to the Scilly Isles are all the result of personal observation. The reappearance of "The Flight", then, is an important addition to Bennett's work, representing one of his last completed pieces of fiction and alerting biographers to an under-researched period in his life where all the evidence suggests that he was undoubtedly happy in his newly discovered holiday retreat and continuing to make plans for future novels and film adaptations.[3] When not correcting the proofs of his last great novel, *Imperial Palace*, or writing and posting his review columns to the *Evening*

3. My research into this period is to be found in "Arnold Bennett's Cornwall". *The Flagstaff*, The Lamorne Society Magazine, Issue No 16 Winter 2005, pp. 12-14.

Standard, he was in a relaxed mood, meeting many of Lamorna and Newlyn's famous artists, such as Lamorna Birch and Dod Procter. This relaxed mood may be gauged from his taking on something of the disguise adopted by Jack Wren who, in the story, buys a second-hand suit of clothes and a cap enabling him to change from his "stylish to the shabby blue suit". Dorothy Cheston's memoir describes Bennett's shedding of his usual smart holiday apparel to "change into the somewhat slighter person in round and floppy tweed hat (the old travelling hat) who strolled down the Cove road, hands in pockets and cigarette dangling, brightly observing the odd variety of inhuman events on every side" (p. 152).

Bennett himself was in flight to Lamorna, happy and relaxed at an otherwise stressful time in his life both in his relationship with Dorothy Cheston and in his financial dealings. "The Flight" encapsulates these concerns, pondering a work-happiness balance—"I've worked awfully hard and I was beginning to suspect that the brilliant results might not bring a lot of happiness"—hinting at Dorothy Cheston's mercurial nature—"He loved her bitterness and sudden anger"—and suggesting a rare contentment— "A sensation of happiness permeated his being".

Published over a period of forty years, Bennett's stories are almost unique in encompassing the early great days of magazine short stories to their decline and near demise with the onset of the 1930s depression and changing habits of popular cultural consumption. His late-Victorian stories found a ready and eager market amongst a newly literate public liberated into mass print culture by the Education Act of 1870. Whether writing about hospitals, the New Woman, séances, artists, aesthetics, industry and business, anarchists, the fire-service, or crime, Bennett's stories provide the literary-historical background to the formation of opinion and attitudes of a growing middle-class readership. Readers of this collection may be surprised to find that not only did he take for granted a familiarity with the political and social debates surrounding the emergence of the New Woman, and the cultural discourse swirling around the aesthetics of *fin-de-siècle* productions, but also that he had no hesitation in introducing his readers to the work of Continental European writers in his own translations. This latter aspect of his work has never previously received any acknowledgement. The Great War may, in retrospect, be seen as bringing to an end what was for Bennett and his contemporaries a Golden Age of storytelling. American money now dominated the market and this is well attested to in Bennett's case by his agent concentrating his efforts to sell his work transatlantically. By the time "The Flight" was published the newer media of radio and cinema had captured much of the more lucrative market for mass entertainment. The thirties also saw a rapid expansion in large-scale cheap book production—something Bennett had long championed in his *Evening Standard* columns—concentrating on the novel and the anthology at the expense of the magazine short story. Bennett's story-writing career, then, provides a microcosmic study in the rise and decline of the genre. He was one of its great practitioners and the present availability of all his short stories, particularly the late-Victorian ones, makes possible a comprehensive critical re-appraisal of his contribution to the popular fiction of late nineteenth and early twentieth century fiction. In his practical guide *How to Become an Author* (1903) Bennett wrote: "It has been asserted that Englishmen cannot write artistic short stories, that the short story does not come naturally to the Anglo-Saxon. Whereas the truth is that nearly all the finest short-story writers in the world today are Englishmen...." (p. 94). Bennett takes his place as one of the finest of these and this collection is but one of the recent contributions to the critical re-evaluation of this most talented, prolific, entertaining and influential of England's writers.

John Shapcott

ACKNOWLEDGEMENTS

It was six years ago that Martin Laux first suggested to me that it might be possible to find, transcribe, edit and publish all of Arnold Bennett's uncollected short stories. I, and all Bennett enthusiasts and scholars, owe him an enormous debt of gratitude for undertaking a vast amount of diligent research and painstaking transcription. We met and talked many times over the six years and never once did Martin's enthusiasm for the task flag.

I would like to thank Peter Preston who generously agreed to read the first draft of my Introduction. Peter's invaluable suggestions have helped to make it read more accurately and smoothly.

I am indebted to George Simmers for locating the British version of "The White Feather" and for providing me with the publication details of H. G. Wells's wartime articles.

Xavier Legrand-Ferronnière went to a deal of trouble to find and send me a copy of the original French newspaper version of "The Silken Serpent"—Bennett himself would surely have approved of our academic *entente cordiale*.

It is high time I thanked my publisher, Bruce Richardson, whose friendliness, patience and support have always been much appreciated.

Finally, heart-felt thanks to Linda for all her help and loving encouragement throughout the project.

BIBLIOGRAPHY

Barker, Dudley. *Writer by Trade. A view of Arnold Bennett.* London: George Allen and Unwin, 1960.

Bennett, Arnold. *Fame and Fiction.* London: Grant Richards, 1901.

The Truth About an Author. London: Archibald Constable, 1903.

How to Become an Author. A Practical Guide. London: C. A. Pearson, 1903.

The Savour of Life. Essays in Gusto. London: Cassell, 1928.

Letters of Arnold Bennett. Vol. I. Ed. James Hepburn. London: Oxford U.P., 1966.

Letters of Arnold Bennett. Vol. II. Ed. James Hepburn. London: Oxford U.P., 1968.

Letters of Arnold Bennett. Vol. IV. Ed. James Hepburn. London: Oxford U.P., 1986.

Our Women. Chapters on the Sex-Discord. London: Cassell, 1920.

Bennett, Dorothy Cheston. *Arnold Bennett. A Portrait done at Home.* London: Jonathan Cape, 1935.

Broomfield, Andrea L. "Eliza Lyn Linton, Sarah Grand and the Spectacle of the Victorian Woman Question: Catch Phrases, Buzz Words and Sound Bites." *English Literature in Transition 1880-1920, Vol. 47 No.3.* Greensboro: University of North Carolina, 2004.

Egerton, George. "A Lost Masterpiece". *The Yellow Book.* Vol.I. London: John Lane, 1894.

Ermarth, Elizabeth Deeds. *The English Novel in History 1840-1895.* London: Routledge, 1997.

Grand, Sarah. *The Heavenly Twins.* London: William Heinemann, 1923.

Heilmann, Ann. *New Woman Strategies. Sarah Grand, Olive Schreiner, Mona Caird.* Manchester: Manchester U.P., 2004.

Johnson, George. M. *Dynamic Psychology in Modernist British Fiction.* Houndmills: Palgrave, 2006.

Lafourcade, George. *Arnold Bennett: A Study.* London: Frederick Muller, 1939.

Laux, Martin. "Damned if you do, damned if you don't." *The Arnold Bennett Society Newsletter, Vol. 4, No.8.* Ross-on-Wye: Arnold Bennett Society, 2008.

Pound, Reginald. *Arnold Bennett. A Biography.* London: William Heinemann, 1952.

Roby, Kinley. *A Writer at War. Arnold Bennett, 1914-1918.* Baton Rouge: Louisiana State U.P., 1972.

Shaw, Bernard. *Heartbreak House, Great Catherine, and Playlets of the War.* London: Constable, 1924.

Wells, H. G. *The War That Will End War.* London: Frank and Cecil Parker, 1914.

NOTE ON THE TEXT

All but two of the stories in this first edition of Bennett's uncollected short stories are transcribed from copies of originals held in the British Library. The two exceptions are "The Railway Station", in the Stoke-on-Trent City Archives, and "The White Feather", in the Bodleian Library.

The majority of the stories made their first, and, in the early days, only, appearance in British magazines. Where they also later appeared in American magazines, publication details are given in the "Notes" appended to the relevant story. In a minority of cases where they appeared only in American magazines the original American spellings have been retained. The original spelling and punctuation has been faithfully reproduced except where typographical or punctuation errors threatened the sense of the text. In the very few instances where it proved impossible to decipher document copies with absolute certainty square brackets [ ] are inserted to indicate an element of doubt.

Below is a chronological list of borderline items omitted from this collection—parodies, opinion pieces, translations—together with bibliographical details:

"The Advanced Woman". *The Sun*. 29th July 1893, page 1. Signed A.B.

"Restaurant Spooks". *The Sun*. 5th August 1893, page 1. Signed Enoch Arnold Bennett.

"Little Popow, from the French of Georges D'Esparbés". *Woman*. 21st March 1894, pages 14-15. Signed E.A.B.

"Varnish and Vanity at the R.A.". *Woman*. 9th May 1894, pages 3-4. Signed Sarah Volatile.

"Fiction of the Future. A Prophetic Fantasia". *Woman*. 1st May 1895, page 18. Signed Sarah Volatile.

"On Growing Old". *Pall Mall Gazette*. 29th June 1895, page 5. Unsigned.

"How Percy Goes to the Office. By his Sister". *Woman*. 23rd August 1899, pages 17-18. Signed Sarah Volatile.

The British Library holds the originals of all the above.

PEARS' CHRISTMAS ANNUAL, 1914

"In ten minutes the scissors had done their task"

Bennett's Illustrators

Bennett worked during a Golden Age of magazine story writing that also saw an increasing use of line drawings by a host of British illustrators. Frank Dadd (1851-1929), who illustrated "Nash Nicklin", was in the front rank of these artists. After working for the *Illustrated London News* from 1878 to 1884, he went on to complete some 100 drawings per year, illustrate many books, and exhibit at the Royal Academy.

PART I
BEGINNINGS

Arnold Bennett became Assistant Editor of *Woman* in late December 1893, and the Editor two years later.

HE NEEDN'T HAVE TROUBLED HOW HE LOOKED.[1]

He was suffering the worst of torments; that is, he was in the dentist's chair, with a horrid rubber apparatus between his teeth to keep his mouth open. He looked—well, you know what a perfect object one looks in a dentist's chair.

Just then she came in.

She was only seventeen—young enough to giggle excusably—and she was very pretty. She wore a grey gown, with hat to match; and from the tips of the ribbon bow on her turban to the toes of her patent-leather boots she was bewitching.

She was tall and slender, with roguish blue eyes and yellow hair, and a complexion like a wild rose. And her ears! Ah! those pretty pink ears—so alive to every sound!

He was neither too young nor too old to be susceptible to the charms of a pretty girl. That might make him anywhere from eighteen to eighty, you know.

These sweeping statements are better than more exact facts sometimes—it gets more people in sympathy with one's hero. And when I add that this man was neither too tall nor too short; neither too thin nor too stout, and that he had a face which many would call handsome, I am sure that some will follow my tale with interest.

The man in the chair saw the flutter of a grey gown and he grew damp with perspiration. The agony of the dental operation was over for a time and the dentist had gone into another room—but this—this was worse.

He tried to remember if he had groaned. He believed that he had. Perhaps he had even yelled. What grimaces he must have made too! He recollected that the dentist had asked him if he ever had witnessed an Indian war dance. What had suggested such a thing to the mind of the dentist unless he had yelled and cut capers like an Indian? And now he sat with the cold chills running over him as he thought what a fool he must look. Good gracious! What would she think? And she was so pretty.

Then he grew wroth. What business had a dentist to put his chair in such a place and leave him sitting there with his mouth wide open and filled with india-rubber? It was an outrage. It was monstrous! All of this the man muttered through his teeth as he eyed the corner of the grey gown.

And the girl? That's what I'm coming to. She came into the next room and picked up a book which she had left there, then she turned and went out without so much as glancing his way, and she never knew that the man was there. Romantic, wasn't it?

NOTES

1. *Tit-Bits*. Volume XXI. 20th February 1892, page 338. All three of Bennett's 1892 articles for *Tit-Bits* were unsigned. George Newnes's *Tit-Bits*, launched from Manchester in October 1881, was an innovative late Victorian weekly, aimed at a newly literate mass-market readership.

THE ARTIST'S MODEL.[1]

I

"Now," said Richard Lacy, with a sigh which denoted intense joy, "my chance has come at last."

He threw down the letter and re-lighted his pipe, smiling quietly to himself. An old friend of his, who had made great fame and some money as a novelist, Edmund Shelton to wit, had selected him to illustrate an edition de luxe of his famous novel "Claire Ingelow", which you have no doubt read, and had offered very liberal terms. Here was the opportunity for which Richard Lacy had been waiting ever since he came to London a youth of seventeen more than ten years ago.

He was a struggling artist, who painted pictures (which never sold) in the daytime, and earned his bread and cheese at night by designing for the stationery trade, and such black-and-white work as he could get hold of. He managed to make about £150 a year, one third of which went for the rent of the gaunt, bare studio in which he worked, and the little bedroom attached in which he slept. The purchase of materials exhausted another third, and on the remaining £50 he lived, but did not grow fat.

Unless he could in some way arrest the attention of the public he would probably remain all his life an ill-paid designer. True, by some freak of fortune, one of his pictures had once been exhibited at the Royal Academy. But it was "skied"[2],—not a single critic noticed it and it was reproduced in none of the illustrated catalogues. Even now he was in debt for its very gorgeous frame.

But surely Fate smiled at last. As illustrator of a celebrated novel he could not fail to be talked about. He must at once consider what models he would require for the work. If he could only . . . . .

A timid rat-tat at the door interrupted his soliloquy. "Come in."

A tall young girl stood before him. She was not exactly beautiful, but with an artist's instinct he at once noticed the fine poise of her head and her shapely hand. She was meanly dressed, and she hesitated.

"Good morning," he said, at length. "Model?"

She nodded gravely, and handed him a card. "Mary Blackwood" was the name it bore. Evidently she was a beginner at the business. The old hands never called on him, for they knew his means would not allow him to engage a model, except very occasionally. Besides, her manner seemed to indicate that she had never been inside a studio before. He was rather attracted by her erect bearing and simple air. Models are usually inclined to be stagey.

"Well, I may be wanting a model shortly," Lacy said, "may I ask what your terms are?"

She stated them. They were ridiculously low.

"Perhaps you could call to-morrow, and I could then say

whether you would be likely to suit me."

"Very good, sir. I will call at two o'clock. Thank you." And with a quiet "Good morning" and another grave little nod she was gone.

Soon afterwards he caught himself trying to imitate her deliciously low voice. She ought, he said to himself, to make an admirable model for Claire Ingelow.

II

When Richard Lacy had had three sittings from Mary Blackwood, he began to wonder how in the world he would have got on without her. Not only had she read "Claire Ingelow", but she seemed thoroughly to understand the somewhat difficult character of Claire. She was ever ready with useful suggestions. He admitted to himself that she really inspired his pencil. He looked forward with eagerness to her visits. Not that they were particularly lively affairs. Miss Blackwood spoke only as occasion demanded, and Lacy was not one of those artists who can talk and work simultaneously.

From chance remarks he gathered that she had no relations, and that she lived with a friend older than herself, who was also a model, and who had persuaded her to follow the same calling. He also learnt that his was the first studio in which she had sat.

One day when she came he was almost prostrated by a more than usually severe headache, a complaint from which he frequently suffered. In the middle of the morning's work she suddenly jumped up.

"Why, Mr. Lacy, you are ill!" she cried.

"Only one of my headaches," he said, faintly and wearily. "You know I often have them. But I think I will sit down a bit...."

Then he fainted.

When he recovered consciousness he found himself lying on the only couch which the studio boasted, while Mary Blackwood stood over him with a bottle of smelling salts.

"Where do you keep the tea?" she asked, with a smile. "I must make you a cup of tea at once.

He pointed to a cupboard.

Years afterwards he remembered the quiet joy with which he watched her quick, graceful movements as she set about preparing that tea. To a man accustomed to living alone and "doing for himself" nothing is more delicious than the sight of a charming and sympathetic woman performing those simple domestic offices which an unkind fate has compelled him to do (how clumsily!) for himself.

"By the way," Lacy said, as he contentedly sipped the tea, "how came I on this couch?"

"I carried you there," said Mary, with a suspicion of red in her cheeks.

"Oh .... er ... I see."

"I nursed my mother for three years before she died, and I know what to do; and . . . you aren't very heavy."

"Far too heavy for your strength," he said. And then he thanked her, quite prettily, and she said that really it was nothing.

Really it was a very great deal. From that day they were no longer artist and model, but close friends. Richard suddenly discovered that it was necessary for Mary to sit four times a week instead of three. He explained that if she did not he would have difficulty in finishing the drawings by the appointed time. Then he said he would like to paint her portrait as "Claire Ingelow" for the Academy, which would open in a couple of months.

"But how about finishing the drawing for the book?" she questioned, with a laughing glance from beneath her long eyelashes.

"Well, I think that painting a portrait of you would help me considerably with the black-and-white work. It's rather difficult to explain," he added, after a pause, "but I'm sure it would help."

"Quite so. I think I understand," she replied, sweetly.

No doubt she did.

It was about this time that Richard found he could talk and work as well. They discussed everything; and the man discovered to his surprise that in all domains of knowledge outside art, the woman was his equal. It was remarkable that their discussions never ended with their sittings. Richard said that perhaps if he took more exercise he might have less headache, and so he fell into the habit of escorting her to her rooms. And even at her door he remembered many things he wanted to say. During one of these walks Mary remarked that the portrait was nearly completed.

"Of course you will call it 'Claire Ingelow'?" she said.

"Yes; I suppose I must," was the reply, "but I could suggest at least two better titles."

"Indeed! And may I ask what they are?"

"Well, one is 'The Dearest Girl in the World,' and the other: 'Portrait of the Artist's Wife.'"

She was silent. It was dark and the road was deserted. His arm crept round her waist. She looked up, and her lips met his, descending to meet them.

And so it was arranged.

III

The picture being at last finished was dispatched with much trembling. Richard said it ought to be accepted, the subject was so fine. Mary said it ought to be accepted, the handling was so masterly. They both were right.

The eagerly expected and much-prized varnishing ticket duly arrived, but Lacy was unable to make use of it, in spite of all Mary's nursing. His attacks of headache had lately become more frequent and more severe, and on the eventful day he was incapable of movement. It occurred to Mary that he ought to see a doctor. The doctor cross-examined him closely, and then said, "I think your best course is to consult an oculist."

"I can see perfectly well," Lacy said, with some astonishment.

"I know you can now," the doctor answered; "but I feel convinced that your headaches proceed from weakness of the eyes."

Richard's brow became clammy. He said nothing about it to Mary, and went privily to a great specialist in Harley Street.

"You must have absolute rest for two or three years," said the great man.

"But I can't . . . . I must live!"

"If you don't rest, you will be blind before you are thirty-five."

Every word knocked heavily at his heart, and he left the consulting-room in a maze. With great difficulty he gathered sufficient courage to tell Mary. She remained silent a little.

"Then, of course, you must give your poor eyes a rest, dear," she said.

"But how?"

"Well, you will have the money for the 'Claire Ingelow' drawings, and perhaps the picture will sell. Someone is sure to buy it."

"The money for the drawings won't last six months, and pictures by unknown artists never sell."

"Then how do unknown artists become known artists?"

"It's a mystery. How does a chrysalis become a butterfly?"

"Well, I can earn a little." She was determined to keep cheerful for his sake.

He closed her mouth with a kiss.

"No!" he said, "I shall give myself six months' holiday; that is all I can afford. And then I must begin again and take my chances. Perhaps the doctors are mistaken. They often are.

"Yes, very often," echoed Mary.

With a smile and a glance which expressed her sympathy better than any words could, she left him. When she was alone, she began to cry very quietly.

Poor fellow! None but those who have been in the same

awful predicament can realize his feelings. He must work or starve; yet if he worked darkness and black despair would surely overtake him.

IV

It was the day of the Private View, and Lacy sat in his studio wondering if any among the brilliant crowd at Burlington House had cast a passing glance at his picture. The day wore on. Towards dusk a telegram came, reply paid, "What is the name and address," it ran, "of lady who sat for Claire Ingelow. —Mark Ffolliott. Bedford Row."

Now, everyone knew Mark Ffolliott. He was *the* solicitor, and acted for half the aristocracy. His was a familiar figure in the artistic and theatrical circles. Of course, he had attended the Private View.

What could it mean?

Lacy telegraphed back the required information.

He went to see Mary next morning.

"Richard, dear," she began almost immediately, " I know I am a brazen minx, but I think we ought to get married at once. Then I can keep an eye on you to see that you don't work."

"Don't joke old girl," he said, with a tremor in his voice. "I've been thinking, and I've made up my mind that I ought to release you, as there's no prospect now of my being able to keep even myself, to say nothing of a family."

"What if I refuse to be released?"

"I must insist on it."

"Then I shall sue you for damage for breach of promise."

Richard seemed to be in no mood for pleasantry, and looked out of the window. Mary went softly up to him.

"Well, diddums," she prattled, throwing her arms around his neck, "Mary, naughty to tease him like dat. Naughty Mary."

Then she showed him a letter which she had that morning received from Mr. Mark Ffolliott, of Bedford Row. It set forth, with the usual legal formality of phrase, how the writer, catching sight of Mr. Lacy's picture at the Academy, had been astonished at the likeness which it bore to a Miss Norris, who, twenty years since, had several times visited his office in company with her uncle, Sir James Norris, who was an old client of his; that Sir James Norris had died about a year ago, intestate; that it had been discovered that the deceased left no relations except his niece, and that the latter had married a gentleman named Blackwood, and subsequently died leaving a daughter; that Mr. Ffolliott had hitherto been unable to trace the issue of this marriage; and finally, that he was convinced that the original of 'Claire Ingelow' must be the daughter of Mrs. Blackwood, and heiress to £30,000 and a country house.

"I remember," said Mary, when Richard had read the letter, "that mother used to mention her uncle Sir James, sometimes, and tell me how rich he was. That was after father died," she added thoughtfully. "And we were very poor then."

"Mary," Richard said, "accept my congratulations. But of course a girl with £30,000 and an ancestral hall won't throw herself away on a penniless artist."

"Won't she?" was the reply. A kiss momentarily stopped the progress of the conversation. "Just try her."

Richard Lacy had a holiday extending over three years, and so saved his eyesight. He puts A.R.A. after his name now, and paints portraits for £1,000 apiece. But Mary always tells the children, that the best portrait their father ever did was that of 'Claire Ingelow'.

NOTES

1. *Tit-Bits*. XXIV, 6th May 1893, pages 83-84. The story was printed under an introductory paragraph identifying the author as "Mr. A. Bennett, 6, Victoria Grove, Chelsea, S.W.", as their prize-winning writer of the week. Bennett's friends were trying to convince him that he should write a novel, and this short story was written in response to their pressure. The magazine's circulation was built on the back of prize contests and insurance offers, and Bennett's story won the guinea prize for that week's issue.

2. Painters submitting their works to the Royal Academy's Annual Exhibition were always anxious not to find their picture(s) hung at an unfavourable height - "skied" - making viewing difficult and carrying a suggestion of lesser artistic merit.

IN A HOSPITAL.
A BROKEN-OFF MATCH.[1]

I

It was half-past eight and Nurse Parker had retired for the night. Her hours of duty were from 6.30 a.m. to eight p.m., seven days a week, and when, as frequently happened, she had a headache and a footache she went straight from the ward to the bedroom, which she shared with two other nurses, and got to sleep as soon as barrel-organs and her companions' chatter would allow.

To-night she was too exhausted for sleep, and lay reading a dirty copy of "East Lynne"[2] by the light of a candle which was artfully attached to the bedpost. The room was singularly squalid in appearance. Three small untidy beds and a combined washstand and dressing-table constituted its furniture. The floor was strewn with boots, brushes and boxes of all sizes. The wall-paper hung down in festoons. The window was dirty and looked on a blank wall at a distance of 18 inches. The ceiling was on a level with the street, and the vibration of constant traffic had shaken down most of its plaster.

Her room-mates happened to be out for the evening, and Nurse Parker was congratulating herself on the peacefulness of the scene, when a woman unceremoniously walked in. She was a stout person of forbidding aspect, dressed in red uniform with a large white apron and a large white cap.

"I'm sorry Nurse Parker," the woman said in a sharp, unpleasant voice, "but Nurse Smith is suddenly indisposed and I shall have to ask you to take charge of the accident ward to-night."

A contretemps of this kind occurred not seldom at the Royal General Hospital for the reason that the nursing staff was kept at the lowest possible limit.

Nurse Parker, scarcely looking up from her book, said, "Very well, Nurse Reid, I will come in a few minutes."

II

In two more days she was to leave the hospital in order to get married. The event might have occurred three years ago had she listened to her lover, but she was gifted with a very delicate conscience, and was moreover, almost aggressively independent, and it had taken her so long to ascertain her own feelings towards him.

She knew now that she loved him, and, although no one would have guessed it from her calm and impassive features, she felt an exultant joy. Oh! To be the loving wife of a loving husband! To have a home! To be out of this place with its horrible scents and sounds! To have time to cultivate oneself! Already she had told the patients and the staff that she was about to leave, but no one suspected the reason, and no one, at least among the nurses, was sufficiently interested to ask.

She was lightly dozing in her chair, when a well-known sound roused her, a shuffling of many feet in the corridor, and a murmur of carefully subdued voices. A casualty!

One of the porters and a policeman were carrying a stretcher, upon which lay a well-dressed man. His head was invisible, being covered with a stained white cloth. Another policeman followed behind.

"It's a suicide, miss," the disengaged policeman said.

"He done it a treat, nurse," added the porter. "One side of his face is blown clean off."

"Take him to No. 7," Nurse Parker said. "Have you told Dr. Heap?"

None of them seemed moved in the least.

Two large screens were put round bed No. 7 and the body was quietly placed on it. The porter removed the cloth, and exposed to view the man's mangled face. One cheek was almost torn away. Nurse Parker turned white, and grasped the bed-post. She steadied herself, drank a glass of water, and began preparations for the doctor's visit. The porter noticed her white cheeks, and hinted that he was rather surprised that she should "have a turn." He knew that three years' acquaintance with the operating theatre will harden the most sensitive nature.

"You must remember I've been on duty all day," she said, as she gently sponged the suicide's uninjured features. Her voice trembled and she nearly dropped the sponge.

The suicide on the bed was her lover.

III

Presently the house-surgeon strolled leisurely in. He was wearing a coat which was rapidly falling to pieces, and brought with him a strong odour of tobacco.

"A bad job, this, nurse," he remarked, gruffly.

"I think so, sir," said nurse, mechanically.

An Eastern monarch in his palace is not more autocratic than a doctor in the ward. No one speaks except in reply to him, and even then as concisely as possible. His least requirements are watchfully anticipated, and the nurses tremble before his frown.

Dr. Heap turned up his sleeves and set to work on the patient's face. He was in a captious mood and grumbled intermittently. If she had thought of it, probably nurse would have fainted, but the idea never occurred to her. Her mind was fully occupied by the work in hand. When it was finished she brought the doctor a basin of water that he might wash his hands, and at the right moment handed him the towel.

"I sha'nt come in again, nurse," he said, carelessly. "He can't last above an hour or two."

"Very well, sir."

Then she preceded him to the door, and opened it for him to pass out.

The patients were disturbed, and one of them spoke to her as she went by his bed.

"What's up nurse?" he inquired.

"It's nothing," she said. "Try to go to sleep."

IV

This being a case of suicide, one of the policemen remained. She offered him a seat by the fire, and herself disappeared within the screens which surrounded No. 7.

Then she tried to realise what had happened, to think clearly and grasp the fact. Had Robert indeed killed himself? Impossible! But the policeman had told her that he heard a pistol shot in an entry, and found the man apparently lifeless with a revolver in his hand. That was all. Neither the policeman nor anyone else could throw further light on the affair. Indeed, the policeman seemed hardly interested in it at all. But probably cases of suicide were as common to him as broken limbs to her.

Why had this happened? Why, why, why, why? The thoughts ground against each other in her brain, but no answer, however improbable or absurd, formulated itself. And the wedding was really to have taken place in two days! Was there a God in heaven? She laughed queerly and then wondered what she would do with her wedding clothes. Wedding! She a bride! Wilt thou have this suicide? "He can't last above an hour or two." So she must stand and watch him die.

The policeman snored by the fire, and a little boy cried out for water from the far end of the ward. She took no notice.

"Nurse, I'm thirsty," the small voice began again. She must go to him before [he disturbed] the whole ward.

When she returned No. 7 was stirring uneasily. His lips moved. On account of the bandages his mouth was the only part of his face exposed to view.

"Robert," she whispered, "it's me."

The man attempted to speak, but she only caught an inarticulate sound.

"It's me, Robert."

Then he spoke.

"Four to one, Goldfish." The words came rapidly. His tongue fell forward a little. He was dead.

When the night superintendent came [around] at two a.m. she found Nurse Parker [stretched out] on the floor in a faint. The little boy at the other end of the ward was crying.

"Overwork," she ejaculated, as she bent [over] the girl.

NOTES

1. *The Sun*. 5th August 1893, page 1. Signed A. Bennett. T.P. O'Connor, Irish Nationalist M.P. and radical journalist, founded what is generally regarded as the first modern newspaper, *The Star*, in 1887, followed by *The Sun* in 1893.

2. Mrs. Henry Wood's first novel, *East Lynne*, published in 1861, was an immediate success and became a recognised literary signifier for sensationalism and sentimentality.

THE HEAVENLY TWINS ON THE REVOLT OF THE DAUGHTERS.[1]

The Twins, who had been finding it rather dull at Morne, where they were staying with their grandfather, the Duke, were strolling idly through Morningquest. They were tired of baiting Father Ricardo, whom they had thoroughly worsted in theological controversy, until the worthy priest had grown devoid of articulate utterance, and could reply to their severely logical onslaughts only with a sullen scowl. "Like Torquemada," said Angelica, "he's reduced to his last argument—the stake. Wouldn't he like to, if he only could?" The Twins were arm-in-arm, each, as usual, in the other's clothing. This had now become so common as to excite no remark in the streets of Morningquest. Angelica yawned.

"I know what you want, Angelica," drawled Diavolo.[2] "You want a fresh audience. Let's take one back with us."

Half an hour later, as the Twins entered the study, followed by three ladies, the Duke, who had been reading, with Father Ricardo's help, a ponderous tome of Thomas Aquinas, looked up with a visible air of relief and pleased anticipation. He was about to ask to be introduced to the charming strangers, when the deep solemn notes of the chime were borne through the open window. The Duke and Father Ricardo bowed their heads reverently, while the visitors stared at them in some surprise, and the Twins giggled audibly.

"Come," said Father Ricardo, sternly, to the Duke. "Four o'clock. Vespers."

The Duke humbly followed him out of the room, though not without a regretful backward glance, and the suspicion of a sigh.

Angelica rang the bell sharply, and ordered tea.

"Now," she said, seating herself, as usual, among the theological works that strewed the table, and putting one arm round Diavolo, "I suppose we must discuss something."

"I hate discussing things," said Diavolo sleepily. "We have to use such absurdly long words."

"Who cares?" said Angelica. "Haven't we used absurdly long words ever since we were three years of age? It has never been any trouble to us. And as to arguments, we've never had the worst of one as long as we can remember. Have we?"

"Well, what do you want to discuss now?" said Diavolo sulkily.

"'The Revolt of the Daughters', I think," said Angelica, with her mouth full. The Heavenly Twins were now seated side by side, sharing a huge slice of bread-and-jam. The guests, who by this time had been helped to tea, looked appalled at the prospect, and then distinctly relieved when Diavolo protested:—

"Why 'The Revolt of the Daughters'? We're not in the least interested in it."

"You stupid!" replied Angelica, banging his head with her own, which was considerably the harder of the two. "We are interested in all sorts of things that don't concern us in the least."

"Why?" said Diavolo.

"Why!" said Angelica. "What do you suppose we are in

the book for at all except to introduce all the questions, and propound all the theories, that can't be worked off by the other characters?"

"All right," said Diavolo, submissively, "go on."

"I should like to know," continued Angelica, "where is the essential difference between the unmarried girl of eighteen, whom everyone wants to keep 'innocent and sheltered,' and the *married* girl of eighteen whom everyone is content to call emancipated."

"My dear, men like innocence in girls," said the third Mrs Tanqueray,[3] who was doing some fancy needlework, which she always carried about with her, "and by that they mean ignorance. I was perfectly innocent myself until I married. There will be no chance for girls if it becomes fashionable to know things; besides, girls take things so terribly seriously, and men don't like wives with ideas. That is just the difficulty I'm having with—"

"Thank you," said Angelica; "I suppose that *is* the conventional view. I don't see how any other could be expected from you. Of course we all know that Aubrey Tanqueray married you as a suitable companion for that minx of a daughter of his."

"You mustn't mind Angelica," said Diavolo hastily; "she doesn't like saying these rude things, but she *has* to, you know. We are really most charmingly well bred, and we hate hurting people's feelings, but you know how it is in a novel with a purpose; the things must be said somehow, and we're only thankful—"

"Shut up," interrupted Angelica, cramming the bread-and-jam into Diavolo's mouth: "let me finish what I was saying. Doesn't it strike you that the innocent girl develops into the fast young woman very easily when she marries? That magic business at the church is supposed to fit her all at once for coming into contact with everything she has been jealously guarded from hitherto. Can you be surprised if her head gets turned? How on earth is she to know where to draw the line?"

"There *was* something about a Tenor,"[4] murmured the third Mrs. Tanqueray.

Dodo, who had been standing at the window, looking bored, burst out laughing at this, and turned round as if to speak.

"*You* needn't say anything," exclaimed Angelica throwing a crust at her. "You're not a type, you're a portrait, and as such you don't count. Diavolo, what was the next thing we had to say?"

"Well, as to wild oats," drawled Diavolo, "people don't seem to realise that a girl's wild oats must necessarily be of a very harmless kind. There is the *Speaker*, now, adopts the regular old woman's view, and supposes we want to lower the moral standard. Why, the effect would be all the other way—"

"Of course it would," broke in Angelica, decidedly. "Let the young girl loose on society, and what is the result? Suppose she goes in force to music-halls (intolerably dull places *I* call them) don't you see that *she* would not deteriorate, but the places would improve? Where men would take their mothers, wives, and sisters, and meet their girl friends, they would very soon insist on having the entertainment modified to suit the new audience."

"Then there's the question of age," prompted Diavolo, as Angelica stopped to take breath.

"Oh, yes, that's another thing. Why should it be necessary for a girl to marry in order to gain her freedom? Isn't it ridiculous that a bride of 17 is considered competent to chaperon an unmarried woman of 25? Why not give a woman her freedom, married or unmarried, at 25—or at 30, if you like? Or give her a certificate of freedom when she passes a certain standard?"

"I've got an idea," said Diavolo dreamily. "I don't know whether it's relevant. Try keeping the men 'innocent and sheltered' for a generation or two, and give the girls unconditional freedom. I wonder how that strikes you."

"It strikes me freedom under those conditions would be awfully dull for the girls," remarked Dodo, yawning.

"I can't understand what you are talking about," said Hilda Wangel. "What does it matter about music-halls and chaperons? Are you serious in that or are these merely symbols? Are you urging the right of each human being to live his life his own way?"

"My dear Miss Wangel," said Diavolo politely, "you don't catch the point of view, and I don't wonder. In your country you take a higher stand than we do. Your thought is for humanity. We think in cliques. This 'Revolt of the Daughters' that is occupying us all is not a vulgar question for the world at large. It concerns a set. Most of us that discuss it would confess if we were honest that we have never met a daughter in revolt. It is a question of little points of etiquette and propriety; it concerns none but the wealthy, the conventional, and the narrow; it has no message for Humanity. Now you, if I may say so without offence, are an abstraction, and you have a way of saying immensely suggestive things about ethical, moral, and social questions, but it is not to be expected that you should have anything valuable to say about chaperons and latchkeys."

"You've spoilt it all by that, Diavolo," exclaimed Angelica sulkily. "I had a good deal more to say if you hadn't interrupted. I was going into the question of literary freedom and the young person, but, of course, judged by Scandinavian standards, I have nothing new to say about that, and it isn't any fun talking unless one is considered 'advanced'."

Nobody made the least attempt to persuade Angelica to continue, so she got up, yawning, and announced that she must finish drafting a Bill for the admission of women to Parliament, which her husband was to introduce, when Diavolo exclaimed with sudden excitement:—

"Angelica, I believe they are killing a pig!" And in a moment the Heavenly Twins had dashed through the window to the scene of the action.

NOTES

1. *The Westminster Gazette.* 10th February 1894, pages 1-2. Unsigned. Founded by George Newnes in January 1893. Issued as a penny weekly and like his *Tit-Bits* laid out in a generous three column format, compared with the tight seven columns of the rival *The Sun*. The story is a satire written in the style of feminist novels of the period, parodying in particular Sarah Grand's novel *The Heavenly Twins*, first published in three volumes in July 1893. Bennett reviewed Grand's work six times between March 1894 and April 1901. The 1901 article was reprinted as "Madame Sarah Grand" in *Fame and Fiction* (1901).
2. Grand's twins are also called Angelica and Diavolo.
3. Arthur W. Pinero's *The Second Mrs Tanqueray* was first performed on 27th May 1893. Bennett's "third Mrs Tanqueray" may well have been part of the audience that flocked to Pinero's melodrama about so-called "fallen women" who had sex outside marriage and condemning those men who thoughtlessly ruin them in a selfish search for pleasure. Her comment that "My dear, men like innocence in girls" might also be read as an epigraph to Grand's novel.
4. Bennett's "There was something about a Tenor" is a direct reference to the novel's "The Tenor and the Boy–An Interlude" [Book IV]. He is particularly scathing about this section in his *Fame and Fiction* essay: "Grandiose to absurdity ....incredibly preposterous ... wickedly distorted ...." (p. 74) At the same time, however, he praises the novel's argument for female emancipation as "the modern equivalent of *Uncle Tom's Cabin*". (p. 75)

Bennett returned to the theme of female education and emancipation in his story "A Modern Girl. The Revolt of My Daughter", published two weeks later in *The Sun* (22nd February 1894). His male narrator collected "all opinions, whether of Mr. Gladstone or of Professor Huxley, of Sarah Grand ..."

A MODERN GIRL.
THE REVOLT OF MY DAUGHTER.[1]

"I am to understand, then," I said "that you have not been led to this decision by any shortcomings in my conduct as a father. You accuse me of no parental tyranny—no Oriental despotism?"

"Not guilty on that count," replied Eugenia with her accustomed vivacity; "certainly not guilty."

"And your mother?" (I looked at my wife, whose face betrayed conflicting emotions.)

"No; nor ma either. How can you ask?"

"And yet you wish to 'live your own life.' That is the precise phrase I believe?"

"You hit it, papa. I wish to do so, therefore I shall. I am sane, and of full age (she was twenty-one years and four days), and I pleases my little self. Q.E.D. N'est-ce pas?"

"I told you how it would be," remarked her mother. I counted a hundred before replying, in accordance with a well-known recipe.

In face of the continuous opposition of my wife and my wife's relatives, I had brought up Eugenia on a novel and audacious plan—a plan which had so far succeeded excellently. From her earliest years I had carefully abstained from assuming a didactic attitude towards her in matters as to which there was or could be any controversy. When a question arose as to religion, the relations of the sexes, female suffrage, realism, crinolines, Ibsen, I would never (as other parents do) take an unworthy advantage of my position to proselytize on behalf of my own views, but contented myself with collecting all opinions, whether of Mr. Gladstone or of Professor Huxley, of Sarah Grand, or Mrs. Lynn Lynton [sic],[2] and placing them impartially before Eugenia. If she asked me point blank, I would give her the benefit of the views which I had myself formed, adding, however, that in all probability they were quite wrong. Thus she learnt to think for herself. Further I permitted—nay, begged—her to read whatever she chose, and to do whatever she chose, provided always she kept on the windy side of the law. Thus she was widely, if superficially, informed and well used to govern herself.

On the whole I was well satisfied with the result of my educational methods. Eugenia was healthy, handsome, sometimes sensible, unfettered by prejudice, warm-hearted, clever and not without wit—of a slangy kind. People said that a well-known novelist had unflatteringly painted her portrait in a well-known novel, but I for one never saw the likeness.

"And when do you think of deserting your heartbroken parents?" I asked, after I had counted my hundred.

"Saturday, daddy. Arrangements are practically complete. I'm going to write for the papers. The editor of the *Sex* has offered me regular work."

"Oh! You'll keep yourself?" This from my wife, sarcastically.

"I'll try, but perhaps daddy won't mind lending me a couple of hundred just to start with."

"Charmed, I'm sure. On what days would you like the carriage."

She jumped up and kissed me, and told me not to be Early English.

"Of course you know," she began, after a pause, "I love you both awfully, and all that sort of thing. But the atmosphere isn't sympathetic; I differ from you on French novels, and from Ma on fashions and filial duty. And then— "

Of course, the affair went the round of the society papers. Some of them said that I was in the habit of thrashing Eugenia, and that she had been compelled to leave. Others genially remarked that Eugenia was in the habit of thrashing me, and that I had offered her ten thousand pounds to go.

About a fortnight had elapsed, when one evening, as I sat in my study reading the report of the Historical Manuscripts Commission, the door opened, and, without the least warning, a tall, broad-shouldered woman walked in. At first I thought it was Eugenia herself, but I was mistaken.

"Good evening," I said, "to what do I owe the pleasure—"

With an imperious gesture she silenced me, and began to fumble with a card-case.

She handed me a card which bore this strange legend:—

"S. S. S. S."

I looked at the woman interrogatively. She was stern, but pretty.

"Come," she ejaculated.

"Certainly, but whither?"

"The carriage waits. The council sits."

I followed her, not knowing why.

The vehicle stopped in an old-fashioned street, unfamiliar to me. Taking me by the arm my companion led me into a house of forbidding aspect and grimy windows.

"No. 243 arrives," she called.

"No. 243 arrives," another voice repeated from an upper storey.

"Send up No. 243," the second voice sang out after a minute, and I went meekly upstairs, and was shown into a large room, furnished with the most extravagant luxury.

On six Chippendale arm-chairs, placed in a row, sat six celebrated women, most of whom were well known to me. There was Lady Harry —, Miss —, the Hon. Mrs. —, the Countess of —, and two others. (The task of filling up the blanks I'd rather leave to you.)

I bowed.

"Your name?" asked the Countess, who, by the way, was an intimate of my wife's.

"Marmaduke Maxwell."

"Occupation?"

"Reviewer of books and drawer of water. I mean reviewer of books. Pardon."

"Secretary," said the Countess; "read the usual explanatory remarks to the prisoner." Uprose Miss—, and began:—

"This tribunal, before which you, Marmaduke Maxwell, are summoned is the council of the Society for the Suppression of Side Saddles. The Society's name does little more than hint at the great ends for which it was established. In the course of its operations it will no doubt, inter alia, suppress Side Saddles; but the purpose of its founders is to emancipate our sex, more especially that part of our sex which consists of daughters. Its power is vast, limitless. Its members are bound by horrid oaths. Its methods are mysterious, novel, entirely effective. Finally, no man who enters this place leaves it alive, except under pledge of inviolable secrecy."

Miss—sat down. The Countess took up the tale.

"In a sixpenny weekly you permitted yourself to joke on the subject of Mrs. Crackanthorpe's article on 'The Revolt of the Daughters.'"

I acknowledged the impeachment with proper humility, for I was beginning to be afraid.

"Mrs. Crackanthorpe is one of our most trusted agents, and you deserve punishment on that score. But let it pass. You have a daughter, Eugenia, and she has been compelled, in order to maintain her freedom and self-respect, to leave you."

"*Not compelled*," I interposed.

"Do not interrupt. I said 'compelled'. I mean it. You dared to differ from her on almost every aesthetic and social question. The atmosphere of your house was uncongenial, devitalizing. What other course was open to her?" I remained silent. She went on:

"Of course you have no answer. This, then, is the sentence. By the way we will take care that your wife does not come to poverty. You will—"

"Papa, papa." A voice cried out from below.

"That is my daughter," I cried. "I must see her before I die." I attempted to leave the room, but was seized roughly by the shoulder. I struggled and suddenly Eugenia was standing by my side.

"Oh, daddy," she said, "I thought I should never waken you. I've—I've come back."

NOTES

1. *The Sun*. 22nd February 1894, page 1. Signed E.A.B. [Enoch Arnold Bennett].
On 10th February Bennett had published "The Heavenly Twins on the Revolt of the Daughters", a satire on the popular feminist novels of the time, in *The Westminster Gazette*. On 28th February he published "The Renaissance of the Romp", a brief drama giving his thoughts on the Women's Movement, in *Woman*. This short period of intense concentration on these topics proved proleptic of his journalistic concerns - particularly with women writers such as Sarah Grand - throughout his time as an editor.
2. Eliza Lynn Linton (1822-1898) offended many of her female contemporaries by her essays attacking feminism and the New Woman values Eugenia is attempting to emulate.

THE SILKEN SERPENT.[1]
A FANTASY.

From the French of
REMY DE GOURMONT.[2]

After the midday repast, which was a court spectacle, a rigid ceremonial of royalty provided for courtiers' admiration, the king and queen were wont to repose in intimate seclusion. Their favourite spot was a small pavilion built on the banks of the great canal. The place breathed an infinite melancholy, the plaintive monotone of poplar trees floated sadly on the air, and sometimes came a noise of the fray of wings, white wings and black, —swans, revealing in vain unspoken mysteries.

When, after traversing interminable corridors, they entered the accustomed chamber, the king and queen found the meal already laid, a simple refection, but royally distinguished by the fantasy of its dishes, the rarity of its fruits, the fabulous age of its wines: tongues of flaming crimson, juniper-smoked, Asiatic peaches as small as walnuts, wine from the Galilean vines which Jesus blessed. But for some time they had taken little pleasure in these their secret dinners, and often, without even glancing at the small table, the queen would begin to plait some silken threads in silence.

For several weeks now, the queen had been working at the silken threads and her fingers seemed to delight in the strange task. Three threads she would take, of colours chosen to harmonise or to contrast, and, twisting them together, she would fashion a triple thread, still very fine, and of surpassing strength.

"What are you doing, my queen?" asked the young king.

"I am twisting my silken threads," answered the queen.

"So much I see," returned the king. "Your slender fingers come and go, you wet your thumb with the end of your little tongue, and you twist, and twist, the dainty threads—but why?"

"To amuse myself," said the queen.

Again the king questioned her: "And when you have twisted all your silk, what then?"

The queen replied: "I shall not twist all my silk. Only the prettiest, the finest, the most supple, do I twist. That is why my work lasts so long; but I am not wearing out my fingers, dear king. My work lasts, but it will come to an end, and that hour will bring a strange surprise."

"For whom?" demanded the king.

The queen smiled without answering, and once and again her hand trembled and the silks became entangled, so gentle were the eyes of the king, so anxious was his voice.

Having received no reply, the king asked no further question, and seated at the feet of the queen, like a dutiful page, he drew long sobs from a dolorous violin.

Was ever king so melancholy! Nothing could minister to his discontents. All pleasures were but half enjoyed, and, sore distressed, he mourned the half-delights which escaped him. They were the best, the purest, the sweetest, and they fled away, passing into the void, a fragrant vapour which exasperated his desires. Every trouble was the more bitter to him in that he felt it twice, and the most fugitive pains, touched by compassion for a heart so tender, settled familiarly upon his forehead, making as it were an aureole of luminous grief.

He pressed his lips to the hands of the queen, and gently, without hindering her mysterious work, he kissed them one after the other several times; then he looked up and said:—

"Queen, why do you love me less than of old?"

"King, why do you ask me that? "

"I ask in order that I may be consoled by the sound of your voice."

The queen replied:— "Well, be consoled. Your question is silly—that is my answer."

"Queen, my question is not silly, since you cannot answer it. If my question were silly, you would have sealed my lips with a long, irresistible kiss—and you have not done so. You have not stirred, you have not even blushed; your fingers have not stayed their dreadful task—"

"Dreadful!"

"Yes, dreadful. The ceaseless movement of these fingers makes me afraid."

"Oh, afraid!"

"Yes, afraid. As a child is afraid when it sees things move which should not move."

"But my fingers are made to move," said the queen.

"Not thus, not thus!"

The king rose. He took a few steps, and then stood still, fascinated by the motion of the queen's white hands. He followed them in their winding but regular course, until he could anticipate every slightest movement. The nail of the ring-finger would pass and shine as it went; the ring on the fore-finger would appear first edgeways, and then it would burn in all its sapphire splendour. . . Then there came an unexpected movement, and the fingers were quiet.

The queen now toyed with the work in her hands, and it was a long silken serpent, rainbow-hued, which seemed actually to unfold itself in living spirals.

The king remained standing quite still, and with eyes fixed.

He did not see the movements which the queen made, but only those which he anticipated she would make, and which she made no longer. She stood up, her eyes more luminous than the scales of the silken serpent which her fingers had twisted, and it seemed that in the very fashioning of it she had acquired a new soul, the hissing and venomous soul of a viper.

The fascination of her eyes had supplanted the fascination of her fingers; impelled by the queen's glance, the king stepped forward. She touched him on the shoulder, and he stopped; at that moment the serpent hissed and bit, and the king fell to his knees, then dropped on his side.

The queen opened the window and made a sign.

The swans were battling in the green water of the canal, where the sad poplars sobbed with all their leaves.

The black wings fought against the white; the white wings were vanquished, and they floated lifeless on the slow waters of the great canal, like crimes unsepulchred.

NOTES

1. *Woman*. 28th February 1894, page 18. Signed E.A.B. The periodical was a penny illustrated weekly which appeared from 3rd January 1890 to 9th August 1912. Bennett, with his father's financial backing, became Assistant Editor in late December 1893, and two years later, the Editor. He remained with *Woman* until September 1901. His first article for the weekly, "Wrinkles. Supper for a Children's Party", appeared on 3rd January 1894. "The Silken Serpent" was his first story for *Woman*.

2. Rémy de Gourmont (1858-1915), French Symbolist poet and critic who was much admired by Ezra Pound and T.S. Eliot. He provided a platform for symbolist ideas through his editorship of *Mercure de France*.

A FIRST NIGHT. "THE FLOODGATES OF SOCIETY."[1]

At the Imperial Theatre the first performance of "The Floodgates of Society," "a new and original comedy in three acts," was proceeding amid considerable disturbance, and even George Falmouth, the experienced actor-manager, felt flurried and nervous, and began to miss his cues. As for Tertia Clayton, [2] his leading lady, a talented girl with the pluck of a lioness, she was outwardly calm, but during a brief absence from the stage, she remarked that she should like to close all exits, and then set the theatre on fire.

"There will be another uproar when I go on again," she said to the stage manager, "I feel it. I begin with a dangerous line."

"Cut it then somehow, for heaven's sake."

"Not for worlds. What a shame to deprive the dear pit of a little fun!" And she went on.

"This is a little likely house to come to for consolation," her speech began.

"Heah, heah," said a voice from the skies, with an affected

drawl which made each word a pronounced dissyllable. In just half a second both pit and gallery were in full possession of the joke, and people in the street mistook the outburst for tumultuous applause.

"Why the devil," said Falmouth, as he stood waiting the pleasure of the house; "why the devil didn't I cut that line a week ago? Why I'll—" But what he said next would not look nice in print.

At length the second act came to an end. Brandies and sodas were much in request at the bars. The original cause of unpleasantness lay in a grievance of the pit. Be it known that a first night pit is delighted to find a grievance. In this case, the stalls, in the opinion of the first row of half-crowns, were carried too far back, an insult not to be silently swallowed by any self-respecting pit. Consequently the harmless, necessary curtain-raiser, which was, perhaps, a thought too harmless for robust enjoyment, had been laughed to shreds, and when the curtain fell on its simple, happy ending the pit said to itself that it was avenged, and, under more fortunate circumstances, might have lapsed into goodwill and peacefulness.

But truly the future is in the hands of the gods. It happened that George Falmouth, who was a rising man, gifted with ideas, some artistic sensibility, and two eyes for the main chance, had abolished the orchestra from the Imperial, hoping to save money and at the same time to please those of his patrons who preferred to be without music, so-called. He wrote a letter to the papers stating his intention, and spoke witheringly of the "irrelevant, soul-destroying waltz"; several editors commented favourably on the proposed innovation, and most folks, including Falmouth himself, thought that Falmouth had scored. But when the eventful night came, and the wait between the lever du rideau and the main piece stretched itself out to twenty-five minutes, the gallery getting every moment more and more restive, and finally breaking into " 'E don't know where 'e are," then Falmouth cursed his scene-shifters, and sighed in vain for the irrelevant soul-destroyer. He knew the piece was doomed, for that night at least.

Their majesties the critics in the stalls smiled to each other now and then, and decided that their notices would have to be short.

"Talk about 'floodgates,'" said the representative of a comic weekly partly to himself and partly to his fair and fluffy-haired neighbour (who was generally taken by unsuspecting pittites for a member of the ancienne noblesse, but who in reality was an industrious lady journalist who got her living and many tickets by 'doing the dresses'); "Talk about floodgates"—and a joke was born.

"Who is the author?" the lady asked. "Now do tell me, I'm sure you know."

"Assure you I don't," he truthfully replied, in a tone of voice which was meant to imply that he did, but wouldn't say.

The secret of the authorship of the play had indeed been well kept. The most that anyone seemed to know was that "The Floodgates of Society" was from the same hand as a certain book entitled "Atmospheres", which, published anonymously a few months previously, had divided the literary public into two camps, on the question of its merits. "Startingly [sic] original, a work of genius," one side said. "Loathsome nonsense," replied the other. Many guesses had been made at the writer's identity, but none appeared to be correct and the situation was interesting. And those who, so far as interruptions would allow, tried to follow the action of the piece, thought that the new play was interesting, too. How indignant they were at the rowdiness of the gods! What an artistic catastrophe was threatened if George Falmouth were defeated, or even checked, in his noble attempt to lift the British drama from the slough in which it had wallowed so long! And to think that the beautiful Tertia Clayton, whose ascending star seemed likely to outshine all other luminaries in the dramatic firmament, should be the butt of an insolent pit and a cat-calling gallery! The serious persons were so angry that they ceased even to cry, "Order, order."

Act III ended amidst unrestrained tumult and loud demands of "Author." The gods were certainly bent on a game of author-baiting, which is a remarkably exciting pastime, especially for the author.

"Author, author. Cock-a-doodle-doo. Author, author," with the last syllable long drawn out.

"Rather rough on you fellows," said pityingly the critic of the *Daily Sentinel*,[3] whose weakness was melodrama, to a confrère, David Powell.

"Perhaps," answered the apostle of Anything New with unruffled mien.

"But it's your readers who are making a spectacle of themselves. I wish you could induce them to let the author alone till the thing's over."

"They won't stand the last act."

"They'll have to. Falmouth's not the man to be beaten."

The cries continued, and at length George Falmouth came before the curtain. The audience would not listen, and he retired.

"Author, author."

Again the curtain was pulled back, and this time Falmouth was followed by another person. It was a woman? It was Tertia Clayton herself!

"Ladies and gentlemen," he shouted; "here's the author."

The cries suddenly ceased, almost with a gasp. The audience wavered a moment and then precipitated itself into one deafening cheer. Five times the cheering rose and fell, and at last Tertia Clayton made a haughty little bow and went off.

The last act was heard in appreciative silence, and the fortunes of the play were assured. Accounts differ as to the number of times that Tertia Clayton was recalled at the end, but the lowest estimate is seven. They tried to coax a speech out of her in vain. When she set those pretty lips of hers, it was a settled matter.

NOTES

1. *The Sun.* 10th April 1894, page 1. Signed Enoch Arnold Bennett. This was the first of many Bennett stories with a theatrical background to be published. Appropriately enough it was printed alongside an article on Sir Henry Irving, the most famous actor-manager of the late-Victorian period - "Irving in America. His Influence on the American Stage" by Boyle Lawrence.
2. An interesting and, for Bennett, an unusual conflation of family names. Tertia was the youngest of his three sisters. Bennett's mother's father married a young woman from Glossop, in Derbyshire, named Frances Clayton. Reginald Pound writes that Clayton was a "surname Arnold Bennett used in his stories, usually to denote a social grade above most of his Five Towns people. This may well have derived from his grandmother Clayton's frequent assertion that she had married beneath herself." (*Arnold Bennett. A Biography,* p.48) Tertia Clayton's curtain calls exhibited a similar superior demeanour.
3. Bennett's first published article, about the Staffordshire Steam Tramways, appeared in the *Staffordshire Daily Sentinel* on 30th April 1887. Founded in April 1873, and printed in Hanley, Stoke-on-Trent (Bennett's birthplace) the paper incorporated the *Staffordshire Post* in December 1895. Today it appears daily from Monday to Saturday as *The Sentinel,* having previously changed its name to the *Evening Sentinel* in 1929.

STRANGE STORY.
IN THE MATTER OF A LETTER AND A LADY. [1]

The *Scot* came into Southampton late in the afternoon; and when Mr. Arthur Rushleigh had stepped off the gangway and had walked up to the train, he gave, out of very gratitude, half a crown to the engine-driver. He had not seen an English engine-driver for six years, and he felt that the spectacle was cheap at the price. There came a cloud over his delight when he saw the words, "TELEGRAPH OFFICE."

"I suppose I must send her a wire," he said doubtfully. "I'd better get over the meeting sharp." So he went into the office and sent the telegram.

MARIE BENTLEY, care Drahm Attic and Co., Strand.

"Am in England again. So anxious to see you. Meet me Waterloo six-thirty— RUSHLEIGH."

He thought of adding "Never forgotten," or "Tout à toi," or something affectionate of the kind, but he decided not to do so. It would be hard enough to have to say all these pleasant things when he met her.

"Good-bye, Miss Fenton[2]—good-bye. I wish you were coming my way. I wonder when we shall see each other again."

The tall slim girl who had been one of his fellow-passengers on the *Scot* hesitated. The train was just about to leave; the Hon. Miss Fenton and her aunt were going straight to Dorsetshire.

"I wonder," she said earnestly.

Then Rushleigh did the rudest thing. At lunch to-day the wily steward, as hint to passengers that the hour for parting was near, had placed a spray of lilies beside each plate, and Miss Fenton was wearing hers at her breast. There was one bud lying loosely, and Mr. Rushleigh covertly took it. Then he stepped into the train, the engine-driver gave a triumphant note on the whistle, and the train started.

"Good-bye once more, Mr. Rushleigh. I—I shall never forget you."

The journey up in the saloon seemed to him to take a deplorably short time. The more Rushleigh contemplated his position, the more earnestly he wished that some accident would happen to prevent him from reaching Waterloo. He entombed the sprig of lilies carefully in his pocket-book when he gave up his ticket at Vauxhall, and he thought again of that mad letter of six years ago. He could remember every word of it:—

My Dearest Girl,—I did not say to you last night what I wanted to, because I hadn't the nerve. I am going away today, perhaps for some time, and I want you to try to think of me whilst I am absent. If when I return you can tell me that you love me, I shall take your hand and claim you for my own dear wife. Do not answer me, but try to think of me always—Yours ever,

Heavens! what a shy stupid fool he was then. He had found himself wishing many times since that he had been a little more shy and a good deal less stupid fool.

"I can't tell you," cried Miss Bentley, in her high-pitched

voice, as with much enthusiasm she shook both his hands, "how delighted I am to see you. You're altered, you know."

"Yes, I'm altered," said Mr. Rushleigh. He looked at her and was about to use the *tu quoque*[3] argument, but he refrained.

"I just got your wire in time, and coming over the bridge I happened to meet—who do you think?"

"I can't imagine," said Rushleigh, with excusable ignorance. He told the porter to put his trunks on a hansom for the Victoria.

"Why, Herr Blitz" cried Miss Bentley. "Odd, isn't it?"

"Is he?" said Mr. Rushleigh. "Who is—what is Herr Blitz? I forget him."

"Oh, I dare say. You never saw much of him. Why I leave nearly all my business to Blitz. He writes my songs, he copies out my parts, he—I say, Blitz. Come here. I want you."

A spectacled man with a fierce beard came forward.

"Herr Blitz, my dear old friend, Mr. Rushleigh. Used to play in amateur shows with me."

"I am broud," said Herr Blitz "broud to have der honour. Velcome, sare. Velcome to your nadive lant."

"Now look here," said Rushleigh nervously to Miss Bentley, "will you come and have dinner with me at the hotel? We have much to talk about."

"Yes, indeed," said Miss Bentley.

"And after dinner we—we can consider it. You know what I mean."

"Engagement?" whispered Miss Bentley.

Mr. Rushleigh sighed. "Yes," he said; "our engagement."

Miss Bentley appeared to have something more to say.

"Shall we bid good-bye to Herr Blitz?" asked Rushleigh.

"Well, you know," she said, "I was just thinking. Would you mind very much if Herr Blitz came with us? It is scarcely the thing, perhaps, for me to be seen dining with you alone at the hotel"—

"My dear girl," cried Rushleigh, gratified to find himself relieved from the *tête-à-tête* dinner, "that's very thoughtful of you. Herr Blitz!"

"Sare?" answered Herr Blitz.

"Will you dine with us at the Victoria at seven-thirty?"

"I meet you there," answered Herr Blitz with much readiness, and looking at his watch. "With much bleasure; half-past seven. I bring mit me also my yoong friend here, ain't it?"

"That will do capitally," cried Rushleigh, glad at the prospect of a further respite. "I shall expect you both, sharp to time."

When he came down into the dining-room at the hotel Miss Bentley and Herr Blitz were entering. The room was rather full, and fish was being served. The head waiter found two vacant chairs together, of which Mr. Rushleigh and Miss Bentley took possession. Herr Blitz was separated from them by three noisily eating Americans.

"This reminds one of old times, to be sitting near you again," said Miss Bentley, with a little sigh of sentiment. "Do you know, I believe I've got *all* your letters."

"I was afraid so," murmured Rushleigh.

"And when I used to play with your old society, we were the best of friends, weren't we? I still take on a good many affairs of the kind, you know."

"Oh," said Rushleigh.

"But I needn't talk about myself. I'm going to ask *you* something."

"Go on," said Rushleigh absently.

He could not eat much; but his companion was atoning in this respect for his want of ability. Looking at her now, he noticed that her curls were skimpier than of yore. There was the old smile and giggle; but they were produced with greater frequency. It chilled poor Rushleigh to think that if she insisted on it he would either have to marry her or submit to a ridiculous exposé; one which would gratify other travellers in Zululand exceedingly.

"I want," said Miss Bentley coyly, as she looked at the menu to see what was coming next—"I want to ask—I'm afraid you'll think I'm rather forward—when you propose to settle down. You know what I mean, don't you? Settle down and marry."

"Well," answered Rushleigh, "I propose to speak to you about that after dinner. It's a serious matter"—

"It *is* a serious matter," she agreed. "But one thing is quite certain. It's of no use your saying you can't afford it, you know. Your book has had a tremendous sale."

"Oh, I don't wish to say that I can't afford it," acknowledged Rushleigh with some warmth; "I'm not urging that for a moment. Only, you see, one isn't now exactly the hot-headed youth that one was six years ago. You must see that yourself."

"I'm glad they've got *vol-au-vent*," remarked Miss Bentley, glancing again at the card before her. "I'm dead nuts on *vol-au-vent*."

The conversation diverted itself to Mr. Rushleigh's book. Miss Bentley had read "Zululand and Its Ways," and remembered bits of it, and remembered them nearly all wrong.

"I didn't write to you," she said, "because I did not know your address, and because"—

"Because I asked you not to," interposed Rushleigh.

"Quite so. I don't complain of your not writing. I thought it better, you know, and besides my movements have been erratic. I've only written to my mother."

"I suppose your mother is not my style at all?"

"Well, no."

He was very thoughtful until the dessert came on. Then Rushleigh took a glass of wine and held the nutcrackers tightly. "Now for it," he said.

"I want to speak to you about our—our engagement," he said.

"Yes," she said with much interest. She was peeling an

orange. "I should like to know what I am to do. What is the date you propose?"

"Oh, well," said Rushleigh hastily, "there's time enough for that."

"Well, I don't know," she said, shaking her head. "There's a good deal to get ready. You men don't understand these matters. What sort of a dress do you think would suit me?"

The Americans near them were chattering so that no other voice could be heard.

"I must tell you," he whispered, "I must tell you the truth. What will you say when I declare that the impetuous youth who wrote you that letter the night previous to leaving England, and thought you were the only girl in the world, is now a man and has long since discovered that he was wrong? He asked you to wait for him, even if it was for years; and you have waited, and his foolish action has wasted the best part of your life. He does not want to be dishonourable; but what can he do? What *can* he do?"

She had pushed back her chair a little. She had been listening to the Americans, who were talking scandal of an interesting nature.

"I can't hear a word you're saying," said Miss Bentley. "Wait a bit till they're gone."

The noisy Americans rose and went out.

"Now then. Did I hear you say that you sent me a letter the night before you went away?"

"Why, yes."

"Well, I"m bothered," she said emphatically. "Of all the—Blitz come here. I want you."

Herr Blitz, on his face the look of content that comes to a man who has dined and dined well, came up.

"Blitz," she said, "do you remember a letter addressed to me about five years ago, signed by Mr. Rushleigh?"

Herr Blitz put his glasses on the better to think, and considered.

"I dink dere vos two tree ledders mit only initials," he said presently; "but, my tear, I will not swear."

"No, but I will," she said crossly. "I told you you could open my letters, but I didn't tell you to destroy them, did I?"

"But do I understand," interposed Rushleigh with much anxiety, "that you never received the note I'm speaking of?"

"Never saw it," she said—"never saw it; I give you my word."

"*Good* business!" said Rushleigh to himself, with intense relief.

"Fact is, that was just after Herr Blitz and I were married."

"Married?"

"Well, we don't brag about husbands, you know, in *the* profession. I told him to destroy all the affectionate letters from strangers; but you weren't a stranger, were you?"

"No indeed."

"And I bet my boots your letter wasn't too affectionate. You were always much too shy and gawky for that."

She was much amused at this possibility, and Rushleigh joined. Herr Blitz did not laugh, because he never had laughed; but behind his glasses his eyelids twitched.

"By the by, Blitz, Mr. Rushleigh is going to settle down and marry shortly."

Rushleigh took from his pocket-book a flat-pressed lily, and put it in the button-hole of his coat. His thoughts went to Dorsetshire.

"Sare," said Herr Blitz, rising from his chair and bowing with great *impressement*, "I gontratulate you on behalf of my wife and meinself; also I gontratulate your doubtless jarming young lady."

NOTES

1. *St. James's Gazette*. 28th April 1894, pages 5-6. Unsigned. Founded in May 1880 the periodical merged with the *Evening Standard* in 1910.
2. Fenton is one of the six towns of the City of Stoke-on-Trent. Bennett caused offence to the town's inhabitants by omitting it from his Five Towns novels and stories. He did, however, use the name for several of his characters.
3. "You too" - Latin.

FIVE O'CLOCK AT THE HEROINES' CLUB.[1]
A FANTASIA.

The fact was that matters had reached a crisis at the Heroines' Club.

What! You never heard of the club? Well, to be quite candid, no more had I till a few days ago. It was Jane Eyre, a particular friend of mine, who happened to tell me about it. I was gently touching on Rochester's alleged boorishness, and she said he had been discussed at the club and pardoned.

"What club?" I asked.

Then she explained that there was actually a club of heroines.

"And just now," she went on, "considerable unpleasantness is afoot. A small noisy coterie of new members have made themselves very conspicuous, and they think they are going to rule the club for their own ends. But," here she assumed that quiet, determined air of hers, "they are mistaken. At our five o'clock tea to-morrow things will be beautifully settled."

"Is the Press admitted?"

"No; but I think WOMAN ought to know about it. *You* can come. I'll arrange."

"My dear Jane," I cried. "I am enraptured."

So I went.

Dodo, and the Keynotes lady, and Hedda Gabler, and a few others, were in the room when I arrived with Jane. They were trying who could smoke a cigarette quickest, and Dodo won easily. When they saw Jane they simply shrugged their shoulders, looked at each other, and laughed.

Then Marcella came in, and began to talk to Jane about the game laws. The others listened a moment.

"I'll tell you what, pals," said Dodo, "the Marcella female's off her chump about poaching."

"Off her *what*?" said I, involuntarily. I had been cautioned not to speak.

"Hush!" said Jane. "That's considered smart conversation nowadays."

Several other girls came in, and Dodo put a chair on the table, and proceeded to climb on to it.

"I'll preside," she began, coolly. "We'll get the business over and have our little snack afterwards. I move—"

"Do it beautifully now, for my sake," interrupted Hedda.

"Look here, old sinner," rejoined Dodo, "dry up, for *my* sake. I move that all women who have been members of this club for ten years or more be compelled to resign, and that their re-election be in the hands of the new members."

"I beg to second the motion," said the Superfluous Woman.

Jane Eyre was just getting up to speak when the door burst open, and a boy and a girl rushed in—the Heavenly Twins, as I'm a living woman!

"No men!" a dozen voices cried. "Turn him out!"

"Pooh!" said Angelica. "Diavolo isn't a man. He's more than a man. He's a portent—a portent of the period. Besides, we are always together."

" 'Course we are," said Diavolo.

Dodo continued to protest vociferously. Angelica flamed up.

"My dear Dodo," she remarked, with suppressed anger, "calm yourself. If you don't, Diavolo and me—Diavolo and I will take you outside and throw you into the Rubicon, just to see whether the Archbishop of Canterbury will fish you out. You won't like it, I tell you—I've had a ducking myself, and I know."

At these last words Diavolo stuffed his handkerchief into his mouth to keep from laughing, and Angelica boxed his ears. However, the incident had the effect of quietening Dodo.[2]

"Well, sit down. Little boys should be seen and not heard," the latter snapped out. "I put the motion—"

"Excuse me." Everyone turned round. Jane was on her

feet. "Excuse me, this meeting was called for five o'clock. It still wants ten minutes to the hour, and I am expecting other members. In fact I have arranged for a full attendance."

"Hear, hear," said Diavolo.

"Silence, child," said the Superfluous Woman.

"Yah!" returned the boy, "Who kissed Colin in the barn?"

There was nothing for it but to wait, and other members began immediately to pour in, in such numbers that I cannot even give you all their names. There were, first and foremost, Rosalind, Imogen, Miranda, and a lot more Shaksperean [sic] women. (How charming they looked! "I bet they're no good at fly-fishing," observed the Keynotes person.) Then came Sophia Western and Elizabeth Bennet (to all appearance neither proud nor prejudiced), and Lucy Snowe and another Lucy—Richard Feverel's betrothed—and Lorna Doone, and Rhoda Fleming, and Daisy Miller, and Maggie Tulliver. Yes, and Tess (poor thing!), and Marty South, and Catriona, and —Oh! I forget the rest. I observed that although few of these were dressed according to the latest modes, yet none of them seemed old-fashioned, while some of the youngest girls, gowned by Worth[3] or Mason, were already beginning to look out of date.

"Of course," Jane whispered to me, "most of the best known women here haven't visited the club for many months."

"Why?" I innocently inquired.

"Well, you might guess. The Dodo clique made the place simply unbearable. Fancy Miranda smoking, or Lorna drinking gin-and-bitters, as these upstarts do!"

I shuddered.

The clock struck, and Angelica sweetly suggested that Dodo should climb down and make way for her betters. There was some discussion as to who should take her place, and in the end my own modest Jane, as being a capable, shrewd little woman, was compelled to preside. She wanted to retire in favour of Elizabeth Bennet, but the majority had their way.

Dodo began to sing "After the Ball." Little Jane, however, quickly restored order. She was always equal to the occasion. She said the question was whether the club should be a bear-garden and a scandal to the neighbourhood—or not.

Elizabeth Bennet, in a cool, satirical speech, moved that all members of less than three years' standing be suspended for a year, when the question of their re-admission should be submitted to a committee, consisting of Miranda, Sophia Western, and Lucy Feverel (née Desborough). This was carried after opposition.

Angelica didn't quite like it. She said it was "beastly unfair," especially towards Evadne. As for Evadne herself, she readily acquiesced. Dodo blustered, and finally sobbed. She undertook never to swear again, but it was in vain. My fear, or rather my hope, is that when the twelve months has expired, she also will have expired. As for some of the other suspended ones, they may have a second chance.

Upon the whole, I rejoice.

NOTES

1. *Woman Literary Supplement.* 2nd May 1894, page 4. Signed Sarah Volatile.
2. Bennett's references to the Heavenly Twins - "he's more than a man", "ducking", "boxed his ears" - all relate to the plot of Sarah Grand's novel. For example: "[Angelica] was teaching [Diavolo] to respect women, for one thing; when he didn't respect them she beat him; and this made him thoughtful." (p. 255)
3. Charles Frederick Worth (1826-1895), widely seen as the father of haute couture, was an English fashion designer who rose to fame after moving to Paris in 1846.

REJECTED.[1]
A GIRL AND ANOTHER GIRL.

I stood at the door of Marston's magnificent studio, hesitating whether to enter and acquaint him with the sad state of affairs at once, or to turn away and enjoy the pleasure of nursing my wrongs in private a little longer. The two pictures which I had sent to the Academy were rejected by the Hanging Committee.

Theoretically, I ought not to have cared. I belonged to the New British Painters, who held their own exhibitions, amusing one half of the artistic public and enraging the other. The N.B.P.s were supposed to have cast off the trammels of commercialism, and they publicly vituperated the trade ring, which is the academy. Nevertheless, I, in common I believe with most other N.B.P.s, sent pictures in secret to Burlington House. If they came back, as was usually the case, we said nothing about it, but if by any chance one was accepted, we explained that it was a potboiler, not good enough in our opinion, for the N.B.P. exhibition.

The difference between the N.B.P. Exhibition and the Academy is that at the former you never sell anything, while at the latter you do—sometimes. And this accounts for much, seeing that even N.B.P.s must live.

The portal of the studio opened, a model came out, and I caught sight of Marston in his white painting smock. Marston, although artistically we are distant as the poles, is a very dear friend of mine. He happens to be a fashionable A.R.A., and gets five hundred guineas for a portrait. Nevertheless, he likes my work, and I tell him everything. He is older than I.

"Well," he said, as he saw me, "what luck?"

I replied, with an air of gaiety which I was far from feeling, that the committee regretted that from want of space they were compelled, &c., &c., and would I arrange for the removal of both my pictures without delay.

"The first time I ever went to fetch a Rejected," he said, "I had a bit of an adventure, which ended in matrimony. I've never told you I think. At first I thought I wouldn't trouble to fetch it, but I changed my mind. And just as the attendant was making the thing up into a parcel, I heard a voice from behind me, which I knew, inquiring for a picture. It was a woman's voice—a young woman whom I had known in the country, and had not seen for two years. I turned round.

"'Mary!'" I cried. Mrs. Marston's name is Mary.

"'Alfred!'" she cried.

"Then I assumed a cool and distant attitude, not because I felt that way inclined—I didn't—but because I thought it was the proper thing to do. The fact was that when last we met, I had asked the lady a certain question, a question which most men ask a lady at least once in their lives, and had received a refusal, kind, but firm, as they say. I came to London in a huff—worse than a huff—determined to forget her. And, as I thought, I was succeeding pretty well in doing so. So well that I had begun to lie awake at nights thinking about Another Girl—a Londoner this time. But as soon as I saw Mary again the image of the Other Girl seemed to walk out of the back door of my affections.

"'And you have come to London to paint, too?' I asked, after we had exchanged greetings.

"'Yes,' she said, 'And I have got one picture in—rather a large one,' she added proudly. 'This little one was rejected. Have you got many in?'

"Oh, that 'many!' How it hurt me!

"'None,' I said; 'I only sent this one, and you see its fate.'

"Her divine face clouded.

"'What a shame!' she said sympathetically, 'what a shame! And you paint ever so much better than I.'

"'Not a bit of it,' I replied; but I felt comforted. I sunned myself in her presence, and even forgot, for the moment, to hate the Hanging Committee. At length her picture was found—not a bad little thing.

"'May I carry it?' I said, and I looked into her eyes. She returned the glance in a manner I can never forget, and we went out into Piccadilly, I with a picture under each arm.

"We walked to Kensington, and what a walk it was! Never once did I think of the Other Girl. Mary was simply bewitching. I can barely remember a word of the conversation. Doubtless to a third person it would have sounded commonplace enough, but to us—to me, I should say—it was heaven.

"As we strolled along past the Green Park I thought: she is flirting. She wants to leave an aching void in my heart. But I don't care. It's nice while it lasts.

"At Sloane-street, I thought: No, this is not flirting. It must have pained her to refuse me, two years ago. She feels that she has ruined my life, and her desire is to be as kind to me as possible. She pities me. I don't like being pitied. But I don't care. It's nice while it lasts.

"At South Kensington Museum I made a discovery. Could it be? Dare I believe it? Had she repented of her refusal? Did she, after all, love me? I trembled with excitement, and one of the pictures slipped.

"'Do let me take mine now,' she pleaded. 'I'm sure the two together are too heavy for you.'

"'Not at all. I would carry forty of your pictures,' I said, accenting the possessive, and looking into her eyes again.

"I could not be mistaken. She loved me! Where was the Other Girl now? I wondered what on earth I could have seen in the Other Girl.

"I would ask Mary a certain question once more and the answer would be different this time. That inexpressible something in her eyes could only mean one thing. And we might get married at once, because, although I was earning but little, I understood from Mary that she was making Art pay. This was a mean way of looking at the matter, and I hated myself for it. But I couldn't help it a bit.

"When we reached her house she asked me to come in. I refused because I felt that if I did so I should assuredly put the question at once, and this might look too abrupt. No, I must be alone with my ecstasy.

"'May I call to-morrow?' I said.

"'Certainly,' she said, 'that will be better. George will be in then, and he will be delighted to see you.'

"'George?'

"'Yes, my husband, you know.'

"'Ah, of course. Exactly. Good-day.' I fled.

* * * *

"I didn't know Mrs. Marston had been married before," I said, filling up my glass. "I suppose George died, did he?"

"She hasn't been married before, my dear Reggie, and I believe George is well and hearty to this day."

"But I thought the adventure ended in your marriage."

"So it did. I married the Other Girl, who is also a Mary; and jolly lucky I was! I went to see her that very evening—to console myself. Afterwards, long afterwards, I told her the whole story. She laughed. Some women wouldn't have liked it, would they? But she's not that sort."

NOTES

1. *The Sun*. 2nd May 1894, page 1. Signed Enoch Arnold Bennett.

AN ACADEMY WORK.
THE MUTILATION OF A STATUE.[1]

Away beyond the great tower and interlaced rigging of many masts glimmered in the strong moonlight a thin stretch of lagoon. She gazed long and silently at the shining strip of water, and her eyes filled with involuntary tears. Was it love, or merely compassion that she experienced for this strong, surly, black-browed man who, seated at her feet on the balcony, puffed fiercely at his cigar, looking down at the dark, uneasy canal?

They had met two years ago in this very palazzo. And four times since then he had torn himself from his Lancashire cotton mills, where money was woven from two thousand spindles, to come and see her. Thrice he had sworn never to go near her again, and thrice he had yielded, in spite of himself, to the compelling influence which she exercised over him.

And now, man of forty as he was, and accounted shrewd even on the Manchester Exchange, he could not decide whether or not he was in love. Away from her, he supposed, with a sigh, that he must be. But when he saw her little, determined face, with its humorous eyes and square jaw (he hated a square jaw in a woman), and heard now her light irresponsible Society chatter, and now her impassioned revolutionary harangues, he wondered sadly at his own surpassing foolishness, and said with emphasis that the thing was absurd. Why, he was a steward of his chapel and a class-leader, and this woman openly railed at Christianity! He was a cautious Conservative, and she—she said there were two sides to the Anarchist question! He cared nothing for literature, never read anything but the *Times* and the *Textile Manufacturer*, while she treated the poets who fluttered around her as if they were young gods, and raved about Coventry Patmore's odes![2] He had no sympathy with art, and the nude disgusted him, and she was always chipping at statues: at this moment her "Mercury," destined for the Academy, was being admired and discussed in the drawing-room.

A woman carving Mercuries and Cupids, and Venuses, and what not! The thought revolted him. She ought to have been married ten years ago, and had a family. The care of a family was the only proper occupation for a woman, and therefore Miss Cartwright was hateful. And yet for days he had been living on her smiles. He was amazed at himself. It never occurred to him, however, to wonder why she tolerated him, nay, almost petted him.

"Well?" she said at length.

"Well."

"It's rude to repeat. Come inside, and see the Mercury. It's going away to-morrow. You must come and say you like it. Come," she went on imperiously, as he did not stir; "the idea of sitting out here all alone: I just came to call you in, and I've been here quite five minutes. I don't know what my guests will think."

They went in together. The high drawing-room, whose vaulted ceiling you instinctively felt but could not see, was dimly lighted by an English floor lamp. The usual Venetian crowd was assembled—an American statesman, who did not look in the least like an American statesman; two Bostonians, who exhaled a delicate aroma of culture, half a dozen art students of all nations, who lived on half-a-crown a day, and gazed with awe on Freddy Marston, R.A., the sculptor, whose house and studio in Holland Park-road are familiar to readers of the illustrated magazines; a woman with a mission, a princess from the Balkans, who spoke German and wrote novels in shaky French; a London musical critic, supposed to be omniscient; one or two Venetian officers, and other individuals too numerous to mention.

Marston was discoursing on the Mercury, which stood on a low table near the lamp.

"And do you think it will be rejected?" said Miss Cartwright.

"I feel sure it won't," was the reply. And since Marston was the only sculptor on the Hanging Committee, and was understood to be an admirer of Miss Cartwright, some importance might safely be attached to what he said.

A chorus of praise followed, and, with an ironical smile, Kitty—that was Miss Cartwright—turned to the man from Lancashire for his opinion.

"I'll tell you afterwards," he said, in the curt tone which a week or two ago had aroused the ire of Kitty's younger satellites. Some of them wanted to fight him or throw him into the canal, but there was a peculiarity in his look which dissuaded them from extreme measures.

Besides, Kitty always treated him with marked favour, and though this made matters worse, the art students were constrained to inaction, and the man from Lancashire was looked upon as a chartered boor.

The woman with a mission said she must go, and one of

the other guests left; the splash of oars died away; only the man from Lancashire remained in the drawing-room. Old Mrs. Cartwright, ancient and deaf as the gods, slumbered beyond the folding doors.

A sound of guitars and strong, clear voices singing, came through the open window, faint at first, but gradually increasing in volume.

"A singing boat," said Kitty. "Let us go out on the balcony." The man from Lancashire followed her.

A large singing boat, gay with red and yellow lanterns, and followed by a crowd of gondolas, each with its swinging crimson lamp, passed down the canal, disarraying the quaint, uncanny patterns which the moonlight had painted on the water. The procession dissolved into the darkness, and the music ceased.

"What a night!" exclaimed Kitty.

The man from Lancashire said nothing.

"By the way, you didn't praise my 'Mercury'."

"No. You must get people who understand such things to do that. You know if I said what I thought, I should say it was—*not* decent."

"Don't say what you think, then." She laughed a little, but not naturally.

"Tell me, Miss Cartwright," he said irrelevantly. "Were your parents Christian people?" She looked at him.

"Yes. They died when I was young."

"Would that they had lived!"

"You think that I should have been different?" There was no shade of vexation in her voice. "It is better as it is. I try to be honest."

"Why haven't you married? A woman's business is to marry, to be a joy to her husband, and to train up her children."

"Ah! I'm not that sort of woman. I can't sacrifice my life to someone else's. I must work."

"You mean you must satisfy your desire for fame, notoriety."

"I mean," she said, "I must work. I work for the pleasure and inward satisfaction it gives me—because I am an artist. Fame is nothing to me."

"You deceive yourself. You are not content to live a woman's life. You want to make a name, you want people to talk about you. Vanity, vanity! You—"

She quelled him with a look.

"Come inside," she said, "it's cold. I will prove to you that my sole pleasure is in the work itself. I'm not vain. How dare you call me vain? Art is my religion. You see this Mercury. It is my poor masterpiece, and it would perhaps cause some talk even in London. It was to go to the Academy to-morrow."

She took up a heavy paper-knife, and calmly knocked the right arm from the statue, then the left, and then the head.

The ruins of the Mercury lay between them, and each looked at the other, breathing hard.

"There," she said, with an attempt at quietness, "I worked six happy months on that."

"Kitty," cried the man from Lancashire, "You love me! I know it"; and he took her in his arms. For one passionate moment she did not resist.

"You will leave all this, and be my wife," he said, a note of triumph in his voice.

She disengaged herself.

"In Manchester?"

"And why not? People love, even in Manchester. You'll be my wife? Say yes. I want to hear it. I've been a lonely man, Kitty. You'll comfort me." He waited, his face white and red by turns.

"No, Robert. It's impossible."

Who shall describe the struggle which these words ended?

"It's impossible. My ideals are not yours. I'm not a man's woman, because I can't subordinate myself. I can't give up my art for your religion. I can't sit by the fire and see that your slippers are warm. I can't expend myself in the management of a household. I can't take my opinions ready-made from a lord and master. Why, I should neglect you horribly, and my escapades would shock your poor dear Methodists." She had regained her composure.[3]

"You shall be your own mistress," he exclaimed fiercely, "I swear you shall only marry me."

"I daren't. It would be the ruin of us both. You know it would. We shouldn't keep the peace a month."

He sat down to think, and she began to remove the broken marble. Old Mrs. Cartwright hobbled in from the other room. The man from Lancashire stood up with a sudden movement.

"Perhaps you are right," he said to Kitty. "Good-bye." And so he went.

Kitty is still Kitty Cartwright. As for him, they say he is the richest cotton-spinner in Lancashire, and all men go in fear of him. He lives alone in a great house, and spends his money on missionaries.

NOTES

1. *The Sun*. 25th June 1894, page 1. Signed Enoch Arnold Bennett.
2. Coventry Kersey Dighton Patmore (1823-1896) published a sequence of poems, *The Angel in the House*, between 1854 and 1863. The work presented an idealised picture of Victorian womanhood celebrated within the unquestioned virtues of married life. Virginia Woolf alluded to the poem in her essay "Professions for Women": "She was utterly unselfish .... She sacrificed herself daily .... if there was a draught she sat in it - in short she was so constituted that she never had a mind of her own ..... Above all - I need not say it - she was pure." (*The Crowded Dance of Modern Life*)
3. Kitty Cartwright summarises the elements associated with the "New Woman": demands for greater freedom from gender, class and religious restraints; enlarged employment and educational opportunities; an end to sexual double standards. In his "Book Chat" review (*Woman*, 13th June 1894, p. 7) published two weeks before "An Academy Work", Bennett reviewed Ella Hepworth Dixon's novel *The Story of a Modern Woman*, dealing with women's employment and criticizing the sexual double standard. The next week he penned an article on "The Lower Education of Men" (*Woman*, 4th July 1894, pp. 3-4) arguing that whilst "women have attained higher education, sometimes to the detriment of practical living, men need lower education, so to speak, to make them more pleasant to live with." (quoted Miller, p. 20)

FENELLA: A MANX IDYLL.[1]

"Richard, you are sure you know how to work all those ropes and things?" said Mrs. Markheim. She was seated in the well of the yacht "Kestrel" (two and a half rater), and the yacht "Kestrel" blobbed [sic] up and down on the waters of the harbour in a manner which, experienced from the well, was the reverse of reassuring to a lady whose years, like her waist, were just upon the poetical side of forty. The young man she addressed was at the tiller, about seven feet from his aunt, but so intent upon keeping the "Kestrel's" course that he paid no attention to the lady's anxious words. The yacht was doing six knots, close hauled to a freshening north wind, and Richard, who had owned her for exactly one week, felt mightily proud of her sailing qualities. As she neared the buoy which marks the end of the sunken breakwater, the waves grew bigger, and Mrs. Markheim's anxiety grew with them. "Richard, you're sure we shall be all right? Dolly," turning to her daughter, who was leaning meditatively over the weather rail watching the foam as it raced by, "Dolly, you're not safe there, come and sit by me."

"My dear aunt," said Richard rudely, " unless you can be quiet, I'll just pile her up on this breakwater, and then there'll be something worth talking about."

"Pile her up," was an expression which Richard had come across in one of Clark Russell's[2] novels—he reviewed novels, wrote them as well, or at any rate stories—and he used it with all the relish which a literary man has for an apposite quotation. Certainly it silenced Mrs. Markheim for the moment.

The "Kestrel" had now passed the buoy and was outside the harbour, and the exultant Richard, who had never before had sole control of a yacht, winked at his cousin Dolly a wink full of high spirits and self-confidence.

"Feel comfy?" he asked her. She smiled a reply.

Judging from his carelessly nautical attire, and especially the knowing angle at which his peaked cap was tilted, the inexperienced person might have taken Richard for a thorough sailor, cradled upon the deep, and probably well acquainted with all the complexities of tide and current which give the southwest corner of the Manx coast an unenviable fame among yachtsmen, and furnish the fishermen of Port Erin with innumerable yarns; but the devious, uncertain course which the "Kestrel" shaped, and the frequent flutter of her badly set mainsail, told a different story. Indeed, the crew of an incoming lugger which passed Richard's craft, discussed in their mild, quiet Manx way the chances of an accident when the yacht got beyond the shelter of Bradda Head. She was destined, however, not to get beyond the shelter of Bradda Head. Before Richard could plume himself upon being absolutely in the open sea, Mrs. Markheim gave an involuntary shudder, and endeavoured to sit bolt upright.

"Richard," she said, "we must return."

"Couldn't think of it now, aunt. We're just beginning to enjoy life."

"I insist. I—feel—unwell." She put her lips together tightly, and for once Dolly was glad to note her mother's firmness. Neither of them was used to two and a half raters in a choppy sea.

"Oh! very well then," Richard grumbled, "I must put the yacht about and we'll run in on the other tack."

He used these sea-terms with considerable fluency, for he had been studying the subject practically during the last week. But when it actually came to putting the "Kestrel" about, his confidence began to desert him. His fisherman tutor had told him that one person could easily manage a boat like the "Kestrel," and Richard, with the omniscient assurance of a man accustomed to patronise the universe in the editorial "notes" of an evening paper, had replied, "Oh! yes, easily." He found the task rather exciting, however. Should the jibsheet or the foresheet be loosed first? He decided on the foresheet, which was wrong, and yet he could have gone through the drill without a hitch—on paper. The foresail was now shaking and he called Dolly to hold the helm down hard while he attended to things generally. Of course the yacht hung dead in the wind, the mainsail flapping in a style which caused Mrs. Markheim to pray for dry land.

"Ah! missed stays," ejaculated the captain of the "Kestrel," with an attempt at calmness, "we'll try again." Not without difficulty he got the yacht under way once more. A second time Dolly was instructed to hold the helm down hard, and a second time the obstinate little vessel stuck in the wind. "H'm! Funny!" said Richard.

At this instant Mrs. Markheim stood up, and the boom immediately carried away her bonnet and part of her hair. She screamed, and, following the flying confection with her eyes, she was brought face to face with the fact that the yacht was quickly drifting towards the rocks of Bradda. She screamed anew, this time in earnest.

"Richard! See! We're on the rocks."

Richard looked, and at once realised that the tide was sweeping them on to the headland, in spite of the wind. He lost his head then, and began pulling aimlessly at ropes, muttering the while, "You're all right, you're all right. Don't get alarmed."

"There's someone in a boat there hailing you," said Dolly, pale with excitement, and pointing to a little cockleshell of a dinghy with a lug-sail, which was approaching them on the lee-bow. Richard listened.

"You'll be ashore if you don't mind," came a thin, far-off shout.

"There, there, I told you!" Mrs. Markheim almost sobbed. Richard called back some unintelligible reply.

"Help! Help!" shouted his aunt with more sense. The little boat rapidly approached them, dancing lightly over the waves like an animated cork. Its occupant proved to be a girl. She was dressed in blue serge, with a Tam-o'Shanter hat. Skilfully steering her dinghy alongside the "Kestrel," she lowered the sail with a run, threw Richard a line, and was on board in a twinkling. Richard raised his hat, feeling exquisitely foolish, and stammered that the yacht would persist in hanging in the wind. They were not seventy yards from the rocks now.

"Oh! do do something," gasped Mrs. Markheim, "you seem to know—er—about these things."

The girl put up the helm, and sharply told Richard to keep it there. He said to himself that he would sooner have "gone down with all on board," than be rescued in this way by a girl. And on his own yacht too! Now she took the helm from him, and Richard saw that in some miraculous way the "Kestrel" was moving again, the sails all drawing, and the dinghy towing astern. They were saved.

This is a story of two meetings, and that was the first.

To say the least, it was ignominious for Richard, and very informal all round. Mrs. Markheim, overflowing with gratitude, renewed again and again the thanksgiving of herself and her daughter, and begged to have their saviour's name. "Fenella Marston," came the shy answer, and Richard, full of discomfiture and speechlessness as he was, had wit enough left to admire in secret such a pretty name as Fenella. It appeared that Fenella lived with her father in a lone house among the hills between Port Erin and Peel, and "she must go at once," she said, when the poor fluttering "Kestrel" had once more reached the shelter of the quay wall.

* * * * *

A year passed, and Richard was again yachting at Port Erin, this time alone. Mrs. Markheim had graciously asked him to join herself and Dolly at Fécamp, but for some inexplicable reason, he had declined the invitation, much to everyone's surprise, for everyone, including Dolly, imagined that he was in love with Dolly. For his own part, he was not quite certain on the point, and he determined to spend a week or two in solitude at Port Erin with his darling "Kestrel," which by-the-way he could now handle with some skill, in order that he might commune with himself and explore the recesses of his feelings towards the adorable Dolly. Adorable she certainly was—that he admitted. Beautiful, just sufficiently retiring, bookishly clever, and full of sympathy for his literary ambitions, she seemed just the woman to make him happy though married. But—but—but—well, it is impossible to conceal the fact that Fenella was continually in the background of Richard's thoughts. Although the memory of her was connected with the one miserable incident of a brilliant career, he liked to call up her picture as she moved rapidly about his yacht, engaged in saving it, and him, and Dolly, and Dolly's mamma, from a watery grave.

One day he had sailed the "Kestrel" to Peel. Tide and wind militated against him getting her back before nightfall, and he determined to walk home to Port Erin, ten miles over the mountains, and return for the yacht on the morrow. The route from Peel, provided one avoids the carriage roads, is as wild and weird as a person could wish. After leaving the quaint old town and the quaint old town's new, vast hotel, one begins to climb almost immediately, and all the way the cloud-wrapped top of South Barrule appears and disappears like a revolving light. It was late in the afternoon when Richard started, and he found the hill paths, at no time congested with traffic, now quite deserted. Four miles from Peel one of those drifting blinding mists for which the Isle of Man is famous suddenly obliterated the landscape, and when it happily cleared away, after about a quarter of an hour, Richard was well lost. He sat down on a boulder to study a small pocket map, but to no purpose. Then he jumped up, for he heard a man whistling. Presently the whistler appeared in sight, but she was a woman, a woman in a serge frock and a Tam-o'Shanter hat and carrying a bag. She was walking rapidly, and when she caught sight of Richard she suddenly ceased making music, and involuntarily slackened her steps. Richard emitted an ejaculation of surprise which it is unnecessary to repeat here.

Now the experienced reader will have guessed that this woman in the blue serge and the Tam-o'Shanter hat was just Fenella herself. Everything points to it, and such was, indeed, the fact.

Richard greeted her, blushing furiously. Fortunately he was spared the necessity of confessing that for the second time she found him in a fix. He said boldly that he was walking to Port Erin.

"But this is not quite the nearest way to Port Erin," she said, "you should have turned off towards Dalby about half a mile back."

"Yes, I know," was the mendacious reply. "But I wanted a long walk."

Miss Marston refrained from referring to the yacht, no doubt out of delicacy, he thought. But she was willing to chatter about the scenery and the people, and Richard said that more delightful chatter he had never heard. Dolly could not talk like that. And Dolly could not walk like that. It took Richard all his time to keep by her side.

"I have never properly thanked you, Miss Marston, for your invaluable assistance last year. Let me do so now. And you may be interested to know that since then I have acquired a little more maritime skill."

"Oh! To a girl used to the sea all her life it was really nothing, Mr. Lacy."

"You know my name, then?" he blurted out, for he remembered that his aunt had introduced only herself to Fenella last year.

"Oh, yes," returned his companion. "I just asked one of the fishermen. I wanted to find out."

What delightful ingenuousness, he mused. What absolute freedom from conventionality! Now, if she only *knew* as much as Dolly. Poor Dolly was very conventional, in spite of certain advanced views.

"By-the-way, Mr. Lacy," she went on, "I have often

thought about you, and I wondered whether you were any relation to the short-story writer of the same name."

"I am—a sort of distant connection," said Richard. "But surely you don't admire that fellow's work."

"Indeed I do. Did you see that tale of his in the last *Yellow Book*?[3] I thought it was equal to de Maupassant's best."

The *Yellow Book*! de Maupassant! He was not much moved at hearing himself compared to de Maupassant. The thing had occurred before, but that the comparison should be made by a girl such as he had taken Fenella to be was certainly surprising. Why, he had imagined her devouring her *Tit Bits* every Friday.

He confessed to being Richard Lacy, the short-story writer. She laughed with naïve pleasure. They began to talk books with great gusto. What did she think of Henry James, of Flaubert, of Prosper Merimée? And what did he think of George Egerton[4] and the other *revoltées*. The air was thick with "views". Richard was enchanted. Poor Dolly! She was a nice girl, but Fenella—Fenella was a revelation. How lucky he had not gone to Normandy!

"That house, there," Fenella said after a long argument upon W. D. Howells,[5] pointing to an old farm-like structure which stood near a tiny hamlet in the valley below them, "is where I have lived nearly all my life. It has a fine library, my father's. He is the local 'littery' gent!"

"Really!" said Richard "And that, I suppose," pointing to an active figure in clerical attire which was rapidly coming towards them up the steep path, "is the local curate?"

Fenella seemed amused. "Yes," she laughed, "that *is* the local curate."

The local curate approached, and carelessly raised his hat.

"Mr. Lacy," said Fenella, dryly, "may I introduce you to my husband? Charlie, this is the Mr. Lacy I met last year—you remember—just before our marriage."

* * * * *

Richard was up very early the next morning taking a last look at quiet, unobtrusive Port Erin and its tiny harbour. Hour by hour of the wakeful night, his ruffled heart had gone out to Dolly in Normandy for solace. Twelve hours ago he was despising her, and now the very thought of her was like a soft pillow. He had finally decided that he loved her. Presently he was at the village post office writing out a telegram.

"What's this?" said the postmaster, who was also a grocer, pointing to a word in the address. Richard informed him.

"What?"

"F, e, c, a, m, p."

And in forty-eight hours he was there.

NOTES

1. *Woman.* 29th August 1894, pages 14, 16. Signed Sarah Volatile. "Fenella" is printed above Part II of Roma White's serial "The Midsummer Mummers". White (1866-1930) started her career as a journalist before writing a generically mixed range of novels, three of which were reviewed in *Woman* and in *Hearth and Home* by Bennett. He compared her *A Stolen Mask* to George Moore's *A Mummer's Wife* (*Woman*, 13th May 1896), the novel that convinced him of the romantic nature of the Potteries.

2. William Clark Russell (1844-1911) was the successful writer of mainly nautical novels, several of which were reviewed by Bennett between May 1897 and December 1898. Prior to making an appearance in Bennett's story, Arthur Conan Doyle's "The Five Orange Pips" has Doctor Watson engrossed in one of Clark's sea stories.

3. Bennett's first self-consciously literary story "A Letter Home" appeared in John Lane's prestigious *Yellow Book* in July 1895, in the company of Henry James's story "The Next Time". Publication marked Bennett's entry into the cultural avant-garde.

4. George Egerton, (Mary Chavelita Dunne, 1859-1945) was a prominent feminist novelist and translator whose work was reviewed by Bennett between December 1894 and June 1899 - the last review being of her translation of Knut Hamsun's *Hunger.* Bennett countered John Lane's claims that his first novel, *A Man From The North*, was a too risky venture for a publisher by pointing to the success he had with George Egerton's first volume of short stories, *Keynotes* (1893).

5. William Dean Howells (1837-1920) was an American writer who was very influential in the late 19th and early 20th centuries, particularly in promoting the cause of literary realism. Fenella and Richard may well have been discussing Howell's *A Woman's Reason* (1883), which explored women and social values in Boston. Bennett reviewed Howell's work on seven occasions between 6th November 1895 and 15th March 1900.

"MY FIRST BOOK."[1]

This is a plain tale of disaster. There is no literary art about it. I have done with literary art.

My first book, *A Go-ahead Girl*, has run through twelve editions in twelve months, and is still selling at the rate of thirty copies a-day. It has "made" my publishers, Messrs. Calkin and Thuey, and it continues to bring in the revenue of an ambassador. My second book (and my last, I swear it!) *Society* appeared about a month ago. The first large edition was exhausted on the day of publication. A second and third were disposed of within a week, and a fourth is nearly finished. Messrs. Calkin and Thuey gave me £2,000 down for *Society*, and a royalty on every copy beyond eight thousand. But, nevertheless, I have done with literary art.

You have probably read or read about *A Go-ahead Girl*. For weeks it was viewed, reviewed, and re-reviewed without cessation. Mudie's[2] subscribers fought for it, and Smith's[3] were unhappy until they got it. Mr. Macaroni, Member of Parliament, and of the County Council, who does his twenty-five columns a-week, and who is reputed to be capable of writing one article and dictating another simultaneously, made it a "Book of the Hour" in the *Satellite*. He said that the fury and passion of it moved him as he had not been moved for one month, and that its "essential note" was "unabashed modernity." The rest of the review consisted of extracts, numbered in Roman figures. As you may be aware, the title of *A Go-ahead Girl* accurately describes its contents. The book analyses the Society young woman as the Society young woman has never been analysed before. It is ill-arranged, but its pictures are unflinchingly frank; and since Society dearly loves to think itself preternaturally wicked, Society read the thing with breathless avidity. And the book was perused with the more eagerness for the reason that its author had the inestimable advantage of being somebody's son. My father is the author of that celebrated work, *The Strife of Sex in Andromeda*, and people are always anxious to test for themselves the theory of heredity.

But what helped *A Go-ahead Girl* more than anything else was the rumour, skilfully floated in a certain quarter, that my heroine was a sketch from life. It soon became a generally accepted fact that Flo Farningham was no less a person than the Hon. Dorothy Califont, a member of a new clique of affected culture, and a well-known figure in those circles known as "really smart." The likeness was so obvious, the minute circumstantial touches with which the book abounded were so exactly true to life that it would have been idle explicitly to deny that the public had the rights of the matter. And this I took care not to do. The portrait was, in fact, clever—clever as a portrait, and more than that, clever as a picture. *A Go-ahead Girl* would have succeeded in no uncertain manner without adventitious aids of any kind. This sounds something like self-praise; but it is no such thing.

I never wrote the book. The Honourable Dolly wrote it herself, and this is the root of my difficulties. Events followed each other in this wise.

I have been acquainted with the Honourable Dolly for the best part of our lives; but it was only two years ago, when we were both staying at Crawle Castle, the Earl of Luxor's place, that I first came to know her with any degree of intimacy. The Countess of Luxor is the author of that terribly dull work, Lord Capple, in one volume, calf extra. Now, Capple at that time, to the intense amusement of Dolly herself, and of Dolly's own particular set, was making love to Dolly. To spur him on to more abject foolishness than he would spontaneously exhibit, she showed a more marked preference for my own poor self, whom Capple secretly loathed.

There was a large house-party at Crawle, including several highly-cultured ladies. Lady Luxor's set is nothing if not literary; and as I was the only male with the least pretension to bookishness, they graciously admitted me to their cultured companionship. I did not, however, gain much instruction by it, the favourite reading of the ladies of the set being the *Sporting Times*. The essential fact was that Dolly began to talk to me about a novel which she said she had almost completed. She wished me to read it, and I gallantly consented to do so. One evening at the witching preprandial hour, I came upon her in the library, seated in front of a pile of manuscript. She made me take a chair by her side.

"This," she said, with a dramatic gesture, "is my novel." The soft shaded lamp-light fell on her upturned face, and I thought she looked very beautiful.

"I will read you a few passages," she went on. For twenty minutes or so I listened to the tones of her exquisitely modulated voice, and when it ceased I begged her to continue.

"No," she said; "you can read it at your leisure. I wanted to tell you, Mr. Tantamount, that I can never publish this novel—at least in my own name."

"Why not, my dear lady?" cried I.

"Because it is solely about myself."

I had suspected as much.

"It is about myself, and people would say that I did it for self-advertisement."

"They would never dare!" There was indignation in my voice.

"And they would be right—in a way, Mr. Tantamount," she resumed, after a pause, bringing her face nearer to mine. "You have literary aspirations; you write, don't you?"

"I have been writing articles for the papers for the past ten years."

"I thought so."

"But they have never got themselves printed."

"Well, never mind. Now will you do me a little favour?"

"If it is in my power, you may rely on me," I said.

"Will you let this thing be published in your name?"

I was dumbfounded.

"Really," I stammered, I can't do *that*."

She looked deep into my eyes.

"Yes, you can, Mr. Tantamount, and you will—to oblige *me*."

If I had not been sitting quite so near, if I could have got away from the sinister seduction of that glance, I might have withstood her. But I could not. I argued that the proposal was absurd, unheard of. But she wore me down, or rather she dominated me, and when the dinner bell rang I had promised to do what she asked.

To lend some colour of reality to the sham, I recast certain portions of the novel, and re-copied the whole of it. Then I sent it, at a venture, to Messrs. Calkin and Thuey, who lead the "new cultured school" of publishers, and they requested me to call on them. They have the most palatial offices and the rudest clerks it has ever been my lot to see. They liked *A Go-ahead Girl*, and they published it at their own risk.

When the first favourable notices appeared, I experienced a sort of vicarious gratification. Dolly sent for me and talked delightedly about the success of "her" novel, and this somehow hurt my feelings. Then the furore and my troubles began. Congratulations rained on me, and I didn't know what to say in reply. All Dolly's friends hoped that *they* were not in the novel; and when I curtly said "No, of course not," they seemed vexed. Some people made excessively impolite remarks, that I (*I*) had exceeded the novelist's licence, and so on. Interviewers besieged my house. Every editor in the country wanted to know how I came to write this extraordinary, audacious work, of which editions were succeeding each other like telegraph posts seen from an express train. Only upon one point was I vague or undecided. I never affirmed that my heroine was a portrait of Dolly. As Dolly industriously sowed the statement herself, there was no necessity for me to say anything. For a time, I was the most envied man in London—I who loathed myself, I whose life had become a burden. I had forty invitations to dinner a week (Dolly had fifty), and because I could only accept seven, people said I was proud; that success had turned my head.

In the end, I retreated to the country for a space. It was there that I conceived the idea of really writing a novel myself which should surpass *A Go-ahead Girl*. I felt that this was the only way in which I could recover my peace of mind and my self- respect. It would be easy then, Dolly's permission having been obtained, to disclose the authorship of my first book, because the world would not be able to say that I had taken credit for work which it was beyond my powers to compass. I had an excellent opinion of my literary possibilities, and, urged on by the solicitations of my publishers, I wrote *Society*. During the fever and stress of composition, I thought well of the book; but when I came to read it in proof, my hopes of its success were less sanguine.

It appeared; it sold rapidly. But it was ridiculed, mildly at first, then fiercely, cruelly, and I cannot say that it has not had its deserts. And here comes the very coping stone of my shame. The rumour is abroad that I am not the author of *A Go-ahead Girl*. It can only have sprung from one source, and I have been to see the Honourable Dorothy Califont.

"Yes," she said, coolly, in answer to my question, "*I have* let it out."

"But you place me in a very awkward position," I protested.

"Surely," she said, "you ought to be satisfied with the renown which your own book has brought you. Besides, my purpose has been served, and people can say what they like about self-advertisement. I want to be the author of *A Go-ahead Girl* and I'm going to be. I was thinking it would be a relief to you to be free of the role."

Perhaps it would, but our acquaintanceship has ceased.

[*The above story is, we are assured, founded only on what might happen and is not, as some might suppose, a record of fact*. ED. "WOMAN."]

NOTES

1. *Woman*. 3rd October 1894, pages 23, 25-26. Signed Sarah Volatile.
2. Mudie's Lending Library opened in Oxford Street in 1852. Their selection of titles could greatly influence a book's sales figures and he angered some writers by exercising a form of moral censorship.
3. W.H. Smith, and Son, Ltd. opened as a firm of stationers, newsagents and booksellers in 1792. The business rapidly expanded with a countrywide network of railway station bookstalls. Its first circulating library was opened at Euston in 1848. In 1918 Smith's banned Bennett's *The Pretty Lady* on grounds of offending taste: "Smiths, after doing exceedingly well out of it, have decided to ban it." (*Letters III*, p. 61)

THE REPENTANCE OF RONALD PRIMULA.[1]

The fever and fret caused by the publication of that celebrated Society novel, *The Cream Chrysanthemum* are now somewhat allayed, but it is still being read widely, and some account of a curious incident which befel me the other day, and which throws a new light on a piquant episode, will, I am sure, be received with interest.

You remember, of course, that the novel in question chiefly portrayed, under the thinnest disguise, two men well-known in a certain noisy section of Society. Ronald Primula, the man with a pose, the maker of epigrams, and Lord Cecil Dover, his youthful disciple.

Walking idly along Chelsea Embankment one Sunday morning lately, I observed Ronald Primula himself, whom I knew by sight but not personally, sitting in a meditative attitude upon one of the iron seats. As I passed, he rose and ambled sedately away. I noticed how meek and careworn was his countenance—so different from his usual appearance, for instance, at theatrical first-nights. When he had gone some distance, I turned to take the seat which he had vacated, and found a book lying there—a thin volume, shaped like a Pseudonym, and covered with a gold network of "R.P." monograms. With some curiosity I opened it, and saw that it was a diary, daintily written, with wide margins, on hand-made paper. Assuredly it belonged to Mr. Primula, but he was out of call by this time, and I could not resist peeping into it. Having peeped once, I was lost, and gave myself up to it unblushingly. The next thing I remember was a heavy tread passing in front of me. I looked up; it was Mr. Primula, and he stared at me and the book.

"Excuse me," I said, politely; "is this your book?" He hesitated a moment.

"No sir," he replied impressively, "it is not. That book lay there when I first sat down." I knew that he was romancing a little. Evidently, having seen that I had looked at it, he felt ashamed to own that it was his (who amongst us cares to confess that he keeps a diary?), and followed a natural impulse to deny all connection with it.

"But surely—" I began.

"Nothing of the kind, sir," he interrupted, sharply. "It is not mine, I beg to repeat; and for all I care, you can do what you like with it." And so he walked huffily away, little dreaming that I was a journalist.

Well, I am doing what I like with it. Here are a few extracts:—

* * * * * *

1st April.—At 2 a.m. this morning I was swinging gently in the silken hammock in the library, looking up new epigrams from the French papers. A few tired rays of moonlight crept furtively through the high window and, I believe tinged my back hair. The Moorish lamp, which I have recently shaded with Tonquinese gauze, threw a wan, seaweed-coloured light on my face and the seductive page of the *Figaro*, and altogether I was the centre of a gracious and pleasing picture. How exquisite to make pictures which no one will ever see! The Empire clock intoned two, and after I had adapted my epigrams for the morrow I began to repeat them in a soft, cooing voice, varying the emphasis constantly, so as to get the true purple effect, and smiling indulgently the while at my Moorish lamp.

Then Hawkins came in. I thought at first he wanted to go to bed—servants are always wanting to go to bed. I never want to go to bed except at Mr. Oscar Wilde's plays—but he announced: "Lord Cecil Dover wishes to see you at once, sir."

Now Cessy, with his hair the colour of a picture-frame made in Germany, is beginning to bore me. I retain him because a satellite is necessary to a man in my public position; even Jupiter would be a planet of no importance without his satellites; and fancy the earth without the moon

—fancy my back hair without the moon! Still, Cessy bores me! I was about to instruct Hawkins that I had sought my couch, when Cessy walked hastily into the room.

"Ah, Cessy," I said wearily. "What new thing, what new thing? I pictured you asleep, one pale hand outside the coverlet and your mouth open. You catch me learning my to-morrow's epigrams." (I thought I would be bold.)

"*Learning* your epigrams, my blond Ronald!" he drawled, and from the height of his frail six feet he looked down into my large face with a pained expression.

"Yes, Cessy, I have never told you before. I imagined that perhaps it showed a lack of artistic reticence to reveal even to you all my mysteries; just one little crushed-strawberry secret I have kept from you till this hour. Yes, I learn my epigrams, having first adapted them from back numbers of the French papers. It needs an artist to—er—convey, Cessy. I am an artist."

"Frankly, my Ronald," he said, "I thought you were cleverer." His faith in me seemed shocked.

"So I am cleverer, my young friend. Anybody can make an epigram; one sees them in *Punch*.[2] But constantly to—er—use other people's, without being discovered—often: that is worth doing, that is beautiful."

"And have you always done this?" His admiration for me was returning.

"Ah, no. Only since the death of Sally."

"Which Sally?"

"Sally the first. She was my cook. Imperfectly educated, she used words with a sublime disregard for meaning, which I have only seen equalled in the works of an Archdeacon. I remember once I summoned her into this very chamber to compliment her upon the previous night's supper. I told her it had been an exquisite success. 'I'm glad you thought it was an excess, sir,' she said. And in two hours, two flying, glorious hours, I had fashioned from her artless speech that world renowned epigram, *Nothing succeeds like excess.*"[3]

"How beautiful!" murmured Lord Cecil, "and how simple!"

"Yes," I sighed, "she was very useful. It was she who gave me a true insight into the art of lying, about which I have written so magically. Whenever she wanted a holiday, she would say that her sister was down with indigestion of the lungs, or her niece was suffering from ulsters. Always either one or the other. Of course it was merely an excuse, but one could forgive anything to such an artist. Alas! the impious daisies batten on her grave. But what brings you here now, Cessy, at an hour when to be respectable is to be asleep?"

"I have news," he began solemnly, "Have you read or heard of a new novel called *The Cream Chrysanthemum*? No? Well Hicks put it into my hand as we left the club to-night and advised me to read it. It's anonymous, but he says little Willie Rash wrote it. Ronald, I've been reading it."

"And it's the heroine that has upset my poor Cessy," I murmured, "Is she masculine, or new, or neuter, or only feminine? You shouldn't read novels, Cessy. They are like income-tax notices, they make excellent pipe-lights, and they are printed to be ignored. Don't read them. I never do."

"You'll read this though," he said, "It's a *roman à clef.*"

"I shall do no such thing my dear young friend. I haven't yet recovered from the shock of Lord Beaconsfield's *Endymion.*[4] Novels with a key are never worth unlocking."

"But you—that is, we," he exclaimed, "are the key. There are two heroes, you and I."

"Ah!" I whispered ecstatically, "At last a new sensation! Fancy being a hero? I trust Willie Rash has made us heroic."

"He has laughed at us, my blond Ronald. We are the Aunt Sallies of his wooden wit. Here, take the accursed volume, and read it for yourself."

I began to read.

(The remainder of the entry for this day is scarcely suited to publication.)

3rd April.—It would be impossible for anyone, not an artist to imagine my feelings after the perusal of *The Cream Chrysanthemum*. Let me consider the position. For fifteen years I have done London the honour of laughing at it; there has been only one person too august for my epigrammatic personalities, and that is my wife's husband. I have erected a notoriety for paradox and wit which ensures me more invitations to dinner than I can take the trouble to refuse. How great has been my reputation! Why, if when taking a lady down, I happened to remark (as I frequently did happen to remark) that the back of the woman in front looked hungry, she would laugh immoderately, and tell all her friends that Ronald Primula had made a lovely epigram for her, but she couldn't remember exactly what it was.

Am I not right in calling this fame?

Of late years I have sheltered Lord Cecil under my wing, and we have been artists together. Or to be quite frank, perhaps I should say "scientists." For we have made original discoveries in the science of self-advertisement which eclipse all previous work in the same field. Even Eric McGee, the author of *Love-letters of a Triangle Player*, must acknowledge that.

Everyone knew that we made it our life's aim to be absurd beautifully, artistically. And we succeeded. But there is a wide difference between making oneself absurd, and being made to look absurd by another person. And Willie Rash has made us both look absurd. The fact that he has performed the operation artistically does not mitigate my woe.

I weep—beautiful salt tears, and Cecil joins me.

10th April.—My fame is going; I can feel it slipping, like Sarah in *Walker, London.*[5] London is laughing, and at me! The reviews of *The Cream Chrysanthemum* are most laudatory. Even the *Charing Cross Gazette,* which devotes itself to the justifiable homicide of new literary reputations, says that the wretched thing is amusing. Willie Rash is being interviewed day and night. They say he has not slept for three days, for interviewers. On Sunday he lectured at the Playgoers' Club. I stayed away. I wouldn't care so much if the public manifested a reasonable interest in me. But it doesn't; it simply laughs. The almost incredible fact is that not a single editor has expressed a wish to interview me. And in the *Sunday Smiler* I see that there is even an article by Willie Rash's landlady on his methods of work. She says that to her knowledge the book was refused by four publishers (wish it had been four hundred).

12th April.—Twenty thousand copies of the cream one have been sold. I am thinking hard to devise some method, original, and at the same time dignified, of re-instating myself in the popular esteem. At all costs the public must be persuaded to take me seriously once more.

20th April.—The Prime Minister has awarded Willie Rash a pension for distinguished literary service. I am going to France to recoup, and to arrange a plan of campaign.

17th June.—I have industriously cogitated for two months, and at last have arrived at the only solution of this painful situation. I have always been original, daring, different from the multitude. Now in these days the multitude is smart. In that fact lies the germ of my plan. I will ask the Reverend Mr. Violis to give one of his Sunday "At Homes," at which I may deliver my new gospel to the world, to my world. But it shall be kept out of the papers that is part of the gospel.

29th June.—It is settled. I unfold the new gospel to-morrow (Sunday).

30th June.—I fancy the Rev. Mr Violis received me just a

little coldly this afternoon. Perhaps his attitude was explained by the fact that he wanted me to give the lecture in church at one of his "Pleasant Sunday Afternoons," instead of in his wife's drawing-room, and I refused.

I wore a dandelion, obtained at considerable expense, as florists for some inexplicable reason, don't grow them.

There was a great crowd. Cessy kept the actor-managers at bay all he could. These fellows think that because they have grown rich through misinterpreting my plays under strong limelight, they are entitled to slap me on the back and call me "Ronald, my boy." Young Hannibal shook my hand so brutally (some people would say heartily) that he withered all the petals from my dandelion, leaving only the stamen. "Never mind," he said, "it's a stamen of no importance," laughing. "You're an actor of no importance," I retorted, and Max, of the Whitehall Theatre, laughed immoderately.

There were, besides the actor-managers, a varied assortment of lady novelists; a number of artists, also a few Royal Academicians, Mr. Aubrey Beardsley, and Mr. De La Pucelle, who is universally praised for his novels––by artists, and for his pictures—by novelists; some popular preachers, who preach copyright sermons; a lawyer or two, several music-hall artistes; and a bishop at the rim of the crowd. Mr. Violis introduced me in what the *Daily Telegraph* would call a few well-chosen words, and I rose to deliver my lecture.

"Ladies and Gentlemen," I said, "the subject upon which I wish to speak to you is 'The Beauty of Mediocrity.' For many years I have been searching after a true ideal. I have sought it in paradox, and in epigram; in the art of lying, and in the culture of absurdity; in the sunflower, and in the chrysanthemum; in limited editions, and in foreign language; in knickerbockers, and in knick-knacks. And in all these ways I have walked fearlessly, unheeding of ridicule, intent only upon attaining truth. ('Hear, hear,' said the bishop.)

"Now I have found that none of these paths was peace. My successive ideals were false ideals. They brought no lasting satisfaction. They were like a woman with golden hair and big feet; they began well and ended badly. The significance of what I am now saying had been deepening within me for some time, when one day, as I was walking down Piccadilly with a poppy or a lily, I forget which, in my mediaeval hand, I observed a 'bus-horse. Yes, I observed a 'bus-horse! And an inner voice said: 'Behold the one true ideal!' In these days when the comic papers are sometimes funny, anyone can be what is called smart; even our butlers write for the *Yellow Book*, and when filling our glasses, consult us as to serial rights and the comparative dishonesty of publishers. Things have got to such a pass that the great majority of people are clever beyond the average.

"Now I ask you one question—what virtue, what satisfaction even, is there, under these circumstances, in being clever—in being above the average? None. I have been blind, and therefore the age has been blind, to the beauty of mediocrity. In future, I, and those who are good enough to follow me, shall aim at being absolutely mediocre, and so we shall reach distinction. Consider the beautiful life of the 'bus-horse, placid, uneventful, punctuated only by the silver echoing of a bell, and the occasional consumption of the seductive bran mash. He has no ambitions, and to have no ambitions should be the ambition of the truly enlightened. Henceforward, you will hear nothing of me, for I shall be commonplace with my whole soul. The world will forget me, and continue its restless, pathetic struggle after smartness; but generations yet unborn will recognise me as in the truest sense great—great, because I was the one mediocre person in an age which busied itself in being clever with the new cleverness.

"One word more, in answer to numerous enquiries, I may say that I shall continue to write plays, but they will be mediocre."

Then I sat down.

* * * * * * *

And so the diary ends. The world has been wondering why Mr. Ronald Primula has lately ceased to shock it, in his old delightful manner. The diary, I think answers the question. He is engaged in pursuing the mediocre. They say that a statue to the author of *The Cream Chrysanthemum* is to be erected by public subscription in Leicester-square.

NOTES

1. *Woman*. 30th January 1895, pages 16, 18, 20. Signed E.A.B. A satire upon the Aesthetic movement of the 1880s onwards.
2. *Punch*, an illustrated comic weekly, founded in 1841, was in the vanguard of resistance to the Victorian avant-garde and the Aesthetic movement associated with Oscar Wilde.
3. "Moderation is a fatal thing. Nothing succeeds like excess", Oscar Wilde, *A Woman of No Importance*. (1893)
4. Benjamin Disraeli became Earl of Beaconsfield in 1876. *Endymion* (1880) was his last published novel. Disraeli claimed that his novels were romans à clef, saying that "My works are my life" and that the key to his character was in them.

Ronald Primula's surname links him not only to Wilde's love of flowers - the *Punch* issue of 31st March 1883 included a spoof advertisement referring to Wilde's change of costume after his American tour: "to be sold, the whole of the Stock-in-Trade, Appliances, and Inventions of a Successful Aesthete, who is retiring from business. This will include a large stock of faded lilies, dilapidated sunflowers, ... Also a valuable Manuscript Work, entitled *Instructions to Aesthetes* ...." - but also to Disraeli's favourite flower, the primrose. The Primrose League (1882-2004), an organisation founded for the dissemination of Conservative principles, was named in recognition of his regard for the flower.

5. J.M. Barrie's *Walker, London. A Farcical Comedy in Three Acts* was first performed in 1892.

PART II

STRANGE STORIES OF THE OCCULT

THE
"I.C." PERSEPHONE
FRENCH CORSETS

These elegant Paris-made Corsets are cut in such a manner that they give a graceful appearance to almost any kind of figure, reducing in a remarkable manner the apparent size of the waist, without any undue or painful pressure.

The well-known Trade Mark, "I.C. a la Persephone I.C." (with which every genuine pair is stamped), is a guarantee that the materials and workmanship are the best that can be procured.

MADAME ADELINA PATTI writes:—"I am very much pleased with the Corsets; they fit admirably."

"THE LADY'S PICTORIAL" says:—"The 'I.C.' *a la Persephone* Corsets are beautifully modelled, and cut on so perfect a principle that they cannot fail to give a graceful outline to the figure of any lady who wears them."

"THE QUEEN" says:—"The 'I.C.' *a la Persephone* Corsets are beautifully finished, and very moderate in price. The latest additions are graceful in shape and becoming to the figure, to which they tend to impart that slimness and elegance which is so much desired by the present fashion."

The "I.C." PERSEPHONE CORSETS are made in a variety of Shapes and Styles.

6/9, 8/6, 10/6 TO 25/0 PER PAIR.

TO BE HAD OF DRAPERS AND LADIES' OUTFITTERS.

Wholesale only:

SHARP, PERRIN & CO., *31, Old Change, London, E.C.*

THE "I.C." PERSÉPHONE CORSET."

SYLVIA.

White, Cream, and Dove, 8/6 Black, 10/6

As Editor of, and contributor to, *Woman*, Bennett would have mused over the liberated New Woman of his "Strange Stories of the Occult" being torn between the restrictions of "Persephone French Corsets" and the freedoms of the "Latest Novelty 'Sybil' Cycling Costume" in the same issue of *Woman* (25th March 1896).

A DIVIDED GHOST.[1]

The evening when Clara first saw the apparition was that on which she first said "No" to a request of her lover. Probably there is no connection between the two events; I merely mention the coincidence in passing. It happened to be the year of the *Heavenly Twins*, when even the best of friends quarrelled.

Clara and George were standing at the garden door, under the trellised arch of ivy which the florist and seedsman had but just erected by contract. The ivy looked ill at ease and scraggy, and through it could be seen the cloudy sky of a spring night, fitfully illuminated by a waning, moist moon. The sound of the traffic in Kensington High-street came over the housetops like the distant roaring of surf on a coral reef; close at hand were the lights of a hansom, and a horse worrying its bit, and tearing up the gravel with impatient forefoot.

Even a blind man would have known, from the tones of their voices, that they were lovers trying not to quarrel.

"Why not do it?" the man pleaded.

"Because I don't want, George. If my future husband *does* edit a paper, and my father *does* write novels—should I therefore be compelled to write also? I don't wish to write and I won't. I'm not advanced."

"But you *can* write," said George, purposely softening his voice as the woman's rose, a mean trick which she of course comprehended, and which filled her with a desire to scratch him.

"Pooh! Kitty Mason can write."

"Kitty Mason can put ink on paper."

"Well! Suppose I can write! I lavish my unique gifts of style on you alone, then. That's all. Be content."

"As you wish, dear girl." He stroked her hair half timidly. Then after a pause, "But there's no mistake this *Heavenly Twins* thing is going to make a stir, and no one could have reviewed it as well as you, Clara. I've a good mind to print the letter you wrote me about it the other day."

"You just can't then," she laughed, "That would be against your rules, 'to which we can make no exception'—see notice in every issue."

"How's that?"

"It's written on both sides of the paper."

"A calamity! Well I shall do the review myself, and lift your ideas into it bodily. I shall simply steal whole sentences. Where is the book? I suppose I ought to skim it through."

"Papa is glancing at it, I think. I sent it in to him just now. He'll bring it down to-morrow . . . Good . . . night."

They kissed between each of the last three words, and the man, mischievously snatching a rose from the woman's dress, ran off through the trees. She heard him say "*Sentinel* Office, smart now," to the cabman, and went into the house humming an air.

It was a large, old, invertebrate sort of house, with oak beams and nine-inch walls and other survivals from a dead past; and Mr Paine Grant, the *doyen* of novelists and *chroniqueurs*, with his daughter Clara, had only lately removed to it.

The long side passage, leading from the garden to the entrance hall was quite dark at night except for a dim reflection from the hall lamp. Clara closed the garden door with a subdued gentleness which perhaps indicated regret for having crossed her editorial lover.

She took one step up the passage, and then forgot to continue her singing. There was a figure a few feet in front of her. Its back was towards her, and in the faint uncertain light she could not distinguish whether it was man or woman. Presently the head of the figure turned, and she saw a woman's white, appealing face. From the drawn yet mocking mouth there seemed to issue a thin, greyish vapour, and at about the level of the elbows a tiny point of red fire glowed dully.

Clara's heart ceased to beat for a second, and went on again as if it was anxious to make up for lost time.

She knew it was a ghost, not by any process of reasoning, but by pure intuition. Yesterday, an hour ago, a minute ago, she did not believe in supernatural appearances. Extremely well educated, and inheriting the temperament of her father, a benevolently cynical old gentleman who chaffed the universe and all that is therein in a weekly paper at a fixed rate of seven guineas a thousand words, she was accustomed to make merry when the Occult, with a big round O, came up for discussion. Only the previous Sunday, when a member of the Psychical Research Society[2] was recounting to her his flirtations with a ghost, she had said:

"Show me one, just one, and I will believe."

Well, here was one, just one, now on view. By every law of her father's admirable novels she ought to have felt afraid, but Clara's chief and overmastering sensation was one of curiosity. Standing perfectly still, she examined the ghost with the simple wonder and scientific precision of a boy who is permitted to gaze on the new baby. Its face was now turned from her. It had every appearance of materiality, except that the point of red light seemed to shine through its body, and that its outlines were almost imperceptibly indistinct, as if viewed through a carelessly focussed opera-glass. Its attire, or at any rate part of it, drew a smile to Clara's face, and she *hemmed* slightly. The figure again confronted her, and apparently struggled to articulate something, but no sound came. Then it moved calmly down the passage, and Clara followed. For a moment it stood stationary in the full glare of the hall lamp. The faint, greyish vapour again obscured its head, and then like a flash it had passed upstairs. Clara bounded in pursuit, but, catching her foot in her dress, came down with a prodigious thump which brought her father out of his study.

"What now? What now?" he enquired in his sharp, cheerful voice, his spectacles shining like two moons. "Have you seen a ghost, my dear?"

"Yes, father," she answered lightly, "I was trying to catch it, and fell down. But it's disappeared now."

"Ah! they always disappear when I appear. All my life I've wanted to see a ghost," and the old man sighed as he picked up his recumbent offspring.

That was the first manifestation of the famous spectre of 17, Sillitoe-square. Mr. Grant naturally thought that the matter-of-fact Clara was merely answering his own banter, and returned to his study. The ghost-seer went to bed to think the matter over.

At breakfast next morning she was debating whether or not to brave her father's valuable chaff by acquainting him with the real facts of the previous night, when Jackie, who made a third at table, and had been preternaturally taciturn over his bread-and-milk, suddenly began to cry.

Jackie was the six-year-old son of Clara's eldest sister, and at intervals Clara managed to obtain the loan of him. He acted tonically on both herself and her father.

"It's there again," he whimpered.

"What's there, and where is it?" inquired Mr. Paine Grant, politely.

"Behind the screen there. Nurse said ghosties came for naughty boys, and I was naughty yesterday. It came last night, but I put my head under the clothes, and it runned away. I heard it."

"Well, if you *will* be naughty, Jack," laughed his grandfather.

"What have you been doing?"

"I cut the books."

"Books!" repeated Mr. Paine Grant, becoming serious at once.

"The books auntie told me to take to you. I took them upstairs instead and cut them, 'cause I wanted the musics out of them. Here's the *musics*—I don't want them now," and Jack threw down a quantity of slips of paper, each of which contained the musical phrase from the *Elijah*, which occurs so frequently in the *Heavenly Twins*.[3]

"Go straight to bed, Jack," said Mr. Paine Grant. He was a book collector, and Jack had committed the one unpardonable sin. "Stay," he added, "Where are the books?"

"I don't know. Look, auntie," the child screamed, pointing to the door, and clinging to Clara convulsively.

Then it happened that Mr. Paine Grant, novelist, his daughter Clara, and his grandson Jack, all three distinctly saw a figure pass from behind the screen and through the door of the breakfast room.

"I'll write an article on that" said Mr. Paine Grant.

This was the second manifestation.

The spectre began to show itself frequently; the servants left; new ones appeared and in a day or two disappeared, not stopping even to demand a character. One of them, who practised the calling of a journalist when out of a situation, published what she called "The Supernatural Experiences Of Mary Jane." She wrote that one night as she lay in bed, the handle of the door rattled. Lighting a candle she sat up and watched, "in an agony of terror." She distinctly saw the handle move, as if someone was trying to open the door and not succeeding because it was locked. Then a hand seemed to pass through the door, and in the hand was a point of dull red fire. In the morning her face was drawn out of shape with fright; which curiously enough, was perfectly true.

One day the pretty and vivacious Mrs. Quesnel called—she was the wife of the previous occupant of the house, a young stockbroker, who had gone to live in Queen's-gate—and Clara asked whether to her knowledge the house bore any ghostly reputation.

"Indeed, no, Miss Grant," she exclaimed, "we aren't that sort, you know," with which cryptic remark she made an end of the matter, and proceeded to unfold the object to her visit.

"I want you to join our bicycle club. It'll be an awfully select thing, you know. We held the first business meeting here just before I left. The—er—costumes are all made, but we haven't commenced the club runs yet. The fact is we want a few more members." At this point Clara suddenly saw the spectre standing behind Mrs. Quesnel's chair. She wondered whether it wanted to put up for the bicycle club.

"Oh! you are having—special costumes?"

"Rather; as worn at Pau[4] exactly."

"Then I'm afraid I can't join," said Miss Grant, coldly, as she rose to end the interview. (By way of excusing Miss Grant's absurd scruples, it should be pointed out that this was before the days when live ladies rode on two wheels in Battersea Park.)

There was nothing distinctive in this particular manifestation of the spectre. It is mentioned in order to illustrate one peculiar effect which the appearances always had on Clara, and upon Clara only. They produced in her a feeling of loss, as if part of her very self had left her, and this vanishing part was invariably the progressive, liberal side of her nature.

Of course, Clara would never have joined what Mr. Paine Grant had called Mrs Quesnel's "Society for the Judicial Separation of the Lower Limbs," but it is certain that, had the spectre not appeared at that precise moment, she would have gilded the pill of refusal with a little of her father's suave jocularity.

Everyone began to theorise about the spectre. Jackie, for his part, persisted in believing that it appeared for his own special chastening, and would continue to appear till he had saved enough money to buy a new copy of the dismembered novel.

One Saturday night Clara and her father and George sat

up in order to take careful observations. They had a surprising time, as the spectre happened to be very active just then, and the report which they jointly drew up and forwarded to the Psychical Research Society created considerable sensation. One strange point related to the ghost's attire. The lower part of its body was very indistinctly outlined, but it seemed, so far as could be made out, to wear a kind of Moorish woman's trousers. Now and then it would flourish the right arm and a faint cracking noise would be heard, from which the observers surmised that a whip was being brandished, but no whip could be seen.

Another queer thing was that if fairly cornered the ghost would melt away wherever it happened to be, but if left to itself it always retreated to the low seat in front of the window on the first floor landing. It would there sit down, and lo! it was gone.

Mr. Paine conceived the idea of giving a party "to meet the spectre," and a circle of intimate friends was invited. As the evening wore on and nothing happened, the guests began to fear disappointment; but just as Mrs Quesnel was warming to a circumstantial account of the formation of her bicycle club, and every one was gaping, the spectre visualised itself behind her. Three women screamed and two fainted, but the rest set their teeth.

The point of fire on the spectre's hand glowed fiercely, and a grey mist shrouded its features. After standing a moment it passed out into the hall, and Mr. Paine Grant signed to the company to follow. No one spoke. The apparition proceeded upstairs, stood three minutes, by George's watch, in front of the landing window, sat down, and disappeared. The guests still remained silent, not knowing whether to laugh or shudder. Then Sir Russell Locke, the Q.C., spoke.

"And it always disappears just here?"

"Just there," said Mr. Paine Grant.

"What is under the seat? Skulls or bones?"

Clara explained that the seat was really an old box, never used; Sir Russell Locke requested permission to examine it. He pulled off its cretonne drapery, lifted the lid, and peered into its depths.

"Nothing but a book or two," he said.

Clara and her father looked over his shoulder.

"Why there's the *Heavenly Twins* that Jackie lost," said Clara. "And what's this?" She pulled out a curious blue garment.

"Oh!" screamed Mrs Quesnel, blushing hotly, "that's one of my bicycle costumes. I've missed it ever since we left this house."

Clara looked at her father, and slowly a smile broke over their faces.

"That point of fire, and that grey mist?" said Clara.

"Cigarette," said her father.

"And that cracking noise—" said Clara.

"A whip to belabour the mere male," said her father. Then, turning to the company, he went on: "Ladies and Gentlemen, I think the mystery is solved. The fortuitous combination of a copy of the *Heavenly Twins* and a divided skirt naturally produced an awe-inspiring apparition of the New Wom— "

"Never mind her name," interrupted Clara, putting a white hand over his mouth. "Let her rest. The ghost is laid now."

And it was.

NOTES

1. *Woman*. 9th January 1895, pages 18, 20. Signed Sarah Volatile.
2. The Society for Psychical Research (SPR) was formed in 1882 with its original membership drawn mainly from Cambridge University. Whilst their findings generated a mixture of excitement and scepticism, from the 1880s to the 1920s the organisation remained a highly respected body, responsible for collecting and categorising the evidence for extensions of mental powers, such as telepathy, and legitimising the study of supernormal phenomena.
3. The musical notation for "He, watching over Israel, slumbers not, nor sleeps" occurs seven times throughout the novel.
4. A city in Southwest France.

THE CLAPHAM THEOSOPHICAL SOCIETY. [1]

"You know, my dear Mrs. Calvert and my friends," said a stout middle-aged dame to the company assembled in Mrs. Calvert's[2] drawing-room, "the essential characteristic of theosophy[3] is its intense, its absolute spirituality. Thank you, I will take another cup—three lumps, if you please."

"What *is* theosophy, Mrs. Crackthorpe," drawled a young man carefully dressed in black, whose expression just then seemed to indicate that the universe and all things therein were a delusion and a snare.

"Now, Master Charles," Mrs. Crackthorpe answered, looking benevolently first at her interlocutor, and then at a girl, also dressed carefully in black, who sat by the window, "you are asking one of your questions. I sincerely trust (this with a long drawn sigh and another glance at the girl) that your wife, when you get one, will reform you."

"What I want to know, my dear lady, are the points of the creed. What do you enthusiasts believe in?"

"Ah! that brings me at once to our strongest position. Theosophists are pledged to nothing."

"How discreet!"

"Do stop him, Mrs. Calvert," and Mrs. Crackthorpe gave an appealing look to her hostess, who held up a finger with three rings on it.

"I mean," the expounder of theosophy continued, "there is no *creed*. You know our motto—'Truth is higher than all religions.' That embodies a sentiment worth a library of theology. No theosophist is compelled, as a theosophist, to believe in anything."

"Not in anything?"

"Except—er—truth, of course. But naturally," Mrs. Crackthorpe added with a rush, "I can't explain these things. I am not even a *chela*.[4] Mr. Panting Prawle will convince you at the meeting, I am sure."

"A *chela,* Mrs. Crackthorpe?" broke in the girl at the window. "I am so interested. Mr Panting Prawle is a *chela;* he told me so when I met him at the Cavours' last week. What is a *chela*? I think Mr. Prawle is splendid."

"Isn't he?" returned Mrs. Crackthorpe, rapturously. "I don't quite know what a *chela* is, but he will tell you. And you know he has such whole-souled enthusiasm. He said to me that the aim of theosophy was to make all men brothers. Isn't that grand?"

"And the women?" queried the young man. "Not sisters, I hope. Because I've got enough."

"Mr. Scott! Mr. Scott! *will* you be serious, and drink your tea? I'm sure it's cold." And Mrs. Calvert buzzed round him ministeringly.

The girl in black rose to go. At the same moment Mr. Charles Scott found it necessary to depart.

"You'll come to the meeting, Miss Scott," said Mrs. Crackthorpe.

"*I* shall," said Charles, "and I'll try to persuade Minnie to come too."

"Of course I shall come," said the girl. "I shan't want persuading, Charlie. I'm dreadfully interested."

"They aren't engaged yet, I suppose?" asked Mrs. Crackthorpe when the pair had gone.

"No," said Mrs. Calvert, "but they will be soon."

"Cousins should never marry. They don't in Tibet."

*　　*　　*　　*　　*　　*　　*　　*

The birth of the Clapham Theosophic Society was a sublime function, still vividly remembered among the *élite* of that historic suburb. All her friends attended the meeting which Mrs. Crackthorpe, the indefatigable, had convened at her own home, Devonshire House (Clapham Common). Mr. Panting Prawle was the lion of the night. He had been to India; some said he had seen a Mahatma; and he was full of charm and mystery, like a twilight landscape.

His impassioned speech left many of the ladies in tears, and all the men in a muddle. Doubtless, what Mrs. Crackthorpe called the "majestic personality of the man" prevented him from descending to details; still there were not a few of his hearers who secretly wished that he had deigned to be more specific. None of them, however, made bold to say so, not even Charlie Scott. As for his cousin Minnie, she asked Mr. Prawle for his autograph, and got it, rather to the disgust of Charles.

The society was formed and a committee appointed, of which Mrs. Crackthorpe and Minnie Scott were the two lady members. It is perhaps unnecessary to say that Mr. Panting Prawle was unanimously elected President—at least they called him President until he explained that the proper esoteric term was "Inner Head;" after that he was referred to in bated tones as the "I.H."

He was a tall, middle-aged man, of imposing presence. People quarrelled about his age. Some said fifty, others thirty-two. He had abundant brown hair. The whites of his eyes were dazzlingly white, and the pupils unfathomably black. His full-moonlike face was clean-shaven, but the backs of his large flabby hands were covered with silky hair, of which he seemed rather proud. His dress was unobtrusive. Of his speech it may be said that it was oracular.

"My friends," he remarked to the committee, with one hand on his ample breast, at the end of that glorious birth-night, "let us remember that our one motive, our sole aim, is to unite the warring elements of mankind into a peaceful, homogeneous whole. That is theosophy!"

"What a fine definition," said Minnie to her cousin, as he took her home after the affair was over. "How exquisitely he reduces a complex question to uttermost simplicity!"

Charles wanted to turn the conversation into other channels, but the girl's spirit seemed far away. She experienced vague longings to help the world out of a rut, either by becoming a hospital nurse, a nun, a lady lecturer, or something. She treated Charlie's advances with a gentle, forbearing coolness which would have irritated most men, but which only amused Charlie, and he left her with a parting shot about Mahatmas.

In referring to Mahatmas, Mr. Scott touched, I fear, the root of Clapham's theosophistic enthusiasm. The society waxed unconscionably, and the first question which new members put to the honorary and energetic secretary was: "Shall we see Mahatmas—and things?" The secretary referred them to the committee, and the committee, while really as eager for Mahatmas and astral projections as the outer ruck of members, reproved this "anxiety for a sign," and referred enquirers to the memorable words of the Inner Head. The Inner Head was apt to be unapproachable, but one day Minnie, who had got on best with him, and who had just been privileged to drink wisdom from his lips for a period of two hours, ventured to ask whether he had himself witnessed "phenomena." He said he had received many "precipitated" communications from "Masters" in Tibet, and that probably she herself, or some other member of the committee, might be receiving them soon.

That same night Mr. Panting Prawle's house was burnt out. He had called unceremoniously upon the Scotts early in the evening, and had imparted the information to Minnie and her mother that he felt a curious apprehension of impending danger. Later on, when the police summoned him to behold his blazing tenement, he smiled resignedly, even peacefully, as if to say, "I told you so." The ladies were deeply impressed, especially when it came to be noised abroad that had Mr. Prawle not providentially left home at the time he did, he would assuredly have been burnt to death in his study, which was nearly at the top of the house. Among members of the society, Mahatmas had the credit of his escape. The Mahatmas, however, had not saved the sacred Inner Head from serious inconvenience. His newly and richly furnished house—he had but recently come into the neighbourhood—was a smoky, unrecognisable medley of piled bricks and charred timber, and he was homeless.

The members of the committee competed for the honour of entertaining him, and he elected very decidedly to stay with the widowed Mrs. Scott and her daughter Minnie.

The loss of his household gods, his "poor bachelor's trinkets" as he called them, seemed to affect him deeply, though they were insured; but no insurance, he said sadly, could restore to him his invaluable papers and MSS. relating to the history and secrets of theosophy, which represented the labour of a lifetime, and comprised all the accumulated wisdom of the East. Minnie did what she could to comfort him. They walked out together; more frequently they drove in Mrs. Scott's carriage. Minnie entered on a thorough course of theosophical instruction, and, at the end of about a fortnight, the Inner Head said that if she wrote to a "Master" whom he named, she might probably receive a reply. So she inscribed a timid little epistle, explaining that she was a neophyte in theosophy, and asking for guidance, and put it, at Mr. Prawle's suggestion, on the window sill. It evaporated.

The following morning her mother and the Inner Head had begun breakfast when she appeared.

"How soon may I expect an answer?" she said at once to Mr. Prawle.

"An answer?"

"Yes, I wrote last night to Ko Timai, you remember."

"Oh, I had forgotten, my dear (he was very fatherly), of course you did. You may get no answer at all, or you may get one at once, I cannot tell. I myself had a message this morning. It was precipitated on the back of a letter which I received by post from that wretched Insurance Company. I may not show it to you, but here is the seal," and he exhibited a dull red mark at the corner of a letter which lay folded by his side.

"How marvellous! And that was in the sealed envelope of the Insurance Company?"

"It was." Mr. Prawle smiled deprecatingly. Such wonders were part of his everyday existence.

"Good gracious, Ma!" exclaimed Minnie, a moment later, "what's this in my coffee?" With her spoon she ladled out of the cup a soaked piece of paper, and spread it open. Then she gave a little scream. The paper bore the very twin of the seal which Mr. Prawle had just shown her, and beneath it were the words: "Practise faith, obedience. Have courage to persevere. You are in good hands."

* * * * * * *

The day proved indeed an eventful one for Minnie. After breakfast she had a long talk with Mr. Prawle in the drawing-room. She confided in him all the aspirations which had surged in her brain during the last few weeks. The Inner Head listened and advised, and finally kissed her between her level brows in an ancestral way which could be described as impressive. She did not tell her mother of the incident.

By the afternoon the matter of the precipitated note had somehow got abroad, and all the committee, with many other members of the C.T.S., called to congratulate Minnie, and discuss the miracle.

In the evening, just after Mr. Prawle had gone out for a meditative stroll, Mr. Charles Scott appeared. Minnie received him in the drawing-room, and he happened to sit down in the identical chair occupied earlier in the day by the august Inner Head. There had always been a true cousinly brusqueness and absence of ceremony in the relations between Minnie and Charles, and when the favoured of Mahatmas began to relate her experiences, Charlie cut her short.

"Look here, Minnie," he said shortly, "we know each other, so I'll come to the point. I've come on another matter. I want you to be my wife. Will you—dear?"

She hesitated, and was lost. He had her in his arms.

She spoke seriously to him of her aims in life, the doctrines of theosophy and other profound things; but he said airily that they would be all right, and kissed her again.

"But, Charlie," she urged, "you believe in theosophy, don't you?"

"I believe in you, and you believe in theosophy, so I suppose I believe in theosophy. But we'll talk about that some other time."

Just then the door opened and Mr. Prawle entered. Charlie muttered, "That fellow again," and left the room, saying he wanted to speak to Mrs. Scott.

At breakfast next morning there was another mysterious missive for Minnie. This time it fell from the folds of her serviette, and contained these words, "If you would reach your ideals, repulse C. S." She crunched the paper in her hand, and gazed at her plate during the remainder of the meal.

In the library she consulted the Inner Head. He was afraid the message could have but one meaning. For himself, he was unable to see why marriage with Mr. Scott, who was an excellent young man, should be disadvantageous to her highest welfare; but then, he humbly admitted, he had not the wisdom, the power of reading the future, possessed by Ko Timai. He could only advise her to trust to the insight of the Mahatma. He had never found it at fault. The right path was always mountainous and difficult. She must try to be brave. She *would* be brave, he felt sure. He had the completest faith in her strength of purpose and purity of aim. He would be her companion; and he kissed her—not on the brow.

She dried her tears, and wrote a brief note to Charlie. And so her romance was ended, she thought, and she turned her face to higher things.

Two days after Mr. Panting Prawle was arrested for incendiarism. Then the members of the Clapham Theosophical Society began to enquire as to the whereabouts of the subscriptions which they had paid, and which their Inner Head had kindly taken charge of. The society was dissolved by mutual consent and theosophy became a tabooed topic in Clapham. Only now and then Charlie Scott, when Minnie becomes enamoured of some new craze, gently whispers to his wife the word "Mahatma," and she subsides.

NOTES

1. *Woman*. 23rd January 1895, pages 16, 18. Signed Sarah Volatile.
2. Seemingly by coincidence Bennett's story appears above an advertisement: "Chafed skin, scalds, cuts, chilblains, chapped hands, sore eyes, earache, neuralgic and rheumatic pains, throat colds and skin ailments, quickly relieved by use of CALVERT'S CARBOLIC OINTMENT. Large pots 13$^{1}/_{2}$d. each, at chemists, stores, &c; or post free for value in stamps. F.C. CALVERT AND CO., Manchester."
3. A set of occult beliefs, popular in late-Victorian Britain, rejecting Judeo-Christian theology, and incorporating elements of Buddhism and Hinduism. Bennett read and recommended Annie Besant's book on Theosophist teachings, *Thought Power*. Chapter XIII of his *The Human Machine* looks at her writing in the context of Marcus Aurelius and Epictetus: "In the matter of concentration, I hesitate to recommend Mrs. Annie Besant's *Thought Power*, and yet I should be possibly unjust if I did not recommend it, having regard to its immense influence on myself .... It contains an appreciable quantity of what strikes me as feeble sentimentalism, and also a lot of sheer dogma. But it is the least unsatisfactory manual of the brain that I have met with." (p. 121)
4. A spiritual novice studying for initiation in a branch of Buddhism.

AN ASTRAL ENGAGEMENT.[1]

For several weeks I met her constantly at the "Pioneer". Everyone knows me there, of course, and I have my special corner, away from the light, in the tea-room, which is kept vacant for me by a general understanding. I turned in as usual one afternoon about three, and found her upon my territory drinking tea and correcting proofs at a great rate, but, as I could see at once, doing the latter rather amateurishly. She looked up as I approached the table; I suppose there was an aggrieved look upon my face; anyhow, she smiled in the attractive American manner, and said in a babyish, prattling voice, "Am I sittin' in your seat? So sorry." I said, "Not at all;" but she rose and went away. That was the first time I saw her, and, I believe, the first time she came to the club.

I carefully surveyed her from a distance. When a woman's age is in question, I am only to be convinced by the birth certificate, yet I wouldn't accuse her of more than 27 years. Her complexion, all Devonshire cream and rose-madder, looked eighteen, but her eyes—brown, often merry eyes—revealed secrets. The mouth was too small, and the chin weak; otherwise her features were regular, and beautiful in a characterless sort of way. She was exquisitely dressed, not merely covered with the conventional garments. She wore a quite plain, undraped gown of dark blue, the bodice made with a very effective yoke of crimson velvet. Jet sparkled and gloomed at her neck and wrists, and altogether—well, she knew she was a picture.

Now and then we interchanged a few words, and after a fortnight I was treating her in a benevolent, motherly, forbearing manner which she seemed to like, but there was not the least intimacy. She didn't speak about herself, nor I of myself. I found out she was American, interviewing, and cutting capers generally, for the illustrated weeklies. She interviewed whom she chose—of the male kind. No celebrity, once she got sight of him, could resist her. She smiled, showing her beautiful American teeth, and the battle was over. People said she was a Theosophist, or occultist, or something of that kind.

Her manner was unaffectedly lively and gay, till one wet afternoon, when I noticed a startling change in her face. The tea-room happened to be nearly deserted. She prattled and joked in her usual abandoned manner. "I've done an interview to-day," she said "with So-and-So" (naming the author of *When a Man's Simple*), "that several editors I know would go without their dinners to get. They'll just flock round me in droves when they hear about it, and beg for it." Then she went on to describe this wondrous interview, and I gathered that she certainly had a knack of lighting upon good "copy." After a bit she stopped suddenly.

"See," she started off again; after a pause, coming to sit close by me, "I'll tell you a story if you don't mind. I've got to tell some one, and you'll suit me, I fancy."

"Purely personal?" I queried.

"Yes," with an exaggerated baby tone that just escaped being a lisp. And so I came to be acquainted with the most extraordinary love story I have ever heard—and I have heard a few, for all my friends contract a bad habit of telling me things. She told it throughout in a matter-of-fact, unfalteringly light-hearted, aimless, disconnected manner, which I will reproduce as best I can.

* * * * * *

It seems a long way back to commencement (she said)—centuries, but it's really only about three years. You remember Mrs. Chant Crapper, the occultist woman with a big, heavy face and rolling eyes? I met her over at Schenectady; in fact, I interviewed her for the New Orleans *Picayune* out there, and she took to me. People said she was a fraud, and so she was. She began right off by doing me out of twenty dollars. But there, she's dead; and so's that debt. But she really was an occultist. She had—er—powers, you know, made you creep. And she could teach her tricks to other folk—I call them tricks because they were so amusing, though they weren't tricks at all. There was the Astral Body. She *could* project her astral body almost anywhere. Of course you understand what the astral body is?—sort of a duplicate of the material body, without any of the inner soul. She could project it, honour bright, I tell you! And she made me her pupil, took me through strange physical and mental exercises, and in about six months I could project my astral body, too. Yes, it is true. I, Anna Slosson Mapes, could project my very own astral body. You're not assimilating the fact, eh? Well, you'll see. I'll proceed.

The astral self is a sort of second self, you know. With practice you can make it do anything that doesn't require much brain power. I often used to project mine to book theatre tickets, or to see unpleasant editors—there are so many unpleasant editors on the other side—and that sort of thing. It was awfully useful, and sometimes embarrassing. It caused rows between one's friends; for instance, two of my friends would meet, and one would say, "I saw Anna just now on Fifth Avenue," and the other would answer, "No, you're mistaken; she's driving in Central Park: I've come from her." Then they would impeach each other's truthfulness, and make a scene. Well, Mrs. Chant Crapper died, lamented by all, &c., as you know. Before she "left"—that was how she styled dissolutions—she solemnly warned me about using too freely the astral projection. "Remember," she said, "the astral body has, when projected, a certain ego of its own; treat it well, therefore, or it may play you a trick. Don't give it too many disagreeable tasks."

After her death, I travelled to England here, and soon woke up your sleepy old London. Remember my Amateur Charwoman articles?

You know Rudolf Hickman, the editor of the *Illustrated Trumpet*. Awfully rich you know! Boasts of never having allowed himself to be interviewed. About a year ago the *Meteor* was doing a series of journalistic interviews, and I offered to get copy out of Hickman or perish. Well, I saw him, and saw him, and saw him, but it was no use. He had written on a card, *"I won't open my mouth until you promise not to use anything I say without my permission in writing,"* and he used to hand this to all interviewers. We had the most delightful chats on those terms, but he would never thaw out for an interview. Don't know why. Then we got rather into the same set, and one fine day he considerably startled me.

"Miss Mapes," he said, " I've been thinking things over. You can interview me—"

"There," I said, "I knew I should win."

"If you will marry me." Rather a cooling draught, you think? Yes, it was; I said I would consider the matter. He's handsome, isn't he? I think he has the most wonderful face of any man I ever saw, except one. Grey eyes, as a common rule, seem to me rather steely and hard, you know. His aren't like that, but full of softness and depth.

Perhaps you know Richard Carter, of the St. Stephen's Theatre. You don't? You should then. I met him first at Boston, when he was starring in *Othello*. Of course you know what he looks like? Oh! you've only seen him *on* the stage. Well, his hair is really golden—sandy any other girl might call it; and his eyes light blue. His eyes are five feet ten off the ground.

We met first in England, soon after that little incident with Mr. Hickman; very quickly I began to see that it was all over with dear Mr. Hickman. I felt that if Mr. Carter should happen to want a wife who could write him up well in the papers, I should accept the post—when asked.

Hickman and he, curiously enough, are great friends. I don't know how long the intimacy will continue.

Have you ever had two men making love to you at once. No? Well, be thankful. Don't imagine I didn't like Mr. Hickman. I liked him so much that I felt sorry for him. And I used to project my astral body to see him when I myself was giving audience to Mr. Richard Carter. Of course, I did it merely out of kindness, and Mr. Hickman didn't suspect anything. In fact, no one here knew of my occult proclivities. I thought it wisest to keep quiet about them. I find England isn't like America. It doesn't pay to get talked about *too* much here.

I used to send my astral self to Mr. Hickman's Sunday evening "At Homes," which his sister manages for him. I willed it to discourage him all it could, and although it didn't like the task—perhaps it felt sorry for him, too—it carried out my ideas fairly well. Of course I know, in an indistinct way, what it is doing all the time, you understand. Well, as I tell you, while it was behaving to Mr. Hickman as coldly as it decently could, I was listening to Mr. Carter's remarks on things in general at Mrs. Kirkcudbright's .

Well, on Sunday evening I projected my astral body to Mr. Hickman's "At Home" with strict instructions to settle him once for all, because I felt that Mr. Carter's intentions were probably coming to a head. It went in a bad temper—I felt that. I sat in Mrs. Kirkcudbright's drawing-room—awfully good of her to let me live with her, isn't it?—and presently Mr. Richard Carter was announced. I had given him permission to come.

You're single, I know, but have you ever been proposed to? Of course you have, with such eyes. Well, isn't it delicious? I thought it was just splendid. You know, Mr. Carter and I had got rather into the way of talking baby language to each other. He said: " Me wants to be engaged."

I said : " Does it? Poor little thing! It shall be engaged; yes, it shall."

That's how I was proposed to, solemn, and how I accepted. Not a word more. About an hour afterwards, while we were sitting quiet and Mrs Kirkcudbright was busily engaged in keeping out of the room, I felt that my astral body was misbehaving itself over at the Hickman flat. It seemed to be getting agreeable to someone in a corner hidden behind palms. I understood that it said "Yes," and that someone was kissing it.

I went hot all over. Richard had hold of my hand, and he felt it. I knew for certain that my astral body had been proposed to by Mr. Hickman, and had accepted him. I might, by a strong effort of will, have recalled it, there and then, but that would have made a scene at Mr Hickman's, driven the man out of his mind, or something of that kind. So I just sat tight, and felt my hair going grey. And Mr. Carter was ecstatically happy, and stayed late, and Mrs Kirkcudbright congratulated us, and everyone laughed except me. And when Mr Carter kissed me before he went, he said my lips were stone cold. I told him a girl wasn't engaged every day, especially to such a man, and he must excuse a little temperamental eccentricity. All the while I was thinking, thinking, thinking what to do, and conscious that my astral body was treating me in the most shocking manner over at the

Hickman flat.

It actually didn't come back till midnight, and then it laughed. It laughed inside me, and its laugh was horrible.

All that was only last night you know. I'm still cogitating what to do.

I had a letter, such a lovely letter, from Mr. Hickman by second post this morning—he must have written it immediately after my "Other Me" had left him—just saying he loved me, and that he should call at 9.30 to-night, after dinner. That's the very hour that I told Richard to come—you know he finishes in the first act in the new piece. Richard said he should call on Mr. Hickman this afternoon to tell him of our engagement. He said Mr. Hickman was his best friend, and he wanted to have a talk.

I expect he's there now. Who knows? Perhaps they have quarrelled, and killed each other by this time. What *can* I do? What can I *do*? It simply can *not* be explained. Now be lovely and advise me, there's a true woman. It's comic isn't it, after all?

(The girl laughed.)

NOTES

1. *Woman*. 6th February 1895, pages 15-16. Signed Sarah Volatile.

THE FATAL MARRIAGE. [1]

The clock with the grimy white face on the main departure platform at Victoria Station (London, Chatham, and Dover) indicated twenty-three minutes past three, and the 3.25 express for Chatham, Westgate-on-Sea, Margate and Ramsgate, was upon the point of starting. Porters walked briskly up and down, slamming doors, and shouting—"Take your seats, please;" lampmen scurried along the roof of the train, fixing lamps; wheel examiners, with their long hammers, were monotonously tapping the wheels, and opening and shutting the oil-boxes; and the engine driver was leaning out of his cab, waiting for the guard to give the signal.

That official, spruce and alert, had his eyes fixed with interest upon the interior of the booking-office, from which emerged a truck with two new trunks upon it, followed by a lady and gentlemen, both young, both flushed, and both triumphant.

"Hurry up with that," said the guard curtly to the perspiring porter who was propelling the truck, and then turned deferentially to look after his passengers.

"Where for, Sir?"

"Westgate. Got an empty first?"

"Yes, Sir. Here you are, Sir," and the guard sprang to open a door. A moment later he was pocketing half-a-crown, waving his little green flag, and winking privately at a ticket collector, who winked back, all at the same time. The engine whistled and snorted and the train rolled ponderously out of the station.

When they had crossed Grosvenor Bridge, and duly remarked how picturesque the Thames looked, Willie St. John drew off his gloves, and leaving his own corner, sat down by his wife.

"Providence was nearly behaving very badly to us," he said, taking her hand. "Suppose that dray had struck the cab instead of the horse. What an item there would have been for the evening papers! 'Fatal accident in Victoria-street. Pathetic death of a newly-married couple!' Your dear mother's vision would have been more than fulfilled."

"Don't be horrid, Willie. You ought to have more consideration for the feelings of a bride. We caught the train after all. What more do you want?"

" I want"—He tenderly raised his wife's veil and took it. "You look awfully well, Olive," he added.

"Do I, dear?" she answered naïvely; and he took another one. Then they sat silent and happy, and the hours seemed to pass; and when the train stopped they were surprised to find themselves no further than Herne Hill.

Olive was a beautiful creature, beautiful as only a woman of twenty-six can be, having neither the crude, innocent look of twenty-one, nor the omniscient, collected, self-reliant expression of thirty-one. Her eyes were merry, her voice soft, and her teeth perfect, and if only her mouth had been—but Willie St. John considered her mouth precisely right.

And she was clever. She wrote verses, which appeared in *The Yellow Book.* Willie didn't quite understand them—some lawyers do understand poetry; these are in a minority—but he knew they were delicate and fanciful, because he couldn't imagine Olive writing verses that lacked those admirable qualities. Indeed, he thought, if the truth must out, that Olive's poems were much finer things than her mother's novels, which brought in so much money. Olive's mother was the celebrated Mrs. Prescott ("George Wilson"), whose *Prince Florizel* you have doubtless read.

St. John liked her, for she was Olive's mother, and Olive resembled her; but recently she had joined the ranks of the spiritualists, and had had psychic experiences, and written a book called *Apparitions of the Living*. St. John could hardly tolerate that sort of thing. He liked it the less for the reason that Mrs. Prescott's arguments were so convincing and so difficult to answer, and also for the reason that he himself was not unconnected with one of her "experiences." Even then, in the midst of all his bliss, he was conscious, right down at the bottom of his heart, of a slight uneasiness, an almost imperceptible foreboding, caused by the remembrance of this particular experience. But when his mind recurred to the inexhaustible subject of Olive's talents and graces he nearly forgot the matter.

Olive did other things, too, besides writing. In fact, she was a little—advanced. Willie was not a bit advanced, and he laughed at all advanced women, except his wife.

The train was now in the midst of the beautiful country of the Crays, and husband and wife were side by side again. The previous day Willie had been speculating as to what he and Olive would talk about during the ride down to Westgate.

What did husbands say to wives upon these honeymoon journeys? Husbands and wives, it appeared, said nothing to each other. Words were superfluous. They merely looked into one another's eyes and read whole beautiful poems there. When this particular husband and wife had been studying these poems for quite half an hour, the wife descended to prose. She remarked that her husband seemed tired.

"I don't feel tired, dearest," he said, "though I ought to. Did *you* happen to sleep well last night?"

"Excellently" (she scarcely expected him to believe this).

"Well, I didn't. I was awake at two o'clock, and I got up at four and walked about; and we've had a trying day."

"But I thought marriages were like executions, and the condemned man always slept well 'the night before,' and then 'ate a hearty breakfast.' Perhaps you have some awful confession to make, and the prospect of it disturbed you?"

St. John smiled absently, and looked out of the window.

"Surely," Olive went on, a little anxiously now, "Mamma's absurd 'vision' hasn't been troubling you?"

"Oh, no. Not in the least." This was not the fact.

"It *was* a queer thing," said Olive, becoming thoughtful in turn.

"Yes."

"But it couldn't have been anything but a dream."

"No."

The "vision" of Mrs. Prescott had occurred about a year ago, on the very day, in fact when Olive and St. John were formally betrothed. St. John had dined with the Prescotts *en famille*, and stayed till about eleven o'clock, but Mrs. Prescott had retired to her study somewhat earlier, on the plea of having to put the last touches to *Prince Florizel*.

"George Wilson" was always a little behind with her copy. She was, nevertheless, a methodical, keen-witted, and experienced woman of middle age, not addicted to any of the aberrations which are said to accompany genius.

At a quarter to midnight her task was finished. She had enclosed the MS. in an envelope, and was just rising in order to give instructions to a servant to post it before twelve o'clock, when she became aware that someone was looking over her shoulder. Turning around she saw Willie St. John; and wondered, first why he had come into the room; and, second, how he had come into the room, for there had been absolutely no noise save the scratching of her quill pen. Then she noticed a peculiar expression on her future son-in-law's face, and also that he had changed his dress suit for faultless and elaborate morning attire. Although Mrs. Prescott had already made considerable progress in those psychic researches which shortly afterwards moved her to write *Apparitions of the Living*, she had not till then met with any personal "experiences" of an occult nature, but she was immediately and immovably convinced that the *thing* before her was not Willie St. John. That being so, it was necessarily an occult phenomenon. She was frightened, and lacked courage to test by touch the truth of her conviction; but she retained her presence of mind, turned the switch of the electric chandelier, filling the room with light, and observed the figure more closely.

It was undoubtedly the figure of Willie St. John, with a face drawn out of its natural shape by terror, and wild, appealing eyes, whose glance seemed to burn its way into her soul. In what awful plight was this intangible thing before her? Observing again the beautifully-fitting frock coat and fashionable neck-tie of the figure, it came upon her that the apparition must have some connection with St. John's wedding day. The surmise deepened into certainty. She endeavoured to frame a question, and after a struggle for self-control, she managed to stammer in a queer, hard, dry voice:–

"What do you want? Can I help you?"

The apparition shook its head, while the expression on its face became more and yet more piteously despairing, and at last, with a horrible gesture, it threw up its arms and disappeared.

Immediately afterwards Mr. Prescott, coming into the room, found his wife lying on the hearthrug, unconscious.

All the parties concerned, except Mrs. Prescott herself, tried to laugh the affair into a fancy of that lady's brain, overwrought as it was by the strain of her literary work, the excitement naturally incidental to her only daughter's engagement, and finally her psychic studies. These three things, it was averred, were sufficient to account for any number of apparitions. To do her justice, Mrs. Prescott tried to laugh also, but her success was not striking. Reason how she would, the impression that what she had seen betokened some disaster to Willie St. John upon his wedding day, refused to depart. With the passage of months, however, her mind grew easier; and at length, though her belief in the actuality of the phenomenon remained unshaken, she ceased to attach to it any prophetic importance.

Such was the true history of the "vision," the memory of which, as we have seen, had cast some faint shadow of melancholy upon the honeymoon journey of Mr. and Mrs. St. John.

Between Chatham and their destination, husband and wife discussed the delicious details of housekeeping and domestic economy, and, so far as mortals may be happy, they were happy. Just outside Westgate, the train pulled up with a grinding of brakes, and a disconnecting jar. At first St. John feared a collision, and Mrs. Prescott's apparition again recurred to his mind. Nothing appeared to be amiss, however; the train moved slowly and with many jolts into the station, and at six o'clock Willie and Olive found themselves in a remarkably comfortable suite of rooms, all with the expensive sea-aspect.

It was nearly dark. St. John sat by the fire in the drawing-room waiting for his wife, who was in the bedroom above, to join him. Dinner was ordered for 6.30.

For some inexplicable reason the man's thoughts again hovered round the subject of Mrs. Prescott's vision. Try how he might he could not dismiss it from his mind. Suppose, only suppose, there was something in this absurd psychic business, after all. Similar apparitions, authenticated by people presumably honest and shrewd, had undoubtedly proved to be the heralds of disaster. Certain stories by Rudyard Kipling came into his head, and he remembered to have seen in a newspaper that Rudyard Kipling believed in ghosts.[2]

Pooh! What nonsense! The fact was he needed his dinner. He looked at his watch and wondered how long Olive would be. Then he recalled a parody of Longfellow's *Psalm of Life*, which he had once composed, and began to repeat it:—

> Wives of great men all remind us
> We may have a lively time,
> Tell me not in scornful—

He stopped. There was a sound of quick, firm footsteps in the passage, and without any ceremony, two men walked into the room. They were dressed in a blue uniform, similar to, but distinguishable from, that of a policeman. Their faces were clean shaven and hard set. One of them said:

"Mr. William Bruce Walley St. John."

" That is my name," St. John replied. "May I ask what the dickens you want, if it's not a rude question?"

"We are acting on instructions from headquarters to take you back to London at once, without the least delay."

"Oh, really! That's interesting. What headquarters? Why is my presence in town so immediately necessary?"

"We can't stop answering questions. Put on your hat and come."

"Look here, my men," said St. John, standing up, "clear out, or I'll send for the police."

He was entirely mystified, and he was also angry.

For answer the two men stepped up to him, and in an astonishing short second of time, handcuffs were upon his wrists, and a revolver within two inches of his nose.

"You're the solicitor that practises at Bow-street, aren't you?" said one of the men.

St. John suddenly remembered that he had lately been connected with certain anarchist cases, and thought this was perhaps some scheme of private revenge. The revolver and the handcuffs effectually quelled him—physically he was something of a coward—and he obediently walked out of the room between the two men, marvelling the while that such a monstrous adventure could befall a law abiding individual at the end of the nineteenth century, in the best governed country in the world.

"I must speak to my wife," he said as they reached the hall, which was deserted, "she'll be in a—"

"Silence, Sir." The muzzle of the revolver tickled his forehead. Ever afterwards he remembered that even in that awful predicament he uttered the word "wife" with some diffidence, as a newly-married man might. It was a cold, dull night very late in October, and the lamp-lit streets of Westgate, at no time crowded, were now absolutely deserted. A train happened to be waiting; there was only one porter on the platform, and no passengers, and the two men rapidly conducted their prisoner to a first-class carriage labelled "Reserved." The train started.

It would be impossible to describe St. John's feeling during that memorable, interminable ride to London. He raged, he cursed, he tried to bribe, he implored: all without result. The two men would give him no information, nor would they allow him to communicate with his wife in any way. At last this clever and accomplished St. John, accustomed though he was, through his profession, to witness with composure the strangest accidents of existence and freaks of fate, became thoroughly terrified. There was, then, some sinister prophetic meaning in Mrs. Prescott's vision. He remembered with an added tremor that the figure which Mrs. Prescott saw threw up its arms with a despairing gesture and disappeared. What did that mean? And what was to become of his poor, deserted wife?

At Holborn Viaduct Station a carriage was waiting, and the three men were rapidly driven to Soho. The vehicle stopped before a house with a plain, ugly front, and St. John was taken inside. The hall was merely a long, narrow passage, quite dark. Presently a door opened at the far end, and he was told to go forward. He found himself in a large, lofty chamber, dimly lighted by candles, and draped with grey tapestry. In the middle of the room was a large vase heaped up with withered orange-blossoms. Three very old, stern-looking men sat round this vase, and as St. John entered they gazed upon him with a queer smile.

"Willy Bruce Walley St. John," one of them began, "we saw the announcement of your engagement to the woman Olive Prescott in the *Morning Post*. A representative of our Society witnessed your marriage this morning. The woman Olive Prescott is an advanced woman is she not?"

"She—er, writes," stammered St. John.

"Answer! Is she advanced?"

"Ye—es."

"Just so. Our Society exists for the punishment of men who encourage Advanced Women by marrying them. You remember a little accident to your cab, caused by a dray, in Victoria-street this afternoon. That was arranged by us, but through carelessness of our driver the plan failed. So we had no resource left but to bring you back here. Punishment awaits you! Before proceeding, however, I should just explain to you that the strong and determined men who compose this Society, having observed with pain and astonishment the rapid progress of the Advanced Woman in these latter days—how she essays to fight with Man on his own ground, calling out upon Chivalry if she is beaten down; how she writes; how she paints; how she makes orations; how she trades; how, in short, she threatens completely to extinguish Man—have determined to arrest her march by the simple means of snatching from her any man whom she is clever enough to inveigle into marriage. No surer remedy than this could have been found.

"Now, Sir, will you swear never again to go near the woman Olive Prescott, or will you take the punishment?"

"I will not swear," said St. John, with a firmness which astonished him.

"Then, comrade, give him the kiss of death."

The tallest and ugliest of the three men rose and came towards St. John. But, somehow, as the fellow approached, his withered face seemed to take on a more beautiful expression. It grew quite lovely. St. John trembled . . . .

"Why, Willie," said his wife, who was bending over him tenderly, "you've actually fallen asleep in front of this hot fire. It's through being up at three o'clock this morning, I suppose."

They went into dinner.

NOTES

1. *Woman*. 20th February 1895, pages 15-16. Signed Sarah Volatile.

2. Prior to his son's death in World War I Kipling was, in fact, generally unsympathetic to psychical research and notions of ghostly apparitions. This hostility may have been induced by his unstable sister Trix's enthusiasm for the subject. Kipling's stories at this period exhibited a paradoxical mixture of magic and reality, due in part to his experiences in India. Writing to George Sturt in February 1897, Bennett explains at length his personal antipathy to Kipling's art. (*Letters II*, pp. 77-79)

DR. ANNA JEKYLL AND MISS HYDE.[1]

"So old-fashioned," said one of the women.

"She might belong to Jane Austen's novels," said the second, with a shrug.

"Rather jolly though, all the same," the man of the group put in.

"Yes, in her way, I suppose," assented the third woman, benevolently.

If they had known that I was within earshot, they probably wouldn't have discussed my characteristics with such engaging freedom; but people who go to "At Homes" in "Mr. So-and-So's tiny but daintily-furnished rooms," and talk in their natural voices, must accept the risk of being overheard.

What would they think of old-fashioned Miss Hyde, who is rather jolly though, in her way, could they see her now—the smoke wreath upcurling from her lips and *Children of Plaster*[2] on her lap?—I wonder. But, Arthur, poor mystified cousin, will be calling again soon. I must mix the draught and return to my natural Jane-Austenish self.

I thought it a weird thing, when our old friend Mr. Utterson died, that a packet should have been found among his private papers with the inscription, "For my friend, Miss Anna Hyde only; to be opened by her in private." And the *bizarrerie* of the affair has, in effect, come near to being more startling than pleasant.

You remember Mr. Utterson, the lawyer, the friend of Dr Jekyll whose terrible story Stevenson has told in *Dr. Jekyll and Mr. Hyde*. He died about a year ago. The packet addressed to me contained a bottle of some wine-red fluid, a quantity of whitish powder, and this letter: "DEAR ANNA,—One secret relating to the Jekyll-Hyde affair I have kept from everyone. I make you the depository of it, partly because I have known you since you were a baby, and we have always been happily intimate; partly for the somewhat foolish reason that your name happens to be the same as that adopted by poor Jekyll for his other self; and partly because you are a woman, and courageous enough to attempt a hazardous experiment. The secret is this. The strange and powerful potion which Jekyll concocted and employed to transform himself into Hyde was not, as he himself thought and all the world has given to understand, completely exhausted. I found a considerable quantity of the ingredients in an old cupboard in the room where he died. Those ingredients accompany this letter. Often I used idly to speculate as to the probable effect of the potion upon a woman; idle speculation led to serious study of the problem, and in the result, although I have arrived at no definite solution, I have come to believe that the drug would affect a woman differently from a man. We know that in Jekyll's case it divided the evil from the good, and gave to the former a separate existence and personality. But just as one can divide a square in more ways than one by a single line, so, I reasoned, may an individuality be split in numerous directions by the operation of one agency. We see in the character of every human being not only evil and good, but many other pairs of opposite qualities—the imaginative and the matter-of-fact; the credulous and the sceptical; the conservative and the revolutionary; and so on. Suppose that, taken by a woman instead of a man, the potion gave a bodily form to her scepticism as distinguished from her credulity, or to her radicalism as distinguished from her essential conservatism, or to her dry, hard common sense as distinguished from her imaginativeness; or even say that latent mannishness which slumbers but uneasily in the breast of the most womanly woman—what interesting experiments a fearless woman might then make, if she chose, with this easily-mixed potion. Some people would say I have grown morbid. Perhaps. But for all that, Anna, I will ask you seriously to consider the matter. Will you try it, to gratify the long-cherished wish of a friend who will be dead when you read these lines? R. UTTERSON. P.S.—Whatever your decision, I beg you to make no one your confidant. Be advised upon this point. I know what I know."

A disturbing legacy, was it not, to receive from an old friend, whom one had always believed to be the most humdrum person in the world! At first I rejected Mr. Utterson's proposal, almost with fear. I was not that sort of woman. I could go to church in a *démodé* bonnet and not blench; when two of my portraits appeared in a popular magazine with the legends, "At Seventeen" and "Present Day," I bore the sight with equanimity; but I was not intended by Nature for psychological experiments.

But after awhile, the curious ingredients left by Mr. Utterson—the wine-red liquid and the whitish powder—began to have a fascination for me. I looked at these every day.

Once I mixed together a little of each. The result was a kind of sparkling Moselle. I moistened my tongue with it, shuddered slightly, and dashed the glass to the ground.

Then it came upon me that one day, struggle how I might, I should end by taking the potion, if only to ease my curiosity. That day has come.

I drank the prescribed quantity at 11 a.m this morning. At first I thought I should faint. Life itself seemed to be oozing slowly away at every pore. Then vigour returned, and I ran trembling to the glass. My appearance was not much altered. The features were, perhaps, a trifle harder, the eye more bold, but no one could have mistaken my identity. My hair, however, had become quite short and unkempt, and my dress fitted badly. I christened my new self, "Dr Anna Jekyll."

And did I feel much the same? Yes, at the beginning. My first impulse, which I immediately acted upon, was to get out of the house. I put on my hat and jacket, and was just closing the front door, when I remembered I had forgotten my gloves. "Never mind," I said, and calling a hansom I jumped in, and gave the driver the name of a well-known restaurant in Regent-street.

In Piccadilly it occurred to me that I had no cigarettes, and I stopped the cab at a tobacconist's shop, and bought some, and a box of matches.

Arthur was in the grill-room of the restaurant. I spoke to him.

"Are you alone?" he said (accent on the "lone").

"Yes; of course. Why?" I asked lightly.

"N-nothing."

"Waiter; chop and a glass of Burgundy."

"Yes'm."

"You know your way about, fair cousin," Arthur murmured contemplatively, looking at the table-cloth.

"You may depend on that," I answered.

Afterwards I told him I wished to make a purchase at a bookshop, and he walked along with me to Bumpus's. I asked him if he knew the price of *Children of Plaster*.

"Surely you're not going to buy *that*," he exclaimed.

"I am," I said, raising my chin.

"But both Mudie's and Smith's have tabooed it."

"Yes, that"s why I want it. These libraries are so prim and old-fashioned".

"You're different to-day, Anna, somehow," he said. "It is your hair?"

"Not at all," I replied, hurriedly.

Later on he offered to see me home.

"See me home!" I said in amaze. "Is there any more sense in you seeing me home than there would be in me seeing you home?"

"Well, you're a woman, and I'm a man, that's all." There was some scorn in his voice. "However, as you wish. I'll call this afternoon."

I gave him one glance, and left him.

Well, he will be here directly. I think I'll change back from Dr. Anna Jekyll to plain Miss Hyde. I go to my room, mix the potion, gulp it down. Another spasm, and I am myself again ....

Then and then only, it occurs to me that during the last five hours I have been something peculiarly and strikingly horrid.

"I wish I had never seen Mr. Utterson and his wretched drugs," I exclaim, passionately.

"What's that, eh?" says a voice behind the screen. It is Arthur's voice.

"I was only soliloquising to the effect that I haven't been feeling quite myself to-day." Arthur's look says that he agrees.

* * * * * *

I had solemnly resolved a month ago, after the escapade which I have described, never to touch Mr. Utterson's terrible potion again. For a week I remained firm to my purpose, and then, as before, the drugs in some strange way seemed to call aloud to me, and I looked at them, toyed with them, and to-day I drank the transforming draught once more, in spite of myself. Having become "Dr. Anna Jekyll," I went down into the library, and as luck fell out found Arthur there in conversation with my father. The two men stopped talking suddenly and self-consciously.

"I hope I'm not interrupting the discussion of private matters," I said, rather icily, somewhat hurt by the silence which my entrance had induced.

"Nothing private, my dear."

"Then why did you stop?"

"My dear Anna, there are some painful things one doesn't care to talk about in the presence of a good woman."

"How much longer will these quaint old ideas linger on?" I exclaimed with disgust, and left the room, banging the door.

At lunch Arthur suggested that he should take me to the afternoon "Pop." at St. James's Hall.

"I don't want to be *taken* anywhere," I said. "But if you care to *accompany* me, we will go to the Ladies' Football Match."[3] I could have laughed to see the looks on their faces.

"My dear!" ejaculated my mother.

"And why not?" I queried. "Is it not a woman's sacred duty to develop herself physically? And can there possibly be a healthier exercise than football? The conventionality of my family is becoming positively nauseous."

This didn't seem to convince them, however, and Arthur flatly declined to go. Accordingly I went alone, and paid five shillings for a seat on the grand stand. There was not a large attendance, and nothing appeared to be happening. Then a thick-set, healthy-looking woman announced that one of the players was suddenly indisposed, and there was some difficulty in getting a substitute.

"I shall be very happy to play," I called out.

"Can you play?" the woman asked.

"I can't tell yet, because I've not tried; but I think I can. I'm strong. Feel my arm."

"Will you come down to the dressing-tent?" she said; "I daresay you'll do. You know" she added in a whisper, "*we* can't play *very* well, yet." So I left the grand stand amid the ill-suppressed titters of a few males, and donned what the captain of one of the teams called "our working costume."

Just as I was putting my head outside the tent, I caught a glimpse of the back of a figure on the grand stand that seemed familiar. Heavens! It was Arthur. Without stopping to reason the matter calmly, I rushed back, re-assumed my own dress, took a cab, and went home. I fled to my room, tremblingly mixed the potion, and drank it. Once more I was my old self, plain old-fashioned Miss Hyde.

"Had Arthur seen me?" That was the burning question. It has turned out to-night that he had not. It seems like a fearful nightmare, this afternoon's experience. What is the precise effect of the drugs? I think I can tell. Mr. Utterson's conjecture was not far wrong. The effect on a woman *is* different from the effect on a man. In Dr. Jekyll's case it divided the evil from the good. *In mine it divides the "new" from the "old."* Every woman, even the nicest, feels "new" at times, and the most aggressively "new" occasionally feels "old," or at any rate, middle-aged. But when I become Dr. Anna Jekyll, through the sinister operation of that accursed potion, *I am entirely "new."*

Shall I have the moral strength to resist taking it yet again? I doubt. Thank heaven! there are only two doses left.

* * * * * *

My mistrust of myself was only too well-founded. For the third time I have taken the potion. What will happen I know not, but I am prepared for something particularly awful. For you must know that Arthur and I have fallen deeply in love with each other lately. There is nothing specially terrible in the fact, of course, but the mischief is that he will probably call this afternoon *and I shall probably propose to him!* I feel sure I shall; it will be so beautifully "new." But why not use the drugs in order to become my better self again? Or say, if he should call, that I am not at home, or ill? Alas! I can do neither of these things. So long as I am "Dr. Anna Jekyll" I can only behave as she wills.

I await him in the drawing-room. He is announced. He enters, smiling; we begin to converse.

"If you will allow me to make the remark, Anna," he says, "your dress this afternoon is scarcely so becoming as usual."

"Only doll-women care for dress," I say, " I am surprised that you should notice such a trifle, my dearest Arthur."

He naturally seems rather surprised at the whole of that speech, including the "my dearest Arthur." There is a pause. I feel I am going to do it.

"Arthur," I say, taking his hand, "Do you know what love is?"

"I should think I did," says he rapturously. He would propose himself, if I gave him the chance, but I can't, can't.

"Arthur," I proceed, "*I* know what love is, too. Now what I am going to say to you may seem a little strange, but, as you are aware, I am quite free from the usual feminine slavery to convention".

"Of course," he replies, polite but mystified. I am really going to propose!

"Arthur, will you be—"

"Mrs. Pilchard-Finney and Miss Pilchard-Finney," the servant announces. Those chatterboxes, at such a time!

"*Good* afternoon, dear Miss Hyde," &c, &c. Arthur retires to a window, and my mother opportunely enters. Suddenly, with a mighty effort, I form a resolve. Begging to be excused, I run to my room, drink the last of the potion, and I am saved. Never again can those drugs fascinate me, for they are exhausted. But what a hair's breadth escape! Arthur will surely propose to-morrow.

By the way, how funny it feels to be a "new" woman.

NOTES

1. *Woman*. 6th March 1895, pages 15-16. Signed Sarah Volatile.
Robert Louis Stevenson's *Dr. Jekyll and Mr. Hyde* was published in 1886 and became a bestseller. Bennett indicates a stylistic debt to him in several of his early letters "He deals chiefly with the sweet uses of alliteration - subtle, concealed alliteration of course - & he damn well knows what he talks about" (*Letters II*, p. 26), although "Stevenson only helps me in minute details of style" (*Letters II*, p. 29). James Hepburn believes that Stevenson's influence "upon Bennett was fairly considerable, and elements of his style can be seen especially in *Leonora* (1903) and as late as *The Pretty Lady* (1918), particularly in the closing passage." (*Letters II*, p. 25, note 14)
2. A possible reference to *Children of Circumstance* by Iota (Kathleen Caffyn), reviewed by Bennett in *Woman* on 17th October 1894. Iota's 1894 novel *A Yellow Aster*, about an emancipated woman of the 1890s and the subject of free love, was also reviewed by Bennett in *Woman* on 21st March 1894.
3. The first recorded women's football match took place in Scotland in 1888. In 1895 Nettie Honeyball established the British Ladies Club in London.

THE PHANTASM OF MY GRANDMOTHER.[1]

It began with automatic writing, which was first suggested to me by reading about Mr. Stead and "Julia." You get a clean piece of paper and a pencil, and you empty your mind, so to speak, and wait for events. A psychical friend persuaded me to try the experiment, and, half in joke, I did so. For ten minutes nothing happened. Then, to my complete surprise, my hand began to move of itself, and the pencil formed letters and words. Frankly, I was rather frightened, so uncanny was the business. This was the message:—

The spirit of Edna Clayton controls this writing. You can semi-materialise her if you choose to do so. Get an oviform crystal, and search it alone to-night, about 11 p.m., before the portrait in the dining-room. Then will, *firmly and with all your mind's power, that the crystal vision shall detach itself and separately exist.*

Now Edna Clayton was the name of my paternal grandmother, who died in 1842, at the age of 23, two years after the birth of my father. She was a renowned beauty, and her portrait by Daniel Maclise[2] has hung in our dining-room for fifty years, a dazzling sight. She was a well-educated woman with a pretty wit, and her early death, as may be imagined, was the cause of profound grief to a wide circle of friends.

Was the automatic message merely a trick of my disengaged brain, or was there "something in it?" At first I was afraid to put the thing to the test, afraid to take a step in the dark with a chance of clutching the Unearthly. But that afternoon I went to Burns', in Southampton-row, and paid five-and-sixpence for a crystal, bringing it home in my muff.

Richard Larch[3] came to dinner, and according to his custom gave us much Chopin and Heller during the evening. Whether he noticed that I was not appreciative or whether he wanted to go home and compose another sonata in my honour, I cannot say, but he left early, and for once I was not sorry.

At eleven, father and mother went to bed, and I crept like a thief into the dining room. Lighting two candles on the mantelpiece, over which hung the portrait of my grandmother, I sat down by the dying fire, with the crystal on my knees, and gazed steadfastly into its iridescent deeps.

Presently I indistinctly perceived in it the blurred outlines of a figure, a woman's figure, in a white evening dress; the vision grew clearer, clearer; unmistakably it was the counterfeit of my grandmother that I saw in the crystal. Then something told me to fix my eyes on an armchair opposite me, and to *will*, with all my moral strength, that the vision should materialise itself.

I perspired; my eyes ran; the room seemed to swing round. With an effort I regained possession of myself, and there sitting in the armchair, smiling gaily, exactly as she does in the picture, sat the presentment of Edna Clayton, my grandmother. I looked up at Maclise's portrait; it was strangely dimmed and faded. My brain struggled to comprehend the situation, I felt a fluttering at my heart, and lost consciousness.

When I recovered the figure of grandmother was still sitting opposite me, smiling.

"So you have come round," it said, in a sweet resonant voice. "I am *so* relieved."

"I am quite myself again, thank you," I stammered. "Can I—offer you anything to eat, grandmamma?"

"Don't call me that, Alice," she implored, "although of course I am your grandmother. Still, I don't look it, do I?"

"You look the most beautiful creature I have ever seen," I answered. "But won't you tell me *what* you are? Because I'm rather frightened; at least, I've never felt like this before."

"Ah, dear girl," she said. "Don't ask questions the answers to which would overwhelm you. So far as *your* knowledge can go I am a semi-materialised spirit, brought into a temporary half-existence by the combined exertions of your physical will and my spiritual will. Let that content you."

"But why did you—write to me?"

"Simply for the reason that I felt adventurous. I desired to see my descendants more closely. We never lose touch with you, of course, but I wanted more than that. And now you must take me about, and show me the world; the *fin de siècle* world you call it, don't you?"

My grandmother's tone was so matter-of-fact and so persuasive that I quickly lost my fears. We chatted far into the night and she wove such a spell round me that I sat down at her feet, and would have stroked her long thin hands. Then I bounded away with an exclamation of horror. My fingers had passed through her hand as they might have passed through milk!

"My dear girl," she said, soothingly, "It is unwise to touch me. Remember I am only semi-materialised."

"Then how am I to show you the world?" I asked.

"That we can arrange," my grandmother said confidently. " I must warn you to tell no one of my presence here without my permission. It might lead to fatal consequences. I shall not be able to retain my materialisation for more than thirty hours at most. So it will be necessary to see the sights tomorrow."

"There is the weekly 'At Home' at the Club," I said, "we might go to that."

"Do women follow men into their own clubs now? They were fairly advanced in my time, but—" my grandmother ended with a gesture.

"Not at all, we have are own clubs," I explained.

"Ah, I see, for the discussion of cookery, housekeeping, needlework, dress, &c., I suppose."

"Scarcely that," I said dryly.

"For what then?"

"Well, I can't tell you exactly. Social purposes, mutual improvement—"

"Mutual fiddlesticks," interrupted my grandmother. "It seems to me you just want to imitate men. After women's clubs, I shall not be surprised to hear of men's sewing meetings. But I will go to your club."

"I had promised to take Richard—Mr. Larch."

"Richard—Mr. Larch—Who is he?"

"Well, you see, he's a great friend of mine, I should say of papa's, a musician; he often comes here."

"To see your dear papa, of course. Yes, Alice, they never alter, those Richards. I know them. They used to come to see *my* father. Well, you must put Richard off."

"I can't do that, I'm afraid, grandmamma."

"Then you must tell him about me, and we will go

together. Perhaps that will be more fun."

The next day I explained the matter to Mr. Larch, and I believe he thought I was mad. But when I took him to a disused room at the top of the house,[4] from the window of which my grandmother was eagerly surveying the street, he realised the situation, though not without a thrill.

"Charmed to meet you, Mr. Larch," said my grandmother, bowing low and gracefully.

Richard was entranced with her beauty. His experience was similar to mine, and in a few moments he was perfectly at ease with her.

We got out of the house unobserved, and in a quarter of an hour my grandmother was seated in a quiet corner of the large reading room in which the club receptions are held.

She was, indeed, a vision of beauty: blue eyes, golden hair, a radiantly clear complexion, and a figure unmatched in the room. No woman outside Albert Moore's[5] pictures could have appeared more lovely. Her full, dimpling face had the contour of a young girl's, and yet there was a grave look upon her, even when she laughed her gayest, which indicated ineffable knowledge and unimaginable experience.

Her early Victorian costume and coiffure suited her admirably, and so much weird and fearsome raiment is to be seen at the club "At Homes" that no one remarked on the strangeness of her dress. Our corner was partially screened from observation, and probably such people as happened to notice any peculiarities thought she was a journalist, making copy out of herself for an evening paper.

Mr. Larch and I sat on either side of my grandmother, and in front of us was a small table. The room began to fill.

"Now Mrs. Clayton," began Mr. Larch, seeing that my grandmother sat silent and watchful, "may we not ask you for your impressions?"

"I see that there are still more women than men. It used to be so. Philosophers are right in saying that man is the nobler creature, but they give the wrong reason. It is simply because he is the scarcer. We always worship a rarity. But who is that insignificant man there with five tall girls round him?"

"That is the great Domville, the novelist," said Mr. Larch.

"What, not the author of *Passion Lilies*? I was reading that last night, Alice showed it me."

"Yes. That's the man. What did you think of it?"

"It was like drinking sea-water while a band played 'Home, Sweet Home,' in two keys to soothe your nerves. Why the heroine's simply—"

"Yes, isn't she!" said I.

"I suppose marriage still survives in out-of-the-way corners of the country?" queried my grandmother.

Mr. Larch looked at me, and then at my grandmother, who smiled. "I hope it is not dead yet," he remarked.

"And do all those girls want to—er fascinate Mr. Domville—marry him?"

"Not in the least," said Mr. Larch. "They are competing for the honour of being the heroine of his next novel. You know all Domville's characters are drawn from life, and with each book he publishes a key to the *dramatis personae*. People like it. Once a man brought a libel action against him for this dodge, but Domville got a number of witnesses to swear that it was an honour even to figure foolishly in his novels, and the man lost his action, and had to pay the costs."

"Then all those girls have histories—pasts you call them?"

"Oh, no! They are the most guileless creatures. But it's the fashion now, you know, for a woman to go about with a past, several if possible, and these innocents will expect Domville to write something terrible about them out of his head, and then they will be able to look the whole world in the face."

"I see. Two pasts make one future. How wonderfully the human race has progressed in fifty years!"

At this point there was a slight commotion of expectancy in the room, and a big over-dressed girl entered, alone.

"Lady Winifred Wolstanton,[6] sister of the Earl of Cobridge[7] and Caux," I murmured in my grandmother's ear.

"Famous or notorious?" she asked, adding, "both words seem to have the same meaning now, though."

"She gets £40 a week at the Moon and Stars Theatre."

"Oh!" said my grandmother. "I did hear something once about bringing the classes into touch with the masses. Now I understand. You would call her a philanthropist then—or a social reformer?" Mr. Larch laughed.

"Her story is rather funny. She used to be awfully extravagant, you know, and cajoled so much money out of her brother that at last he cut up rough."

"He what?"

"He turned nasty, I mean, and said she shouldn't have another penny. Soon afterwards she came to him and said she had arranged to go on the burlesque stage, and if he didn't fork out—give her a decent allowance, she would carry out the arrangement and disgrace the family name."

"And he yielded?" put in my grandmother.

"No, people don't do such things nowadays. He said, 'All right!' and at once sat down and wrote a letter to the manager of the theatre, pointing out that under the circumstances it would increase the attractiveness of Lady Winifred's *début* if he had a box, and the manager sent him one, with compliments. The theatre was packed, and the earl applauded his sister most generously."

Shakspere could not adequately have described my grandmother's look.

I had been hoping that as I was not a very prominent member of the club we should be left alone, but happening to look up I saw Mr. and Mrs. Townley aiming directly for me, with the Townley twins. I whispered to my grandmother to turn her head and appear to be deeply engaged in conversation with Richard.

"How d'ye do, Miss Clayton" said the twins almost

together, "we thought we'd pop in because we wanted to see Mr. Domville, and so pa and ma came too." The Townley twins were fourteen, tall and sickly and pert, and they always patronised their adoring parents.

"Dear Charlie has just written a satire on modern society," piped Mr. Townley, "we think it proves his genius."

"Oh! there's no doubt I'm a genius," interrupted the boy confidently, "I'm going to show these musical prodigies the way about. But I must speak to Domville. I've got a new theory about the dawn of love." And he went away.

I fancied I heard Richard saying something to my grandmother about New Woman being a thing of the past, and that the New Child was the phenomenon of the day.

"You know Annabel's got some drawings in the *Purple Quarterly*?" said Mrs. Townley. I said I was unaware of the fact.

"You don't. Oh! you really must see them. Why, Queersley is nothing to her. She has caught the very spirit of decadence."

"Yes," said Annabel, "I flatter myself I can put more meaning into one face than Queersley can get into ten. Ta-ta for the present. I want to chat with Lady Winifred," and the girl was lost in the crowd.

"How wonderfully," my grandmother said, "your club makes clear to me the meaning of our old maxims. Those young Townleys throw quite a new light on the saying, 'The boy is father to the man.' Of course he is. I see it now, and the girl mother to the woman. I should so much like to talk to those two children." My grandmother set her lips.

But worse than the Townley twins was to come. No sooner were they gone than Mr. Tawdry Queersley[8] loomed large and lank and beardless before us. He carried a square volume under his arm, which anyone could see was the new number of the *Purple Quarterly*.

"An interesting face," whispered my grandmother. "Introduce me as a cousin from somewhere or other." I did so.

"Perhaps you would like to see the portraits I have done

for the new *Purple*," Mr. Queersley said.

"Delighted," said my grandmother.

"Well, this is a sketch of our greatest actress." Mr. Queersley opened the book, and exhibited a drawing of a woman with bloated cheeks, a smile like an angry cat, and a protruding under lip which hung pendent like a ripe fruit.

"What a horrible woman!" exclaimed my grandmother.

"Ah! You only say that because you aren't used to my style. I am not afraid to face facts, you know, and I bring out the subtleties of character as they have never been displayed before. That sketch is a masterpiece."

"Really!" said my grandmother. "It's a very extraordinary work certainly."

"Yes, isn't it?" said Mr. Queersley, turning over a page. Now this is a portrait of Mr. Larch here. Observe the quality of line. See how the very soul of music is expressed in the cut of the coat collar." Mr. Larch looked another way. In this picture he had the appearance of a condemned murderer suffering from acute indigestion. "You see," Mr. Queersley explained, "he is in the act of composing a sonata."

My grandmother gasped.

"I'll tell you what," the artist went on, struck with a benevolent idea, "I'll draw your portrait, and it can appear in the next number of the *Purple Quarterly*. You look rather quaint in that costume—I suppose you're going to a fancy dress ball."

"Your smelling-salts, Alice!" my grandmother moaned. I put them on the table, and she bent over them. "It's very good of you, Mr. Queersley," she said, "but to-morrow I'm going on a long voyage—very long."

"That needn't interfere. I'll do it now, it won't take ten minutes, and the people here will be wild with joy at the chance of seeing me at work. I'm the greatest artist of the day, you know. I'll just get some paper and a pencil." He skipped away.

My grandmother looked at me and at Mr. Larch. "Good-bye, Alice. Good-bye, Mr. Larch. Be happy. I've stood your novelists; I've stood your Lady Winifreds; I've stood your New Child—shall I ever forget the New Child? But to have my portrait done by the Tawdry Queersley—I cannot, I cannot; good-bye!" And immediately she faded from our sight.

Then Mr. Queersley came back.

"Why, where's your cousin?" he asked.

I could not speak. Mr. Larch was not in much better case, but he managed to stammer:

"She's gone. She had to go."

"Funny. I didn't see her go out."

"Neither did I," said Mr. Larch, solemnly. I suppose there was something strange written on our faces.

"How queer you are!" muttered Mr. Queersley, and picked up his *Purple Quarterly*, and strode angrily away.

NOTES

1. *Woman*. 27th March 1895, pages 14-16. Signed Sarah Volatile.
2. Daniel Maclise (1806-1870), born in Cork, launched his career as a portrait painter in Ireland after the success of his portrait of Sir Walter Scott who visited Cork in 1825. Moving to London in 1827 his skill as a portrait painter led to an invitation to contribute a series of caricatures to *Fraser*, a popular magazine founded in the 1830s. He was elected a full member of the Royal Academy in 1840.
3. The name of the chief protagonist in Bennett's first published novel, *A Man From The North* (1898). Bennett began writing the novel in mid-April of 1895, some two weeks after "The Phantasm of My Grandmother" appeared.
4. The "disused room at the top of the house" reappears in *A Man From The North*, becoming, in Chapter XV, an important psychological key to deconstructing the text. (See John Shapcott's Introduction to the Churnet Valley Books edition.)
5. Albert Joseph Moore (1841-1893) was an English painter, renowned for his pictures of languorous female figures posed against a decadent and classical background. His subtle juxtaposition of the aesthetic and the classical combined in a way to defy easy definition. Today Moore is recognised as an important symbolist painter and contributor to the Aesthetic Movement.
6. Wolstanton, a town between Burslem and Newcastle-under-Lyme is renamed Hillport in Bennett's books.
7. Bennett lived for a time in his father's house at Cobridge, a middle-class professional district between Burslem and Hanley. It is renamed Bleakridge in his books.
8. A less than subtle reference to Aubrey Beardsley and to *The Yellow Book (Purple Quarterly)*. Beardsley's pen-and-ink drawings from 1894 to 1895 for *The Yellow Book* included portraits of actresses and gave the book its defining look. The description of a "drawing of a woman with bloated cheeks ...." is likely to be a satire upon Beardsley's *Portrait of Mrs. Patrick Campbell*, which appeared in the first issue of *The Yellow Book* in April 1894.

THE CRYSTAL-GAZERS.[1]
(Episode One)

About nine o'clock in the evening, Gatti's Adelaide Gallery in the Strand is not so busy as it has been earlier in the day. The diners have betaken themselves in digestive contentment to the theatre; the hour for supper parties is not yet; and, in the meantime, the dark-featured waiters lounge at the buffets, idly fingering their long white aprons, chattering Tuscan to each other, and eyeing with exhausted disgust any belated customer who may chance to demand their services.

On one particular night during the late frost, as the clock over the north portico pointed to a quarter past nine, the waiter in charge of a table near the corner where chess is played, began to lay it with cutlery and serviette, and the inevitable bread-roll and pat of butter; he had scarcely done so when the golden-braided door-keeper pushed open the swinging glass doors, and, bowing with respectful familiarity, ushered in a lady, who walked direct to the prepared table, placed her muff and an evening paper on one chair, and occupied another herself. She greeted the waiter with an alert smile, and in a surprisingly short space of time was applying herself to a mutton chop with grilled mushrooms, while the waiter carefully poured some white wine from a wicker-covered bottle into a glass. No frequenter of Gatti's got served with such alacrity as this self-possessed woman. For she was thirty and pretty, she was exceptionally well-dressed, she spoke kindly but with the air of one used to the briskest obedience, and she came regularly at the same hour every evening except Saturday.

At quarter to ten the golden-braided door-keeper peeped in, and, catching her eye, pointed to a waiting hansom outside. She nodded, folded up a long and closely written letter which she had been reading, and began to gather up her things, glancing carelessly down the long quadruple row of gleaming, deserted tables. At the far end of the gallery she saw a footman looking about as if in search of some one. He approached awkwardly, finally stopping in front of her, and saluted.

"Beg your pardon, madam, are you Miss Riverdale?"

"I am."

"I'm Mrs. Richmond's footman. She said I should find you at the third table from the top on the left, nearest the wall, and she's sent this note."

Miss Riverdale read the note with some surprise.

"You have the carriage here of course?"

"Yes, madam."

"Well, I must get you to drive me down to Fleet-street first, the *Mercury* office. I shall have to arrange for someone to do my leader, and then we will go to Mrs. Richmond's. By the way, where does your mistress live now?"

"South Kensington, madam, Onslow-square. Mrs. Richmond said we were to lose no time, madam."

"Very well, I am quite ready. Waiter, I shan't want a hansom to-night. Good night."

At the *Mercury* office Miss Riverdale was delayed a little, for her place was not easily filled, and it was half-past ten when Mrs. Richmond's carriage, rapidly drawn by a pair of browns, rolled into Onslow-square.

In another moment the door of the house opposite which it had stopped was opened, and a maid ran down the steps and met Miss Riverdale at the gate.

"Mistress says will you go up to her bedroom at once, ma'am? She's very much upset."

"What about?" Miss Riverdale smiled, reassuringly.

"I don't know, ma'am, I'm sure."

Miss Riverdale and the maid had not got half-way upstairs before a rather large woman, apparently about thirty-eight years of age, robed in a heliotrope tea-gown, appeared.

"Helen!"

"Yes, dear friend; here I am, you see. I don't know what

they'll do without me at the *Mercury*, but I've come like an obedient genii. I do hope it's about something really important that you've summoned me so hurriedly, otherwise I shall cease to respect you, I think." They passed into a bedroom where an immense fire was burning.

"How delicious!" Miss Riverdale went on; "I'm frozen stiff. Come, you mustn't cry, and you mustn't hang on my neck like that. I'm not physically strong. Now what *is* the matter?"

With an effort the stout lady collected herself, and began, almost in a whisper, "It's about Emily and Tertia."

"I knew it. Not secretly married, I hope? Or have they bought themselves a latchkey and joined a club? The servant seemed to think they were out."

"Helen, it's very serious; I have not your strength of character you know, and although the twins are only twenty they do practically as they like. It isn't as if I was their mother. When I protest, they kiss me, and quote you as an example of the brilliant success which a woman is capable of achieving when allowed perfect freedom to control her own actions. For the past month they have been going out frequently at night. They said they joined a society, and that I must take their word that it was a perfectly proper society. And, of course, two girls can go out together where it would be very unconventional for one to go alone."

"And they refuse to tell you what the society is?"

"Oh yes; absolutely. They said I shouldn't understand it. Their poor father believed in giving girls the same freedom as boys, and this is the result. Well, since they've been members of this society a change has come over them. I can't exactly describe it, but they are different. For one thing, they have a constant air of apprehension, as if they were expecting a ghost to appear. And then, too, they quarrel, and you know they are generally the most affectionate pair of twins one could wish to see. I'm sure the other morning, it was when the Indian mail came in, and there was a letter from Jack Winter—you remember Mr. Winter?"

"Oh yes, quite well. He and I used to be great friends," said Miss Riverdale.

"There was a perfect scene over that letter. It was addressed to the 'Misses Richmond,' and they almost fought for it. I believe they're both in love with Master Jack. He's coming home in a few weeks."

"Really?" said Miss Riverdale.

"Yes. I do believe they're both in love with him. After that scene with the letter they didn't speak to each other for two days. And I've been *so* upset. But I can't tell you how I feel; there's something uncanny about their appearance. And I made a discovery to-night."

"Which determined you to send for me?"

"Yes. It's this." Mrs. Richmond produced a small yellow card, which bore these words:—

> SOCIETY OF CRYSTAL-GAZERS
>
> ------------
>
> MEMBER'S TICKET
>
> NAME ———— *Tertia Richmond*
>
> S.S.S.,
> *President.*

Miss Riverdale examined it carefully.

"Do you know anything of it?" asked her companion.

"Nothing at all."

"Nor I. But I'm sure it's terrible—occult, or something of that kind; and so I sent for you at once. Luckily I remembered your restaurant habits, and knew exactly where to find you. I found the card on the stairs after dinner, Tertia must have dropped it by accident. Now, what is to be done? I expect you to advise me. Heaven knows what dilemma my foolish girls may get themselves into!"

When she had unfolded her tale, Mrs. Richmond seemed a little relieved. Her confidence in this self-possessed, bright-eyed woman was complete, and already she felt her anxiety to be diminishing. These two had known each other for many years, and neither an utter unlikeness of character nor a considerable difference in age had prevented their being the closest friends. Even the older woman's marriage to a rich barrister, a widower with two children, had interfered but slightly with their intimate relations, and five years ago, when Mr. Richmond had died suddenly under pathetic circumstances, their companionship had taken a new lease of life. It was the equal regret of both that Miss Riverdale's remarkable success in journalism, and the consequent demands on her time, had of late years made it impossible for them to see as much of each other as formerly.

"Where are the twins?" asked Miss Riverdale.

"Tertia is out, but I think Emily is upstairs. They quarrelled again after dinner about something."

"Will you ring for Emily?"

"Certainly, if you wish it, Helen; but I am sure you will get nothing out of her."

"Well, I can look at her at any rate," said Miss Riverdale.

Mrs. Richmond touched the bell, and a servant came.

"Kindly tell Miss Emily that Miss Riverdale is here and would like to see her."

"Yes, ma'am." The girl disappeared, only to return in a minute with the news that Miss Emily was out in the square.

"In the square, on a night like this!" exclaimed Mrs. Richmond. "There, Helen, I told you; it's all of a piece. There's something uncanny about the business."

"I will go to her."

"But it's so cold."

"Never mind. I shall at least be as warm as Emily."

Onslow-square, with its trees and its carefully tended

shrubs and lawns, has a sufficiently ordinary aspect in the daytime, but at night it takes on an air of mystery and strangeness that is almost weird. The feeble rays from the lamps which outline the square scarcely pass beyond the railings, and the centre of the immense rectangle, with its shadowy, waving forms of trees above, and its impenetrable gloom below, might well be a haunted wood, the rendezvous of elves and sprites and other unworldly things. On this particular evening the ground was covered with hard, soiled snow; a slight yellow fog made the eyes smart, and seemed to intensify the cold.

As Miss Riverdale peered over the railings into the gardens, her mind was filled with queer fancies, and the resonant roar of invisible omnibuses passing down Sydney-place somehow filled her with an indefinable dread. What could have induced this girl to wander in the square alone in the dark, with the thermometer ten degrees below freezing point? She asked herself the question in vain. Presently Miss Riverdale found an open gate. She went into the grounds and called softly: "Emily, Emily!" but there was no reply. For some distance she stumbled along, at every step fancying she saw she knew not what, and then turned back. Suddenly she heard footfalls on the frozen snow. Yes, there was a figure stooping down, and moving slowly about as if in search of some dropped article. She ran towards it. "Emily," she cried.

The figure straightened itself with a start, and Miss Riverdale recognised the young and beautiful face of Emily Richmond.

"Why, is that you Miss Riverdale? How do you do?"

The words sounded curiously commonplace. Miss Riverdale almost laughed, and her nameless fears fled.

"Fairly well, thank you, Emily," she said, drily, standing at a little distance. "But what are you looking for?"

"Nothing," Emily replied, carelessly; and then, with a

little exclamation of delight, bent down again, and seized a round object, which glittered slightly as she thrust it under her cloak. Miss Riverdale forebore to put any further questions, and taking the girl's arm, led her gently out of the gardens and into the house.

"Now take me to your room," she said, "I do so want to have a long chat with you. Your mother doesn't seem very well."

They talked some time, and presently Miss Riverdale returned to Mrs. Richmond's bedroom. "I haven't learned much," she said, "but I'm going out with Emily."

"At this time? Where?"

"I'll tell you afterwards."

"Yes, but"—But Helen had gone.

(Episode Two)

It came to pass that later Helen Riverdale and Emily were to be seen leaving St. James's Park Station on the Underground Railway. They traversed several quiet streets, and at length stopped before a large house, the windows of which were all dark. Instead of going to the front entrance they went down the area steps and rang a bell. A little postern opened, showing a long, gloomy passage. When they had reached the extremity of this passage, a double door, curtained with heavy black plush, barred their further progress. Emily knocked five times slowly, and twice quickly. The door then yielded to gentle pressure, and the two women found themselves in a vast, low apartment, dimly lighted from an unseen source, and dotted with men and women, each of whom was seated at a small table, and gazing with rapt attention at certain objects placed thereon. As they entered, a young girl ran out, apparently without seeing them.

"Why, *there's* Tertia!" exclaimed Emily. Let's fetch her back."

"Very well," answered Miss Riverdale; but just then a hand

was placed lightly on her shoulder. She turned round. A young man, tall, with a striking actor's face, was in front of her.

"Well!" gasped Miss Riverdale; "of all the"—Then she stopped.

"This is Mr. Winter, Mr. *George* Winter—Jack's—that is Mr. Jack Winter's brother," said Emily, and the young man bowed, smiling.

"Mr. Winter and I know each other well," answered Miss Riverdale. "But I have always understood that he utterly scorned the occult sciences, and I certainly was surprised to find him here."

"All initiates do that—in public," said Mr. Winter, easily. "A real occultist has no desire whatever to be the missionary of his faith. He believes that the Truth is not for the herd."

"Am I one of the herd then?"

"Certainly not, since you are here."

Helen looked curiously round the immense chamber and observed, what in the half light she had not at first noticed, that it was divided into a number of small compartments by partitions of thick sheet glass which ran from floor to ceiling. These cubicles, as they might be termed, were ranged on either side of a broad central corridor. Nearly every cubicle was occupied by one or two individuals, but a few here and there were empty. All the people in the room were therefore in full view; yet no sound was heard, though it could be seen that more than one couple was engaged in conversation.

She was about to ask the meaning of this arrangement when an old and distinguished looking man, with short, white beard and white hair, and a face in which benevolence and cynicism were simultaneously expressed, came up, with all the air of one having authority, and called Emily aside.

"That is the mysterious 'S.S.S,' our President," explained George Winter. "No one knows his real identity. He founded this Society, and he is absolute autocrat here. All that he insists on is sincerity of purpose on the part of members, the purpose of course being the study of the occult science of crystal-gazing. If he suspects any ulterior motive—if, for instance, he thinks that a member makes use of the crystals simply to advance his worldly affairs, that member is never seen here again. I believe he imagines that both Emily and Tertia Richmond have joined the Society for ends of their own."

"What insight he must have!" murmured Miss Riverdale, softly. They looked at each other and laughed.

Then the President turned to George Winter, who introduced Miss Riverdale. "S.S.S." bowed.

"The celebrated journalist?" Miss Riverdale bowed in her turn.

"An initiate, I presume?" he inquired, suavely.

"Yes, sir," said George, quickly. The old man made another stately inclination and retired.

"And now, sir," there was some archness in Miss Riverdale's voice, " you may tell me all about this place. You made me an initiate with admirable despatch, but I scarcely feel the part, you know."

"Let us go into one of the gazing-chambers," said George Winter, leading the way to the nearest empty glass apartment. At that moment a faint scream was heard from one of the remoter cubicles, and they saw a woman fall back, apparently in a swoon. Miss Riverdale started, but no one seemed to betray the slightest emotion, and two attendants presently appeared and carried the woman out.

"It's nothing," said Mr. Winter. "That often happens. I daresay she's seen something that frightens her—a death perhaps."

"Seen something? In the crystal I suppose?"

"Yes, in the crystal. Here is one. (They were now seated.) It looks a simple enough sphere, doesn't it? But for ages initiates have used it as a means of foretelling the future."

George Winter proceeded with a very lucid exposition of

the principles of crystal-gazing, and at the conclusion Emily yawned, and reminded Helen Riverdale that they had forgotten Tertia.

"You and Tertia intended to hold another little *séance* here to-night, didn't you?" said George Winter. His tone seemed to indicate an intention to tease Emily, and she certainly blushed.

"It is to be to-morrow night," she said.

"I hope you will come to some more definite conclusion *this* time," George said.

"What *do* you mean, George?"

"I mean nothing, Emily."

A bell rang with startling, muffled solemnity in the still, obscure apartment. Involuntarily both Helen Riverdale and Emily Richmond shuddered. The crystal-gazers rose, and, opening the doors of their glass cases, began to file out.

"We must go," said George Winter; "it is midnight."

Helen was surprised at the lateness of the hour, and she had to admit to herself that she had not penetrated far into the mysterious doings of the two girls. Her suspicions as to the real nature of the case, however, were deepened, and she felt sure that George Winter knew something. She determined to ask him, and at the same time to give him a certain piece of information of which she felt sure he was at present in ignorance.

He escorted the two ladies to Onslow-square in a four-wheeled cab. As they were alighting from the vehicle a figure came out of the gardens and crossed the road. It was Tertia Richmond.

"Why, Tertia," said Miss Riverdale, kissing her, "what is the meaning of this? I found your sister strolling about the gardens about two hours ago, and now you are doing the same thing. Are you in search of treasure, or the influenza?"

"You had better ask Emily," said Tertia, coldly. She had evidently been crying, and she ran quickly into the house. Of George Winter she took no notice at all.

Helen looked at George as if to say, "What does it all mean?" but he only shrugged his shoulders.

Now that the obstreperous twins were once more both at home again, Mrs. Richmond seemed relieved, although Helen had absolutely nothing to tell her. She wished Miss Riverdale to stay the night, but Helen refused, saying that probably Mr. Winter would be kind enough to see her home, and soon they were comfortably ensconced in a belated hansom.

"One o'clock!" said George, with a sigh.

"To a journalist all things are permitted" said Helen, "so don't hint. I want to ask you some questions. Why have those two girls taken up crystal-gazing?"

"Dear lady," he said, "how should I know?"

"You *do* know. Now, has it anything to do with your brother Jack? If you will tell me, I will tell you something."

"Well, tell me something first." Helen involuntarily moved her head nearer to his, and half-whispered a few words in his ear. George was ever cool. He betrayed no emotion.

"I am not surprised," he remarked, "and I am delighted. But I'm sorry I can't tell you anything about Emily and Tertia. I only know there is to be a final scene of some kind to-morrow night at the Society, and I'll take you if you like, and leave you there. Have you told them—what you've told me?"

"No," said Helen, "and I shan't till this thing is cleared up."

When they arrived at the rooms of the Society of Crystal-Gazers on the following night, George Winter contented himself with saying a few words to the President and then left.

Helen found the twins seated on either side of a table in one of the glass compartments, with two crystals before them. To her surprise they greeted her quite effusively.

"We had a note from George Winter this afternoon," Emily began, "saying that if we were in any difficulty to-night, you would be able to help us, as you had special knowledge. So we have determined to tell you *all*. Why didn't you say before that you were an adept crystal-gazer?"

"There were reasons," said Helen, with perfect truth. "But we must begin at the beginning. What were you both doing out in the Square gardens last night, in the frost and fog?"

"Oh! That was simple enough," said Tertia, lightly, "we had a row in the afternoon, you know, and I suppose I got a bit angry over the crystals, and I took Em's crystal and threw it out of the window. She went to look for it after dinner, and found it without my knowing. When I came here in the evening, I had a little unpleasantness with the President, and I went home; I felt rather sorry for Emily, and I thought I would try to recover her crystal for her. I looked for it a long time, but of course I didn't find it."

"I see," said Helen, drily. The two girls were absurdly serious, and she felt that it would be impolite to laugh. "And now what did you quarrel about?" Emily took up the tale.

"It's a secret, mind," she began. "When Jack Winter went away to India we both fancied he was in love with one of us, and we were certain we were both in love with him. Now mind, it's a secret. We wanted badly to know which of us he would marry. Then we heard of this Society and we joined it. When we had finished the necessary studies, you know, and all that stuff, I looked into the crystal, and I saw a picture of Jack Winter proposing to me, and so of course I told Tertia she was out of it."

"But I looked into the crystal, too," Tertia put in, "and I saw the very same thing. That was how we quarrelled."

" It must have been very annoying for you," said Helen. "Are you sure you went to work in the right spirit?"

"Ye-es," said Tertia. "Then we arranged to have another *séance* to-night, and we have had one."

"And what is the result?"

"Same as before. There must be some mistake on Emily's part."

"On yours, you mean," said Emily, crossly.

"I suppose the crystal cannot lie," Helen remarked.

"Oh, no. Impossible. But tell us, what did George Winter mean when he said you could help us? Have you seen anything in the crystal?"

"Many things," answered Helen with due solemnity, "and I am very sorry—"

"Sorry for which of us? Be quick."

"For both of you. Are you sure Mr. Jack Winter is in love with either of you?"

"Well, not positively certain, of course, but—"

"I'm glad of that, because it happens that Mr. Jack Winter has written to me asking me to be his wife, and I sent a letter in reply to catch him at Naples to say that I should—er—be most happy."

"You horrid, dear old thing!" said the twins together. They kissed Helen, and the President, observing this ceremonial, requested all three to leave the Society.

Thus it happened that the occult science of crystal gazing lost two youthful votaries. But there is some satisfaction to be gleaned from the fact that after that night Mrs. Richmond never had to complain of her stepdaughters' nocturnal escapades.

NOTES

1. *Woman*. Episode One published 10th April 1895, pages 15-16; Episode Two published 17th April 1895, pages 15-16. Signed Sarah Volatile. This two-part story was Bennett's first attempt at the serial form.

"Use Dr. Mackenzie's ARSENICAL TOILET SOAP. 1s. per Tablet. Made from Purest Ingredients, and Absolutely Harmless." This image, linking beauty, purity and sexual appeal shared a half-page in *Woman* (25th March 1896) with an appeal from the "Irish Distressed Ladies Fund."

PART III
LATE VICTORIAN YEARS

Up, up, to the attic where Santa Claus was.

Fire rescue stories were very popular in the 1890s. Bennett's 1898 Christmas story for children is a good example of the genre.

A LITTLE DEAL IN "KAFFIRS".[1]

"Presents—clothes—honeymoon. How on earth can one leave out either?" asked George Littlecash of himself, earnestly drilling his penholder into a much furrowed forehead. "There never was a wedding without presents. One can hardly get married without clothes. As for no honeymoon—why, Hetty would be justified in crying off before the very altar."

What had placed our friend in this unpleasant quandary was, to begin with, Uncle Piper's cheque for £500. It was a cheque to marry Hetty and set up house with, and *qua* cash was satisfactory enough; but accompanied with the wise avuncular injunction, "George, marry on a cash basis—*cash*, mind—or never look me in the face again." Such excellent advice, *plus* a £500 cheque, it is impossible for a nephew to spurn—especially a nephew in love.[2]

And then, when he had this gold-mine of untold wealth in his pocket, and a full ocean of happiness to look forward to, George fell into the toils of that plausible fellow Tom Scherer, of the well-known City firm of Mouton Scherer and Walker. Scherer had such a taking way of remembering, and cherishing affectionately, one's Christian name.

"Ah! Congratulate you, my dear George. Coming off next month, eh? Happy man! Some of you fellows have the devil's own luck. And just in time, too, for me to put you on to one of the nicest little chances of making a comfortable nest-egg for the happy home—one of the prettiest chances you ever had. But come into Pipps's and have a coffee."

Pipps's, that long, low, smoky "dive" in Throgmorton-street, was crowded with easy-mannered gentlemen in silk hats, or in no hats at all, who conversed in pairs and in groups with electrical energy. They could not hear themselves for their own talking. "Sell-at-five-three-eight," "Book-you-thousand," "Buy-six-quarter." "Sell," "Buy," "Panjandrums," "Rhodes," "Barney"s stock," "Struck-Bibble-bobble-reef,"

"Last-crushing-ten-ounces"—such were some of the scraps of jargon that emerged above the din in flashes of comparative silence; whilst ever and anon a gentleman would draw from his vest-pocket a little note-book and pencil some entry or other. Almost deafened at first by the hubbub, George Littlecash was soon in the whirlpool himself, an eager listener to Mr. Scherer's glowing tales indicative of the pecuniary advantage certain to result from a small punt in the South African "boom."[3]

"Eighty thou' in one deal, my dear George—what d'ye think of that, eh? Springett went nap on Gold Bug Extensions—put on every penny he could scrape together till he hadn't a cent to swear by—and came out eighty thousand golden sovereigns to the good. And yet you say it isn't worth trying. My dear George—faint heart never *maintained* a fair lady, if it won her."

The upshot was that George figured up his liabilities against his cheque, and handed over to the trusty Scherer £250, to be converted in two days, or some such reasonable time, into £2,500.

"Done!" cried Scherer, as he pencilled the little transaction in his note-book.

And "done" George was; for next day, when he looked at "Mines" in the money column, he found Gold Bugs had crawled downstairs three-eighths.

"What do you advise, Scherer?" asked George when they met in the City.

"Never advise, my dear George. Don't do it—on principle. 'Cut your losses, let your profits run' is our old wheeze; but it's no good being too hasty. This fall is simply due to somebody being in too big a hurry to pocket a profit. But you judge for yourself, dear boy; that's what I advise."

Next day Gold Bugs had crawled downstairs two or three steps more.

"It's nothing, George," said the optimistic Scherer; "weak

holders—couldn't last it out—that's my explanation. Still, don't be guided by me."

Next day after that Gold Bugs had fallen so heavily that you couldn't find anybody to pick them up again at any price. And just then, of course, to make amends, George Littlcash was reminded by his tailor of "that little account" which had been overlooked for so many many quarters. It was in this doleful hour, as he sat savagely biting his lips, knitting his brows, and inwardly cursing Scherer and all his works, that he glanced vaguely at a copy of the *Evening Intelligence*.

"RENEWED ACTIVITY IN RAND SHARES"

was the line in large type that caught the disconsolate investor's eye as the paper lay on his desk.

"Confound Rand Shares!" he ejaculated fervently, wheeling round as though from a too affectionate snake.

Just then, as luck had it, in popped the beaming and expansive Scherer.

"Why, George, my dear boy, you're looking as ghastly as James Canham Read[4] when he was 'taken from life,' as the waxworks bill says. Nothing serious, I hope? Gal chucked you?"

"Look here, Scherer; I don't want you blarneying me again. I've had quite enough of Rand shares, thanks—in fact a long sight too much."

"Rand shares! Why, my dear fellow," Scherer returned, with a look of pained virtue, "you really don't mean to tell me that's what's put you down in the dumps—that little matter of two-fifty, when you stood to win as many thousands! Bless my soul!"—Scherer's eye had just caught the line in the *Evening Intelligence*—have you seen the paper to-night?"

"No," replied George, whose back was turned—"nor want to. I'm sick of the whole thing. You knew, for I told you, I couldn't risk anything under the circumstances unless it was absolutely certain."

"And that"s what you call 'risk'?"

"Oh hang!—I know it's my own fault—only don't bother me with any more of these fine tales."

"Now, I call this very unkind of you, George," said Scherer, injured; "I do, indeed." And so saying, whilst he kept one eye on George's back, Mr. Scherer cast the other down the money column. When it reached "Gold Bugs" that particular eye flared up like a fusee.[5]

"Now, what should you say if Gold Bugs went up again to five and a quarter, eh?"

"Rot!"

"Right you are, dear boy. 'Rot' is it? Well, well. You think I misled you about that little deal, eh?"

"Well, if you want plain-speaking, Mr. Scherer, I think you did."

"And you an' I friends, George! This is what comes of trying to do a man a good turn! Now, what do you say if I offer to take those shares off your hands again, since you're so cut up over 'em?"

"At a shilling apiece I suppose. Ha, ha!"

"A shilling apiece? No, sir! Not at 'a shilling apiece.' I'll give you what you gave for 'em, and a 'shilling a piece' over to soothe your injured feelings. What d'ye think of that!"

Mr. Scherer found his magnanimity so exhilarating that he drew himself up, threw open his coat, and slipped George's *Evening Intelligence* into his own pocket.

"You doubt my honesty and good faith, eh, my dear sir," he said, pulling out his cheque-book and a roll of notes. "Last week you paid me £250; if you will be so good as to hand me back the scrip I shall have much pleasure in handing you my cheque for £262 10s. Or, p'raps," he added, with cutting sarcasm, "since you doubt my honesty, you would prefer Bank of England notes?"

George, who had risen, half-dazed, had just enough presence of mind to gasp, in his astonishment—

"If it's all the same to you, I should."

"Certainly, my dear sir."

"I'm only too delighted to hand it back to you," said George fervently, as he passed over the scrip and received the crisp notes and gleaming gold in exchange.

"And yet, strange to say," laughed Scherer, "I can assure you I'm not less delighted to take it back. Ha! ha! ha! Ha! ha! ha!" For some moments the cachinnation prevented speech. When Scherer found breath he remarked to his bewildered friend, "My dear George, let me give you a word of honest advice—in fact two words. Don't doubt your friend's honesty again; and when you hold active shares keep a sharp eye on the papers—ha, ha, ha!"

"The papers?" echoed Littlecash, "why, no; I haven't seen to-night's paper yet," and he struck a bell.

"Yessir?" said the Office Boy.

"Where's to-night's evening paper, Tippetts?"

"Ain't come in yet, sir."

"O yes it has," corrected Mr. Scherer, choking with laughter as he produced the *Evening Intelligence*. "I just—just—mechanically picked it up for a moment myself."

But the Office Boy triumphed.

"That's a hold won, sir; to-night's ain't come in not yet, sir."

"Not come in?" shrieked Scherer, turning to the date. "Why good lord—the d—d paper's a month old!"

Mr. Scherer's exclamations as he sank into George's chair were so shockingly profane that even the Office Boy turned pale and expected a flash of lightning.

George got his friend out of the office at last, but made a point of handing him back the odd twelve pounds ten—"to soothe his feelings." The wedding took place, and Uncle Piper will never know the particulars of George's first—and last—little venture on the Stock Exchange.

NOTES

1. *St. James's Gazette* XXX. 27th April 1895, pages 3-4. Unsigned.
James Hepburn identifies this story as being referred to in a letter to his friend George Sturt, written on 10th May 1885:

> I wrote a topical story for the *St. James's* last week, & got slated all round for it. Kennerley said it merely bored him; Chapman was "disgusted", but he added his opinion that only E.A. Bennett could have done it. And yet the *St. James's* put it on their placards, an honour not given to a story by the daily press once in a twelve month. What the devil is a fellow to do? Am I to sit still & see other fellows pocketing two guineas apiece for stories which I can do better myself? Not me! If anyone imagines my sole aim is art for art's sake, they are cruelly deceived. An income sufficient to satisfy my naturally extravagant tastes, first, and then as much art as I know how to produce, but not till then. (*Letters II*, pp. 18-19)

2. Writing to his young Potteries friend Edward Henry Beardmore in 1890 Bennett offered similar avuncular advice:

> MY DEAR EDWARD, - I am writing to congratulate you on having reached the mature age of 21.... I find I have no particular suggestion to offer or advice to give, except this. A man in your position, with good settled prospects, and no cares worth a button, can only sail on one course, namely, the matrimonial. I maintain it is your imperative duty to get married, and I would suggest Miss Jones, who lives near you. £40,000 in her own right, my boy! Think of it. (quoted in Pound, p. 78)

3. There was a boom in South African gold shares - known in Stock Exchange parlance as "Kaffirs", a then popular term the equivalent of "niggers", both now equally derogatory - in 1894-95. This resulted from the realization among stockbrokers of the great potential value of the Witwatersrand gold seam.
4. On 4th December 1894 James Canham Read, a middle-aged, married book-keeper at the London docks, was executed for the murder of one of his several mistresses, 18 year old Florence Dennis. He was arrested after police traced a telegram he had sent to a relative. His waxwork effigy appeared on the grand staircase at Madame Tussaud's.
5. A match with a large head, able to burn in a wind.

THE ADAMLESS EDEN.[1]
A NEW FAIRY TALE.

"And a jolly good thing too!" the King said, when he heard the news.

"I *beg* your Majesty's pardon!" exclaimed the Prime Minister, who had a careful eye for his royal master's dignity.

"I should say an excellent thing too." The King corrected himself with a blush. He was rather new to his position, and ill-at-ease under the shocked gaze of the venerable vizier. "An excellent thing too! Let 'em go. I'm delighted. It will save me twenty thousand crowns a-year in dressmaker's bills alone, to say nothing of temper. What good *are* women, after all?"

And the courtiers grouped round the throne dutifully echoed:— "Aye! What good *are* they, after all?"

Now this was the news that had been told to the King. All the ladies and handmaidens of the Court had left the capital in a body, under the leadership of the Princess Cecily, and withdrawn to a remote plateau, far beyond the Yellow Mountains. Their purpose, so the tale ran, was to form a community from which man should be rigidly excluded. The Princess Cecily, whose faculty for logic was proverbial throughout the kingdom, had clearly demonstrated that man was no essential part of the Universe and could be dispensed with; also that man was a tyrant, a fool, a loathsome insect, and several other things which ought not to be encouraged.

"Besides," said the King, after a pause, "they'll come back sharp enough."

"Of course they will!" the courtiers responded, eagerly.

At that moment the King's three sons entered the audience chamber. The King had no daughters, and his wife was long since dead, but the five daughters of his late brother Carl, Princess Cecily, Princess Gertrude, Princess Magdalen, Princess Margaret, and Princess Rosalys, resided in the palace and attended to the household affairs of their uncle and Sovereign.

"Where is Princess Gertrude?" asked Prince Eric.

"Where is Princess Magdalen?" asked Prince Sigurd.

"Where is Princess Margaret?" asked Prince Wilhelm.

No one asked for Princess Rosalys, perhaps because she was little more than a child; nor for Princess Cecily.

The King told the three Princes, with many jokes and quips, exactly how affairs stood, and then said, "Did you want your cousins very much this morning?"

"Oh, no!" each of the Princes answered nonchalantly, "I was merely enquiring."

And with that, the huntsman's horn winding merrily beneath the castle windows, the whole company trooped out, for this was one of the King's hunting days.

In the meantime the ladies of the Court, after incredible

hardships nobly endured, had reached the plateau beyond the Yellow Mountains and instituted a new kingdom, of which Princess Cecily, who was the eldest, and wore spectacles, was proclaimed ruler. Princess Cecily allotted to every individual a task suited to her powers; some had to make a wall round the plateau, others to plough and sow, others to bake and draw water, others to attend to the livestock, others to work in clay, others to spin, others to stitch, others to cobble, and still others to attend the tobacco plant, which grew luxuriantly upon the plateau. There was no need of house-builders, for the land was full of green shelter and shadow, and the nights were warm like new milk. Princess Rosalys, being young and unfit for toil, was appointed to watch from a little tower on the west wall. Upon the summit of this tower stood a pole with a sharpened end, and the orders of Princess Rosalys were, if she saw any male creature approaching the plateau, to stick a large green apple upon the pole, so that all might see it and be warned. And so weeks grew into months, the days being given to honest labour and the evenings to innocent pleasures; and all the ladies declared that, through the wisdom of Princess Cecily, perfect happiness had been attained.

As for the King and his Court, they laughed for awhile, but presently a grey sadness filled the palace. Yet when some forward fellow suggested that the women should be brought back to reason and the city, the King flamed up and swore he would die first. He called for his diamond-studded cigarette-making machine, that he might be soothed with the blue incense of tobacco, but it was nowhere to be found and someone said: "The Princess Cecily has taken it."

Then Prince Eric called out: "Sire, this is too much. The women, I well know, are better away, but it is meet that thieves should be brought to justice. Therefore I will go to the plateau, and—and—talk with them."

And the King, secretly glad of an excuse for altering his royal mind, said "Go."

Now, when Prince Eric reached the plateau, and observed the high wall with never a gate, by which it was surrounded, his heart sank; but after a time he saw three stairways at some distance apart, cut into the solid stone; and he laughed, knowing not that those stairways were a malicious lure of the Princess Cecily.

He ran lightly up the nearest stairway, and put his head over the wall.

"Hold, miserable male!" a voice cried. It was the voice of Princess Cecily, who had been warned by the apple on the pole that a man was approaching. "Hold! What is your errand? "

Somewhat taken aback by her vigour and determined appearance, Prince Eric replied: "I would help you if I may."

"What can you do that a woman cannot?"

"I can teach you feats of strength and bodily skill," said Prince Eric, for he was an athlete.

The Princess smiled scornfully, and all the ladies by this time having gathered together, they went through every imaginable physical exercise, until Prince Eric marvelled.

"Shall not this intruding male be punished?" asked Princess Cecily, whereupon everyone answered, "Yes," except the Princess Gertrude, who would have saved Eric, but lacked courage. And Princess Cecily cast a spell over the man, so that he could move neither tongue nor hand nor foot, and his neck was cricked round till his eyes saw the small of his back. And thus they left him.

After a certain period Prince Sigurd left the city in quest of his brother, and, seeing a stairway, climbed the wall of the plateau; and when his head appeared over the wall, Princess Cecily questioned him as she had questioned Prince Eric, and he answered:—

"I will write stories for you," for he was an author.

"Pooh!" said Princess Cecily, "How many books have you written this year past?" And he replied that he had written one.

"And I six!" exclaimed the Princess Cecily. "Shall not this

intruding male be punished?" And everyone answered "Yes," except the Princess Magdalen, who would have saved Sigurd, but lacked courage. And Princess Cecily cast her spell over him.

After a certain period, Prince Wilhelm left the city in quest of his brothers, and seeing a stairway, climbed the wall of the plateau; and when his head appeared over the wall Princess Cecily questioned him as she had questioned Prince Eric and Prince Sigurd, and he answered:

"I will keep your accounts," for he was a mathematician.

"Ah!" said the Princess Cecily, and bit her lip. "Who has skill in ciphers?" she asked, looking round. Then a handmaid approached and said "I, Princess," and Princess Cecily smiled.

"Question the maid for yourself," said Princess Cecily proudly to the Prince.

Prince Wilhelm considered.

"Eleven elevens?"

"132," the maid replied smartly.

"There you are, sir! Right first time!" and Princess Cecily laughed with cruel glee. "Shall not this intruding male be punished?" And everyone answered "Yes," except the Princess Margaret, who would have saved Wilhelm but lacked courage. And Princess Cecily cast her spell over him.

When six moons had gone and nothing was heard of the three Princes, the King and the whole city fell into great sorrow and alarm. And none dared follow the three Princes to the plateau, for men muttered in the streets —"Surely Cecily is a sorceress." At last came to the King a pale little curate who was employed in the Chapel Royal, and said—"*I* will seek your sons, sire." Now, this curate had conceived, a passion for the Princess Rosalys, and the Princess Rosalys had regarded him with favour.

"Good!" answered the King. "Don't forget about my diamond-studded cigarette-making machine."

"Never fear, sire," said the curate, and set out.

It happened that one afternoon the Princess Rosalys had

with her in the tower on the wall of the plateau, to relieve the tedium of solitary watching, a certain tire-woman,[2] who had been her nurse.

"My child," said this woman, just before the sun sank behind the Yellow Mountains, "my eyes are dim, but I think I see a little man in black on yonder hill."

The Princess Rosalys looked out anxiously, and then started as if she had received a shock.

"No, no, good mother," she murmured uneasily, "your old eyes mislead you. I see nothing."

"I see a little man in black," repeated the tire-woman stoutly.

"What! You dare to contradict me? I tell you there is no one. Leave my presence." The Princess Rosalys feigned to be in a passion. After the woman had descended, she gazed long and eagerly into the west.

On the following day, before the Princess Rosalys had gone up into the tower, the Princess Cecily, being in the pleasure gardens with her youngest sister, exclaimed,

"Why, what is that queer thing on the tower-pole?"

"I will go look," said Princess Rosalys, blushing, and ran off. On the pole was stuck an embroidered slipper, one of a pair which Princess Rosalys had once secretly worked for the curate. She removed it from the pole and hid it, and went back to her sister.

"What was it?" asked Princess Cecily.

"A fig-leaf blown against the pole by the wind," answered Princess Rosalys; she guessed that in the night, the curate, who was skilled in games of ball, had cast the slipper on the pole with his hand, for a signal.

The next morning Princess Cecily exclaimed:

"Heavens! That fig-leaf is there again!"

"So it is!" said Princess Rosalys, and ran off to get the other slipper, in which she found a paper containing these words: "Put the paper, which you will find within this, at some convenient place where your sister Cecily may discover it to-morrow morning, and keep a watch for me. I must see you.—Charles." Charles was one of the curate's names, of which he had seven. On the inner paper was written: "From an ardent admirer." The tenour of this latter message somewhat annoyed the Princess Rosalys, but she determined to obey the curate, for she was heartily sick of watching in the tower, and the next day before dawn she put the paper in a crevice in the eastern wall, at a spot where Princess Cecily usually repaired to witness the sunrise.

When the Princess Cecily awoke and went to look over the wall, she observed the paper, and peered at it through her spectacles.

"What!" she cried, "And do my subjects revere me so deeply that they are fain to relieve their feelings by means of ink and paper! To think that I was foolish enough to imagine that they chafed under my rule. Ah! How even I may be deceived! But stay!" She paused a moment. "This is a man's handwriting! Can it be that I am beloved for my own sake? It is, it must be so! At last! At last!" And she waved the paper over her head. For the Princess Cecily had never been loved of a man; some said this why she took to spectacles.

But be that as it may, she gazed at the paper again and again, and moved not from the spot for several hours, entranced by the vision of a man's homage.

The Princess Rosalys, having watched her sister read the paper, sped to the tower, and leaning out, saw the curate beneath.

"How may I ascend, my darling?" asked the curate, "I observe that the stairways are—er—occupied."

"Alas, yes!" said Princess Rosalys. "Can you not scramble up?"

"It would not be seemly, my love," answered the curate. "But see! Take the pole from its socket, and drop it down to me and I will vault to the summit of the wall."

In a few moments the curate was safe within the tower. The Princess Rosalys descended alone into the pleasure gardens, and called out loudly:

"Girls, girls! I have something in the tower." And everyone came up to her, some hastily, others slowly.

"Another fig-leaf perhaps!" laughed one.

"No! Something alive."

"A mouse?"

"No! Bigger than that!"

"A dog?"

"No! Bigger than that!"

"*A man*?" It was the old tire-woman who spoke.

"Yes."

Many clapped their hands, but not a few walked away in disgust.

"But something more than a man—a curate!"

At the word "curate," those who were departing retraced their steps and participated in the general glee, and the curate himself, at that moment appearing, was joyfully saluted. He told them of the sorrow of the city and the Court, and asked if they would return with him; whereupon everyone cried "Yes!"

Then came a sudden silence, for each was afraid of Princess Cecily. The uproar had roused the Princess from her dreams, and she could be seen rapidly approaching through the orchards, all trace of emotion gone. She hated the curate with a deadly vindictiveness, for certain reasons of her own, and immediately set about to cast her spell upon him. But the look on his face stopped her.

"False woman!" he began with uplifted finger, "Where is the King's diamond-studded cigarette-making machine?"

At these words Princess Cecily, sinking to the ground with shame, pulled the article from the pocket of her gown, and begged to be forgiven.

"Upon one condition only," said the curate, "and that is that you release the three Princes from your wicked spells."

And this she perforce did.

Then the whole body of them, the curate conducting Princess Rosalys, Prince Eric with Princess Gertrude, Prince Sigurd with Princess Magdalen, Prince Wilhelm with Princess Margaret, and the others following behind, set out upon the journey home. When they arrived within the King's palace there were great rejoicings, and four marriages happened in as many days. As for the Princess Cecily, she expired of chagrin. The curate was raised to an arch-bishopric, and with his wife, Rosalys, lived happily ever afterwards.

So ends the true history of the Adamless Eden.

NOTES

1. *Woman*. 23rd October 1895, pages 15-16, 18. Signed Sarah Volatile.
2. A lady's maid. An archaic term well suited in the context of a fairy tale.

JOHN AND THE LOVELY STRANGER.[1]

I.

"Surely," said Anna Smith to her younger sister Mary, "surely we know that girl standing by the lamp-post. Just turn around and look at her."

"Can't!" Mary answered, "You know perfectly well I should fall off if I did."

"What a duffer you are! If I'd had four lessons, as you have, I could do anything, anything."

"You'd better apply for a place at Olympia at once," Mary rejoined sarcastically. "But why you didn't turn round yourself— "

When cycling,[2] it is a mistake to get too interested in a conversation. As the dialogue grows keener, the attraction of your machine for your companion's becomes more and more imperious, and often before you know what has happened, pedals and feet are interlocked in a mad and complicated whirl, the solid earth leaps up to greet your nose, and the policeman laughs softly behind his white glove. This is precisely what happened to Anna and Mary Smith.

"There," said Anna, when they had arisen from the ruins of fifty pounds' worth of machinery, "That's your fault!"

"No, it isn't. It's yours," Mary answered, "and I do believe my left hand is hurt, and I shan't be able to play tonight. That's the worst of riding with a novice."

"Novice, indeed! Why, John says I shall be a better rider than you."

Being strong and healthy girls, with minds of their own, and a brother (the said John) whose name was a household word in households where they play football, the two sisters often quarrelled in this manner, but no ill was meant, and soon they were walking, rather shakily, up a side avenue of the park where cyclists are not allowed either to ride or to fall, a boy having been instructed to take the wrecked bicycles to the infirmary.

Almost exactly alike in appearance, Anna being twenty-six and Mary twenty-five, they were very different intellectually. The daughters of a successful Q.C., both had received an excellent education, and Anna, having evinced a partiality for natural science, had been to Newnham and attained distinction there. Mary, on the other hand, was an artist by temperament, and had, indeed, acquired so considerable an ascendancy over the violin, that she was sometimes asked to play at charity concerts of no small importance. The halo which encircles the head of every good violinist was not absent from Mary's, but as she knew nothing of natural science, couldn't argue, couldn't even talk about music with any subtlety, Anna found it quite easy, in spite of the sacred halo, to keep her proper position as elder sister and mistress of the house, and never allowed herself to be outshone, even when there happened to be a musical evening at the Smith's. Not that there was undue jealousy between them! They were just human beings.

"Look! There's that girl again," Anna exclaimed, when they had walked a little way. "I wonder what on earth her name is. I know the face quite well."

The woman in question stood some distance in front of them. She was distinctly beautiful, though in a French kind of way, and wore a broad coquettish hat and a gown which obviously had come from Paris, and upon the whole she made a very pretty picture against the trees. An enigmatic smile rested upon her infinitesimal lips. As for her age it might have been anything between twenty-five and thirty-five. When the Smith girls came up to her, the enigmatic smile became less enigmatic, and it appeared that she intended to speak to them.

The sisters returned her greeting amiably, all the time trying desperately to recollect her name, but without success.

"We haven't seen you for quite a long time," Mary ventured, and then branched off volubly into a description of their accident. Nowadays bicycles form the chief, indeed the only topic meet to be discussed in polite circles. No matter to whom one is talking—a dowager, a poet, a painter, a serious-minded person—or where one is—at dinner, in a picture gallery, at a dance, or coming from church, the word "bicycle" immediately arouses intense interest, and from the moment it is introduced the conversation runs along as smoothly as a Dunlop tyre, opinions are freely interchanged, and under the magic influence of this wonderful subject strangers become acquaintances, acquaintances friends, and friends inseparable intimates.

But strange to say, the unknown girl exhibited but little interest in the matter.

"*We* don't cycle yet, as *you* do," she said, laying a particular stress upon the pronouns as if she belonged to another nation or continent.

"Really!" said Anna. "Do your people object?"

"Oh, no," the girl returned, and her smile expressed melancholy amusement. "It isn't that. But we don't. It hasn't reached us, you see. In about a year I expect we shall all be going in for it madly. But, of course, *we* are always a season or two later than *you* in our fashions."

There was the same peculiar stress on the pronouns.

"What on earth do you mean?" Mary was on the point of exclaiming, but she checked the impulse.

Then the stranger neatly turned the subject, and began to talk about herself in a very clever manner; so clever that Anna and Mary were amazed and fascinated, and both of them felt dimly that they had heard this girl talk before, but where and when they could not recall. She said she was living alone, knew scarcely anyone in London, hadn't a soul to speak to; and she moved her hearers to such sympathy that they asked her to lunch.

"We are all alone just at present," Anna said, "as father is on circuit; but perhaps John may drop in unexpectedly."

"I shall be delighted to come. I love going out to lunch. With *us* lunch is frequently the most interesting meal of the day, especially when a poet or something of that sort happens to be invited."

"I don't think I can supply the poet," Anna laughed.

"No, we don't know any poets," Mary added.

"You don't know even one poet! Well, I never heard of such a thing. With *us*, every girl knows a poet. With *you*—"

The stranger gave an odd little "oh!" and then stopped.

"I was forgetting," she said, almost to herself. "Of course, they wouldn't understand."

By the time the two had reached Onslow-square, where the house of Mr. Lockson Smith, Q.C., was situated, the stranger had ingeniously contrived to make the two Smith girls aware, without actually telling them, that her name was Muriel Start; had asked them for their Christian names; and had most completely entered herself in their good books. Both Anna and Mary had, however, a disquieting consciousness that there was some touch of the uncanny, some hint of other-worldliness, about this delightful creature who called herself Muriel, and neither was quite free from apprehension.

II.

Such apprehension was well-founded. Emphatically, Muriel Start was no ordinary girl.

I am approaching a part of my story which needs to be told with the greatest tact, in order to command credence. I may fail in that tact, but the tale is nevertheless true.

Muriel was not a human being at all! She belonged to that world in which the characters of novels live and move and have their being. Many confiding individuals suppose that novelists invent their personages. This is not so. The secret has never been divulged before, but for reasons of my own I divulge it now. There is another world side by side with ours, and what is called "the imaginative faculty" is merely a disposition to see this world in dreams. The verity of the statement ought to be apparent to anyone who has read novels, and who thinks a moment. The people in novels are entirely different from the people one meets in daily life. Therefore they must either be mere inventions or the inhabitants of another world. But if they are mere inventions, how comes it that all characters in all novels have the same or very similar qualities—qualities so at variance with our own? Do all authors invent alike? The notion is preposterous, and we are led naturally to the conclusion that novelists merely describe people whom they have seen in that other world—that world which is hidden from the sight of ordinary mortals.

Muriel Start—this was not her real name in "Noveldom," she had assumed it in order to hide her identity from the Smith girls, whose recollection of her face and talk was due to the fact that they had lately been reading about her in a novel by a new author of some power—Muriel Start had been "seized with an uncontrollable desire" (after the manner of her kind) to investigate this prosaic world of ours, so different from romantic "Noveldom;" and she had accordingly left her own land—by what means I dare not say—and come to earth, like Mr. H. G. Wells' angel, whose iridescent pinion was pierced by the rector's bullet.[3]

III.

The luncheon hour passed away gaily to the accompaniment of Muriel's chatter. Just as they had risen from the table a young man entered, of medium height, and quick, alert movement, and Anna introduced her brother John. John, in the intervals of athletics, was studying for the bar, and intended to step comfortably into his father's practice when the great Q.C. should retire. He was immediately attracted to Muriel's personality, and made up his mind that he had never seen anyone like her before, which was truer, perhaps, than he knew. Very soon they were gossiping freely to one another.

"I always thought," Muriel said, "that athletic young men were invariably tall and brawny, and said nothing but 'By Jove!' and 'W.G.'[4] At least, that is the sort I have been accustomed to. Now, you aren't big and you aren't brawny, and really, you talk quite well. Why, you take an interest in books, and the woman question, and music, and—and lots of things."

He was enchanted with what he imagined to be her humour. It was at his instigation that Anna, when Muriel said she must go, insisted on her returning to dinner, and the *musicale* which was to occur subsequently; and all the afternoon the sisters and the brother analysed the qualities of their new friend, and decided that she was bewitchingly quaint. John was so busily employed in singing her praises (he was a frank boy) that he forgot to inquire very minutely who this Muriel Start was, and neither Anna nor Mary cared to confess to him the extent of their ignorance on that point.

She came in a dress of some indescribably soft, white material, and in her dark hair were some violets. She was the only guest to dinner. John sat next to her.

"What puzzles me," she said sweetly, during the soup, "is that you folk never give your opinions on abstract subjects. And you make such short, scrappy remarks—never a speech that would fill even half a page of a book. Surely you must feel deeply on some question or other."

Here was a chance for an epigram, as Muriel thought, but neither John nor Anna nor Mary accepted it. They simply laughed, and then Mary asked John, in a matter-of-fact tone, if he had practiced the clarinet piece of Brahms' which he was to play.

"Brahms!" exclaimed Muriel. "Ah! Brahms and Wagner! Those are the only musicians in whom *we* interest ourselves. Perhaps we like a nocturne or a ballade of Chopin, or the 'Moonlight Sonata', but that is the limit. Tell me the names of other composers. I scarcely know them."

And John, who found a charm even in her naïve ignorance, instructed her for many minutes in the history of music.

In the drawing-room, when the other guests began to arrive, she bade John sit near her and describe their peculiarities. He did his best, but she speedily discovered that she was bored.

"There is nothing strange about any of these people," she complained, petulantly. "Have none of them an idiosyncracy, or a scandal, or a bit of pathos attached to their persons? Where is the young violinist, with a tragedy hidden in his soul, who is starving while he lives for art alone? Where is the ugly girl whose face is miraculously transformed as soon as she sits down to the piano? No proper *musicale* is ever conducted without the assistance of these two." But John, though he had the best will in the world to do so, could not produce either of them.

Mary took part in a violin and piano sonata of Mendelssohn, playing with great taste and fire, and the performance was loudly applauded.

"And now, my dear," said Muriel, getting up excitedly, "Improvise something. Give us some wild, desolate melody direct from your heart. I love that sort of thing, and some of *my* friends can do it awfully well."

"I never improvise," Mary said, "and that is the last item of the programme. I wonder why the iced drinks haven't been brought up."

Muriel was dumbfounded.

"But you are an artist?"

"I try to be, but I don't know anything about wild and desolate melodies from the heart."

"Well then, you can't be an artist."

"You are candid," Mary replied, drily. Both she and Anna were losing their good opinion of Muriel.

But John was still enthusiastic.

IV.

It soon began to be clear that John was in love. His sisters laughed; his father, who, by this time, had returned from circuit, sneered; but it made no difference. John insisted on Muriel being frequently asked to the house, and she showed no unwillingness to leave what she called her "lonely lodging" for the comfortable and even luxurious domesticity which was to be found at Onslow-square.

Everyone, including John, felt that a climax was quickly approaching.

On a certain evening, John found himself alone with Muriel in the drawing-room. Anna and Mary, though they had now ceased to have any warm regard for John's enchantress, were anxious to please their brother, and had absented themselves with ingenious excuses.

"The moment has arrived," John remarked to himself, and then he began to direct the conversation towards the subject of Love. Muriel seemed to have no distaste for it, and dissected the emotion with great skill.

"Have you ever been in love?" John asked.

"I have often imagined myself to be in love," she said, "but until this moment I have never experienced the true passion."

"Then you care for me Muriel," he exclaimed, happily, and made as if to kiss her.

"No, no," she exclaimed. "Wait! What I said was merely a

formula which is quite *de rigueur* with *us*. I must think, I must think."

She covered her face with her hands for a moment, and then looked up.

"You know nothing about me?"

"I know that I am in love with you."

"But about my parents, I mean."

"I understood that your parents were dead," John said, scarcely comprehending why she should introduce the matter at that particular juncture.

"Yes, they are dead — dear old people, but I must tell you about them. They were little better than peasants, Dorsetshire peasants. You will wonder how it is that *I* came to be the daughter of people who are little better than peasants. I dress well, I talk correctly, my habits of thought are those of what the world calls a lady. How is it? I cannot tell. But such things happen with *us*. Girls who have sprung from the commonest stock carry themselves like the descendants of half-a-hundred duchesses."

"My dear young lady," John put in. "To me it is a matter of the utmost unimportance who your parents were. I love you, and that is enough for me."

"A most proper answer," she returned queerly, "and just what one of *our* young men would have said. But there is my inevitable brother."

"Your inevitable brother?"

"Yes, don't you know that *we* always have a brother or some other near relation, whose misdoings have cast discredit on the family, making it impossible for the girls to marry?"

John laughed.

"What has this brother of yours done?"

"He committed forgery— that is the usual thing."

"And how can that possibly affect you?"

"Of course I know it's only a question of sentiment, but I couldn't do less than mention it."

"Miss Start," John said, "if you had a hundred brothers, and each had committed a hundred forgeries, I should love you just as much as ever."

"You are very kind," she returned. "I expected as much."

To a man not in love the conversation must have seemed strange, especially Muriel's share of it, but John was in love; her strange, exotic beauty enthralled him; to him her utterances were quite natural and right.

"I have had experiences," she began again, after a pause. "You are not—the first. A man proposed to me once in St. James's Hall at a Wagner concert."

"But you refused him?"

"Yes, though he drove me home in a hansom, and we parted at my front door. The next morning he sailed for the East. That is the correct sequence with us—Wagner concert—hansom—the East."

"Will you marry me, Muriel?" John inquired pointedly.

"I love you, John," she said simply. "But my heart is old and tired. And there is this to be thought of: you are to be a great orator, are you not?"

"I hope to be a good pleader."

"Well, I too have my little talent, and it is the same as your big one. I speak at public meetings; in my humble way I can make thousands hang on my lips. Supposing that I married you, would you compel me to give that up? Would you say to me 'My wife must not speak in public. Let her attend to her house.' Would you treat me as a toy? Would you laugh at my serious aims, and tell me my highest ambition should be to assist you? Answer."

There was a moment of tense silence.

"No," said John, who was a broad-minded fellow, "I would never dream of behaving so unjustly. I should do everything to encourage your talent. Why should you not fulfil yourself just as well as I."

"Those are your sentiments?"

"Emphatically."

"Then," she said, with set lips, "then I can never be yours."

"Why?" he gasped.

"Can you ask? With *us*, the husband *always* does that sort of thing, and if he didn't, the wife would scarcely consider herself married. Moreover, life would not be worth living unless one was crushed, snubbed, subjugated. One would have no motive for drowning oneself when the crisis came. No; I am disappointed in you, John—I will call you so this once—I imagined you had a finer conception of what a husband should be. I will tear your image from my heart, and henceforth we shall never meet."

"But I—I"

"It is useless," she smiled radiantly. "This has been a delightful experience. Let us close the chapter."

Just then Anna Smith came in, and John was obliged to swallow his mystification, his chagrin, and his arguments. He wrote her a long letter that night, saying that he could only suppose she had been joking, and hinting that a joke was occasionally out of place. But the letter was returned through the post-office, and no one ever heard of Muriel Start again in this our prosaic world.

NOTES

1. *Woman*. 25th March 1896, pages 24, 26, 27-28, 30. Signed Sarah Volatile.

2. Bennett himself was an enthusiast for the 1890's passion for cycling: "Bicycling is the rage now. I got my machine about 3 weeks ago ....I find cycling a most excellent practice. Weather permitting, I spend the afternoons upon two wheels .... Distances entirely disappear." (Letter to George Sturt written on 31st March 1896. *Letters II*, p. 42.)

It is no coincidence that the opening page of Bennett's story is accompanied by a large half-page advertisement from Peter Robinson of Oxford Street, offering the latest fashionable ladies' cycling costumes, and "reliable" ladies' cycles, with "all the latest improvements from 10 Guineas."

3. H.G. Wells, *The Wonderful Visit* (1895). In Chapter IV of Wells's novel a Vicar shoots an Angel – –"clad in robes of saffron and with iridescent wings, across whose pinions great waves of colour pursued one another as he writhed in his agony."

Bennett reviewed Wells's novel as the lead item in his "Book Chat" Column in *Woman* on 9th October 1895, page 7, signing himself Barbara.

4. Dr. William Gilbert Grace (1848-1915), universally known as W.G., is still regarded as one of the all-time great English cricketers. He was arguably the most famous Victorian celebrity.

THE MARRIAGE OF JANE HENDRA.[1]

Heathfield Junction is by no means an interesting station. Situate on an insignificant branch line that connects the southern edge of Dartmoor with the Great Western main line, it derives a certain importance among its fellow-stations from the fact that it is the point of departure for a still more insignificant branch line running towards Exeter—a thread of rails which for the last ten years has been trying to reach Exeter, has not yet succeeded in the attempt, and probably never will succeed. Most junctions are ineffably dull, and Heathfield, with its silent platforms and its fictitious air of importance, is more ineffably dull than most.

On that particular morning, however, the up-platform of Heathfield Junction was less blank than usual when the train was due from Chudleigh Bridge. The porter on duty—a porter of a giant species which seems to grow only in Devonshire—regarded its approach with a certain pleased expectancy, and there appeared to be actually someone awaiting its arrival. This was a young man of about twenty-five, tolerably well-clothed in a suit which denoted sporting proclivities. He belonged to the farmer class. For the rest, his appearance had nothing remarkable, except that he was evidently in a state of extreme annoyance and anxiety.

Suddenly he accosted the porter, and pointing to a small wagonette and a large four-horse char-à-banc which stood waiting outside the station, he said,—

"Expecting anyone by the Chudleigh train?"

"Ess, sir," was the reply in the rich roll of the Devonshire accent, "a wedding party—that's what the wagonette's for. They be driving to Buckland in the Moor, to be married there, as I hear. The Hendras, sir, two cousins. Happen you know 'em?"

As a matter of fact the young man could have told the porter far more than the porter knew, but he chose to appear ill-informed.

"I know the name," he said.

"Ay," the porter went on reflectively, "folk will wed, whatever happens, and it's right they should."

"Yes?" the young man put in interrogatively.

"Ay, they will wed. It is but two years last month as the news come to Chudleigh, and Silver, the guard, told me of it same marning."

"What was that?"

"Well," and the porter settled himself in his shoes for a narration, "old John Hendra and his brother Will, as each had a farm up to Chudleigh, went out to Australia, partly for business and partly for pleasure. They was both doing well, and when the other brother—Charles, they call him—asked 'em to go out for a cruise like, and look at a mine as he wanted 'em to speculate in, they accepted and went. Young John Hendra, him as is going to wed Jane Hendra to-day, he was Will's son, and he was left in charge o' both farms. Will Hendra's wife was dead. Well, as I'm telling you, they both went out—to Perth, I think it was—and said as they'd be back within a twelvemonth. I saw 'em go myself from this station, and I remember how old John Hendra kissed his wife and daughter, Jane—her as is going to be wed to-day. Well, about six months afterwards, or it might be seven, Silver, the guard, says to me one marning, 'Jolliffe,' he says, 'hast heard about old John Hendra and his brother Will?' 'No,' I says. 'Sad news,' he says, 'sad news! Mrs. Hendra had a letter this marning to say as they'd both died o' fever in some mining place about a hundred miles from Perth.' Ess, fay! Silver told me that, and I could scarcely get the train out o' th' station."

"I heard something of it," the young man said.

"You did? Ess, it was in the *Mercury*. Well, that was two year ago, and now young John Hendra's going to marry his cousin Jane. Folk will wed, and quite right, I say ..... Here she comes."

"She" was the Chudleigh train, whose steam showed in

the distance.

"Train from Newton Abbott's very late, isn't it?" the young man asked, his anxiety perceptibly increased.

"Indeed you'm right, sir. It's due ten minutes 'fore Chudleigh train, and Chudleigh train's eleven minutes behind."

As the train, with a jar and clash of brakes, rumbled into the station, the young man walked uneasily away to a distant part of the platform.

Three passengers alighted; an alert, grey-haired woman, whom the porter hastened to assist from the carriage, and a young couple. They all three greeted the porter, who then went off to have the usual morning chat with Silver, the guard. These three were the Hendras. They were all dressed in black, but the girl wore a starched white blouse which looked finely fresh and feminine in the July sunlight, striking a note of subdued joy amid the austerity of the black.

Few people would have guessed that a wedding was afoot; the trio were so quiet, so sedate. Yet the girl's eyes told tales, and beneath the sober attitude of her squire there was to be observed a highly unusual excitement.

"Now, mother," said the girl to the grey-haired woman, who was staring about her with a tranquil gaze, "let us get into the wagonette. I can see that Cousin John is worrying lest we should be late."

"Yes, Jane."

John Hendra laughed at the "Cousin John." It sounded strange from the lips of the woman so immediately to be his wife. But there was no getting over the fact that they were cousins, and Jane would always be having her joke.

"It's about the last time you'll call me cousin, Cousin Jane," he said, with a clumsy attempt at repartee.

"Why?" she asked, innocently. "My being your wife won't stop me from being your cousin. You'll be 'Cousin John' to the end."

The elder woman looked suddenly sad.

The driver of the wagonette touched his hat to them over the palings which separated the station from the white high-road, and they crossed the platform, old Mrs. Hendra between the bridal pair. Some whim caused Jane Hendra to scan the station as she was leaving it; at the far end of the platform she espied the young man.

"If that isn't Harry Penfold!" she exclaimed.

"Harry Penfold!" Mrs. Hendra repeated.

"What's he doing here, I wonder?" John Hendra murmured, inimically.

"I must go and speak to him," Jane said, leaving her mother's arm.

"Not now, Jane; not now. Come along to the wagonette." Her lover's tones were curiously urgent.

"Better come along, Jane," said her mother, quietly.

"But why not? I must. Besides—there, he's seen me." And, walking quickly, she went to meet the young man, who was coming towards her.

As a rejected suitor, Henry Penfold had an attraction for her. And she was as cruel as only a good woman can be.

"Good morning, Mr. Penfold," she said, her rosy face all smiles and good-nature. "What are you doing here all alone?"

"Why shouldn't I be going to your wedding?" he answered. "You're being wed to-day, I'm told."

"Yes," she said, modestly, looking at the stitching on the front of her blouse. "John and mother are just getting into the wagonette. I'm to be married at Buckland Church, you know, because mother was married there. Mother was born at Buckland. We had to have a special licence. It's such a pretty old church."

Penfold made no answer; he was marvelling at her beauty, and cursing it.

"Well, I must be going on," she said. "You wish us luck, Mr. Penfold?"

He stared at her, and then looked away.

"I may and I mayn't," he said, bitterly.

"But you will shake hands, Mr. Penfold, on my wedding morning? You've stopped caring for me, I'm sure, long ago."

He put his right hand behind him.

"Look here, Jane," he said. "Plain speaking's my motto. You know well enough I love you, and you're only here to torment me."

She gave a gesture of pained remonstrance, but he went on.

"Yes, I love you, and I only wish I could hate you. I only wish I could prevent your marriage to John Hendra."

Silently she left him, and in another minute the wagonette was bearing the little wedding party along the mountainous route to Buckland.

Penfold walked across to the down platform, following the porter, who, having finished his gossip with Silver, the guard, had sent the Chudleigh train on its way. The other train—that which came from Newton Abbott and the world in general—arrived instantly, and Penfold scanned its carriage windows with eagerness. Several farmer folk alighted, but in these he took no interest. His attention was directed to a man who descended from a first-class compartment.

"Mr. Stokes," he said, hurriedly, going up to this person. "They've gone on."

"I feared so. Without discussing anything now, Mr. Penfold, we'll follow them. It's a long drive, and we can catch them."

In the presence of this calm, confident man of forty, even Penfold could put on a certain appearance of coolness, which, however, he was far from feeling. As for Mr. Stokes, he accosted the porter, and, dropping into the dialect, asked where a good conveyance could be most quickly obtained. The porter stared with awe and wonder at Mr. Stokes's superb tourist suit, and answered that no conveyance could be obtained within three miles—of that he was sure.

"Then what about that char-à-banc?" Mr. Stokes asked imperiously, pointing to the vehicle which, with its driver, was still waiting outside the station.

"That'll be hired by a party, I'm thinking, sir."

In a moment Mr. Stokes, with Penfold like a dog at his heels, was in the road talking to the driver of the char-à-banc, and in another moment he had learnt that the char-à-banc was destined for a party of Sunday-school teachers coming down from Moretonhampstead.

"Look here," said Mr. Stokes to the driver, "I must have this thing. What's the figure for the day?"

"Sorry, sir; there is no figure."

"Who's the owner of the turn-out?"

"I am, sir," said the driver, not without pride; "I'm Bagley, of Bovey Tracy—the Dartmoor coaching excursions, you know."

"Ah! well, Mr. Bagley, you have four fine animals there. I daresay they are worth £30 apiece, and the char-à-banc, say £100. Put on £30 for forced sale. I'll give you £250 down, in Bank-of-England notes, for the turn-out."

Mr. Stokes spoke quite in his ordinary tones, without ostentation, without the least sign that he had said anything uncommon.

Penfold was staggered. "This comes of living in Australia," he muttered to himself.

The driver looked hard at Mr. Stokes, who met his gaze, and then he got down from his box.

"You mean that?" he said.

"Here are the notes," and Mr. Stokes took out his pocket-book.

"I take ye," the driver said, laconically, his eyes glistening. In a surprisingly limited number of seconds the transaction was complete.

"You'll want a driver, I reckon," said Bagley, of Bovey Tracey. "My man, Jim, here's as good a whip as you'll get. Where are ye for?"

"Buckland," returned Mr. Stokes. "But we shan't need a driver, thanks. I know these roads as well as any man in Devon, though I haven't been over them for seven years, and I can see the horses are steady. Up you get, Mr. Penfold."

Mr. Stokes was already on the box. Before seizing the whip he looked at his watch. "Four-and-a-half minutes," he said.

"It's the queerest business as I ever had," said Bagley of Bovey Tracey afterwards to the porter, Jolliffe, "and how I shall settle up with them Sunday-school folk from Moretonhampstead, I don't know. Who is the gent?"

The porter shook his head.

"I remember his face—that's all. He must ha' been to foreign parts and come back."

It was plain at once to Penfold that Mr. Stokes was a skilful driver. In a couple of minutes he seemed to have summed up the little peculiarities of each of his animals, and they were bowling along at some twelve miles an hour. From his perch on the high box-seat, Penfold could just see over the high Devonshire hedges, and as he gazed at the rolling country in the direction of their flight, he had a sense of elation, of being in the midst of exciting events. He made no attempt to anticipate what would happen when they overtook the Hendras, and how Mr. Stokes would conduct himself. He had an admiring awe for Mr. Stokes. He did not dare to question him, preferring to wait till Mr. Stokes should think fit to speak.

When they had done about a mile, Mr. Stokes spoke:

"How much start had they?"

"Seven or eight minutes."

"And it's twelve miles, up hill and down dale, rough surface most parts, unless the new County Council's altered things. They had a one-horse wagonette, hadn't they?"

Penfold nodded.

"Good horse?"

"Yes, one o' Bagley's."

"Hm! we shall catch 'em, if I have to kill all this team for it."

He was silent and then went on:

"You were rather staggered when I bought this turn-out, Penfold. Well, few men would have done it, or thought of doing it. But it's my way. If I've set my mind on doing a thing, I do it, whatever the means, and whatever the cost. I only returned to England from Australia two days ago. I was in Exeter night before last, and last night I heard as Jane Hendra was to marry her cousin. I said to myself, 'I know something that would stop that if it got about, and it ought to be stopped,' I said. I don't mind telling you that I wanted to stop the marriage. I had a reason—never mind what it was. Then I thought of you. I knew all about your affair, because I'd been told that very day, and I said to myself that you would give a lot to stop Jane Hendra's marriage, and so I sent you a message to meet me here. I thought to have had a scene on Heathfield Station with the Hendras, and I should have done if that d—d train hadn't been late. However, we shall have the scene in the church instead. Get up there."

He flicked the off-leader on the ear with the whip, and the horse plunged forward. They were making a hot pace up a long curving incline.

"Yes," Penfold said, "I'd give anything to stop that marriage. Jane Hendra would never have me now, but it would spite Johnny Hendra. And I hate him."

"So do I," said Mr. Stokes.

"Why?"

"Well, er—I hated his father, and I'd good reason to. It'll give me much pleasure to put the brake on this precious wedding."

"How shall you do it?"

"I've got a little bit of information that will do it, or I'm mistaken. You know that old John Hendra and his brother died of fever up behind Perth, both on the same day?"

"Yes."

"Well, they didn't."

"What?"

"They didn't die of fever."

"But the other brother—the Australian—I forget his name."

"Charlie it was."

"Well, he wrote himself to Mrs. Hendra, and told all the circumstances."

"Yes, I know he did. But he only did that to spare Mrs. Hendra's and Jane's feelings, and to stop a scandal. Everything was hushed up; out there, you know, these things can be arranged."

"Then aren't they dead?"

"They're dead right enough. Old John shot his brother, by accident, with a revolver, and then shot himself—he was so mad with grief and remorse."

As he uttered these words, the features of Mr. Stokes were marked by a strange delight.

"Do you think those youngsters 'll marry when they know that? Do you think young John Hendra will wed the daughter of the man who murdered—I mean killed—his father? Not he. It would be against nature. How will they look when we march after them into the church and tell 'em that?"

"She wouldn't marry him, that's certain," Penfold murmured, and a sort of dim hope seemed to spring up within him.

They drove on in silence, the horses now and then cantering and the coach gently swaying from time to time.

"What's *your* grudge against the Hendras?" Penfold asked his companion presently.

"That's my business," returned Mr. Stokes, promptly. "I've brought you along to see this marriage stopped, and you'd better be content with what I've told you."

"Certainly. No offence. I merely asked. I reckon it's a pretty big grudge, Mr. Stokes."

"It is," was the reply. "It's as big as yours."

They were passing through the little hamlet of Ilsington, when Mr. Stokes hailed a man who was breaking stones in the road.

"Seen a wagonette pass this way?"

"Ess, sir."

"How long since?"

"Might be ten minutes."

"God! they've got a good horse," said Mr. Stokes under his breath. "We aren't gaining. And I wouldn't miss the chance for a thousand pounds."

He whipped his horses almost savagely, and the vehicle plunged forward at a tremendous pace.

"Steady," said Penfold, who was timid.

"Look here"—Mr. Stokes turned to him—"would you like to get down?"

"Oh, no."

"Very well; sit tight."

The next two miles, along an undulating and fairly smooth road, were covered in nine minutes, and the horses were getting excited and beginning to show signs of the strain.

"When we are at the top of this next hill," said Mr. Stokes, "we can see two miles of road. I remember it well. We shall see that cursed wagonette then," and he urged the pace still more.

The coach breasted the hill in superb style, and the driver and his solitary passenger could discern in front of them a long, rather steep hill, and a similar ascent further on.

"See it?" asked Mr. Stokes, his eyes staring in the effort to pierce the distance.

"No," returned Penfold, moodily.

"Curse them—and curse you, you lazy devils!" He laid the long whip viciously about the panting animals, who, seeing the descent before them, first hesitated from instinctive caution, and then, still feeling the whip, broke into a gallop.

"We shall catch them before the service yet," Mr. Stokes shouted; "they're bound to dawdle a bit. We shall do it."

Down the slope they flew, as though flying from a thousand fiends. The village of Buckland lay below the crest of the next hill, and Mr. Stokes knew well that at best he could not arrive within less than ten minutes of the Hendras. He pictured the marriage ceremony as having already commenced, and the vision seemed to rouse his fiercest wrath.

Penfold clung to the seat. Alarmed though he was by their speed, he could not help being struck by the skill of Mr. Stokes's driving. The horses were well in hand, that is to say they had not run away; they were responsive to hints from whip or reins; they knew that they were under a master. But no earthly power could have stopped the vehicle in its descent. Fortunately the road was straight and clear, though rough, and as they neared the bottom, the pace still increasing, Penfold said to himself that nothing but a mishap could cause them trouble.

The thought had barely crossed his mind when the two leaders collided with a violent impact. A trace had broken. The near leader stumbled. In an instant all four horses were entangled, their heads thrust upwards in the desperate effort to stay their course. The coach swerved with a frightful movement. Penfold screamed, and almost before the scream was finished, found himself on the top of the hedge. He wondered how he had got there.

By a miracle he was unharmed, except for a badly-scratched face and torn clothes. He looked down, and then, the branches giving way, fell into the roadway. Mr. Stokes was lying on his face, six yards away. The coach was propped up against the bank from which the hedge grew; two horses lay quiet, and two others were struggling violently.

Trembling, Penfold walked to the unconscious man, and, turning him over, looked into his face. There was no sign of hurt there. Presently Mr. Penfold opened his eyes.

"Where—what .. ?" he exclaimed weakly. "I know. There was an accident. Trace broke. Run on, run on, Penfold, and stop that wedding of Jane's. Stay, I'll tell you something else."

He stopped a moment, possibly for lack of strength. Passing his hand along his body, and trying to move his legs, he said,—

"It's all over with me, my spine's broken. But you'll run on and stop it, Penfold. I've not told you all. I kept back something because I wanted it to be a surprise even to you. It wasn't an accident—I mean the shooting. John and Will Hendra had a quarrel about some mining shares, and there happened to be a revolver too handy, and John used it before he thought what he was doing. Yes, it was murder right enough. Then John killed himself. Run on and tell 'em that, and see if they'll marry."

Penfold began to speak, but Mr. Stokes, with a movement, stopped him.

"And I'll tell you my grudge now. Seven years ago, when you were a boy, and Jane was a girl of seventeen, before I went out to Australia, I fell in love with Jane, and I asked her to marry me, and she said she'd sooner be dead than wed me. Think of that. That's my grudge. That's why I went out to Australia. Run on, and tell Jane that dying Dick Stokes sent you. Run on, lad, it isn't a mile and a quarter from here. Run...."

The man's speech grew incoherent, and his eyes closed. Penfold, in an agony of fear, grasped his arm and wondered whether he was dead. He turned to the horses; they were now quiet. With a supreme effort to collect himself, he cut one loose from the medley, and, mounting it, rode off up the hill. He could not decide whether his object was to fulfil a vengeance or merely to obtain help for Mr. Stokes. Yet he felt convinced Mr. Stokes was dead, and in this he was not mistaken. Slowly he mounted the hill, and so, passing through the quaint little village, came into view of Buckland Church, in front of which all the inhabitants seemed to have gathered.

A man and a woman were just coming forth from the church, arm-in-arm. They were John Hendra and his young wife.

NOTES

1. *Woman*. 26th October 1898, pages 12, 14-15. Signed Sarah Volatile.

THE CHRISTMAS CHIMES OF MALYPRÈS.[1]

I

HOW ROSALYS RESTED IN THE BELFRY.

The beating of some distant reverberation seemed to set astir my sleeping senses. My eyelids rose heavily. I saw a shaft of light, and coming hastily down the steps towards me a man dressed in a costume of the last century. He bent, and, my eyes closing again, I resigned myself to his arms. I scarcely knew that he lifted me up, but soon I was consciously sitting in an easy chair, with a flask at my lips. When I had sipped from it, I gently pushed it away.

"I am quite strong now," I said, "except in my foot."

In the background hovered two dark, dwarfish men with strange faces.

"A hassock, Jacques," said the young man in Flemish to one of these; the creature disappeared. I could feel the warm blood coming back to my cheeks, and when my shoe had been removed and the hassock placed under my foot, I was sufficiently recovered to smile some thanks to my rescuer.

"You are comfortable?" he said, in a foreigner's English.

"Deliciously."

"And you will not faint again?"

"Under no circumstances."

He looked hard at me, apparently uncertain whether or not I was to be trusted. My answering glance must have showed that I read his hesitation, and firmly rebutted it.

"Then we will talk afterwards," he said abruptly. "I must play now."

He balanced himself on a high worn stool in front of a double line of projecting pegs, and having wrapped strips of white linen about the little fingers of both hands, he began furiously to strike the pegs with clenched fists, while his feet ranged in mysterious motion above a row of pedals. The place was filled with a deafening clatter of wood and metal, and beyond the clatter, as it were far away, one heard faintly the music of the obedient bells.

As soon as my eyes could resist the fascination of this noble, richly clad figure, attentively rapt in its weird office, I turned to examine the chamber. It had no regular shape, and the greater part of it was occupied by a huge brass cylinder, slung horizontally, from which a forest of wires rose to disappear in the punctured roof. Grouped round this was a multitude of wheels and levers and handles and notched bars, some rough and dull, others scrupulously polished. By my side, through a longitudinal hole in the floor, I noticed that a pendulum of incredible dimensions swayed majestically to and fro; I peered half timidly into the depths, but the end of the rod lost itself in obscurity. Here and there in the white washed walls were tiny windows through which, in the late dusk, dim outlines of flying, tattered cloud could occasionally be distinguished. A lighted lantern already hung over the head of the *carilloneur*, and presently one of the dark, dwarfish men kindled another one in a remote corner. The appearance of these two men as they crouched behind their machinery, peering at me with black eyes through the interstices of cogwheels, was grotesque and almost disconcerting. They seemed, either by long residence in the altitude of the tower, or from some other cause, to have become denaturalised. Day and night, so I guessed, summer and winter, they had inhabited the belfry, keeping alive the great clock, and nursing the delicate mechanism of the bells, until in the course of years they had lost kinship with humanity and the lower world, and had degenerated to the condition of gnomes, rational, canny, astute—but not human.

The playing ceased, and in the unaccustomed stillness which followed the gigantic tick, tick of the pendulum beside and beneath me asserted itself with solemn distinctness. The *carilloneur* turned round on his stool. A fine, serious face he had—the face of a thinker and of an artist. I thought of the city full of people massed in the streets and squares below to enjoy the fruits of his genius.

"How splendid," I said enthusiastically, "to have an audience of two hundred thousand! The greatest singer in Europe couldn't hope for a twentieth of that number."

He smiled.

"Do you ever feel nervous up here?"

"I was nervous to-night," he said.

"My accident must have discomposed you. I am very contrite, and you must forgive me. I was walking with my cousin in the Grande Place, listening to your carillon, and while my cousin was busy talking to someone about a street improvement, I had the idea of climbing the belfry to see the great Quentin Claes, of whom I had heard so much, actually at work. My cousin didn't see me go, so of course he didn't object. The concierge objected, but I arranged matters there, and then I began to mount those interminable stone steps that led up to this eyrie of yours. It was dusk when I started, and before I had mounted ten steps it was pitch dark. Do you know there are strange noises to be heard in your tower? A sudden wind blew my hat away. I must have been very frightened, with no companion but the hand-rope. When I had been climbing for hours and hours and could scarcely get my breath, something flew against my face. I tripped over a step, and I fell, and I sprained my foot, and I fainted."

"And now," he said composedly, "you are certainly thinking that the sight of the great Quentin Claes actually at work is but a poor recompense for your perilous exertions."

"Indeed I am not!" I answered. "I am delighted with everything—except my foot. By the way, how did you know I was lying at your door? Did I scream so loudly?"

"Jacques came to tell me there was a ghost on the stairs. He had been outside for something, and caught sight of your white dress .... My last piece," and he turned back suddenly to his instrument. Once more the strange medley of cacophony and music filled the room.

Even in England my adventure might well have been called an escapade, and judged by the light of the Continental proprieties, which are cotton wool and a glass case to the young spinster, it must have been accounted the shameless caprice of a maiden who had forgotten to be maidenly. It was inexcusable, especially in one who intended to submit herself permanently to the social laws prevailing in this funny little country of belfries and burgomasters. So much I afterwards acknowledged, but at the moment I had not the faintest consciousness of indecorum. And if the attitude of Quentin Claes was not misleading, he, too, scarcely regarded my behaviour as other than ordinary.

I have been always frank with myself, and during the conversation that ensued after Quentin Claes had finished his concert *au carillon*, I discovered and privately admitted that inarticulate whispers, unspoken tidings of concord, sympathy and regard were passing between us, hidden in the intensity of a swift glance, the inflection of a syllable, the smile of anticipatory comprehension. Who shall describe this subtle, delicious commerce of spirits from which springs love? Love! Did I think of it thus early? Girls are taught to manipulate their feelings so that love may take them by surprise, seize them, as it were, from behind. To be aware of his coming, to beckon him onwards on tip-toe, to watch him from afar, with a hand shading the eager eyes, is, even by our modern code, unseemly in a woman. But all these things I did (as indeed, what live woman has not?), and to-day I take no shame for them. We spoke only of common matters: of his daily visits to the belfry in the performance of official duty, of his antique costume, which he told me was of the pattern worn on festival days by every *carilloneur* of Malyprès since the belfry existed; of the two clock-winders, who after all, it appeared, had wives and children down in the under world; of the expanse of country which might be seen from the windows of that chamber on a propitious day; of England and London, and so forth. And we were intently interested, not in what was said, but rather in what was left unsaid—what could not be said. We became forgetful—the singing birds in our hearts growing each instant more carelessly gay—of that underworld where the gnomes of the tower had wives and children. I was enamoured of the sound of his voice, and he, I knew well, not indifferent to mine. We recked little what the words were—in fact, uttered the most foolish remarks time after time in a short half-hour. He was he, and I was I. We had found each other.

We paused in our talk once in order that he might explain to me the movement of the great cylinder in ringing the tunes which the clock played every quarter of an hour.

Once again the cylinder moved, and amid the rattle of wires and concussion of jacks, I distinguished a peculiarly jerky, jig-like air, which seemed unsuited for so solemn a clock as that of Malyprès.

"That is the Burgomaster's tune," Quentin Claes explained, with a satiric laugh. "He composes one specially every year, and compels me to put it on the cylinder. The chimes are changed once a year," he added, "at Christmas."

I had forgotten: the Burgomaster *had* a turn for music.

"The Burgomaster is my cousin," I said.

"Then you are Miss Coore?" he exclaimed, with a falling face.

"You have heard of me?"

"I heard that you were to come."

A chill seemed momentarily to enwrap us. I gathered that Quentin Claes did not love the Burgomaster. Almost before we were aware of it the hour struck.

"What time is that?" I asked, starting up nervously, and then sinking down with a sigh because of my foot.

"Ten o'clock."

"The Burgomaster will wonder what has become of me. I

have been here half an hour." (Half an hour, was it only?)

Quentin Claes hesitated.

"I can't stay here," I half whimpered, "and I can't walk down, though my foot is not very bad. But I must, emphatically must, get down somehow."

"It is simple," Quentin Claes said; "I shall carry you."

"What! down those dark, dangerous stairways ?"

"Certainly," he answered; "Jacques will light us."

II

ROSALYS ENDS BY REFLECTING.

My position in the household of the Burgomaster, though easily defined, was unusual and difficult to sustain without a troublesome feeling of self-consciousness. M. Karl Dierickx-fisschers—such was his name—happened to be a bachelor and I had come from England into his house in order that he might woo and marry me. Our agreement had been scarcely so explicit as that, but in plain English it amounted to as much. The son of my mother's cousin—my mother being of foreign extraction—the Burgomaster had visited us several times during his travels in England.

My mother liked him, and I teased him—undaunted by the halo of greatness and success which was supposed to encircle his brown, curly head. In my mother's eyes Cousin Karl was the wealthiest and most renowned printer of his country, a famous scholar, a member of learned academies, in short, a personage; in mine he was simply a short spare man of thirty-eight, with little eyes and a jerky walk, who took himself and the world too seriously, and who could seldom speak to me without blushing. He used invariably to call me "*Cousin* Rosalys." One day I asked him to omit the "cousin." "If you wish it—Rosalys," he answered, hesitating and shamefast. "There, that's a brave man!" I applauded, with the ingenuous glee of a schoolboy watching a fly on a pin.

The letter which I received from him after my mother's

death, suggesting that I should take myself to Malyprès and form a third in the household nominally presided over by an aged aunt of his, was without exception the most curious document I have ever seen. I accepted the quaint proposal, partly out of an adventurous spirit, partly on account of my solitude and mere weariness, and partly from another feeling, dim and refusing analysis—product, perhaps, of our intricate modern temperament. Those few of my acquaintance who were told about the matter took my decision as of course, and plainly thought me fortunate ..... Will the time ever come when love shall really be the unique condition precedent to marriage, when women shall have ceased to be auctioneers disposing of themselves with a merchant's astuteness? At moments I can see glimpses of that era—an era in which mate and mate shall stand equal and single-eyed before each other. But it is not yet. Though this is a surprising age of upheaval, and many think that the summit of civilisation is close upon us, I imagine that the world has still far and painfully to travel.

As I sat in a corner of the Burgomaster's soberly magnificent salon one night at the close of a reception, I wondered at the temerity of my early attitude towards him. The immense room, hung with the very flower of Flemish painting, lined with rare cabinets, and lighted by three huge dazzling chandeliers, was nearly deserted now. Half an hour previously it had decorously echoed to the conversation of the assembled aristocracy of the second richest town in north-western Europe, all ceremonious and deferential in the presence of one dignified man, a printer—a printer, however, whose salaried proof-reader was a *savant* and the founder of a school of thought. Could this be he whom I used to flout and ridicule? It seemed impossible, and yet—

He was talking quickly in that resonant voice of his to Quentin Claes. Save for these two, Karl's aunt, who in her prim purple sat dozing in an arm-chair, myself, and a couple of footmen in a doorway, the great chamber was empty. I could never quite make out the relations which existed between my cousin Karl and Quentin Claes. They respected, liked, hated one another; were fond of being together, and were always apparently at a difference, disputing on equal terms in spite of a marked inequality of age and of prestige—though, indeed, the *carilloneur* was famous enough in his own profession.

They were arguing now, my cousin, stately and sneering, Quentin Claes rather heated and aggrieved. Presently they gave up, each with a shrug of the shoulders, and came towards me. I had scarcely yet recovered the use of my foot, though six weeks had gone by since the accident in the belfry, and all that evening I had been bound to a chair, receiving with what queenliness I could command such people as the Burgomaster introduced.

Quentin Claes begged to take his leave.

"I have offended the Burgomaster," he said airily, as he bent, rather longer than the dozing aunt would have thought necessary, over my hand, and the two exchanged looks of supercilious defiance. As the younger man left the room, my eyes involuntarily followed him; he turned half round at the door and his gaze met mine; he stopped an instant; neither of us moved; then he was gone.

I glanced up suddenly at Karl, and just as suddenly Karl fell guiltily to examining a picture on my left. Where was that municipal dignity which had clothed him so amply during the reception?

"Why do you look at me in that way, Karl?" I asked.

"In what way, Rosalys?"

"As if you suspected me of some secret shame," I said, with a spurious accent of protesting innocence, which had gone forth almost before I was aware of it.

"I beg your pardon," he said, his hands behind him, and one toe drawing patterns on the carpet.

Some wicked and extravagant impulse to pose took hold

of me, and, as I examined his downcast face, my breast trembled with inimical passion. Is it not said that the only people we cannot forgive are those we have injured?

"You are pleased to think I am doing you a wrong," I exclaimed.

"A wrong, cousin?"

"Yes, cousin. Ever since I was unfortunate enough, in an innocent caprice, to hurt my foot at the top of your foolish old belfry, and Quentin Claes was kind enough to carry me down in his arms and across the Grande Place to this house, you have looked askance at myself and at him. Did you always bicker with Quentin Claes upon trifling matters which one would fancy should be left to his discretion? Or is it not rather a recent innovation?"

"No innovation, surely!" Karl tried to laugh, "we have always quarrelled about music. But we have been friends, in a manner. As for what you—"

"Ah! Music!" I interrupted, scornfully. "The Burgomaster, not content to be foremost in handicrafts and philosophies, must also cut a figure in the art of music. He composes little airs, and, so that all may hear and wonder at the Burgomaster's myriad gifts, he abuses his official authority in order to have the little airs played by the belfry clock. *Quelle folie de grandeur*! Naturally Quentin Claes, being an authentic musician, takes exception to the little airs."

"They are good airs," he said, firmly.

"And if they were finer than Van den Gheyn's[2] own, would you force them on the *carilloneur*? Already the clock plays one of your little airs at the third quarter twenty-four times daily; and now I understand that when the chime-tunes come to be changed at Christmas you want all four quarters to be announced by the ingenious melodies of the Burgomaster."

"Who told you so?" he asked, with that outer quietude which nothing ever disturbed.

"Quentin Claes told me," I answered. "Is he not frequently

in this house to inquire about my poor foot? But let us get back. You think that Quentin Claes and I have taken a fancy for each other. You think I would seek to break that contract under which I entered your dwelling."

"There was no contract," he murmured. "You were and are free."

"Nonsense, Cousin Karl. There was a contract, though it was neither formally written down nor spoken of at all. Else, why your jealousy, which hangs over me like a cloud? But be re-assured," I went on, "I shall marry you. And there is nothing whatever between Quentin Claes and your ever dutiful and grateful Rosalys."

I got up, and with the aid of a stick began a limping journey across the chamber.

"Let me help you," he said, starting forward.

"Thank you," I said, "I can walk perfectly," he fell back-again. The dozing aunt had silently disappeared, and I left the Burgomaster standing alone under the central chandelier. His face showed a curious alloy of chagrin and happiness.

* * * *

It was a humid November evening. I opened my window, and went out on to the balcony overlooking the Quai Vert. In front of me the long, winding canal slept under the susurration of the curving poplars, and all around were the towers and steeples and stepwise gables of this magic city of Malyprès, vaguely black against a mysterious midnight sky.

A servant was bolting the ponderous gates of the mansion. He vanished with a jingle of keys. Then the belfry clock struck the quarter before one, and my cousin the Burgomaster's "little air" came to me over the chimneys. The hour and the scene were propitious for reflection, and, indeed, I began to reflect. Why, in the thoughtless impatience of a petulant mood, had I lied to Karl? Had I but invoked his magnanimity instead of casting jeers at him, all might yet have been well. But now I had effectively closed the one avenue towards freedom.

III
ROSALYS GOES AGAIN TO THE BELFRY.

The winter was mild. On Christmas morning, as, returning from the church of S. Jean, we walked, Cousin Karl and I, along the tortuous Quai de la Poterie, there was not a vestige of ice on the waters of the canal, which were rippling under a light breeze. The sky was a clear weak blue with scarcely a cloud, and the bare trees in the sunlight seemed almost to give a faint budding promise of spring. The boats and the great barges showed no hint of life, but the Quai was gaily busy with holiday folk, even at that early hour.

The Burgomaster was somewhat quiet, and returned the salutations which beset us at every yard of our route, with a preoccupied, perfunctory air, quite different from the diligent suavity of his usual manner in the streets. But we were at peace, we two, and I had reason to think that he was in a pleasant, meditative temper that day. Certainly, he answered very kindly whenever I chanced to let fall a remark; which was not often, for I had my own thoughts, grave enough.

"The chimes recommence this morning," I said, as, upon turning a corner, we came in sight of the belfry tower. They had been silent for a week past in order that the new tunes might be arranged on the cylinder.

"Yes," he said, with a smile, "at ten o'clock."

I had not heard whether his own melodies had after all been selected, and I did not care to inquire directly. Discretion forbade any reference to that topic.

In passing the Fishmarket, we noticed a crowd of children round some street performers, and the Burgomaster stepped aside to watch. There was a cart with several monkeys in it, drawn by a caparisoned pony, and close by a camel, the whole in charge of two Italian-looking men, one of whom continually beat a drum. The monkeys leapt from cart to pony, from pony to camel, sitting upright now and then to eat a biscuit or piece of bread thrown from the crowd. Everyone laughed heartily at their antics, and one very tiny monkey that had perched itself, with the most horrible grimaces, between the ears of the immobile camel, garnered a rich harvest of tit-bits. Suddenly a stone flew up out of the press of people, and the little animal dropped heavily to the ground, shrieking with pain. The Burgomaster darted forward, the crowd dividing before him, and had lifted the animal before its owners knew what was happening. I can never forget the passion of tenderness which shone in the eyes of this strange, self-contained man, as, with my lace handkerchief, he bound up the hideous little creature's bleeding paw. The incident in itself was trifling, but it had a deep-reaching effect upon myself.

We continued our way home immediately afterwards. At the door of the great house on the Quai Vert he left me to enter alone.

"You have elsewhere to go?" I said.

"Yes," he answered, smiling, and then growing grave. "There are several matters waiting my attention."

The accident of his sudden departure seemed to have been contrived by Fate to render easy a scheme which might otherwise have proved at least embarrassing. I had a tryst in the belfry to keep with Quentin Claes. I had granted it not without certain hesitations and not without compunction, and both of us understood that it was to be of a decisive nature.

When the time came, I tried to walk across the Grande Place without timid, guilty side glances to right and left in search of a wronged Burgomaster, and I do not think that I succeeded.

"M. Claes has gone up?" I enquired, with a pitiful assumption of nonchalance, of the concierge on the first story of the tower.

"Yes, mademoiselle," she curtsied, "scarcely a moment ago. The new chime strikes in half an hour. Mademoiselle wishes to ascend?"

I went up in such haste that near the top I overtook Quentin Claes.

"Who is that?" he said, seemingly startled at the sound of my footsteps and panting gasps in the dark. I stood a moment, irresolute.

"Rosalys," I murmured.

He groped for my hand, and I gave it him.

"Quentin Claes," I began feverishly, as soon as we were in the clock-room, and he, having satisfied himself that the machinery was in smooth order, had dismissed the two winders to their own devices on solid ground, "Quentin Claes, I did ill to meet you here, but now that I am come there is a confession to be made."

He took my hand again, but I withdrew it, and for a few seconds we stood silent, facing each other, the ticking of the clock heavily distinct in our ears. The door leading to Quentin Claes' little retiring room was slightly ajar. Stretching out my arm mechanically I latched it.

"We have seen each other alone many times during the last month," I went on, "and yet I have never told you about a little conversation between myself and Karl on the night of the reception after you left. I informed him then, though he did not ask me, that I did not care for you—that I was nothing to you."

"But you are, and the Burgomaster must know it."

"Am I? Let it be granted that I lied. But the Burgomaster must never know it."

I felt stronger then than Quentin Claes, whose expressive face had a baffled, nervous look.

"Why are you bound to him?" he asked plaintively. "Why cannot we put our case before him, so that he may—"

"I am bound to him because he has faith in me, and because he is a kind and an honest man. There must be no more indecisions, temerities, no more playing with fire. Our—friendship sprang up swiftly; as swiftly let it die. It was all wrong."

I had not intended, heaven knows, to be eloquent in this strain; I had credited myself with less firmness of resolution; but an imperative, masterful impulse possessed me that morning, and no opposing consideration could stand before it. In vain Quentin Claes sought to move me. I met his arguments with set lips and silence.

"You do not love me," he said at last.

"Oh Quentin!" I whispered. Tears were in his eyes, but I felt none in my own.

"Kiss me—just once—and I shall know."

I kissed him. "That is the end," I said.

There was a whirr above our heads, and the chime began to strike—a jerky, jigging tune, Cousin Karl's, I felt sure. I could not avoid even then, a sad smile at his little vanities.

Suddenly the door of the retiring room opened, and Cousin Karl stood before us. He looked at each of us in turn, with quiet, undecipherable eyes, then walked solemnly across to the turret door, and disappeared. The chime was still going.

In that dreadful instant I clung to Quentin Claes and he to me. After perhaps a minute there was a strange noise outside the door. Quentin Claes went timorously to open it, and looked down the stairway. He looked a long while. Then,

"Come here," he said to me, without turning round.

I obeyed. The Burgomaster lay below us, self-slain.

*　　*　　*　　*

It happened twenty-five years ago, and to day I am more than ever sure that Cousin Karl did his deed in no spirit of hysterical altruism. He was not an altruist. He desired a woman's fealty, and he believed a woman's word, and when he discovered himself to be both disappointed and deceived, he took a dramatic revenge, planned in a second, and in a second carried out. A woman's remorse and repentance availed nothing to stay his inexorable hand. Well and clearly he foresaw, at the supreme crisis, the heavy punishment he was meting out for that woman. Cousin Karl was a great man.

I have seen many strange things since then, and heard of stranger. There have penetrated, this December of seventeen hundred and ninety-three, even to the seclusion of my retreat at Dimsdale, in Staffordshire, rumours of the sanguinary turmoil in France, and the sinister activity of M. Sanson and his plaything.[3] But nothing moves me, not even that. I have lost the capacity for emotion.

NOTES

1. *Woman*. 9th December 1896, pages 20-23. Signed E.A. Bennett. Illustrated by Gertrude Demain-Hammond.

Writing to Sturt on 21st October 1896 Bennett reported: "I wrote a story last week for our Christmas number, with a Flemish scene. When I began I thought it was going to be something rather good, but I'm not ecstatic about it now. Quite out of my usual run, & therefore artificial, a mere *tour de force* .... the writing will pass in a crowd, & the idea is not inane" (*Letters II*, p. 66). Bennett was to explore further the stylistic possibilities of a female narrator in his 1905 novel *Sacred and Profane Love*.

2. Gheyn van den Gheyn (1721-1785) was a Flemish organist, composer and virtuoso carillon player, famous for his ability to improvise.

3. The French Revolution was four years old when, on June 2nd 1893, a mob invaded the Tuileries and evicted the elected representatives from the National Convention, thus unleashing a year of terror. The Sanson family was famous for its efficiency as public executioners.

DRAGONS OF THE NIGHT. [1]

The *Swift*—everyone knows the little old G.S.N. paddle-boat which has been plying this fifty years between London and Ostende—was being warped from St. Katherine's wharf into mid-stream. The fore-cabin passengers—seated on camp-stools and standing—were looking over the starboard bow, and the saloon people—who had graciously visited the forward deck to see the fun of the start—took an intelligent, condescending interest in the donkey-engine, which was spitting and swearing furiously as it gathered up the hawser.

"Slack that rope there, quicker! You'll break it," the captain yelled from the bridge.

"Shan't break it, sir."

Before the passengers had noticed anything, the ship had passed the warping buoy, and was pulling on the hawser fit to wrench the ring out of the buoy's nose.

"Cast of," called a deck hand pettishly to the man in the dingey waiting round the buoy, and the next moment the ship was on her way, and had begun to dodge the barges that were sprawling and lounging up-stream on the evening flood.

It was a pretty scene, though as common as dirt. The hundred million lights that light the Thames were just beginning to show, timidly, in the green and pink of the August sky. They moved queerly over the river, and flickered away down the banks of it; and the river ran between and under, as black and mysterious as Styx—or the canals at Runcorn. The men on the barges loomed large, and made big, beautiful movements, with sweeps as long as a mast. The tugs lost that air of agitated ducklings which they have, as they fume and splutter about, and seemed to glide along with dignity in the evening glow. The big ships at moorings looked bigger and more sublime than ever. The wharfs wore a mediæval aspect. Even the Tower Bridge, which is one of the seven ugliest things in Europe (all the other six are in London), rose vaguely and dimly imposing, as it arched its back to let through an Aberdeen cargo boat.

Yes, it was a pretty scene, and it made the steerage passengers feel sentimental (the saloon folk had gone back to inhabit their own place). They were rather crowded up—it was the Saturday before Bank Holiday—and many of them were dirty, and they spoke to each other in various European and Asiatic languages, but they were, most of them, animated by that tender sentiment which departure by ship never fails to arouse. They were only going a hundred and forty miles, yet they felt just as poetically and sweetly sad as if the *Swift* had been a Lamport and Holt liner bound for Valparaiso.[2]

Ninety per cent. of them were men, and the few women were in charge of omniscient husbands and lovers, who spent themselves in trying to show their utterly unfamiliarity with the deck of a ship. Only one girl seemed to be alone. She was tall, and she stood apart, against the rail, her head thrown proudly back, one hand guarding her straw hat, and the other clutching a parasol and the rail. She was not well dressed, but she had a fine nervous style with her, and she looked out of place in that crowd—like a racehorse on a cab-rank. Her appearance and her solitude had already drawn the attention of several men of the preening peacock kind, and by these she had been marked for inquiry during the voyage.

She seemed to be deeply engaged with herself: as though the glance of her eyes were turned inwards to behold a heart peopled by Strange Things. She absolutely ignored even the sailor who was rummaging about her feet to get a rope off the bitts.

"*If* you please, Miss," the man exclaimed angrily at last.

She sprang away, angry in her turn. She would have glared at him, but he was a grey-headed man and looked worried, so she merely apologized. Still it struck her as unseemly that she, private secretary to Henry Arnhout (Arnhout and Arnhout, West India Docks), who owned the largest and finest fleet of cargo steamers in the wide world, should be snubbed by a deck-hand of a miserable old ten-knot toy like the *Swift*. She was accustomed to writing out telegrams which sent monsters of eight or ten thousand tons dead-weight capacity flirting off from one side of the world to the other. Captains courted her favour, and Chief Engineers paid her compliments in the Scottish language, because it was only through her door that Henry Arnhout could be approached. She was a personage at Arnhout's. And her salary was twenty-eight and six a week. Next September it would have been thirty, if—

The deck-hand was looking at her thoughtfully. She sustained his gaze for a moment, and then blushed red and glanced down at the deck-seams. Other people also glanced at her, notably a slight, dark man with twinkling eyes.

Could it be that anyone knew—so soon?

No, it was impossible. She decided that it was absolutely impossible. And then, as men and women must who have unexpectedly met Fate walking abroad and been flustered by the sight thereof, Nellie Crane deliberately went through the Event again in her mind. It was horrid, horrible, but she felt she had to do it.

Time, only sixty minutes ago.

Ah! But she must begin earlier than that. She must begin with Paul English.

Paul English, Arnhout's cashier, bachelor, young, had left the office very early in the day to catch the noon boat at Dover for Ostende. He was to spend his holiday at Ostende, and she had permitted herself to hope that he would not spend too much of it at the "Cercle privée," which offers to the simple stranger "the same attractions as at Monte Carlo." He was six years older than she, being nine-and-twenty, but her interest in him was maternal.

So much for Paul.

She had been with Mr. Arnhout for a short time in the morning, but afterwards was engaged solely with her typewriter in her own little room. Although an immense amount of work waited to be done, there was no reason why she should have finished it that day; but she had felt in the mood for hard labour, and the office seemed more pleasant to her than her bed-sitting-room in Muscovy Court. Moreover, Mr. Arnhout had said he was leaving early and had exhorted her in his kind fatherly manner not to do too much. Therefore she had stuck by the Remington[3] for eight mortal hours (and Saturday, too!), going out at one for a bun and some tea, and at five for a bun and some tea. It was Nellie's whole-hearted enthusiastic way.

At 6.30 the Remington was put into its tin night-cap, and Nellie, having locked the door of her own room, walked down the corridor, a little pleased with herself. The place was long since deserted. The door next to hers was that of Mr. Arnhout's room. It was marked "Private," and no one used it but Mr. Arnhout himself, for there was a law that all others should enter that sanctuary by its other door, through Nellie's room. Nellie tried the lock to make sure it was fast (Mr. Arnhout was so careless, she often said to herself benevolently), and to her surprise the door opened. She went in just to see if the key was on the inside, and she saw Mr. Arnhout lying queerly back in his armchair. No, she didn't scream, though she knew at once that he was dead. She went up to him. (Afterwards she wondered how she could have done this, she so nervous and excitable; but the thought of a dreadful thing is always more dreadful than the thing itself.) His head was twisted a little, so that his silky white beard lay over the right lapel of his frock coat. His face calm, creased, waxen; his hands hanging limp. On his waistcoat (how the starched white front bulged out!) were two clots of blood, near the bar of his watch-chain, which, as usual, was in the top buttonhole: that was all.

A stab, a stiletto, she said. The most terrible thought was that the murderer had done his deed while she was in the next room, separated only by a door. She clicked the typewriter—and dear old Mr. Arnhout died; the idea desolated her. He was stiff; must have been dead for hours—hours. *It* might have happened as early as a quarter to ten, for since then she had heard no sound in Mr. Arnhout's room.

She looked about and saw his private safe open, and one Bank of England note on the floor. Why had her thoughts then turned to Paul English, with an exquisite overwhelming tenderness? She knew not, but she knew at once that Paul English would be suspected, and that he must be warned: was not justice subject to the most frightful accidents? Paul was said to be somewhat wild when he chose. His reputation amounted to this: "A good fellow, but—" She alone really understood and fathomed Paul. He must be brought back from

"HIS HEAD WAS TWISTED A LITTLE."

Ostende at once, so that there might be no appearance of flight.

A telegram? Too public. A letter? Too slow: the post had gone. Then it was that she thought of the *Swift*, and looked at some lists of sailings which hung on the wall. In a single busy instant she resolved to go to him. She knew his hotel, the Wellington; she would get to Ostende at breakfast-time on Sunday, and by the evening they would both be back in London.

She had twenty-five minutes. Closing the door softly, she went away, speaking to no one of what lay within.

*　　　*　　　*　　　*

She was staggered to find the vessel in mid-ocean. How it had got there she could not tell. The full moon shone down over the blackened foremast, lighting the ship and the immense flat uneasy circle of sea. The deck was now deserted, save for a couple of men who were gossiping with the look-out, and someone who stood behind her, gently stamping his feet. She was cold to the bone, and lifting her shoulders she turned around. The slight dark man, with twinkling eyes, faced her.

"A beautiful night," he said.

She had taken him for a Frenchman but he spoke as a Londoner.

She assented.

"You are shivering," he went on. "Have you no rug?"

He looked up at her—for he was somewhat less than she—apparently sympathetic, respectful.

"No."

"I will get one."

"Please don't," she observed, peremptorily, wise with the wisdom of the girl who had to support herself unaided and alone in a large city.

"As you please."

He turned his head seawards, and she noticed the weakness of his thin pale face—the restless mouth, the receding infinitesimal chin. But his eyes had fire; it was as though they had burnt their way into the sockets.

Still looking seawards, he addressed her again.

"You must have started in a hurry. Did you happen to hear of the murder of Henry Arnhout before you set out, Miss Crane?"

She felt as the hunted pickpocket feels when, fleeing from one policeman, he sees in front of him another, with arms extending across the street. She was sick with a dread which she could not define, and if the man of twinkling eyes had not looked persistently seawards he would have noticed the sudden whiteness of her face. Already, in a sort of delirium, she saw the net of circumstantial evidence closing round Paul English. Of herself she never thought once. She desired to seize the little dark man and pitch him into the sea; then she wanted to bury her face in her hands and cry; and she could do one thing no more than the other.

"Who are you?" she asked; and it seemed that she was listening to someone else's voice.

"I am Andrews."

The word conveyed nothing to her.

"Andrews of Scotland Yard," he explained.

Then she had a vague memory of assize reports and marvelous feats of detection as related with cross headings in halfpenny papers.

"I am the detective in charge of the Arnhout case," he continued, while she looked at him dumbly. It seemed to her that he was proud of the impression he had created, and the thought stiffened her back and put a curve into her nostrils. She had an absurd desire to argue with him that he was mistaken, that there was no Arnhout case. Half an hour before the *Swift* sailed, none, not even herself, knew of the murder. And in thirty minutes the police had not only discovered it, but had tracked her to the steamer? Impossible. Nevertheless she just had to believe it. Her eyes were suddenly opened to the terrible organized might of British law. She gasped at her foolishness in leaving England. She had not helped Paul, and she knew that she was a suspect. She ought to have gone direct to the police—those police of whom she had now made enemies.

Her haughtiness collapsed, and she grew sullen.

"You are here to arrest me, I suppose?" she said at length. He looked at her. She saw in his eyes a hundred subtle schemes, and she shrank away.

"That depends," he answered cheerfully. "At the moment I am merely investigating. I try to explain to myself your presence on this boat. I wonder why you did not leave London at the same time as your lover."

"My lover!" She gasped the words, and all the colour flew back to her cheeks, signalling dire outrage.

"Yes, Paul English, who, having killed Mr Arnhout, has gone off with five thousand or so in cash."

She rose at him, dumbfounded; attempted to speak, failed, and turned away.

"Either arrest me or leave me." She threw forth the words furiously over her shoulder, and the little detective quailed before the scorn in her voice.

"Of course, that's only my theory," he said, apologetically, and put out a hand as if in appeal; but she walked to the other side of the ship, and fell into an empty deck chair. The universe whirled before her and then tumbled roaring about her ears.

* * * * *

She had dozed, and she was roused by the slow settling of a rug on her shoulders. It was still night, but over the gently heaving surface of the sea moved mysterious faint whitenesses, heralds of the dawn. Sirius low down on the verge blazed fiercely, in an unwise attempt to outshine the Dunkerque light to starboard. Nellie looked up, dimly conscious. It was Andrews who held the rug.

"Forgive me," he half-whispered, nervously hurried, "I

thought I could do it without wakening you up. Now, please," he lifted his hand with the protective appealing gesture characteristic of him, "please don't throw it off. Forget what I said just now."

She was weary and full of the sorrow of Mr. Arnhout's death and the sorrow of his own foolishness, and the man's deep eyes glowed with kindness and soft contrition. So she accepted the rug.

"Thank you," she murmured, and then, when he came round to the front of her chair and bent down, the sight of his concern for her and his repentant, serious features nearly made her laugh. "You are a queer detective," she said.

"Detectives are like other men."

He might have added in explanation that she looked superbly tragic in that deck chair under the fading moonlight. The wide-brimmed hat tilted forward, and the pose of the long arms .... (How in the name of Aphrodite do women manage these effects?)

"Detectives are much misunderstood," he went on. "We—I—am not without feeling."

"But you must get hardened," she answered. "How many people have you caused to be hanged?"

She was instantly sorry. His expressive eyes were damp.

"You are cruel," he said sadly, and then pulled himself together. "But you have the right to be. Let me tell you that I have been thinking over your—your case, and I am convinced now that Paul English is as innocent as you are. And—and—you must let me help you. A certain amount of suspicion, of course, attaches to him, but it will be easy to clear that away. But you must tell me all you know."

So she sat up, and with a pressure of the hand forgave him, and told him all. Secretly she pitied him because his eyes were so sad. Then the sun rose, and the grey-haired sailor who hauled down the mast-head light observed the two in converse and thought things.

"There's one point you haven't explained," said Andrews later, "and it's very important. Why are you on this boat?"

"I thought Mr. English ought to be told, warned, and so—I just came along at once."

"I see," he said, tactfully examining the broad ocean. "Are you and Mr. English—"

"Mr. English is just a colleague of mine, and—and—No, we are not, certainly not. Far from it. Mr. English is my colleague . . . . There has never been a word . . . . If a man may be loyal to a colleague, why not a woman?"

She was of the Fabian Society[4] and held views.

"Just so," said Andrews. "I will get you some tea, if I may. It will do you good." And he went off towards the saloon.

The rumour of the risen sun drew the passengers up from the doubtful tenebrous forecabin, where the berths were four deep and the smoky swinging lamp mingled its own special odour with the fumes of French Government tobacco. The damp deck was inhabited once more, and pale-faced people stamped about yawning, and pointing out to each other Heyst and Blankenburgh, and the dome of the Kursaal at Ostende. Nellie waited, expecting Andrews and the tea; but he did not come. Presently a steward approached, balancing a steaming cup after the manner of an equilibrist.

"Gentleman sent this for you, Miss."

An hour or more passed, which she employed in considering what precisely should be her demeanour to Mr. English when she met him at the Wellington.

Then the *Swift* glided up the narrow creek that Ostende calls its harbour. The other people crowded to the gangway, but Nellie sat still. Just as the first rope was thrown ashore the detective appeared before her again. He was agitated, and once or twice he swallowed.

"You'll pardon me, Miss Crane," he began, and as he spoke his voice calmed and hardened, "but I mustn't let you go. My duty, you know. A British ship is British soil, and I can only allow you to leave it on condition that you promise to return to England with me at once. We should just catch the first Belgian State steamer."

"But Paul—Mr. English?"

"*Of course* I can't let you communicate with him. Recollect my position. It'll be all right. I'll see to him."

"Mr. Andrews, you are on our—on his side?"

They exchanged looks. His restless eyes dropped before hers. A pause. Then:

"I swear it," he said quietly.

"Then I put myself in your hands," she said, smiling gravely.

* * * * *

Aboard the big Belgian State steamer *La Flandre* Andrews had insisted that she should retire to the ladies' cabin for rest, but she could not rest there. There was the usual desolating delay at the Admiralty pier, and other steamers came in and added their quota to the train load of Sabbatic misery. Andrews passed the time in sending off telegrams. For her there was nothing but to wait; throughout the whole of the journey he industriously avoided her. When they got to Victoria, in the afternoon, she was so weary that she could have slept on a rail-fence.

He called a hansom, saying that they must drive straight to "the station," and Nellie took her seat. He spoke to the driver, and she was vaguely aware of the horse's steady trot and of occasional changes of direction as the vehicle swung round a corner. It all seemed a dream to her, and she half expected to awake in her three-foot six bed at Muscovy Court. It was a year to her since the previous evening.

Then the cab stopped in a mysterious street, which she recognized at once as being a tributary of Tottenham Court Road. In another moment Andrews had led her into a house, the door of which was closed behind her. A dirty old woman, with grizzled, grey hair and a spotted apron, stood at the foot of the stairs. Andrews had vanished.

"Is *this* the police station?" Nellie asked.

"Come in, dearie, come forward," the old woman invited, with caressing gesture; and Nellie, shivering at the touch of her, went.

It was a rather spacious room in which she found herself, with a large, thickly-curtained window. The floor was bare. Windsor chairs stood around the walls, which were decorated with printed and written notices. At the far end were a deal table and four arm-chairs. Two of these chairs were occupied by unkempt, dark-browed men of foreign appearance, so alike in looks that they must have been brothers. The others were empty.

The two men were conversing in Italian, with all the acrobatic gesticulations that the Italian tongue seems to need. As Nellie entered, they turned upon her a double gaze—cold, callous, sinister, brutal; a gaze under which she had a fear like the sudden fear of death, which once felt is never forgotten.

"Is *this* the police station?" she questioned again.

"No, it is not." The elder of the two answered her. His tones were crisp, short, neat. It was the English of a thorough linguist, but not the English of a Briton.

"But Mr. Andrews, the detective, told me we were going to a police station."

The two brothers exchanged a faint grin.

"So Dennis called himself Andrews, did he—Andrews of Scotland Yard? Dat was good, Luigi, *es*pecially for Dennis."

"I must go," she said, almost dropping.

"Now do not move." Just then she noticed that a revolver had been used as a paper-weight for a little pile of telegrams on the table. "People—strangers, dat is—who come into this house do not go out so quickly as dat. Once involved in the affairs of the Dragons of the Night, it is not easy to extricate one's self, Mees Crane."

"Let me see Mr. Andrews," she appealed, unable to believe that Mr. Andrews' eyes had cheated her. "He said he would help me. He will tell you."

"Ah! He will? Mr. 'Andrews' is ver' busy just now. Attend to me. You are here to answer one question, my girl. Will you swear on the Holy Cross not to reveal anything dat you know about the death of Henry Arnhout?"

"No, I won't," she cried, and there was despair in her voice.

"The consequence of *re*fusal will be of the most serious."

"I won't, I won't, I won't." She hid her face in her hands and sobbed.

"Then we will consider what to do." He struck a bell and the old woman entered. "Take careful charge of this girl."

"Come along, dearie," the old woman mumbled, as though she were a hideous doll-mechanism contrived to utter only that one phrase.

Limp, unopposing, Nellie allowed herself to be led into a small cubicle, apparently at the back of the house. At first, when the door closed, she was in absolute blackness, but soon she noticed a shadow of a glimmering square high up in the wall, just sufficient to make the darkness visible.

It is one thing to be intellectually aware, from paragraphs in the papers, that secret societies exist. It is another thing to believe and know by actual experience that they exist. Such belief and knowledge are disconcerting. We are so accustomed to the power of public opinion and the fear of the law that we forget there are places even in London where the one never penetrates and the other goes but seldom. And to get, by mischance, into one of these places means that the getter-in must entirely reorganize his notions of things in general and adjust his point of view to meet the case. Moreover, he must do this quickly. For some people the shock of the change is too much. They lose their heads for a time, or for ever. The new knowledge swamps them. The brain, suffering from an indigestion of sensation, gives way. That is the simple psychology of the matter.

Fortunately for Nellie, being weak and weary, she merely fainted. And then gradually coming to, she grasped the situation by degrees, what time [sic] she had a vision of her typewriter as an infernal machine, with the man who called himself Andrews as a horned devil in charge of it.

More than the death of Mr. Arnhout, more than the peril of Paul English, more than her own danger, it was the falseness of Andrews which affected her. For she had trusted him.

The torment of her reverie was suddenly interrupted by a slight noise in the region of the faintly-glimmering square. There were movements, and then the thin clatter of falling glass in the darkness, and a body slipped down the wall and landed with a thud of boots on the ground. Nellie screamed. The dim outline of the owner of the boots seemed familiar to her. There was an ineffectual attempt to strike a match.

"Cuss!" This viciously.

Another attempt, and a vesta flared in the cubicle. The two examined each other, Nellie on the floor, the visitant standing.

"Nellie!"

"Paul!"

(Up to now it had always been Miss Crane, Mr. English; but circumstances alter cases.)

He bent down to her, and her head was in his arms, and in a moment she was crying, and exquisitely, painfully happy, and her interest in him had ceased to be maternal.

The match burnt on the floor, and went out. But she had seen his shrewd, careless, open face, and his curling yellow hair.

"What in heaven's name is all this?" he burst out. "I was out on the quay at Ostende this morning—hadn't been to bed"—she thought of the "Cercle privée" at the Kursaal—"and I saw you get off the *Swift* with a strange-looking fellow and run with him on to the *Flandre* just as it was starting. I was too surprised to do anything, and besides there wasn't time. But I felt sure something was up. Another steamer followed the *Flandre* immediately to meet the holiday traffic at Dover, so I took it, and I got there soon after you. I came up to Victoria in the same train as you, and I followed your hansom in another one. You see, I'd no right to intrude till I knew something. Immediately you got to this street and entered this house, I knew the fellow was fishy. This street's a bad 'un. I tried to follow you in, but an old hag at the door wouldn't let me. So I went round to the back, and, well—I got in anyhow, and here I am. What's up?"

"Paul," she said, "what are the 'Dragons of the Night'? And oh! don't you know about Mr. Arnhout?"

"'Dragons of the Night!'" His tone altered. "That's the great Anarchist society. What about the old guv'nor?"

"Mr. Arnhout has been murdered, and we are in the clutches of the Dragons."

Then, as he struck match after match, she recounted to him the whole story. He listened in silence, except at one point, when he exploded:

"What! You went straight off to warn me! Well, of all the splendid—! And I never guessed. Go on, go on."

* * * *

The door was opened, and the two Italian brothers entered, followed by a third man.

"Oh, Paul! These are the two!" the girl cried, and clung to him—blinking in the sudden light.

He sprang forward, but they overpowered him, and in an instant, as it seemed, his limbs were bound. The curious thing was that none of the three Anarchists appeared much surprised at the sight of Paul. They looked up at the broken glass in the wall—it gave on a staircase—nodded to each other, and escorted their prisoners—Paul fuming and threatening, the girl white and silent—into the council chamber, where Nellie had originally been interrogated. The third man held a revolver and had charge of the mobilisation. He placed Paul on one side of the room near the fireplace and Nellie on the other. Then, with the two brothers, he sat down, putting the revolver in its old place—on the telegrams.

Nellie started to see Andrews occupying the fourth chair at the table. He looked steadfastly at a paper in front of him. His eyes were dull.

"Now let's have an end to this nonsense," Paul said. "What are you going to do? You'll suffer for this."

"It is due to you dat I should explain," the elder of the two brothers replied judicially. "I am president of the great and powerful society, The Dragons of the Night, and I am feared in the police bureaux of seven European capitals. Anarchism—but I will not trouble you with an explanation of the theory which is our religion. Let me only say, that for us that theory is sound, sacred. You do not tink so. But it will be no matter. To proceed: We have our schemes, and our schemes need money; for if one makes war on society one must use the weepons of society. When we need money we get it—from capitalists, those human fiends who rob the fatherless and grind the faces of the poor. Dat is in the Bibel. In this inst*ance* we selected Henry Arnhout to supply money, and he did supply it—through the perzuazi-on of my excellent fellow-councillor." Here he pointed to the third man, who raised his brows and shrugged his narrow shoulders. "People will say dat he was murdered. Well, he was *re*moved and the eart' is better for his loss. May others follow Henry Arnhout. We got the money, and there would have been no trouble if you, Nellie Crane, had not stayed late at your office yestairday, and discovered by accident the affair. The resspectahble corpse would have been so quietly taken away at night, and dat would have been the end. But it was not the end. You, Nellie Crane, knew, and it was ne'ssary to *ar*range. My excellent fellow councilor, Dennis," he pointed to Andrews, "followed you—"

Here the spurious detective suddenly glanced up at Nellie. Again his eyes had the appealing look in them; but the tremendous contempt of her silent stare shattered him, and he bent his head once more. Then murmuring something in

Italian to the other three, he went quickly from the room.

"Followed you," the orator continued, "and ver' cleverly brought you back from Ostende before you had opened your mouth. Good so far. With you we might have *ar*ranged. We might have contrived a means to be merciful. But yet again we are meddled. By some means you, Paul English, poke your nose into our private business; you force yourself into this building, and—from Nellie Crane, presumably—you learn all. Two outsiders now share with us a secret of which the knowledge should be fatal. There is only one remedy—death; death for Paul English and Nellie Crane!"

The cold, steady, impassive, brutal tones ceased, and the three men in the arm-chairs looked at their victims. In the short awed silence that followed Dennis crept back into the room and resumed his seat, always avoiding the glance of the girl who had been his dupe.

Paul English opened his mouth in furious protest, struggling to free his bound limbs.

"What!" he cried. "You would murder a woman, you—"

"Why not?" was the calm rejoinder. Women are ressponsible for the state of society which it is our sacred mission to altair. And what, after all, is a woman? Like a man, she is in our sight a unit—a ting to be used or thrown away. We have not time to pity women, the origin of every evil on the planet! It is death for both, my colleagues, is it not?"

"Yes," said the speaker's brother.

"Yes," said the murderer of Henry Arnhout.

"Yes," whispered Dennis.

There was a noise in the passage.

"What is dat?" asked the chief.

"It is the police; I have just been to fetch them," Dennis answered quietly, at the same time reaching over for the revolver. He looked full at Nellie, and then at his friends. "I have betrayed you, my colleagues. I have broken the solemn oaths of our society—and I have done it for a woman. Ah!

"THERE WAS NOISE IN THE PASSAGE."

Moonlight and the sea and a girl's face! What is a man when he ranges himself against these? A few hours ago, in a foolish madness, I swore to that girl that I was on her side. A hundred times since I have tried to persuade myself that the oath was nothing—a mere form to enable me to carry on our work. But I cannot stand in her presence and be false to it—I cannot—I cannot. Colleagues, I have betrayed you and the society, and I die!"

He put the revolver between his eyes and fired, and fell across the table, and the legs of the table scraped along the floor. At the same instant a group of constables rushed into the room.

"Moonlight and the sea and a girl's face!" Nellie repeated under her breath, and then, with a cry, flung herself into Paul's arms. The police had cut him free.

NOTES

1. *Hearth and Home*. 1st December 1898, pages 118-121. Signed E.A. Bennett, Author of *A Man from the North*. Illustrated by Shepperton.

The journal began publication in May 1891, and ran until January 1914, before merging with *Vanity Fair*. Bennett wrote for it from September 1897 until November 1903.

2. The Lamport and Hill Line was founded in 1845 by W.L. Lamport and George Holt (brother of Alfred Holt of the Blue Funnel Line). By the time of Bennett's story both brothers had died and the firm was a limited company with twelve new ships delivered or under construction. Sailings were made to Valparaiso, Chile, in the 1880s.

3. Probably a Remington 6 typewriter, made in 1894, the most popular of all Remington models. In the early 1890s a Remington brochure claimed that more than 100,000 of their typewriters were in use, compared with 40,000 of all other brands combined.

4. The Fabian Society, founded in 1884, advocated a policy of gradual social and political reform, as opposed to revolutionary action. *Woman* started as a moderate feminist paper with the motto "Forward! But Not Too Fast".

THE GREAT FIRE AT SANTA CLAUS' HOUSE.[1]

It was Christmas Eve.

All the children in London were asleep, but something caused Jack and Tommy Martin, who lived at 99, Domesday Street, to wake up at the same moment.

"We must dress quickly," said Jack, the eldest.

"Yes," said Tommy.

And so, without a candle—the moon shone in at the window, they flung themselves into their clothes. They didn't know why they did this: they simply felt that they had to do it.

"Come on," said Tommy, and they were out on the landing. There they met their two sisters, Lizzie and Annie, both younger than themselves, and both fully dressed, too. This in itself ought to have been surprising, yet none of the four felt in the least surprised. It seemed right.

"We must creep downstairs," said Lizzie.

And they crept downstairs ever so softly.

"We will put comforters round our necks," little Annie said. "It is freezing hard."

"Yes, yes."

Then Jack, the tallest, undid the latch of the front door, and they ran lightly down the front steps and so into the street. At the house opposite lived the Ravenshaws, and a little higher up on the same side the Pinkertons, and still higher up the Flacks. And just as the Martin children ran down *their* steps the Ravenshaw children ran down *their* steps, and the Pinkertons down theirs, and the Flacks down theirs.

There were twelve of them:—

The four Martins already mentioned; Alice and Mary Ravenshaw; Willie, Harry and Ernest Pinkerton; Percy, Jane and Jemima Flack: six boys and six girls.

"Hurry," called the Pinkerton boys, "we must catch that 'bus."

The 'buses went along the main road which ran past the end of the street. The 'bus to which the Pinkertons had pointed stopped for them, and one after another they clambered on.

"Let's go inside, it's so cold," the little Flack girls cried,

Jack undid the latch.

but the conductor stopped them.

"No," he said, "it's full inside."

Now all the children could see quite well that there was absolutely no one inside the 'bus. However, they didn't argue, but went at once on top, and the 'bus started.

The streets were brilliantly lighted, and the shops full of good things, and there were thousands of people walking about—grown-up people, that is to say. The children wondered what time grown-up people went to bed. The boys noticed that the men flourished sticks and smoked, and the girls noticed that the women carried purses in their hands and wore veils. And each thought how fine it was to be able to do these things.

Presently the 'bus went quicker and quicker and quicker. Then Jack Martin observed something.

"I say," he shouted to the others, "have you noticed there isn't a driver to this 'bus?"

And sure enough there wasn't. The horses were flying along—and no reins, no whip. Yet somehow the children weren't frightened.

"Hadn't we better tell the conductor that there's no driver?" suggested Annie Martin. She was a thoughtful child.

"Yes," said Percy Flack. "Here, Jemima, you're nearest, run down and tell him there's no driver."

Little Jemima went hurriedly down, the 'bus jolting her, and her heart beating. In a moment she came back.

"The conductor's gone, too," she twittered like a little bird, "and—and—it's full inside."

"What sort of people?" Percy asked.

"Not people, but something else," she said, solemnly.

"Never mind," the others said, and the 'bus flew faster and faster.

Soon they went across a big square with huge buildings all about.

"That's the Houses of Parliament with the clock tower.

Look, it's ten o'clock," Jack Martin explained. He had travelled. As they flew by, the clock face opened and a man put his head out.

"Lord Salisbury![2] we know his beard!" they cried.

And it was Lord Salisbury, and this time they were just a little surprised.

"Good luck. Get on! Get on!" shouted Lord Salisbury, and then popped his head in, and the clock face went back, and it was ten o'clock again.

They were dashing along the Strand now at a terrific pace, and they noticed that all the grown-up people stood still to watch them pass, clapping and cheering; and all the other 'buses and cabs and vans drew up at the sides of the road so as to give them a free passage.

The next thing was that all the twelve children at once began to roar in deep, hoarse voices, and then Tommy Martin bawled out,

"We aren't on a 'bus at all; we're on a fire-engine. Look! here's the funnel!" And sure enough there it was stuck up at the front, and shining like glass. "And we've got brass helmets on, and axes in our belts." And so they had, girls and all.

"Hooray!" they yelled.

Then they passed the Mansion House. And on the steps of the Mansion House stood the Lord Mayor and his beautiful daughter the Lady Mayoress, both dressed in their official robes. And these two waved their hands and sang out,—

"Quick, quick! You'll be in time yet."

Faster still they flew. Now they were in a long, long street, and at the end of the street they could see a big building with a sign sticking out,—

SANTA CLAUS' HOUSE.

And there were hundreds of windows to this house, and out of every window came a little tongue of flame. The 'bus, or fire-engine rather, got nearer and nearer, and then suddenly it stopped plump—dead sudden, and all the children were thrown over the front, and found themselves standing on the pavement in front of the burning house. And there were no grown-up people to be seen; only themselves.

"To work!" cried Jack Martin, and they turned to the 'bus, or rather the fire-engine, and discovered that it *was* full inside, full of Boiler.

In a very few moments they had got out the hose and connected it with the water-main; the engine began to spit fire, and jump, and throb, and then the water shot out from the hose-pipes, with a grand *Z z z z p*. There were three hose-pipes and these were held by the two Martin boys and Willie Pinkerton. The girls piled coal in the furnace of the engine, and the other fellows stood by with their axes. The fire had now obtained a good hold on Santa Claus' house. The flames roared and sent a great light far up into the sky, and the heat was tremendous. It was an exciting scene, but all the children kept their heads steady, and appeared to know exactly what to do and how to do it. The water spouted up into the top windows, and you could hear it go *fizz* as it met the fire.

Then little Jemima shouted out suddenly, and the others noticed that her chubby face was black with coal.

"Look, look! There's poor old Santa Claus at the attic window."

And there the venerable old man was. Santa Claus put his hands round his mouth, and called in his magnificent voice:

"My children, some of you must hasten to the back of the house and get the reindeer out of the stables. You can carry the presents out that way. The fire is burning less fiercely at the back."

Without waiting to hear more, Harry and Ernest Pinkerton and the two Ravenshaw girls scurried off according to directions.

"And now a fire-escape before I perish," Santa Claus cried.

"The fire-escape, the fire-escape—where is it?" the

children shouted, but there was no fire-escape. That was the one thing wanting. Horror! Despair! Was it possible that Santa Claus would be burnt to death?

Just then one of the horses turned its head, and said quietly to Jack Martin:

"Get the Waterproof Plasters."

"Of course! How silly of us!" Jack exclaimed.

And Jack rushed to get the Waterproof Plasters from the box behind the engine.

"Here, Tom and Willie, come and have these stuck on your backs! Here, girls, take the hose a bit."

What with the roar of the flames, the throb-throb of the engine, and the hissing of the water, Jack had to shout pretty hard. He stuck the round plasters on the backs of Tom and Willie, and then called to Harry Pinkerton, who was leading some reindeer into the street, "Harry, you take one hose, I'll take another, and we'll hoist these chaps up. Lean backwards, Tom and Willie."

So Jack Martin and Harry Pinkerton took the hose and directed the full force of the water at the Waterproof Plasters on the backs of Tommy and Willy, and these two rose in the air on the columns of water, up, up, to the attic where Santa Claus was.

Santa Claus put an arm round the shoulder of each and slipped off the window-sill.

"Gently, gently," the old gentleman cried.

"Now, Lizzie and Annie," directed Jack Martin, "turn the taps off slowly."

The force of the water gradually decreased, and in this manner Santa Claus, supported by Tommy and Willy, who lay on their backs on the two columns of water, safely descended to the ground.

"My children," he said, gravely, "you have saved my life by your heroic efforts, and I shall never forget it. Not only *I* am indebted to you, but also all children over the whole earth. For think what would have happened if I had perished! There would have been no more Christmas presents. I thank you from my heart."

Whereat they all blushed with pleasure under the grime of coal-dust that was on their cheeks.

The hose was still playing on the fire, and with old Santa to help and encourage them the children soon had the fire under control. Moreover, the reindeer had been led out into the street, and the presents were being carried forth and stacked up in huge piles on the opposite pavement. There you could see every imaginable toy, game, puzzle, and useful thing that ever was, is, or will be.

At last Percy dropped his hose, and said modestly to Santa Claus: "Your house is ruined, but the fire is extinguished."

And Harry Pinkerton said:

"The reindeer are safe."

And Alice Ravenshaw said:

"We have carried out all the presents, and not one is broken."

"But my sleigh, my sleigh?" he inquired.

Off like a shot ran Harry, and dragged it from the stables. Only one corner was a little charred.

Then the old man said:

"Once more, dear children, I thank you. My reindeer are scathless, and my store of presents is complete. True, my house is burnt out; but I can build a new one for next Christmas, and this time I will build it not of bricks, but of Love, for in that commodity you have made me rich; and it will never burn again. And now, you must start homewards."

"May we not see *you* start?" little Jemima asked.

"No, little one. No mortal eye may see me when I mount my sleigh, and with a pile of presents behind, flick with my long whip the manes of my reindeer. Good-bye, good-bye!"

And he blessed all the children, saying:

"Once more, dear children, I thank you."

"Christ bless you."

And they jumped on the fire-engine, and the horses broke into a gallop. The streets were silent and empty now, for it was very late; or rather, I should say, it was Christmas morning.

Just as they got in sight of the Strand they noticed that they were no longer on a fire-engine but on a 'bus, and their brass helmets had given place to hats and caps, and their axes had disappeared. Soon, very soon, the horses galloped less furiously, fell into a trot, and then stopped opposite the end of Domesday Street. The children went down the steps. The conductor was standing on the platform, and the inside was empty.

"Good night," said the conductor.

"Good night," they answered.

And ran off to their homes and crept upstairs and undressed, washed themselves, and got into bed, and slept—slept hard.

Slept, slept hard.

NOTES

1. *Woman*. 7th December 1898, pages 1-3. The story appears in "The Children's Supplement" to the *Woman* Christmas number. Signed E.A. Bennett. Illustrated by Adrian Field.
2. Lord Salisbury (1830-1903) became leader of the Conservative Party following Disraeli's death in 1881. He was thrice Prime Minister, his third administration running from June 1893 June 1902.

THE ROMANCE OF BOBBY LEMPRIERE.[1]
PART I.

His two grandmothers settled it all between them. His mother was a poor, weak thing, wrapped up in her own health, and, moreover, abroad, so she was not even consulted.

"He is such a dear boy," they said, "though he is so unfortunately plain, and always in scrapes or in debt. He means well, but he is instability and impressionability itself, and easily influenced. He ought to have had some profession—we told Louisa so. Only, with his uncle in such a shaky state, it hardly seemed worth while, when he might succeed him at any moment. Marriage is by far the best thing for a young man inclined to be a little wild. Some nice, lively,—Bobby would never stand anything dull—sensible girl, with a head on her shoulders, rather older than himself—and with a little money, shall we say?"

So they cast an eye round all the young ladies of their acquaintance. And soon he was sent to stay down on the river with the Hultons (of Manchester fame) for a few days.

He was rather bored at being persuaded to leave London in June. Miss Hulton was not a beauty, though an awfully jolly girl—up to anything: could play the banjo and sing a comic song to perfection, and ride like a bird. She looked very nice, too, in light flannels and a sailor-hat in the country, if a trifle dairy-maidish at the end of a hot and crowded ball in town. He also afterwards discovered that when she laughed and talked, which she did incessantly, one forgot that her mouth was large, and her nose of the unpiquant, *retroussé* order. Also she moved well, and had an excellent figure. Her people were kindness itself. There was no one else staying with them, and he and Polly seemed to be left alone together a good deal, he found. However, she kept him fully amused and contented, and the few days somehow lengthened themselves out into a week, and the week became a fortnight.

The grandmothers, up in London, smiled and nodded.

Then one evening in the punt—how it came about exactly he never quite knew: whether he had proposed to her or she to him—but that, of course, was impossible; what was he thinking of?

Anyway, when they arrived rather late for dinner they were certainly engaged, and went directly and told the Hulton parents. And there was great rejoicing over him.

The next day he flew up to town and broke the news to both his grandmothers; and they were quite delighted, and so surprised, they said!

They chaffed him, too, awfully at the club, and he rather enjoyed it. "What! little Beetroots and Carrots, with his sandy hair and pink face, going to marry Polly Hulton, the great heiress?" And they said, "Did Polly ask 'Beetroots,' or did 'Beetroots'ask Polly? Which was it?"

Odd again, wasn't it? He didn't care about that so much. But then Polly was always up to her jokes. And so popular! Half the young men about town knew her so intimately, they called her by her Christian name to her face.

She had any amount of great, great friends amongst his male acquaintances.

"Fancy little 'Beetroots' carrying off Polly Hulton before them all! Lucky dog!"

And they all laughed, and slapped him on the back, and he laughed too.

"Of course he was a lucky dog, and Polly was far and away too good for him."

So, for the next week, Bobby and Polly paraded at every "function" in town as "the engaged couple." And they had a real good time, and no end of fun together.

But at the end of seven days' felicity he received one of the periodical telegrams from his hypochondriacal mother, at Chamounix: "Come at once. I am worse."

He was very much upset, and rushed about from his

grandmothers to Polly, and from Polly to his grandmothers.

They said: "It really was very sad. Too tiresome of Louisa. But they supposed he must go."

So he went and said good-bye to his Polly, very much down on his luck, and kissed her affectionately on both cheeks.

"This has happened before, old girl," he said. "It means nothing. I shall be back by return of post."

And he went off sadly by the mail train.

He hated travelling, and he hated being abroad, and he could speak no language decently but his own. Also, I am afraid, he was not very fond of his mother. And Chamounix is such an impossible, un-get-at-able place. So when, after journeying night and day, another telegram met him at Martoban in the Rhone Valley—"I am better. Coming back by easy stages. Stay where you are"—there is no doubt he stamped about his uncarpeted hotel bedroom and swore. "To be stuck in that hole for probably a week, in the middle of the season, it really was—" He was barely twenty-one, and still thoroughly enjoyed the way in which society appreciated him, or, perhaps, to be more correct, his prospects. When he grew calmer, he threw open the window and hung out of it, wondering how on earth he was going to amuse himself there for a week. Then he strolled into the public room and found an English paper six weeks old; from thence into the coffee-room, where there were dismal tables spread with not over-clean cloths and fantastic napkins all ready for *table d'hôte*. He groaned, and went out-of-doors. The little town was all asleep in the mid-day sun—white road, dirty houses, and many smells.

He wandered down to where the milky river, white from many glaciers, raced through the village to meet the Rhone, and was crossed by a wooden bridge with its picturesque roof sloping down to the water. Here he paused and threw many small stones into the stream, much too cross to notice any local attractions. After about half an hour, he raised himself with an impatient sigh, walked from under the bridge and surveyed the country. There was the church to his left, on rising ground, overlooking the town—whitewashed, with an extinguisher-crowned tower, and the church-yard was carpeted with faint-coloured pink instead of grass, but otherwise did not seen to afford any particular attraction or peculiarity. Straight up high in front of him, on an isolated and unpremeditated-looking rock, stood an ugly round tower, of no apparent architectural or historical object or age. He walked towards it aimlessly, and began to climb the rough and broken path of the hill, deep in his own indignant thoughts—flicking viciously and unseemingly at the pink, star-like sedums that somehow had found a hold in the bare rock for their neat round coil of blue-bloomed leaves.

He stumped doggedly on and up till he was brought to an abrupt standstill by the wall on the summit, and an untidy wooden door up a flight of steps.

He ran up them. The door was on the latch, and he found himself in a small, high-walled yard partly paved with cobble-stones, and with bright green tubs of oleanders standing about here and there. The base of the tower in this enclosure had all the appearance of an ordinary dwelling-house. Small latticed windows, open door, a spinning wheel and empty chair, and a cat on the threshold. A buxom old woman, in a very *négligé* cotton bed jacket and sabots, was sousing some linen up and down in a large pail set on a stool.

He dropped his stick in surprise, and stood open-mouthed. The old woman looked up at the noise, and, wringing her sodden hands, came forward, smiling.

"Monsieur est venu voir le chateau? The view—but it will be *superbe* this afternoon! The finest view to be had anywhere in the valley of the Rhone. Gretchen!" she called, without waiting for his halting, "Gretchen!"

Bobby turned round, and there, in the doorway, stood Gretchen, a very pretty child, apparently about thirteen, with a small Madonna like face, slightly tanned by the sun, very large pathetic eyes, and a long fringe of silky fair hair, almost sweeping her eyebrows.

"Gretchen," said the old lady, "take the Monsieur to the 'summet' of the tower. Give him the opera-glasses. Show him the view. Make him inscribe his name in the book"

"Oui, Gran'mère."

She was knitting, and did not look up, but simply turned for him to follow. Then he noticed her plaits which fell down her back nearly to the hem of her striped skirt.

"What hair!" he thought; "Polly couldn't do it, or anything near it!"

She led him through several doors and up a spiral staircase, lighted at intervals by narrow loopholes, giving him at the same time a rapid description of the tower, in which there was some vague allusion to "erige au douzieme siecle," ending with what sounded like "les Romans." But he was too absorbed in her hair and neat ankles—rough stockings notwithstanding—to notice any discrepancies.

At the top was a small kind of observatory, with a little table, a large ink-bottle, and a still larger visitors' book; also a telescope on legs, and a very indifferent pair of opera-glasses.

The view, if not "superbe," was, at least, extensive, both up and down the Rhone Valley.

She pointed out the various objects of interest gravely, in the most charming patois.

"There was the great river, monsieur might perceive 'a l'oeil nu'—all milky-white from the glacier torrents. There, too, he could just see far away the blue waters of the Lake of Geneva. That was the village of Visp. It was about there that the road would pass through the mountain to Zermatt, and the road to Chamounix was close by to the right."

"Es-cur voos avvy jammy etay a Chamounix ?" he asked, breaking through the shyness of the Gallic tongue.

"Non, monsieur, jamais."

"A Geneva?"

"A Geneva? Non, monsieur, never out of the valley of the Rhone. Will monsieur have the bonté to inscribe his name? Gran'mère is very particular about that."

She opened the book and dipped the pen in the ink.

What dear little hands! Strong and rather brown, but so very, very small. He wondered how old she really was; she hardly seemed quite a child.

He took the pen and scrawled, "Robert George Lempriere, London, England."

She turned over the leaves of the book, looking for a piece of blotting-paper, and as she leant over the table one of her plaits fell over her shoulder and on to the page, smudging the writing beyond all deciphering.

"Oh, monsieur!" she said, clasping her hands in horror, "what have I done? Oh, comme j'étais stupide. Pardon, mille pardons!"

What a lovely face when it had a little colour in it! What liquid blue eyes!

He became a great deal redder than she was, and stammered:

"Ne le mentionnez pas, mademoiselle, ne le mentionnez pas!"

"What will my grandmother say?" she said, standing before him with her hands still clasped, and her eyes very wide open.

What long lashes! and her eyebrows looked as if they had been drawn with a very dark lead-pencil.

"Will she be angry, the old brute?" he said, relapsing by mistake into his native language.

He could not think of "angry" in French, and so was obliged to repeat it again:

"Ne le mentionnez pas, sar ne fay ree-ang."

She applied the blotting-paper to it in great distress.

"Si maladroite! How could I be so maladroite? May I trouble the monsieur to write his name again?"

He sat down and wrote once more, "Robert George Lempriere."

And if Robert George Lempriere No. 1 had been scrawlly, Robert George Lempriere No. 2 was also extremely agitated.

* * * *

"It is odd that we haven't heard from Bobby for so long," said his paternal to his maternal grandmother. "He wrote last, if you remember, from Martoban, very angry with Louisa for changing her mind, and keeping him there for some days. But they must have met long ago by now. And I suppose he is tied too tightly on to her apron-strings to be allowed to write letters even, poor boy! I know the sort of life he leads when he is with his mother."

"Louisa may be fanciful, but she is my daughter, please remember Maria," said the other.

"I beg your pardon, my dear, I'm sure," answered the paternal grandmother. "I forgot at the moment."

But Polly Hulton had also not heard from Bobby for a fortnight, and she thought it not only odd but unkind. And she let him know it, too, several times, and then she maintained a dignified silence, and hoped his letters to her were lost.

And, in the meantime, Bobby, as his grandmothers, and Polly, and London in general knew him, had quite disappeared from the face of the earth, and there was in his stead at Martoban, in the Rhone Valley, a Bobby who lived and slept and walked in the clouds, who had completely forgotten his past, and was oblivious as to his future. Who disappeared all day and came back at casual and impossible hours for his meals, and then knew not whether he dined off *sauerkraut* and *lager-biere* or nectar and ambrosia. A Bobby to whom the whole world consisted only of a high-walled yard, pink oleanders in green tubs, a spinning-wheel, and—Gretchen!

It was really too absurd! Little boys with red hair and pink faces, and the nickname of "Beetroots and Carrots," only make themselves appear ridiculous under these circumstances.

Their exteriors do not admit of high-flown romance becoming them gracefully. One must be cast in a romantic mould outwardly, as well as inwardly, to command sympathy under the sometimes rather trying influence of strong emotions.

Who would have thought it of him? Who would have believed it after the sensible, matter-of-fact manner in which he had been brought up, and from his former choice of companions and mode of life? Where in his flippety, everyday young heart had his germ of medieval madness been hidden away all these twenty-one years?

And there they all were in England, quite unconscious of the calamity that had engulfed him, thinking him too encumbered by "Louisa's" apron-strings to write. While "Louisa," having intimated that she had again changed her plans, and was returning slowly the other way by Geneva, stopped some days in Paris, and imagined him already safe in high-hat and patent-leather on the London pavements.

There he was, sitting on the stone steps below the spinning-wheel, quite happy, quite uncaring.

There he had been yesterday, and the day before; there he would also be to-morrow and the day after, and to all appearances the day after that again.

She was sixteen, he had discovered. It was only her extreme slightness and smallness of make, and the glorious plaits that gave her at first appearance so very juvenile an air. What was the charm? She was very pretty, with an extreme sweetness of manner and inborn courtesy that might well pass for refinement and breeding. But she represented to him a hitherto unknown and unimagined type of young-womanhood—the embodiment of an ideal that he seemed unconsciously to have entertained, and, perhaps, sought for in vain in a vague way all his life—a fair, gentle soul, simple and sincere, set on a pedestal as far from him and his as the sky from the earth, high above all worldliness and frivolity, all chaff and slang, to be loved reverentially with her mystic eyes and deep rooted, religious faith.

If she had been English she would probably have left out her "h's," and have outraged a cultivated eye by the blending of many colours in her dress. But a foreign language—even though it be the broadest patois—covers all defects of grammar and expression to one but slightly acquainted with it in any form. And a striped petticoat, a velvet body, and a white chemisette have a fascination of their own, even though they are of the coarsest material and shabby.

He wound her yarn for her. He understood all the mechanism of the spinning-wheel. He made friends with the grandmother; he even proffered humble overtures to the solemn cat. Also his French became rapidly more fluent.

The grandmother shrugged her shoulders, and paid no attention to his daily and prolonged visitations. He never failed to produce the prescribed 30 centimes for the privilege of the "superbe" view and the use of the indifferent opera-glasses, though he had long since given up the form of mounting the tower and availing himself of either.

"Ills sont droles, les Anglais!" was all the old lady remarked, and went about her work.

To Gretchen he read poetry; English, of course. Bobby, who had never been known to open a book, actually unearthed a dilapidated volume of Tennyson from the public room of the hotel, and carried it about in his pocket. Life seemed to have become all poems, all romance, all dreams.

"O sweet, pale Margaret,
O rare, pale Margaret."[2]

With "eyes of tearful power" you could not appreciate it very much, could you, seeing that you did not understand one word? But you always stopped your wheel or your knitting whilst he read, and sat listening with polite interest, your little hands clasped demurely in your lap. And when you felt quite sure he had come to the end you would say quite prettily, "Merci, monsieur; c'est très joli!" and begin your work again.

And though you never inquired what it was about, Bobby seemed quite satisfied.

She must have thought him "un peu fou," this young Englishman, all the time!

He told her a great many things about England and London—to him it seemed a far-off dream, a story of the long past—and in this she was deeply interested, specially in parts concerning "les demoiselles Anglaises," and the manner of their clothes.

She was also very deferential, very quiet and grave. She rarely smiled, but when she did Bobby held his breath in enchantment. It came slowly, first in her eyes, and then gradually curved her mouth into surpassing sweetness, and there appeared on one cheek an unexpected dimple that he could have fallen down before, quoting,—

> "The very smile before you speak,
> That dimples your transparent cheek,
> Encircles all the heart."

PART II.

Long, cloudless summer days up there under the old tower, with the hot sun beating down on the cobbles till midday, and then the little court in pleasant shade from the neighbouring mountains. A deep azure square overhead, and through a narrow loop-hole in the wall—

> They saw the gleaming river seaward flow
> From the inner land, far off, three mountain-tops,
> Three silent pinnacles of aged snow,
> . . . the shadowy pine above the woven copse.[3]

And that was all of the outer world.

Gretchen framed in the doorway, with a distant look in her beautiful eyes, that probably saw only as far as the lizard on the opposite wall.

Gretchen; a cat; a spinning-wheel; sometimes a grandmother; and Bobby Lemprière, lost to all the rest of creation in a blissful sea of love—or madness, which you like. He never ventured to analyse his feelings for her, or look beyond the present; there were no to-morrows, only unreasoning and happy to-days.

One afternoon he persuaded her to take him to see the church, and they clambered down the rock and through the narrow, dirty streets, where the flat-faced, tow-haired women and blue-bloused loungers stared at them agape.

They wandered round the churchyard. He picked her a handful of fragrant and nodding pinks, and gave them to her shyly.

He had never attempted to make love to her all this time. Perhaps it was his unfamiliarity with the language that had restrained him; perhaps he did not know how. Making love to Polly Hulton and to Gretchen would be two very different things. And I don't know that he ever had made love to Polly; they chaffed each other a good deal, but that was all.

Gretchen showed him her mother's and father's graves, and many curiosities in the way of wax flowers in glass cases. They came round a corner suddenly upon a niche in the wall of the church, filled full of cross-bones and skulls neatly piled up, dozens and dozens of them all grinning out. It was rather a shock.

"Ah! Comme c'est horrible!" he exclaimed.

"They dig them up from time to time, monsieur," she said simply—there was nothing remarkable about it to her; "the churchyard is so full."

He stood looking at them with a gruesome fascination and disgust, whilst she absently pulled one of his flowers petal from petal. Generations of peasants who had lived and were still living, down in the town, their stupid lives contentedly, accomplishing little, enjoying little, as we account it, and ending it all like this. And Gretchen was of them too! He looked at her.

Sunlight on her neat, fair head. Eyes downcast. There she would stay in the tower till one of those bebloused boors came and claimed her for his wife, and then she would go and live down in the dirty town with him, and waste her dear little life away in a dull monotony of hard work, month after month, year after year, washing his clothes, cooking his dinner, mending his horrid socks to the end of all time. And she would sleep beside him when her span of years was told—an old woman, worn out, perhaps, with weary toil, and it might be ill-treatment; sleep beside him under the pinks, till she in her turn would be dug up, and put to grin to all eternity amongst that ghastly crew in the time-worn wall. The thought of it made him quite sick.

"Oh, come away, come away!" he said, almost in tears, in his anxiety laying his hand on her arm. "No; I don't want to see the inside of the church. Let us go right away." And they went down the tortuous streets again.

He was very silent. The skulls and cross-bones hung over him like a cloud of evil portent. He accompanied her up to the rock, and to the door of the yard. Then he clambered down again alone, and wandered off into the mountains for many hours. He was building castles and dreaming dreams all the way. He tramped along among the whortleberries. Sometimes on the path and sometimes off, his thoughts turned completely inwards.

Not until it was almost dark did he retrace his steps—coming back into the village with a swinging step; and the cloud of skulls and cross-bones wholly dispersed as the clock struck nine. He had formed his resolution. There was an intense happiness on his plain face.

By very force of habit he found himself turning over the bridge in the direction of the tower. Dear little noisy river! how he had hated it that first day, and thrown stones at it viciously, and been so bored! He laughed now at the thought.

He had never visited them so late. But they always made him welcome. He would just look in and say "Good-night"—not interrupt their humble supper; just say "Good-night," and that was all, and then to-morrow—to-morrow! His heart beat very fast.

*　　　*　　　*　　　*

There was just light enough to clamber up the familiar rough path. The crazy yard-door was wide open, and as he set foot in it he heard Gretchen laugh from within the house. Never could he remember having heard her laugh before. She, too, had caught his gaiety and lightness of heart. She, too, perhaps, felt a glad foreboding of to-morrow.

He went up the stone steps to the kitchen door, and then stood still. There, certainly, was Gretchen. The room was all ablaze with fire and candles—and she was still laughing; her face, in fact, was alight with happiness and charming, dimpled smiles. And—he could hardly believe his eyes—she was leaning against the table; and sitting on it, holding both her hands, was a large, black-bearded man in the inevitable blue blouse.

That was all he saw, and then everything began to swim. The old grandmother came out, and stumbled over him in the darkness, as he was propped against the door post.

"Mais, monsieur!" she exclaimed.

"Qui-est-ça?" he said, faintly, pointing in the direction of the blouse.

"Oh, c'est le fiancé de Gretchen, who comes from arriving unexpectedly. He is menuisier[4] at Lausanne. Will monsieur not do them the honour to enter?"

But "monsieur" had stumbled out at the stone steps, and was crashing down the hill, quite regardless of his neck.

By the time he had arrived at the bottom he had remembered that there is really such a place as England, and a London of grand-mothers, and high hats, and clubs, and civilization, and—oh, terrible beyond words—of Polly Hultons!

Arcadia was at an end.

He walked unsteadily along the road to his hotel, standing whitewashed, green-shuttered in the moonlight. He went to his own room, shut the door, and flung himself down, half in, half out of the window, with his face buried in his arms.

Oh, hateful river, with its all penetrating cracked voice! It seemed to be running in his own head. Surely she might have given him one hint—one word. A little sooner it would not have been so bad. But to-day of all days! It was very cruel. Could she have been so blind? Though he had spoken no word, she must have seen, surely, how he loved her. But she was so young, perhaps she did not understand. It must have been that; she did not see what it all meant. So this was the end of it all! What he had foreseen in the churchyard was already in near fulfilment. He had been mad—for how long? When did it begin? He could not quite tell—about three weeks. Quite mad! And now he was gradually becoming sane again, and he did not at all enjoy the recovery of his senses.

His mother! His grandmothers! And—a thousand times worse than all—*Polly*!

No, he could not face them again. He would telegraph to his mother. He would say he wanted to travel and see the Continent. It would do him good. It would enlarge his mind. It had ever been his most ardent desire. Anything—anything in the world, only he could not and would not go back and face them all.

Beyond that, for the moment, he did not get; nothing mattered much, only he could not stay there, and he would not go home.

Polly!—he loathed her very name. Her bouncing figure, her high coloured face ("blowsy," he called it in his bitterness) rose up before him and he groaned aloud!

Oh, little peasant Gretchen! Will that great hulking lout ever appreciate all your pretty ways, your gentle charm? Would not any one of those tow-haired, flat-faced, large-waisted maidens from the village have been all the same to him? Oh, many times blessed and happy lout! Oh, most miserable and ill-starred Bobby!

A solicitous and greasy waiter knocked at the door. "It is

late, but monsieur has not dined. The table-d'hôte has long been over; but— "

"Monsieur does not want to dine."

It would indeed be sauerkraut and bière to-night!

"Monsieur is not ill?"

"No, monsieur is not ill."

But monsieur seemed very surly. The waiter was sympathetic, and shut the door gently, and went away. "C'est la maladie du coeur, pauvre garçon!" he said to himself, beating his left side dramatically; "ah, je la connais aussi, moi!"

Bobby got up and lit a candle. It was no good, he must go home. He sat down on a chair and reviewed his situation.

There were all their tiresome letters that had come bothering from time to time—piles of them—on the dressing-table. What were they all about? He had not the very vaguest notion. Some of them he had even forgotten to open. He tore them up wildly, and stuffed them into the stove. Well, they would have him back amongst them again in about two days.

He packed his portmanteau in a dazed way with trembling hands. He had only half regained his senses. Between London and Arcadia— between Gretchen and her spinning-wheel and Polly and her banjo— there, was indeed a great gulf.

Forty-eight hours later a haggard and wild-eyed "Beetroots and Carrots" descended on to a London platform with an expression of set tragedy stamped upon his round, young face. He drove to his rooms and straightway dressed himself with scrupulous care in his London clothes. Then he went out and sought the abode of Polly Hulton.

His knees knocked together as he walked up the well-known staircase.

How do fellows get through these sort of scenes? How do they break these ghastly kind of things?

Miss Hulton was very much at home, and alone. Hardly had the servant closed the door behind him than she sprang from the recesses of a large chair and seized him by both shoulders, almost shaking him—she was by far the taller of the two.

"Bobby!" she cried, surprise mingled with reproach, "*where have* you been all this time? Why did you never write? It really was *too* bad of you!"

He freed himself from her grasp.

"I—have—been—at—Martoban, in—the—Rhone—Valley," he said, jerking out the words slowly.

"What! You don't mean to say your mother stuck there all this time?"

They had both sat down. She was watching him intently. He was much changed; he looked a great deal older.

"I have not seen my mother," he said, almost inaudibly.

"*You have not seen your mother*? Then what on earth made you stay at Martoban for over three weeks? I thought it was all mosquitoes and smells. Why, you were furious at first being kept there only a day or two! Were there mosquitoes?"

He gazed all round the cornice, and up at the struggling cupids on the ceiling. Then he looked her straight in the face, and said calmly, "I haven't the *least* idea."

"I don't believe you've been at Martoban at all," she said, suspiciously.

"Oh, very well. I can show you my hotel bills, if it will give you any satisfaction," he answered grimly.

They sat looking at each other in silence.

"Bobby," she said at last, "what is the matter with you?"

He shrugged his shoulders, and said airily, "Nothing."

"Well, but *something* must have kept you at Martoban," she persisted. "I suppose you found someone you knew?"

Come what might, he was quite determined wild horses should not drag from him any mention of Gretchen.

"There was no one there I had set eyes on before."

"Well, then," she said impatiently, "I suppose you *met* some people you liked. It is all the same thing. Americans probably. A pretty American"—jumping at conclusions rapidly one after the other— "and you went excursions up the mountains with her, all day long, and imagined yourself in love with her, of course! And she led you on, as they always do. Platonic friendship, etc., etc. I know the sort of thing! I don't mind your amusing yourself, goodness knows! But you might at least have written. You are not to be trusted out of my sight for a day! And we had only been engaged for a week! It really was *too* bad of you!"

"There were no Americans and no English," he answered desperately; "nothing of the kind. You are completely wrong. I was mad for a little while out there, that was all— off my head, I think! I can't tell you anything more. But now, as you see" —with an attempt at a smile— "I am clothed and in my right mind again. And what I have come to say—that is, to tell you"—he got up and began to walk about— "to explain, to— to say— I mean—" All his carefully-prepared speech had forsaken him.

"To tell me! To say, to explain!" she repeated, mercilessly; "to say—*what*?"

The extreme gravity of the situation had not in the least dawned upon her.

"To say— to explain—" he stammered; "that is, to ask you—to ask you"— he dropped into a chair, his courage completely deserting him— "to ask you how you are getting on with your skirt-dancing?[5]" with a gasp and a rush.

* * * *

The Morning Post, July 28th:—'The marriage arranged between Miss Polly Hulton and Mr. Robert Lemprière will not take place, as announced."

* * * *

One afternoon, in Piccadilly, his best friend overtook him, and caught him by the arm, and said, "Look here, old chap; you'd much better tell me all about it. You'll feel ever so much better. It shan't go any further, if you wish. Only don't go about any longer looking like a lost dog, and cutting all your acquaintances."

"There is nothing to tell," said Bobby, evasively.

"No, of course not. There never is when a fellow goes and buries himself in some unheard-of place abroad, and then comes back and jilts the girl he's engaged to, for no rhyme or reason that anyone can discover. Out with it, like a man. I know those Americans!" with a voice of personal experience.

Bobby sighed a huge sigh, and began,—

"Well, then, it was at Martoban, you know; and I was so wild at being kept waiting for my mother—a beastly little hole, and there was nothing to do. And there was a sort of ruined-tower place on a rock, you know. And I went up it the first afternoon, and she lived up there—"

"I can't imagine an American living in 'a sort of ruined-tower place on a rock'; but go on."

"There was no American at all about it," he said; "she had plaits. I never saw such hair, *never*!" and he wandered on and got very incoherent, and raved a great deal, and quoted Tennyson, and mixed up the grandmother and the cat hopelessly. And Gretchen seemed sometimes to spin pink oleanders, and sometimes green lizards. His friend looked at him in anxious and sorrowful silence.

"I was a *fool*!" he said bitterly, in conclusion.

"I think you were!" answered the other, suppressing a smile.

Little pink-faced, sandy-haired boys, who so far forget the fitness of things as to indulge in sentiment, cannot, in the latter end of the prosaic nineteenth century, even expect sympathy from their best friend. It is really too absurd! What should we all come to if this sort of thing were encouraged?

NOTES

1. *Woman*. Part I published 8th February 1899, pages 10-12; Part II published 15th February 1899, pages 10-12. Unsigned.
2. Alfred Tennyson (1809-1892),"Margaret" (1833).
3. Alfred Tennyson, "The Lotus-eaters" (1833).
4. Carpenter.
5. Skirt-dancing was a popular music hall mixture of ballet steps and acrobatic kicks performed so as to keep the full skirt in motion and display just enough too maintain male interest. Kate Vaughan created the skirt dance at the original Gaiety Theatre around 1876.

THE SCRATCHED FACE.[1]

I.

When Edward Dumayne descended from the boat-train at Charing Cross that hot afternoon of July, he told a porter to put his portmanteau on a cab, and then stood still a moment, twirling that sparse black moustache of his. In his loose travelling attire he looked like a man who not many years ago had been an athlete, and whose abnormally developed muscles were now beginning to be but the framework for a super-structure of fat. And this was the case. Having achieved distinction at Cambridge by means of athletics, he had suddenly put them aside for something more serious. There is not much scope for athletics in Fleet Street, and it was to Fleet Street that Dumayne had devoted his energies. After nine years' labour, he found himself the editor of an extremely modern, smart and epigrammatic evening paper, and rather a personage in those circles where they write.

He was returning from a business mission to Vienna. For three weeks he had been separated from the daily journalism of London, and, returning thus to London, it seemed to him that he felt vaguely interested in the news of the day, as an outsider (that is, a person not a journalist) might feel interested.

So, seeing his porter still patiently waiting at the doors of the luggage van for a chance to seize the portmanteau marked "E. D." in red letters, he sauntered slowly down the platform towards the bookstall. Several people turned to look at him, for he had the air of being a celebrity, in spite of his youth. He was thirty, one of the youngest editors in London.[2] Further, he had but recently engaged himself to marry a young lady whose charm, wit and solid sense were—he was solemnly convinced—unsurpassed in the wide world. (Even editors suffer from the old universal illusions.) What wonder, then, if he appeared a little self-conscious and a little self-satisfied as he traversed the platform? He had been an editor only a year, and engaged only four months.

He mechanically felt in his ticket pocket, and finding only a French penny there, wondered if Messrs. W. H. Smith and Son would accept that coin. He tossed it up meditatively, and just then his eye caught the yellow contents bill of his own paper, *The Afternoon*. In another instant he could read the legend upon it, and the words ran:—

MYSTERIOUS DEATH
OF
LEONA LISS.

He did not stagger; no one could have detected a tremor in his body; but, nevertheless, his heart stood still for a moment. He was conscious of having received the severest shock of his smooth and successful life. He halted, and wondered when the machinery of his pulses would begin to move again. Then he walked quickly up to the bookstall and demanded a copy of *The Afternoon*, tendering the French penny.

"Sold out, sir," said the clerk.

Even at that juncture the journalist in him felt proud; but the pride was short-lived.

"What evening paper have you?"

"None, sir, all gone. The extra special *Afternoon* 'll be here in five minutes or so."

Dumayne set his teeth and turned round. He heard half-a-dozen other men ask for papers within the next thirty seconds, and, looking about him, discovered that everyone was in a state of strange excitement. He comprehended suddenly that London was enjoying one of those supreme and utterly surprising sensations which happen only once in a decade.

And well might it be so! For Leona Liss—he should have dined with her and her niece that very night—was the most celebrated, the most talented and the most beautiful woman in the country, perhaps in Europe. She was an Englishwoman, and the goddess of three European capitals, not to mention the cities of the New World—a combination of facts sufficient to make her unique in the annals of the stage; continental stars have a habit of not being born in Great Britain. She was an actress of genius, with a divine voice and a miraculous gift of humour; and her realm was that of comic opera. It had been said of her by a great statesman and wit that she had invented comic opera. Her vogue was incredible. Scarcely a month back she had told him, Edward Dumayne, that she had declined an offer of £750 a week for ten weeks in America. She was thirty and looked twenty, and she stood at the very height and summit of her career. Her photograph was everywhere. The record of her delicious whims, her innumerable charities, her myriad suitors, was continued from day to day in the press of England, France, and the United States. Prime Ministers had kissed her long thin hand; a Queen had kissed her cheek.[3]

As a member of the public, Dumayne was acquainted with these matters. In his private capacity, as the accepted suitor of Leona's niece—the young girl who so quietly shared Leona's wonderful existence—he knew more. He knew the woman beneath the actress, and it seemed impossible to him that this woman, so full of gaiety, and goodness when he last saw her, so childishly exultant at the prospect of an approaching holiday cruise in the Mediterranean, was dead.

In the midst of his excitation he could not help sardonically smiling at the fact that he, intimately connected with the tragedy, could not buy a paper containing the news of it. Just then he espied an old gentleman folding up a copy of *The Afternoon*. He hesitated and approached him.

"Excuse me, sir," said Edward Dumayne with careful politeness, "will you allow me to look at your paper? There are none to be obtained here, and I have a special reason."

"Take it, by all means," the old gentleman answered, and hurried off to the platforms. Dumayne bowed to his back.

In a fraction of time he had read the brief paragraph, which under heading of a stupendous type, flared on the fifth page of *The Afternoon*. It ran:—

"We deeply regret to announce that Leona Liss died very suddenly yesterday afternoon at her seaside residence at Port Erin, Isle of Man. A correspondent gives currency to the rumour that her sister, Miss Lotta Liss, the well-known author, was with the deceased lady at the time of her death. It is well known that the sisters had not spoken to each other for many years, but it would appear that the unhappy difference which separated them had at the last moment been healed. No further details are at present obtainable." That was all.

Dumayne muttered an anathema against Studforth, his senior assistant, for having allowed the reference to the family quarrel to go in. Then he stuffed the paper into his pocket, found the cab and sent it to Fulham with his portmanteau. Calling another vehicle for himself, he sprang into it.

"24, Kensington Court Mansions. Quick!" he said to the driver. The man saluted, and whipped viciously at the horse, recognizing instinctively in his fare a practised and generous taker of hansoms who would pay for speed.

II

As the hansom sailed along Pall Mall, up St. James's Street and down Piccadilly, Dumayne had full opportunity to judge of London's excitement. The newspaper boys were disposing of their bundles at a prodigious rate, and the people who bought papers stood still on the spot of purchase to open and read them. In omnibuses men and women could be seen talking eagerly to one another over their newspapers; even the conductors seemed to have acquired an interest in life. Presently one of the *Comet* carts, travelling as if pursued by the infernal powers, passed even the swift hansom, and in its progress belched forth packets of papers to boys who stood expectant at various points. The contents bill on the back of the cart said, *Leona Liss—Special*. Dumayne speculated upon what Studforth would be doing just then to preserve the renown of *The Afternoon*, and whether this rival publication with the crimson cart had really obtained a special account of Leona's death. He almost stopped the cab in order to buy a *Comet*; then he thought of the *Comet*'s reputation and refrained. He knew the *Comet*'s ways.

He leaned back in a corner of the hansom and, closing his eyes, endeavoured calmly to view the circumstances. His mind ran upon Lotta Liss, that dark and sinister figure, the estranged mother of his Edna. He remembered that Lotta was the origin of his connection with the Liss family. Nine years ago, when he was the callow sub-editor of a weekly organ of politics, literature, and art, his chief, Murchison, had introduced him to Lotta Liss, who, though retaining her maiden name, was the widow of a friend of Murchison's, with one child, a shy little girl of nine years. Even at that time Lotta, though only twenty-six—she had married at fifteen—was famous as the wielder of the most pungent and sarcastic pen that ever woman held. Her novels encountered terrific opposition, but they sold freely, and editors were content to print her at her own price. He called to mind clearly the small, hard, vivacious face of the diminutive brunette who, dressed with extravagance, had talked to him brilliantly but cruelly, showering upon him and his sex the profusion of her wit and mordant satire, taking advantage of his youth and exulting in the fatuity of his stammering replies. In spite of his discomfiture, he recollected that he had found a naïve pleasure in the fact of the terrible Lotta devoting so much attention to him. At that time, Leona Liss was only on the threshold of her fame, and she was somewhat overshadowed at first by Lotta's greater renown. But how quickly their relative positions had changed! Leona had appeared in *King Cole*, that most entrancing of all operettas, and suddenly London had humbled itself before her. Instead of Leona being known as the sister of Lotta, Lotta descended to the position of the sister of Leona. Then Leona went to Paris, to Madrid, to South America, and returned in two years a *diva* of the first magnitude, to compass new and more splendid triumphs in her native city.

It was soon after her reappearance in London that the estrangement had commenced. Jealousy on the part of Lotta was, without doubt, at the root of the quarrel which, so far as Lotta was concerned, had long been simmering. A trifling incident—the exact nature of which none, save the parties most interested, ever knew—and Lotta found excuse to pour out the vials of her bitterness in a scene which (Leona had once told Dumayne) was engraved forever on the memory of the shocked younger sister. Lotta retired from London, taking her daughter with her, and her writings became more pungent and not less popular than ever. Leona lived chiefly either in her Kensington flat or at a beautiful house which she acquired on Wimbledon Common. It was only recently that she had bought the house in the Isle of Man.

As for Edna, her mother had strangely enough frequently allowed the girl to visit her Aunt Leona. Two years ago, when Edna was sixteen, mother and child had coldly agreed to separate, and Edna came to live permanently with her aunt. She was a quiet, studious, determined girl, who had contrived to keep her own individuality and ideals even in the vortex of Leona's brilliant circle. She seldom spoke of her mother, and Dumayne himself knew merely that the two had had serious differences. The truth was that no one could have lived in comfort with a woman of Lotta's temperament, and the distinguished author had lucid moments when she recognised this.

Edna had her mother's literary bent, and it was in his professional capacity that Edward Dumayne had renewed his acquaintance with her, whom he remembered as a little shy girl of nine years. The acquaintance had developed into something else, and now for some months they had been betrothed.

Such in brief was the history of Dumayne's connection with the Liss family—a connection which, by the way, was not precisely the least of his claims to distinction.

He was wondering whether the death of Leona would necessitate the hastening of his marriage with Edna, when the cab stopped. Jumping out, he looked up at the large and stately windows of the flat which had been Leona's London home. At the same moment, a girl's figure appeared at the left-hand window. She smiled gravely down upon him with a look of relief.

III.

The first greetings and hurried explanations were over, and the two sat side by side on the Chesterfield sofa which flanked one side of the fireplace. The room was large, and furnished mainly in the style of Louis Quinze. It had been a subsidiary reception-room till Edna came. She transformed it into a study, added the Chesterfield sofa, a couple of Chippendale bookcases, and a typewriter, which stood on a table by itself and looked somewhat bizarre amid its surroundings.

"And you know absolutely nothing?" he was saying. He held her hand.

"Absolutely nothing," Edna answered, in a quiet, sad voice, "beyond the telegram that came at two o'clock."

"Let me see that telegram again, dear." She took from her pocket the crumpled salmon-coloured bit of paper. He read, meditatively:—

"'Your aunt died suddenly yesterday afternoon, failure of heart's action.' There's no signature," he added.

"No, but it's from mother. No one else would have telegraphed—quite—quite like that. As she spoke the girl looked down at her dress and reddened a little. She was plainly attired in a close-fitted check-gown, and she wore the white linen collar and cuffs which seem essential to the happiness of so many literary women. Her face was set and sad, but there was no sign of tears in her black, brilliant eyes.

"Of course," she went on, "I wired instantly for further particulars, but there has been no reply—it is three hours ago now. I shall go to Liverpool to-night, and catch the two o'clock steamer to-morrow morning. I felt somehow as if I must start off at once, but then I remembered that you were returning this afternoon, and I felt sure you would come straight here. If you hadn't come I believe I should have done something silly. I've lost all my nerve."

"You don't look as if you had, darling," he said. He was marvelling at her self-possession. "Why not let us go together to Port Erin to-morrow? I can't possibly leave to-night; have to meet my confounded proprietors; but I can leave by the 5.15 from Euston to-morrow morning. Won't that do for you?"

She shook her head.

"No," she said; "I must be *on the way!*"

Dumayne did not discuss the point.

"It's all horribly mysterious," he began, after a pause. "Your aunt, on the very day before she was to have started for Marseilles, goes off to Port Erin, and within fifty hours of her departure she is dead... I never knew she was subject to heart disease."

Edna nodded.

"Yes; mother has it too. I think I have it."

"Nonsense, darling; don't begin to imagine things."

She smiled contemplatively and went on, gazing at the floor:

"I ought never to have left mother; though Heaven knows I've had a happy enough time here with Auntie. In spite of all the admiration and the homage and the fuss that was made of her in that big drawing-room on the other side of the passage, Auntie was always just a kind woman to me. But I ought never to have left mother."

For the first time tears came into her eyes, but she did not cry.

"But why," Edward said, "why should your thoughts turn to your mother now? Is there any connection between her and your aunt's death?"

"Edward!"she sat up straight in sudden protest, "what do you mean?" She seemed to tremble.

"My dear girl"—he put his hands on her shoulders—"the strain of all this is too much for you. I simply meant, will your aunt's death affect her in any way disadvantageously?"

"Oh! I thought... I beg pardon... I didn't know what you

meant." Edna flushed and put her hand to her forehead, and then gently removed her lover's hands from her shoulders. "I seemed surprised when you told me the newspaper said that mother was at Port Erin. But I wasn't really. I haven't told you that on the morning auntie went away, she received a letter addressed in mother's handwriting."

"A letter from your mother?"

"Yes, it was the first time mother had written to auntie for years."

"And did your poor aunt say anything about it?"

"No, she read it and put it in her pocket. So naturally I didn't ask questions. And it was that morning she went away to Port Erin."

"Do you think she went because of the letter?"

"I—I—don't know... Yes, I think so."

Edna controlled herself with an obvious effort.

"O Teddie," she burst out, "I wish I had never left my mother. She has been alone now for two years. I might have changed her attitude towards auntie a little. I might have softened her. Instead of that, I feel sure she grew harder and bitterer. And auntie felt it, we both felt it... And then that letter. And the death... Oh, what can it all mean?"

She sank backwards. She had swooned.

IV.

It was not surprising that Edward Dumayne felt restless and excited that night. Few such days had been his lot, and although he practised the journalist's pretence of remaining impassive under whatever circumstances, he had been profoundly agitated more than once during the few hours that had elapsed since his return to London. Not the least of his agitations was due to the sudden indisposition of Edna. But that was not serious. He had obtained a doctor, and Edna had shortly recovered consciousness, and was now under orders not to get out of bed for a couple of days. That prevented her from going to the Isle of Man. For some reasons he was not sorry that she could not go.

He had transacted some urgent business with his proprietors at the office of the paper, and now, having dined at home in Fulham, he lighted a cigar, and opening the French window of his dining-room sat down in a corner and gazed meditatively out into the obscurity of the garden. Rather large, the garden was of peculiar shape—rhomboidal—owing to the immediate proximity of the Wimbledon branch of the District Railway, which ran on its brick arches at an angle of about 70 degrees to the back of the house. Trains passed, one way or the other, about every five minutes. One could not see them very distinctly at any time of day, owing to the line of tall poplars which a thoughtful landlord had planted along that side of the garden abutting on the railway, and which were now in fullest leaf. Some people would have preferred not to see the trains at all, but Dumayne rather enjoyed, in the evening, the thunderous procession which threw the glare of lighted panes on to the grass of his lawn. He often sat up watching till the trains ceased for the night.

And they had another interest. Leona Liss used constantly to travel by the last train to Wimbledon. It was a whim of hers. She averred that the forty-five minutes journey punctuated by regular stops at stations monotonously alike, soothed and prepared her for sleep. Accompanied by her maid, she practised all sorts of subterfuges in order to avoid the attentions of the idly curious on these night journeys; but, nevertheless, thousands of people boasted of having travelled down with her—immeasurably more than could possibly have done so. Indeed, it was the correct thing for the *jeunesse dorée* of Earl's Court, Fulham, and Putney to remark casually: "By the way I travelled down with Leona last night. Deuced well she looked, too. And that maid of hers isn't bad either."

Dumayne tried to read a novel, and then, not succeeding, bent his mind frantically on a book of naval tactics. But in vain. The night was hot, and his brain was hotter. He threw the naval tactics on the floor, where they underwent a critical examination at the paws of a kitten. He tried to entice the kitten to his knee, but that failed also, though he gave so much attention to the business that his cigar went out. Then he lighted a pipe, and under its influence all the thoughts which he had kept by main force in the background of his mind, crept forward and assailed him.

Why had Studforth put on the *Afternoon's* placards, "*Mysterious death*"? Studforth was a clever chap, and he must have had some reason for that word, though there was nothing on the face of the telegram to justify it. He had seen Studforth that evening at the office, and yet had not cared to put the question to him. There was, of course, nothing "mysterious" in Leona's death. Thousands of people died suddenly of heart disease every year. It was sudden; that was all.

And yet . . .

Fifty times his reflections covered the same ground—dismissing a horrible idea as preposterous, then finding suggestions, hints, reasons, in support of that idea. Why had Lotta, after years of silence, written to her sister, and what was there in the letter to cause Leona to abandon a holiday and rush away to Port Erin?

"I want a drink," he said aloud, with a sort of laugh, and he got up and went to the sideboard. He noticed that the large hanging lamp burnt low and was beginning to smell. He put it out. Then, with the grateful taste of spirit in his mouth he returned to his chair. The last Wimbledon train swept past the garden with a roar.

"Poor Leona will never travel by that line again," he murmured.

After a long time, during which his mind seemed vacant, he woke to the consciousness that another train was approaching, and also to the fact that he was alone on the ground floor of the house. As he had ordered breakfast for four o'clock the next morning, his servants had probably retired hours ago. He felt afraid. The kitten lay asleep. He had an impulse to waken it, but he laughed at his cowardice and refrained from doing so. He could not hear the train; he saw it approaching through the two lime trees at the end of the garden; those trees which he well knew completely hid the approach of any train till it was within a few yards of the garden. Yet he could see plainly the headlights of the engine, and a faint glare from the carriages. Then the train came up in full view; and it stopped exactly opposite the garden. No train had ever done that before. Even now, he had heard no noise whatever.

He jumped up hastily and kicked the kitten; but the kitten merely looked at him in mild infantile wonder, and went to sleep once more. He went again to the liqueur stand, and this time drank out of the bottle. Then he walked steadily back to the window. The train was still there. As though in impalpable thin mist, he could count its lighted panes. But there was something else. There was something on his lawn. Emerging from the shadow of the poplars, and approaching him, came a white, swathed figure. Dumayne supposed vaguely that it must in some way have descended from the train, got down the masonry of the arches, and so over the wall into the garden. It took short slow steps.

"God!" he exclaimed, at length. "It's Leona Liss!"

Wrapped from head to foot in white, and moving with difficulty because her feet were trammelled, she came nearer, with a deliberation which maddened him. He recognised the marvellous glance of those Liss eyes, and all the lovely features, now set in a sweet and changeless calm. She walked across the lawn until she had passed over the yellowish reflections thrown from the train on the grass. And now she was within twelve feet of Dumayne—only the half opened window between them. He dropped his eyes, and looked again, fascinated. What was that on her face? He saw plainly across her left cheek and left temple a long thin, red wound. It seemed like the freshly made scratch of some gigantic blunt pin.

He didn't remember any more. The next sensation was a feeling of chill. He opened his eyes, and found himself on the floor. The dawn was just coming, and the train, with the figure of Leona, had vanished.

V.

The interminable journey to Port Erin wearied him, but at the same time it gave him opportunity to gather himself together for a scene to which he could not but look forward with apprehension. As he idled about the extraordinary toy railway station at Douglas, waiting for the extraordinary toy train for Port Erin, he said to himself with a sort of satisfaction that in a few hours' time he would have probed to the foundation of this mystery. He was a man and a journalist again now.

At Port Erin station he put aside the greetings and the curiosity of the boatmen, whose acquaintance he had made on previous visits, and who seemed to spend their lives in meeting trains. He hired the solitary Port Erin fly, and drove by precarious cliff paths, straight to Leona's house, which stood solitary half-way up the hill that flanks the western side of the harbour. The servants of the house knew him, and they met him with an apologetic confidential air; but he uttered no word except to inquire if Lotta Liss was there. She was, and in what appeared an incredibly short space of time the interview was upon him.

In a small room with a sea-prospect, Dumayne found himself facing the mother of the girl whom he was to marry, the dark, mysterious Lotta Liss. It was years since he had seen her, but she had not greatly changed. Her black eyes glinted at him. Her small frail body seemed to exude a nervous defiance of him. Her attitude implied that she was at bay. There were dark lines under her eyes; her lips were pallid; her cheeks dead white against the black satin of her dress.

"Mrs. Crowdy," he began to speak.

"Miss Liss," she corrected him, haughtily.

For an instant he felt abashed.

"Your daughter calls herself Crowdy, and your late

Dumayne found himself facing the dark mysterious Lotta Liss.

husband—" his tone was bellicose; she stopped him.

"I choose to keep my own name, as you very well know, Mr. Dumayne. The world knows me as Lotta Liss."

He bowed. She went on contemptuously.

"So you have engaged yourself to my daughter, without her mother's consent."

"You cast her from you."

She made a gesture of denial, and then seemed to dismiss that trifling matter.

"What is your business?" she asked.

He hesitated a moment, framing his words.

"Edna is ill," he said. "In her behalf, as her future husband, I have come to see the remains of your sister."

"You cannot."

"Why? I insist."

"She was buried this afternoon."

He was astounded into silence, and there was a pause. Then his words came coldly, cuttingly: "Why did you consider this indecent haste to be necessary? The whole affair is well—singular. Your sister receives a letter in your handwriting, the first for years." Lotta sat up straighter. "She comes suddenly away to Port Erin, although she is on the eve of starting for France. She had been here scarcely a day when she dies of heart-disease. You, who have not seen her for many years, happen to be here, but you send no word to Edna, who was your sister's dearest companion, till twenty-four hours have elapsed. I travel with all haste to attend the funeral, and arrive only to find the poor lady already buried."

Lotta smiled imperturbably.

"In this hot weather, you know," she began, and left him to complete the sentence for himself.

"But," he resumed firmly. She cut him short.

"*But!*" she exclaimed, leaping up from her low chair. In the deepening twilight of the summer evening her figure showed black against the window. "*But!* What do you mean?

Who else should take charge of Leona's body but me? Must I await my daughter's instructions? As for the telegram being late, that was an accident. I forgot to telegraph."

"You forgot?"

"You heard me, Mr. Dumayne."

There was another brief silence. Lotta had sat down again. Dumayne carefully schooled his voice:—

"If your sister is buried, then her body will have to be exhumed."

"Do you dare . . . ?"

"I dare nothing. *But I want to know whether her left cheek and temple are marked by a recent wound, and if so, how that wound came there.*" He italicised the words.

He appeared cool, but his heart was beating heavily. The woman's nostrils dilated and contracted with a quick movement. Dumayne could just see that in the gloom. He waited. "Shall I ring for a lamp?" he asked at length.

"No, no," she cried out imperiously. "Sit still. Wait a moment."

So they sat for a few seconds, she looking out of the window where the sea was, and he contemplating her steadily. Presently she turned towards him.

"So you know about Leona's face?"

"I have seen her spirit," he answered quietly.

"It must have been so for none else in the world but myself knew it. You have seen her spirit. I believe you. I will tell you about my sister. I killed Leona."

He opened his mouth to speak, but she went on quickly.

"Yes, I killed her; but not in the way you think. Listen... Do you know why I hated Leona? You don't? Nor I. It was one of those unaccountable hatreds. Possibly due to jealousy. I had a great name when she was a little pink chorus girl. I would have kept her and shielded her like a mother. But she was too independent for that. She wanted to make a reputation for herself. She made it. She eclipsed me. Did I hate her for that? Who can say? I had always hated her. And yet I had always loved her, too. My influence with the press, powerful as you know, was always used in her favour, even at the very time when she took my daughter from me. Why did I quarrel with Edna? Perhaps because she was so like Leona. Perhaps because I cannot live in peace with anyone. No one understands me. Spiritually, I am alone. I married at fifteen, and at sixteen, I was a widow. I have been too much solitary. I am 'queer,' as people say. My books are 'queer.' But they are the books of a genius. During these latter years I have changed, I, even I, have become religious. Some months ago I determined to forswear literature, the world, everything, and to enter a convent. I am superior to fame now, I wish to relinquish all that. But before I retired there was one duty which called aloud to be done. I had a confession to make to Leona.

"You remember Lord Belfort, who died a long time ago in some trumpery frontier skirmish. Lord Belfort loved my sister, and Leona him. Well, I parted them, out of pure causeless spite. Oh!— and by the simplest expedient. I sent for Lord Belfort, and I told him that Leona was secretly married already. He went away and got killed, and Leona never knew why.

"The other day I wrote to Leona, informed her of my intention to enter a convent, and that I must see her first. We met. In this room I told her what I have told you, and she fell dead from the shock. And now, Edward Dumayne, you know."

The rich deep tones of her impressive voice ceased, and she lay back in her chair. The rim of the moon suddenly appeared at the window.

"What about the wound?" Dumayne asked, with an assumption of incredulous sarcasm which did not in the least represent his real feelings, "you have not explained that."

She sat erect again, and put her feet on the floor.

"I had forgotten it. The explanation is simple. Last night I went into the room where my sister's body lay. I—Iwanted to kiss that cold and beautiful mouth. It was quite dark, and as I groped, bending over the coffin, my brooch wounded her face. At that moment my remorse was greater—but what has that to do with you? I put the lid on the coffin, and forbade anyone to lift it again, and so none knew of it, save you. You saw her spirit. To you such an occurrence was no doubt surprising. To me, not at all. I know what I know. As for your talk of exhumation, that is nonsense. Of course you believe me."

"I do," he said.

She laughed sombrely.

"And if you didn't," she added, "there is the death certificate of Sir John Queech, who happened to be staying in the village."

"Is that all you have to say?" he queried.

"That is all. And now you can go back to your Edna. To-morrow I find my convent. You think, probably, that your and Edna's lives are shadowed for ever by this tragedy. Not so. You will live and you will forget. In half a year's time you will be a hundredfold happier than you now deem possible. I advise you to marry at once. As for me, in my convent, I shall never forget. Good night. You had better sleep at the Falcon's Nest; it is the best hotel."

He rose.

"Stay." She paused, got up, and lighted a candle which stood on the mantelpiece.

"Edward Dumayne, do not go away under any misapprehension. I hate you. I have been compelled to tell you my secrets, which I had sworn never to tell to anyone—not by your astuteness, but by an accident, the accident of an apparition. I hate you; but you will be happy nevertheless."

With a gesture she ordered him from the room.

NOTES

1. *Woman*. 21st June 1899, pages 12-15. Signed Sarah Volatile. Illustrated by M.E. Thompson.
2. Bennett was appointed Assistant Editor of *Woman* in 1893 at the age of 27, becoming Editor in 1896.
3. The alliterative Leona Liss suggests the actress Lillie Langtry (1853-1929), one of the most famous of actresses who drifted into drama on the strength of her notoriety in other spheres. A celebrated society beauty, she was a mistress of the Prince of Wales and friend of Oscar Wilde.

A MILLIONAIRE'S WIFE.[1]

Francis Dumayne, the millionaire, lay dying. The wealthiest man must ultimately relinquish his wealth, but to Francis Dumayne the separation had come earlier than usual. He was forty-five, in the prime of life, and a fortnight ago he had been in the full vigour of manhood.

Now, the great mansion in Piccadilly was hushed from basement to attic. The white-calved footmen moved on tip-toe in the hall. The maids talked in whispers. A couple of grooms constantly renewed the straw which, for eight days past, had carpeted the busy noisy street.[2]

In the master's immense bedroom, furnished in the style of Louis the Fifteenth at the cost of twelve thousand pounds, there were four people—the millionaire, two nurses, and Marian Dumayne. The dying man was on the last lap of life, and he knew it; you could tell that by his anxious, grey face.

"Marian," he whispered, scarcely audible.

One of the nurses went over to his wife, who was sitting by the window, thirty feet from the bed. Marian came to the bedside, and Francis Dumayne, with a weak but imperious gesture, waved the nurses away.

"Marian," he whispered again, and he looked long at her. She was a beautiful girl, not more than twenty-six. She might have been his daughter instead of his wife. Pale, with heavy dark eyes, and black hair slightly dishevelled through long watching, she stood moveless, silent, her hands clenched, gazing at the man whom death was gripping from her.

"Marian," he said, "I am dying."

She stretched her hands towards him.

"You will have all my money," he said. "It will come to nearly a hundred thousand a year. You are young. You should be happy."

"Why talk of wealth now, Francis?" she said, entreatingly. "I love you."

He lifted his hand.

"Don't lie to a dying man," he said, and there was something curious in his voice which stopped her from making a reply. She merely started. Her heart seemed to flutter and then lie still. "You never loved me!" he went on. "See; you do not cry."

"I do not cry because I cannot," she put in, softly.

"The farce has been kept up long enough," he resumed, painfully ignoring her interruption. "It is well that it should cease. I say you never loved me."

"How long have you thought so?"

"I have known it for seven years."

"Before our marriage, then?"

"Three months before."

"And yet you married me."

"Yes, because I had plighted my troth, and I never draw back . . . and because—"

"Because?"

"Because I loved you. I die loving you, Marian; be sure of that. I love you, though you lied to me before our wedding."

"Lied to you, Francis?"

"Yes, when you said you loved me. Ah! You little thought that all these years I have known that it was my wealth you married, not me. I kept the secret well, did I not?"

"Why did you keep it? Why did you not accuse me before?"

"I was too proud, Marian. But death humbles a man."

"Oh, Francis," she cried out, so loud that both the nurses turned at the sound, and then she sank to her knees by the bed. The millionaire fell back exhausted, a faint groan in his throat, a bitter smile on his pallid lips.

The next moment one of the nurses was leading Marian from the room. She made no resistance. Presently she found herself on the couch in her own boudoir. She was dimly conscious of having passed on the stairs Sir Edgar Dumayne, her husband's brother, and the old white-haired physican. She remembered that they had spoken to her, but she had taken no notice of them.

She closed her eyes, and tried to realize all that last brief, amazing interview with the dying man meant for her. Their married life, though comfortable, had fallen short, she admitted, of her girlish dreams. Of course the reason was now obvious. He had deemed her guilty of an infamy—for she could call it by no other word. To tell a man that you loved him when in fact your sole desire was to possess his wealth, seemed to her nothing less than an infamy, though she knew the trick to be common enough. Yet he had never once fallen short in affection, courtesy, respect. What self-control, what inflexible purpose he must have had! In that moment she loved him more than ever—for his strength.

How had the first suspicion been planted in his mind? She could discover no answer to that question, tease her brain as she would. Besides, what was the use of answering it? The only important fact was that he had thought her guilty, and that there was no means now of clearing herself before him. He was dying, dead, and death is irretrievable . . . His wealth was hers. Ah! That wealth! She would never touch it. She would walk out of that gorgeous abode with nothing but her widow's mourning, back into poverty from which he had raised her. Not even to save herself from starving could she have touched a penny of his hundred thousand a-year. She had often longed for a child. Now she thanked God that she had none; a child would have complicated matters.

As for the money, that should be Sir Edgar's. She had never liked the baronet, who to her had always been cold, proud, distant, resentful. In Sir Edgar's eyes when Marian, the orphan of a poor country solicitor, married the millionaire, who was old enough to be her father, she committed a crime. She was well aware of this attitude, and the two had scarcely taken the trouble to keep up an appearance of friendship. Still, he was Francis' brother, and the money must go to him.

So the thoughts ran round and round in her brain, and at length, from the weariness of long watching, she fell asleep. How long she slept she could not have guessed, but she was conscious of being awakened by the physician's arm on her elbow.

"Mrs. Dumayne, Mrs. Dumayne," he said, in his sharp curt tones.

"Well," she said, dazed, looking up at his wrinkled yellow face.

"Drink this," and he gave her a glass of brandy. She drank it.

"Ugh!" she shuddered.

"Mrs. Dumayne," he said, "I want you to prepare yourself for a shock. Keep calm. Joy never kills. Your husband is better. He will recover. There, there! You shall come and see him presently."

And the old man was gone.

She clasped her hands tight over her forehead, and set her brain to this new task. Francis, then, would live. Could she explain to him his mistake? After the seven years' mental torture which he, unknown to her, had endured, could they be anything to each other again? Would it not be simpler if she ...

Mechanically she pulled from her hair a thin silver dagger which she always wore in her coiffure. She gazed at it, fascinated. It was a beautiful instrument.

Would it not be simpler.... He might think better of her then, when she was gone whither he had nearly been.

She stopped. Sir Edgar was in the doorway.

"You have heard the good news, Marian. What a relief for you!"

She fixed her dark eyes on him.

"Come in, Edgar," she said, quietly.

He obeyed and sat down, smiling. As she examined his face, it seemed to her that she read his soul and despoiled it of its secret. Everything was plain to her. And her own soul blazed up in anger.

"Listen to me," she said. "My husband has told me that for seven years he has known that I never loved him, that I married him for his money."

"A sick man's delirium," Sir Edgar said lightly.

"No, no," she protested. "He spoke sanely what he believed to be the truth. But it was a lie, Edgar. You know it was a lie."

"Really," the man began.

"Who told my husband that I did not love him, that I wanted his wealth merely?"

"I must say, Marian—"

She swept his feeble interruption aside.

"You told him, Edgar. You hated the thought of our marriage. You tried to poison his mind against me, and you succeeded."

There was a pause.

"Well," he said, at length, "I admit it." He laughed cynically. "What were you to us? I admit that I did what I could to put you and him apart."

"And now," she towered over him like a figure of fate, "you shall undo what you did." She felt herself lifted up on a torrent of wrath.

"What do you mean? "

"I mean that you shall go upstairs to Francis, and confess that seven years ago you lied to him."

"I won't."

"You shall."

She approached him, and the silver dagger trembled in her fingers. She herself wondered what would happen next. Sir Edgar, as he caught the lightning in her eyes, began to temporise.

"Any shock might be fatal to him," he said.

She remembered the doctor's words, and repeated them. "Joy never kills."

"Marian, really... is not your own place now by his bedside?"

"Not till you have been there: that I swear. You will go?"

For a few seconds the two confronted each other, eye meeting eye.

"You will go," she repeated, superbly insistent.

His glance quailed at length before hers.

"Yes," he murmured, "I will undo what I once did—seven years ago."

"Thanks," she said coldly. "It is the least you can offer."

And as she watched him leave the room, she replaced the dagger in her hair. Some women might have been afraid lest he would not keep his word. But Marian had no such fear. She knew that their souls had met in conflict and that hers had won.

Just as he was closing the door she called him back.

"Edgar!"

"Yes," he answered.

"Good-bye," she said meaningly. "We shall not see each other again."

He bowed and disappeared.

Then she sank down in a chair. The reaction was upon her.

"Mrs. Dumayne!" It was the doctor's voice again at last.

"Your husband would like to have you near him."

"I will come," she said rising. "Do you know where Sir Edgar is?"

"He has just left Mr. Dumayne, and is gone out. Did you want him?"

"Not specially," she said.

"Shall I tell someone to call him back?"

"Pray don't," she said.

She went upstairs, and entered once more the great

bedroom. The two nurses were by the bedside, just as though they had never moved. When they saw her, they stepped noiselessly away. She crept towards the bed.

"My husband!" she cried, and kneeling down seized his wasted hand.

"You have forgiven me—already?" he whispered.

"I can cry now," was all she answered.

And his hand was damp with her tears.

NOTES

1. *Woman.* 6th December 1899, pages 9-10. Signed E.A. Bennett, Author of *A Man from the North, The Gates of Wrath* &c. Illustrated by Lance Thackeray.
2. As Bennett lay dying in March 1931 the local council allowed straw to be laid on the road outside his home at Chiltern Court to deaden the traffic noise. This is the last recorded occasion of this custom in central London.

THE PHANTOM SNEEZE [1]

It was close upon twelve o'clock of a warm June evening, and Mr. Percy Oscroft and Emily, his wife, were sitting side by side in the drawing-room of their suburban house, a detached abode of the superior order, with a garden all round it, electric light, and a lawn only just too small for a lawn-tennis court. They were a young couple, both under thirty, well-off (as things go), and of a cheerful, optimistic, sane, sensible turn of mind. Both were tall; the husband was handsome; the wife was alert and straight, and her expression was charming. Fifty trifling indications proved that they were still pretty violently in love with one another. Percy was an A.L.A.,[2] and occupied a somewhat exalted position in the head office of a large insurance company. When lunching with colleagues in the City, he was prone to discuss the uses of differential calculus as applied to insurance tables; also the possibility of one man hoeing the tenth part of an acre after business hours. The Oscrofts were an indefatigable couple; they rented a plot of ground near to their home, and grew thereon beans and potatoes—not because Percy's salary of seven hundred and fifty a year was insufficient for the purchase of beans and potatoes, but because, out of their abundant health and energy, they positively enjoyed the cultivation of vegetables. Their establishment consisted of themselves, their two healthy and naughty boys, Arthur and Lionel, aged respectively five and six, a cook, a parlour-maid, and a nurse. Mrs. Oscroft was her own governess; before marriage she had earned a living in that precarious vocation.

These facts are recited in order to show that there was nothing morbid, weird, unusual, or eccentric about the Oscroft household and its inmates.

On the night in question they had given a small impromptu supper to a few friends who lived in the neighbourhood, and now, as their custom was, they sat up together talking in easy intimate comradeship of the day's doings. The guests had departed about a quarter of an hour ago.

The grandfather's clock in the hall struck twelve.

"To bed, girlie, and please see that I catch the 9.24 in the morning," said Percy. "I have missed it two mornings running."

"I can't catch your train for you, you idle boy," said his wife. "Is the dining-room window fastened?"

The dining-room was at the back of the house, and had a French window which gave on to the garden.

"No."

"Go and fasten it, then."

"Me daren't go by myself. Wifie come wiv' me."

(At the office Percy was regarded as a model of the sober, phlegmatic and unsentimental Englishman.)

So they went arm-in-arm, *viâ* the hall, to the dining-room. This apartment communicated with the drawing-room by means of heavy sliding doors; but when these were closed, as to-night, it saved exertion to reach the dining-room from the drawing-room by means of the hall. Percy turned on the electric light as they entered the room. The French window was blowing open, and he closed it.

"Shall Percy lift girlie up to push the bolt?"

He lifted her, and she pushed home the top bolt.

Then they left the room, Percy switching off the light as they passed the door. No sooner was the light out, and they in the hall, than the sound of a sneeze came from the dining-room. It seemed to have had its origin near the French window. It was a tremendous sneeze, and they both stood still a moment, startled.

"What was that, Percy?" the woman exclaimed, clutching at him.

"The cat, of course, you trembling little bird," he said, and pinched her. "You weren't frightened, were you?" He looked at her, and guessed that she had been perhaps a little frightened. "You mustn't let Jack Fenton's tales get on your nerves, you know," and he kissed her.

Jack Fenton had been one of their guests that night. He was an active member of the Society for Psychical Research; said he didn't believe in the supernatural a bit, and yet was always recounting authenticated ghostly stories which admitted of no explanation save the supernatural.

They returned to the drawing-room to turn off the light there. Emily went into the room first. As she did so, she stopped, her eyes on the sofa, and clutched again at Percy, pointing mutely but frantically to the sofa.

The cat lay on the sofa asleep.

"Then it wasn't the cat," Percy remarked, with an air of carelessness. "Perhaps—"

He stopped, and raising his head in the hesitating anticipatory manner usual at such physical crises, gave vent to a noisy and reverberating sneeze. Almost in the same instant his wife also sneezed with equal emphasis. Yet the night was warm.

It was so sudden, so unexpected, and so comical, that they burst into a simultaneous laugh, and amid the laughter Emily's vague apprehensions as to the first of the three sneezes were somewhat assuaged. Nevertheless before retiring they revisited the dining-room in search of a possible strange cat. But this quest was unrewarded.

. . . .

The next morning they had other things to think about.

"A letter from Aunt Julia," Percy said as, at 9.3, he sat down hurriedly to the breakfast table, intent on consuming two slices of bacon, one egg, three pieces of toast, and two cups of coffee in seven minutes. "Just open it and read it to me, will you, Em? Are my boots ready? Pass my coffee."

He assaulted the bacon, and Emily opened the envelope.

"Oh, dear!" she said, after a minute, "Bad news. Oh, Percy, your poor Uncle Edmund died last night. Influenza. Whatever will Aunt Julia do? He had only been ill a few days. She didn't telegraph because she had no idea he would die. The doctor hadn't either. She wants you to go down to Woking at once! She says, 'I know my dear nephew will come to me at once in my great trouble, and see after all the necessary arrangements for me. Your afflicted and sorrowing Aunt Julia.'"

Percy said nothing at first. In fact he went on eating for a moment, and then stopped.

"Pass the letter, girlie. So the old boy's dead!"

Just then the two children ran into the room laughing and shouting; they had breakfasted in the nursery. Lionel, the younger, held the cat insecurely in his little chubby arms. Suddenly the cat sprang free, and walking sedately into the corner by the French window, sneezed with great violence. The two children laughed a gay united peal at this exhibition.

"Hush, my darlings!" Emily said. "I want to tell you something very sad. You remember Uncle Edmund?"

"Him that came here long time ago, and had a funny black cap on all the time?" said Arthur, who usually acted as spokesman for the two.

"Yes, dear. Uncle Edmund is dead."

"Dead?"

"Yes. He died yesterday evening."

"What is 'dead'? Like the canary last week? Is he gone to heaven? Shan't we see him any more?"

"Perhaps, if you are good," put in Percy, sententiously. "Now clear out, both of you, I want to talk to your mother."

The cat sneezed again.

"And take that sneezing animal with you. Em, where's the *Bradshaw?*"[3]

. . . .

That morning Mr. Oscroft went to Woking instead of to the office. He was away four days, and returned after his uncle's funeral, very late on the fourth day. Only his wife was sitting up. They supped together in the dining-room, while Percy gave Emily all the details, mournful but interesting, of his absence. Edmund Toodle had been Percy's only male relative. He had lived with his sister, Miss Julia Toodle, at Woking for many years, in the enjoyment of leisure and a respectable fortune amounting to some twenty thousand pounds. He possessed a reputation for eccentricity. He had a marked tendency towards the hypochondriacal, and it was certainly the irony of fate that he should have died of influenza, for he spent the major portion of his existence in taking precautions against cold. It was on this account that he seldom left home. There, the regularity of his habits and the safety of his life seemed assured; in a strange house he was at the mercy of other people's habits: such was his theory. The sole visit of his old age had been paid to the Oscrofts about a year ago, when he came to London to consult a specialist about his eyes.

"The old boy has done the right thing with his money," Percy said. "He's left it in trust for aunt for life, and afterwards it all comes to me. I'm the trustee and executor. Of course I'm awfully sorry, especially for aunt's sake, that uncle's dead, but twenty thousand is a lot of money, Em, you know. By the way, I've asked the old lady to come up next week and stay with us for a bit."

"I'm glad you asked her to come," said Emily, quietly, and then they got up from the table and left the dining-room. Percy switched off the light in going out, and just as he did so there was the sound of another immense sneeze in the old spot.

Again Emily clung to him. He turned back into the room.

"No," she said, imploringly, "don't go back, Percy."

"Why?" he asked. "Yes, of course I will. It's only the cat."

"The cat's in the kitchen. I fastened her up in her cage myself."

Nevertheless, Percy went back, turned on the light, and searched. But he could find no explanation of the sneeze. Nightly for several nights the strange phenomenon of the sneeze recurred and a certain atmosphere of disquiet seemed to permeate the house. Emily was obviously uneasy, and Percy, while pretending to laugh, shared her uneasiness.

"Look here," said Percy, at length temporarily forsaking his attitude of assumed scorn, "I'll get Jack Fenton to come down and spend the evening with us. He shall investigate, and report to his Psychical Society. It will amuse him, and probably some ridiculously simple explanation will be forthcoming. What do you say, girlie?"

Girlie concurred, and three nights later Jack Fenton came to dinner. It was on the same evening that Aunt Julia arrived from Woking. The old lady was primly cheerful, bearing her sorrow well. The children, being on very intimate terms with Mr. Fenton, were allowed, most improperly as Emily said, to come down to dinner, and the meal, was a merry one.

Nothing was said as to the object of Mr. Fenton's visit until the children had been forcibly carried off. Then, in the drawing-room, while the men smoked cigarettes and Aunt Julia knitted with ceaseless industry, Percy and Emily related to Jack Fenton all they knew of the phantom sneeze.

"Do you think it's occult, Mrs. Oscroft?" asked Jack.

"Well—er—no; but I must say I can't understand it."

"Now be candid. Do you think it's occult?"

"Yes."

"Well, then, I don't," said Percy. "What do you say, Aunt?"

"Nay, my dear ...." Aunt Julia shut her lips tight.

"Let me see," the psychical expert said. "You didn't tell me, Oscroft, when your uncle died."

"Last Wednesday."

"And when did the sneezing begin?"

"Wednesday night."

"Curious," said Jack Fenton. "Excuse me, Miss Toodle, but can you throw any light on this?"

Aunt Julia shook her head and went on knitting.

"Curious," Jack repeated.

"Now, Jack," exclaimed Percy, "no rot! You don't really think the two things have any connection?"

"Frankly," said Mr. Fenton, "I don't. But we'll make an experiment. You say the sneeze doesn't happen till after midnight, and that you've never been able to see anything. This is my suggestion, Mrs. Oscroft. The sliding doors are closed now, and we'll keep them closed; but if you don't mind I'll bore a hole through the panel of this left hand door, just big enough for me to look through into the dining-room. It can easily be repaired afterwards, and in the meantime the curtain will hide it."

The suggestion was agreed to, and a large gimlet sent for.

"Why not two holes?" said Percy, while they were boring. "Then I can look as well as you."

"I should prefer to look alone," said Fenton.

The hour approached. At half-past eleven Percy went into the dining-room to switch on the electric light there, and then returned. Jack Fenton took up his post of observation. Twelve o'clock struck. The four people in the drawing-room remained still and silent, straining for a sound. The clock struck the first quarter after midnight.

"It's no go, I'm afraid," said Jack, looking away from the spy-hole for a moment. "Our preparations have frightened the phenomenon, whatever it is. Perhaps it objects to being overlooked."

He laughed.

At that instant the sneeze sounded, as loud and startling as ever. Jack Fenton whipped his eye back to the hole like a shot, while Aunt Julia gave a slight scream and Percy soothed her.

Then Jack faced the company, faintly smiling.

"Servants gone to bed?" he inquired, cheerfully.

"I asked Maria to sit up," said Mrs. Oscroft.

"Is Maria your pretty parlour-maid?"

"Yes."

"Then will you ring for her?"

Mrs. Oscroft rang; the parlour-maid appeared.

"Maria," said Jack Fenton, addressing her, "will you kindly go into the dining-room. On the carver's chair near the window, you will see—er—something. Please bring it in."

Maria departed, and in a moment returned with the cat in her arms.

"There is your ghostly sneeze," said Jack Fenton, with pride and a smile. "There is usually some very matter-of-fact explanation of these things. I may tell you now that I felt sure from the first, in spite of what you said, that the cat was the true cause of this famous sneeze. Maria, you may deposit the cat on the sofa."

As Maria left the room both Mrs. Oscroft and Aunt Julia observed that she was pale and trembling. Jack Fenton must also have noticed something in the girl's demeanour, for he said,—

"Doesn't Maria like cats?"

"Oh, yes, I think so," answered Mrs. Oscroft. "Anyhow she feeds Smut every day. Poor old Smut! The lazy animal's asleep already," and Mrs. Oscroft fondly stroked the alleged author of the sneeze.

"I'm very glad it was the cat," said Aunt Julia.

"Cat!" laughed Percy, brutally. "Of course it was!"

"But it must have been some other cat the other night," said his wife.

Percy merely grunted the male grunt which is designed to sweep away all feminine argument at a blow.

Jack Fenton walked off home, feeling as though he had discovered the identity of the Man in the Iron Mask.

Everyone retired to bed.

. . . . .

The next morning, after Percy had left for town and Aunt Julia had gone out with the children, Maria came into the dining-room, where Mrs. Oscroft was casting up household accounts.

"If you please, ma'am, I want to speak to you."

Mrs. Oscroft looked up.

"Certainly, Maria."

"I wish to leave, ma'am."

"Aren't you satisfied, Maria? I thought the place suited you. You have been with us nearly six months, and that is such a very long time for you modern servants to stay that I imagined you were quite settled down."

"I'm satisfied with the *place*, ma'am. But I can't stop in this house not another day; no, not if you was to cover me with silks and satins for it."

"But why, Maria? Why this violent dislike to the house.

What has the house been guilty of?"

"Look here, ma'am." The pert, pretty face grew firm. "I must leave, and I'm going now. I've packed my box."

"Then you had better unpack it," said Mrs. Oscroft, decisively, "for you certainly are not going now. Since you insist on leaving you must give me proper notice—a month's."

"Excuse me, ma'am, I knows the law. If you wanted for to get rid of me, you could give me my month's wages, that's thirty shilling, and tell me to go. And I can do the same. Here's one pound ten in loo of notice ma'am. I pays it willingly. I'll do fair by you. I wish you good morning, ma'am, but in this house I don't stay."

Maria placed two gold coins on the edge of the table, and walked out of the room.

. . . . .

That night Mrs. Oscroft and Aunt Julia were chiefly occupied in discussing this singular fancy of Maria's, and bemoaning the inconvenience thereby caused; for Minnie the nursemaid had been transformed into housemaid for the time being, to the neglect of some of her own duties, and the children had taken full advantage of the situation. Percy stood smoking with his back to the fireplace, silently attentive to the conversation.

"Don't stand there, Percy, for goodness sake," said his wife. "You rather get on my nerves with your superior masculine smile."

Mr. Oscroft yawned and obediently moved to the sofa.

"Stop!" cried his Aunt, "You'll crush the cat."

Smut lay just where Maria had placed her on the previous evening. Apparently Smut had slept twice round the clock.

"Poor old Smut!" murmured Percy, and tweaked its whiskers. "By jove! Em, the animal's dead."

Smut was not only dead, but stiff.

Mrs. Oscroft wept a little over the corpse, and then Percy delicately picked it up to carry it out of the room. He opened the door, and immediately two white-clad figures came pattering forward in a state of high excitement. These were Arthur and Lionel, supposed to be long since fast asleep in their cots. Mr. Oscroft was so surprised that he dropped the extinct cat behind the door. By all the laws of fatherhood he should have been angry at this gross breach of faith on the part of his offspring, but he could never be angry with Arthur and Lionel.

"Ah!" he said calmly, "You've got up early, my friends. Breakfast won't be ready for quite ten hours yet. What is the meaning of this excursion?"

Both ran direct to their mother.

"My darlings, you are very, very naughty."

"We comed downstairs to find some dessert in the dining-room, muvver, 'cos Minnie wasn't in the nursery, and she forgot to give us a chocolate when we went to bed." This from the first-born.

"Muvver," said Lionel, breaking in, "why did you tell us Uncle Edmund was deaded?"

"He is dead, my pet."

"Well then, he just isn't"

"'Cos," interrupted Arthur, asserting his right as the elder to tell the tale, "we seen him in the dining-room just now. He'd got his little black cap on and he was turning his coat collar up. He frowned at us, and then we runned in here."

The boys stopped breathless, and all looked at one another.

Suddenly came the sound of a huge sneeze from the dining-room.

"There, that's him!" said Lionel triumphantly.

There was the thud of a falling body. Miss Julia Toodle lay extended on the floor. She had fainted.

. . . . .

The next day at breakfast Aunt Julia seemed to have recovered. At that bright morning hour, when the chirp of sparrows came in from the garden and sunshine filled the room, the affair of the previous night had assumed an unreal, remote aspect. Percy, by his demeanour, tried to indicate that he despised and had forgotten it. Emily did not refer to it, but her attitude implied a special sympathy towards Aunt Julia, and a scorn of Percy's scorn. As for Aunt Julia, she was silent till breakfast was nearly over. Then, pushing away her plate, which she had scarcely touched, she burst out.

"I must tell you something," she began. "You remember when your poor dear Uncle stayed here a year ago. He took cold then, or he thought that he did." Aunt Julia paused, and then continued in her thin, deliberate, rather quavering tones. "He was very liable to colds, was your Uncle. He told me he caught this particular one in your dining-room, through the French window being open."

"I remember he said something about it." Percy remarked, "But it was the height of summer."

"He also told me that on the following morning, the day after he had taken cold, he asked at breakfast for a piece of red flannel to put round his neck, but you, Percy, laughed so much at the idea of red flannel that he said no more about it. That laugh annoyed your uncle very much."

"I quite recollect Percy's laugh," said Emily with a look of proper disapproval at her husband.

"He didn't get over it for a long time; and as for the cold, he said that he never did get over that. He made up his mind that he would never be able to shake it off, and he firmly believed that it was the cause, directly or indirectly, of his last attack of influenza. Just before the end he was delirious, and several times he spoke vaguely of red flannel."

"Poor old dear!" murmured Emily.

"The very last thing I heard him mutter was, 'What about

that red flannel, Percy?' or something like that."

Aunt Julia's feelings were a little stirred by this recital, and she began to cry softly.

"How strange!" Percy ruminated.

"You may well say so," said Aunt Julia, brightening, and looking at Percy with a certain timid courage. "There *are* strange things in this world, Percy. Now, my dears, I have been wondering whether—that is—whether your poor Uncle's spirit was unsettled for want of that red flannel. If so, it would be easy for us—"

"My dear Aunt," Percy interrupted her, "please don't be–-well, ridiculous is the word."

"That's all very fine, Percy," said his wife; "but how do you explain—"

"I don't explain," said this matter-of-fact, sternly common-sense man, with terrific firmness. "But it might be explained—that business of last night—in fifty ways. As for this red flannel idea, it is too absurd. What! Offer red flannel to an alleged ghost! Good-morning, both of you."

Then, lofty, superb, superior, Percy departed.

Nevertheless, despite this outburst of pure intellect defying superstition, Aunt Julia and Emily went forth to shop, and came back with a very small parcel, which showed a red tinge through its tissue-paper.

Just as they were preparing to go to bed that night Emily said to her husband: "You look very tired, love. I'll lock up." And without waiting for him to reply she went into the dining-room, taking something from her pocket immediately she was out of range of Percy's eyes. She returned with a great air of nonchalance.

"Coming to bed, dear?" she asked.

He hesitated.

"Yes, love."

They had scarcely reached the bedroom door when Percy stopped.

"You're sure you made all safe, darling?"

"Of course, darling."

"I think I'll just go down and see," he said.

"Don't be absurd," she answered. But Percy went down into the darkness. As he descended the stairs he took from his trousers' pocket a small parcel, unwrapped it, and threw the paper over the banisters. Then he crept into the dining-room, and without turning on the light found his way to the corner by the window, and dropped a bit of soft stuff on the floor. So double-faced and hypocritical creature is man!

Thus the spirit of Uncle Edmund was furnished with two pieces of red flannel.

The next morning Emily, happening to wake up, found Percy dressing. She looked sleepily at her watch; it was twenty-five minutes past five.

"What on earth, Percy—?" she began and then stopped in amazement at this strange freak of a man who daily found it impossible to arise in time for an 8.45 breakfast.

"I was very restless," he said calmly, "So I'm going to do a bit of work in the garden."

"But the servants aren't up."

"I suppose not," he said.

Percy, being dressed, issued from the bedroom. Aunt Julia's chamber was on the opposite side of the passage, and it happened that her door opened at the same moment.

"Aunt!"

"Percy!"

"What are you doing up so early?"

"I was very restless," Aunt Julia replied sweetly, looking down at her black silk dress, "So I thought I would get up and go into the garden."

"Good!" said Percy, after a pause, "I'm going to do the same."

They both went downstairs with singular haste, and their entry into the dining-room was simultaneous. Each glanced surreptitiously into the corner by the window and then looked quickly away.

Only one piece of the red flannel lay in the corner.

"What a lovely morning!" exclaimed Aunt Julia, and they passed into the garden. It was a rather large garden and they seemed to avoid each other.

Later, Percy stole back to the dining-room. The piece of red flannel was gone, but the servants were about, and he was glad to think that they had swept it up and removed it. He hoped he might never see or hear of it again. At that moment, Aunt Julia was in Emily's bedroom.

"Well?" Emily inquired.

Aunt Julia shook her head sadly, and exhibited the flannel.

From that day the mysterious sneezes resounded no more in Percy Oscroft's dining-room. Percy on the one hand, and Emily and Aunt Julia on the other, cogitated privately and in vain to imagine how it was that the phenomenon had so suddenly ceased. It could not be due to the red flannel, they said to themselves, because each had put down a piece of red flannel at night, and each had seen a piece of red flannel the next morning; so that the ghost of Uncle Edmund could not possibly have taken it.

But then, you see, neither of them knew that Uncle Edmund's ghost had had the choice of two pieces.

Anyhow, though the scoffer may scoff, it is indubitable that the phantom sneeze never again did vex the drowsy ear of night.

NOTES

1. *Woman*. 20th June 1900, pages 16-18. Signed E.A. Bennett.
Bennett's *Journal* entry for 5th November 1899: "I have now decided, acting upon Phillpott's [his friend and fellow writer] advice, to write a short story *every* month. I finished my November story this morning: "The Phantom Sneeze", a humorous ghost tale, 4,500 words." (*Journal 1*, p. 98)

2. Associate of the Institute of Actuaries.

3. George Bradshaw (1801-1853) published the world's first compilation of railway timetables in 1841. By 1898 the original eight-page edition had become a 946 page *Guide*.

December 5, 1900.

THE STRANGE SHELTER.[1]

I was walking out one night, about eleven o'clock, down a short side street which branches off at right angles from one of the best-known thoroughfares in the West End. As there are reasons why the name of the street should not be printed, I must content myself with stating that it is within a few hundred yards of Piccadilly Circus, that it consists chiefly of chambers, the offices of moneylenders, and a few surgeries of American dentists, and that at the far end of it is a cabmen's shelter. Doubtless many readers will recognise the street from this description. During most of the day it is well stocked with waiting hansoms, but late in the evening, when all the cabmen in London are engaged with theatre business, it is, considering its nearness to a crowded highway, curiously empty and deserted.

As I passed the cab shelter I observed that the attendant (the man whom you may see peeling potatoes at a pail in the forenoon) stood at the door of the shelter, looking first within and then into the street, his face pale and distorted. I halted in order to watch him, and to my astonishment he suddenly fell down on his back like a log. Running to him I found that he had fainted. He soon revived, and then I hoisted him on to one of the narrow deal seats in the shelter, and told him to rest his arms on the table at which the cabmen have their meals. In a few minutes he was to all appearances perfectly recovered.

"Do you often do that?" I asked him, smiling.

"I have never fainted before in my life," he said, gravely.

He was a man of thirty-five or so, with a pleasant, sensible, honest face, and he looked strong and healthy. I felt that there must be something behind this swoon, and was just going to question him when I heard the sound of a dog barking. It was a feeble, distant sound—the *yap-yap* of a little dog—and for the life of me I could not be sure whether it was in the shelter or not.

"Where is that dog?" I asked, somewhat mystified.

"Ah!" he exclaimed, with evident relief. "You hear it?"

"Distinctly," I said. "But where is the animal?"

"It isn't anywhere," he replied laconically, "and it isn't a dog. It's only a sound. But I'm glad you hear it, because now I know I'm not going mad; I know it's not my fancy. The fact is, this is a very strange cab shelter, and I'm thinking of leaving it, though I've only just taken the job on. It's ghostly, that's what it is. I've stood it a week, and to-night I fainted with fright, as you saw with your own eyes; and the wages isn't worth it, and wouldn't be if they was doubled."

"You mean—"

"Look here," he said, "I'll tell you the story of this shelter. I know every bit of it, because my uncle, John Craggs, was here before me, and he was *in* the story. I feel as if I want to tell someone. It'll relieve me."

And this is the tale the man told me. I do not give it in his words, but the facts are accurate.

. . . . .

At three o'clock on the morning of March 13, 189-, a constable in the course of his beat found a four-wheeler stationary in the main thoroughfare to which I have already referred, almost exactly opposite the end of the street containing the cab shelter. The horse, an aged white mare, lay on its side on the ground; it was dead. Neither driver nor fare was to be seen. The cab could not have been there, the constable said, more than a few minutes, for even at that hour there are occasional wayfarers in the main highways of Central London, and such an object must have attracted attention almost instantly. The constable found that the mare had been stabbed in the breast, and there was a quantity of blood in the road. That was the sum of his observations.

But a detective from Scotland Yard, who was upon the scene with laudable rapidity, discovered other things. He discovered that the near foreleg of the mare was broken; and later, with the aid of an expert, he was able to assert that though most of the blood was that of a horse, there was also a little, a very little, human blood in the road.

The detective was a young Scotchman named Sandy Stewart, rather new to his work, full of zeal and professional pride, and extremely jealous of newspaper men. Several reporters scented a mystery, but they were positively informed that the affair was an ordinary accident, and since no one save the police knew that the cab had been deserted, they accepted the statement, and nothing whatever appeared in the papers. In thus keeping the matter secret Stewart was not only following his own inclination, but also obeying strict orders from headquarters; for Scotland Yard instantly connected this dead horse and deserted cab with another affair, as to which they had received communications both from Paris and from St. Petersburg.

On the previous evening a celebrated French dancer named Liane had finished an engagement at a theatre of varieties in Leicester Square. Now Mademoiselle Liane, as many people behind the scenes knew, was the morganatic wife of a Russian Grand Duke, and a few months previously had left her husband against his will, and declined under any circumstances to return to him. She was an extremely beautiful woman, and the Grand Duke was beside himself with anger. Scotland Yard had been informed from Paris that on that night an attempt would be made, on behalf of the Grand Duke, to kidnap the errant Liane, and to take her willy-nilly out of England. From St. Petersburg came an urgent request, backed by the highest diplomatic influence, that the authorities in London would, to use historic phrase, "put the telescope to the blind eye," for this occasion only. There were special reasons at that time for being complaisant towards Russia, and by way of compromise Scotland Yard determined to do nothing, unless, by anyone's indiscretion, action was practically forced upon them. When, however, the landlady of the house where Liane had been lodging went to the police and said that her tenant had never returned from the theatre that night, it was deemed advisable, having regard to the coincident and highly suspicious mystery of the deserted cab, at any rate to prosecute a private inquiry, for the laws of England must not be too flagrantly defied even to please the most autocratic Sovereign in Europe. In this case, murder, or at least violent assault, was to be presumed, and therefore Sandy Stewart had instructions to find out things and report.

From the license-plate of the four-wheeler he was able to trace its owner (a well-known firm of livery-stable keepers in Westminster) and from them he got the name of the driver who had "taken out" the vehicle. The name was a curious one, Adolph Dacosta. The books of Scotland Yard gave this man's address as No. 54 Fetter Lane, but no one in the whole of Fetter Lane would admit any knowledge of Dacosta. Stewart went into the shelter, to which he knew the cab had been attached, and had an interview with my friend's uncle, John Craggs, who was the attendant in charge. John Craggs was almost a celebrity in the world of cab-drivers, and he was also favourably known among the police of the quarter. A poor but highly respectable old man, he performed his humble duties with thorough conscientiousness, was of a very good-natured and obliging disposition, and always struck one, by the neatness of his appearance and his quiet dignity, as being too good for his position. Stewart accordingly approached old Craggs in a most friendly and confidential way, without any of that professional suspiciousness which detectives usually assume when unearthing a mystery.

Judge, therefore, of his surprise when Craggs, at the first mention of the business, was visibly perturbed, though making a violent effort to appear calm. Craggs stated that he knew nothing whatever of Dacosta, except that he was reserved, that everyone called him "Frenchy," and that he was said to have travelled a great deal and seen life.

The detective was so much impressed by Craggs' agitation that he began to question him, and at last put to him the point-blank query:

"Do you know anything of the affair?"

"Me?" exclaimed Craggs. "Me?"

"Yes, you."

Craggs tried to laugh, but was not very successful.

"Nothing except what you tell me, and that's sure. How should I know anything?"

Then, murmuring an excuse, he disappeared within the shelter and busied himself with his pots and pans. Stewart followed him.

"I came down to see you yesterday," said the detective—this was the day after the discovery of the deserted cab—"but you—weren't here."

"To be sure I wasn't," the old man muttered, swiftly. "I was ill ... I had—a cold."

"Did you stay at home, man?" asked the detective.

"Yes."

"What is your address?"

"Now what do you want my address for? You can always find me here."

"I should like it just as a matter of form," the detective said soothingly. Craggs was growing angry in his nervousness.

"18, Chichester Rents," he snapped out, after a meditative pause. He was as unlike his usual self as possible.

For several days Stewart made no progress in his investigations, and then one morning a constable on duty in the neighbourhood informed him of a rather curious thing, namely, that no dog ever passed the shelter without stopping to sniff round it, and that sometimes there would be as many as four dogs at once nosing the ground about the shelter.

Without another word to Craggs the detective seized the first opportunity of the attendant's temporary absence to take up some of the floor boards of the shelter. There was a space of about a foot between the floor and the road, and to examine this space was the work of only a few minutes. The search was not in vain, for the detective found a corpse.

It was the corpse of a little dog, a white King Charles spaniel, with a crimson ribbon round its neck. The animal had no mark of ownership, but the detective had been round to the photograph shops collecting portraits of Mademoiselle Liane, and one of these showed her as nursing a white King Charles spaniel with a ribbon round its neck. White King Charles spaniels are very much alike, especially in a photograph, but there was no doubt in Stewart's mind that the corpse was that of the dog in the portrait.

Here, then, was a very palpable clue. The dog could not have put himself under the floor of the shelter. He must have been put there. Further, the boards exhibited clear signs of having been recently tampered with.

Several cabmen had witnessed the search. Stewart instructed them to say nothing whatever to Craggs about it, and then having replaced the boards, he awaited Craggs' return. The old man, however, did not return; and as he had provided no substitute, the cabmen had to manage as best they could that day for their dinner.

In the evening Stewart, tired at length of lingering near the shelter, went to 18, Chichester Rents, which proved to be a house of four floors occupied by some eight families. The people on the ground and first floors knew no one named Craggs, but on the second floor an old woman stated her belief that the father of Mrs. Macnab, who had two rooms on the third floor and did plain sewing, was named Craggs. Whereupon the detective proceeded yet higher. He found Mrs. Macnab to be a widow of some forty years of age. She was working at a sewing-machine, by the light of a candle, and five children were playing on the floor.

"Do you know an old man named Craggs?"

"That'll be my father," the woman said, looking up from her machine "God send nothing 'as happened to my poor dear father. He's been the best father to me as ever lived."

"So far as I am aware," said the detective, "nothing has happened to him."

"Thanks be to God! You gave me quite a turn."

"Mr. Craggs lives here, I believe?" the detective said.

"That he doesn't."

"But he gave me this as his address."

"I'd swear he didn't. You're mistook, sir. My father lives in Kingsgate Street, off Holborn, and has done this many a year, and every night of his life he comes in to see me, as is a poor widow with five childer, on his way home. I should 'a' been in the workhouse months ago if it 'adn't been for my father. You go to No. 142, Kingsgate Street, sir; that's where you'll find Craggs, sir. At least, you won't find him there now, sir, because he doesn't leave his shelter till 'alf-past eleven of a night, and then he calls here, and then he goes home. If you want to see him particler, you'd best go down to his shelter, sir, in—Street. Everyone knows John Craggs down there."

Without giving any further explanation of his presence or saying anything as to the disappearance of Craggs, Stewart made his way to Kingsgate Street, and there another surprise awaited him. The house was a lodging-house. The landlady said that Craggs had rented a room from her for nearly fifteen years, but had left three months ago, without giving any reason. She had been very sorry to lose him, for he was a tenant after her own heart.

Baffled once more, Stewart the next day circulated among

the Metropolitan policemen a description of Craggs. The old man turned up ultimately at the West London Hospital in Hammersmith Broadway. Someone had found him late one night at Addison Road lying delirious in the private footpath leading to Olympia, and had taken him to the hospital. He was suffering from brain fever. For weeks he was under treatment, and in the meantime Stewart made no discovery whatever in relation to the disappearance of Mademoiselle Liane or to the deserted four-wheeler. After nearly two months Craggs was convalescent, but on the very day before that named for his discharge he fell down some stone steps and broke his leg. He was transferred to another ward in the hospital, and Stewart was informed that the patient would probably be a prisoner for another month. At last the matron said that as Craggs was progressing very favourably, it would be safe for Stewart to interview him within the walls of the hospital.

At the detective's request the interview took place in a private room instead of in the ward. Craggs could now walk with the aid of a crutch, but Stewart was astonished at the change in him. He looked ten years older; his hair had turned from iron-grey to snow-white, and his thin, pale hands trembled continually.

Craggs was comfortably fixed in an easy chair. As soon, however, as Stewart entered the room he tried to spring up, and then sank back with a sort of despairing groan. Stewart, moved to compassion, endeavoured to reassure him by saying that he had come merely to ask a few more questions.

"And the first of them is," said Stewart, "why didn't you give me your proper address?"

"You've found out, then?" the old man stammered.

Stewart nodded.

"I'll tell you everything. I'll tell you everything," moaned Craggs. "I'm not long for this world, and I mustn't have anything on my conscience. Give me time, and I'll tell you. Don't hurry me—I'm not the man I was three months ago."

And then, with many digressions and halts and appeals for patience, old Craggs told his tale. The story amounted to this.

Somewhat less than a year before, his daughter's husband, a meat salesman, had died suddenly, leaving Mrs. Macnab and her five young children absolutely penniless. Mrs. Macnab contrived to earn a little by sewing, but the family would have either starved or gone upon the parish if John Craggs had not intervened. In a very short time he had expended upon the Macnabs the whole of his small savings, and after that he was obliged to assist Mrs. Macnab out of his weekly earnings. These were distinctly limited; nevertheless, the supply to the Macnabs went on as usual, and Mrs. Macnab was told by her father that his savings were still holding out, and would continue to hold out for a long period; she therefore accepted his charity without scruple. Craggs, however, was at his wit's end how to manage. At last he hit upon the plan of giving up his lodging in Kingsgate Street, and living by stealth at the shelter. He said nothing, of course, to his daughter of this manoeuvre. He called on her every night as usual. She thought that he left her to go to Kingsgate Street. In reality he left her to return to the shelter for his night's sleep on the wooden floor. Not a soul in the world suspected that the respectable John Craggs was so poor that he could not afford a lodging. If the fact had become known Craggs would have been ready to die of shame, for his respectability was the very breath of life to him.

One bright moonlight night he was awakened in his corner in the shelter by a thud against the door. "By thunder," said a man's voice, "it's open. We'll take her in here." Two men entered, bearing the body of a girl. One of the men was Adolph Dacosta, otherwise "Frenchy." The other was a dark fellow with one eye. Craggs, paralysed with alarm, dared not move, and made no sign of his presence, which was completely hidden by the shadow of the table. The men closed the door of the shelter, and the man with one eye, who spoke

Two men entered, bearing the body of a girl.

with a foreign accent, began to explain things to Dacosta. Craggs gathered that the former was an old acquaintance of Dacosta's in France, and that he had specially sought out "Frenchy" to help him to carry off the girl.

It appeared that the man had inveigled Mademoiselle Liane into "Frenchy's" cab, and that when they had proceeded a short distance the girl, suddenly suspecting a trap, had produced a dagger and threatened to kill the man if he did not let her go. He grappled with her. Just then the old white mare, through some unevenness in the roadway, came a cropper, and in the sudden jerk that followed Liane's dagger had somehow entered her own breast. "Frenchy" and his employer were then in a terrible quandary. They could not move the mare, who was kicking and squealing from the pain of her broken leg, and though the street was for the moment deserted a policeman or someone would certainly be along in a moment, and then they would be caught with a dead or dying girl in a cab. They decided to lift the girl out of the cab, and carry her away, and, having stabbed the mare, they proceeded to do so. Their invasion of the shelter was an after-thought, a piece of pure chance which depended on the door having yielded to "Frenchy's" push.

Craggs heard them discuss what they should do with the girl's body. Ultimately they decided to put it under the flooring of the shelter, as a temporary measure, and this was done. The man with one eye then dived into the pocket of his great-coat and pulled out a little dog, which he strangled on the spot and threw down by the side of the girl's corpse. Then the two men replaced the flooring, destroyed all traces of their visit, and made off, never suspecting that Craggs had witnessed the whole operation.

As for Craggs he was beside himself with terror, anxiety, and indecision. His inclination was naturally to go for the police at once, but he was deterred by two reasons. First, the fact of his sleeping in the shelter would become common property; secondly, he had a foolish fear that if he informed the police, one or other of the men might take vengeance upon him. He was especially afraid of the man with one eye.

He spent the whole of the next day and night in wandering about the streets. On the following morning he gathered courage to return to the shelter, and he found that in the meantime the corpse of the girl had been spirited away; but he forgot to look for the dog.

He saw then that it was too late to tell the police without getting himself into trouble. And so he determined, if anything was discovered, to deny all knowledge of the affair. The evident suspicions of Stewart, however, unnerved him. The matter preyed on his mind, and ended, as we have seen, in brain fever.

. . . . .

"And what was the end of it all?" I asked my intelligent friend in the shelter.

"Perhaps it isn't ended," he said. "Stewart never found out anything else. 'Frenchy' and the man with one eye have never been caught, and the corpse of Liane hasn't been seen, at any rate not in England. They must be clever chaps, those two. Only one thing is known, and that is that the Grand Duke, or whatever he is, has built a grand mausoleum—that's the word?—in the gardens of his palace outside Moscow, and visits it every day for two hours. So I suppose the girl's body has reached Russia. But how—no one knows. Yes, it's a queer world."

"And poor old John Craggs?"

"My uncle is dead," he replied. "The old man never recovered from the shock, and he died in the hospital. Just before his death he got me his place here, and I promised to see after my cousin, Mrs. Macnab. And so I shall do. But I shan't stop here. Should you?"

And as I thought of all the dreadful circumstances, and of the faint ghostly barking, I said to my friend that certainly I should not.

NOTES

1. *Woman*. 5th December 1900, pages 18-20. Signed E.A. Bennett. Illustrated by T.W. Boyington.

PART IV
EDWARDIAN YEARS

He ground his teeth, as though that operation might serve to hurry her.

"The Railway Station"—Bennett's newly rediscovered Christmas story in the Hanley Library Archive.

36 THE STAFFORDSHIRE SENTINEL CHRISTMAS NUMBER.

PUBLISHED BY SPECIAL ARRANGEMENT. COPYRIGHT.

THE RAILWAY STATION.

By ARNOLD BENNETT.

Author of "Love and Life," "A Man from the North," "The Gates of Wrath," "The Grand Babylon Hotel," &c.

THE RAILWAY STATION.[1]

I.

Railways are contrivances for moving parcels of matter from one part of the earth's surface to another part of the earth's surface, at certain times. The parcels vary in size and value and constituents; one parcel may consist of oranges encased in thin wood, another may be a fowl tied up with paper and string; another may be a beautiful woman wrapped in delicate rose-coloured skin, with an outer covering of pretty clothes, and that parcel goes in a first-class carriage, and the guard smiles on it. But, as far as the railway is concerned, they are all merely parcels. Some parcels can talk; others can moo, or grunt, or neigh; others maintain a strict silence: there is the chief difference. And one is apt to wonder, in one's more philosophical moments, why this business of moving parcels from one given spot to another given spot should be considered so very important, and why these enormous and complex and expensive organisms called railways should have come into existence, and why the speaking parcels should be so extremely tragic when they undergo the experience known as "missing the train." What does it signify, anyhow?

Well, you know, it does signify something, sometimes.

II.

If you had been at the vast London terminus of the Grand Junction Railway, which, as everyone is aware, is the greatest and finest railway in England, and therefore in the world, on a particular evening towards the end of last year, you would have been impressed by the importance, and the significance, and the intense urgency of this business of shifting parcels from spot to spot. The evening in question was Christmas Eve. Need I say more? Christmas Eve has a peculiar quality of bringing out the secret significances of things in general, and especially of parcel-shifting, and most especially of human parcel-shifting; it puts things in a new and clearer light. Had you been at the Grand Junction terminus then you would have perceived instantly various wonderful meanings of life (and of railways), which, on any other evening in the year you might have failed to perceive. That is why Christmas is Christmas.

And you might, if you had been lucky, have perceived a young man, not very tall, and not very strong, and rather pale, but very obviously happy, tottering proudly along Platform No. 8 with a heavy portmanteau in his right hand, another heavy portmanteau in his left hand, an umbrella under his right arm, a rug under his left arm, and two green tickets between his teeth. One portmanteau was labelled R.C. in black letters, and the other was labelled M.M.M. in white letters; and both had the humble, retiring air of portmanteaus that are not very often carried by porters, at twopence for ten yards. The young man rammed his way in a straight line, through the bustle of the interminable platform, gazing in front and on either flank as if in search of something that he had wanted all his life. At last he came to a long train of many carriages, and all the carriage doors were opened wide, and over every doorway was printed in bold characters, "Manchpool (Central)." The young man beamed as though he had discovered America, and paused before the entrance to a third-class compartment. He read again carefully the sign "Manchpool (Central)," and then he turned to a passing and extremely pre-occupied porter and bunted him in the side with one of the portmanteaus. The porter stopped, aggrieved.

"This train goes to Manchpool?" the young man demanded.

"Yes," said the porter.

"Central?"

"Yes," said the porter.

It is a peculiarity of human parcels on Christmas Eve that they are extraordinarily suspicious; they fancy that railway companies have arranged a colossal combined conspiracy to take them where they don't want to go. They will not trust printed notices, and they will scarcely trust porters. In fact, they decline to believe that they are really moving towards the desired spot until they actually get there.

The train had but just taken up its position on the platform, and there were only two other people already in the compartment. The young man occupied the two remaining corners with his two portmanteaus.

"This train goes to Manchpool?" he murmured to one of the other travellers.

"I believe so; I hope so," was the smiling reply.

The young man threw his umbrella and rug on the rack, put the green tickets in his pocket, hung up his hat on the brass hook, and replaced it by a soft cap which he took from the mysterious inward depths of his overcoat. Then he whistled and jumped out of the compartment, into which six other people immediately stepped.

He looked at the long train, and the two mighty engines in front, and he was veritably under the delusion that the entire train existed, that indeed the entire Grand Junction system existed and always had existed for the sole purpose of shifting himself and another from London to a particular spot in the north of England, and on that particular evening. All the rest—all the other trains, and all the other people—were a dream, a figment, a nothing.

He returned up the platform in the direction of the clock and the book-stall. The clock showed nearly one minute past six; he had therefore nearly half an hour before the blissful and ecstatic moment of departure. The book-stall made a tremendous effect, and was doing a tremendous business under its six Welsbach[2] lights, which threw down a flood of radiance on evening and morning and weekly papers. Christmas numbers, sixpenny editions of masterpieces and of trash, six shillings editions of all that was newest and smartest in modern fiction, rugs, mauds, jug-purses, reading candles, and umbrella-rings. Men were continually passing, flinging coins at the clerks entrenched behind the ramparts of literature, and snatching up papers in exchange. Other men and many women paused and gazed long in front of the stall, incapable of making a choice from this bewildering mass of print, amusing and instructive. The young man was among the latter. After several minutes he saw "Woman's Life" on the stall, and he bought it because he remembered that she had once said she liked it. And on the book-shelves, between "Famous Criminals" and "The Early Homes of the Prince Consort," he saw Mrs Peel's "How to Keep House," and he bought that, too, not without a blush. He purchased nothing for himself, because he did not feel like reading.

And he lapsed into a reverie, there in the middle of Platform No. 8, with bangs, shouts, rumblings, and whistles reverberating all around him in the vast terminus while the hand of the clock crept downwards and the crowd surged on every side, hurrying to and fro, and porters cried out, "By leave!" and his toes had narrow escapes from the murderous wheels of luggage trucks. And he thought of an immense draper's shop in Oxford-street, and then of Manchpool, that great manufacturing town in the north, and then of a little branch railway that runs away from Manchpool into the dales, and then of a small old-fashioned market town, in the dales, and then of a house in the town, and a warm room in the house .... And then he was back again in front of the great draper's shop in Oxford-street, and he saw the shutters going up and the assistants covering the goods with enormous grey sheets.

"Aha!" he exclaimed joyously and almost challengingly.

For Christmas Eve was in his heart.

Cold feet induced him to stamp and walk about. And this perambulation brought him opposite to the little chocolate emporium between the book-stall and the first-class waiting-room. The chocolate emporium in the Grand Junction terminus is a longitudinal hole in the wall, about six feet by three. There is a narrow marble counter within the aperture, and right at the back of the aperture are a few shelves; and the counter and the shelves are loaded with every conceivable and inconceivable form of chocolate. You can buy a pennyworth of chocolate in three wrappings of fancy paper and you can buy an elaborate half-guinea basket of chocolate, constructed of gilded wickerwork and silk ribbons, with a glazed card attached upon which to write the name of the goddess for whose consumption it is intended, and the name of the goddess's worshipper. And between the counter and the shelves there stands always a girl with frizzy hair, dressed in tight black, with white collar and cuffs, and a touch of red ribbon at the throat. She is not always the same girl, perhaps, but she is always there and looks very nice and neat in her cage, surrounded by that tempting and variegated display of bonbons.

Now the young man chanced to get a glimpse of her, in the corner of his eye, as he walked past the chocolate emporium, and he looked quickly away, as modest, shy people do, when they think they have seen someone they know but aren't sure. In a few seconds he retraced his steps, and made a careful inspection of the face behind the counter from a safe distance. Yes, it was she. It was the girl who used to serve him with two poached eggs, a cup of tea, and a victoria pudding every day at one o'clock at the A.B.C. shop[3] in Cheapside.

III.

He wavered as he approached her lair again, and then turned definitely towards her. She recognised him at once.

"Who'd have thought of seeing you here, Mr. Churner," she said smiling, and putting up her hands to her frizzy hair.

"Nay," he said; "who'd have thought of seeing you here?"

And he bought a shilling packet of something which she had specially recommended, while she told him that she had been in her present situation for three months, and didn't like it, though it wasn't so monotonous as the A.B.C., and there were no white aprons—she hated white aprons.

"Still at the old place?" she inquired.

"Oh, no!" he answered. And there was a note of pride in his voice. "I left Pawson and Leaf's last month. I'm setting up for myself in the drapery at Tarnside—a town in North Lancashire, you know."

"Are you now?" she exclaimed. "I do hope you will succeed, Mr. Churner."

"Yes," he said, "I hope so, too." He tried to restrain himself from adding further personal details; but he could not—he could not keep the thing to himself. "I've come into a little money," he added.

"Some people do have luck!" she said. "Much?"

"About a couple of thousand," he answered nonchalantly, as if it was threepence three farthings.

"Good gracious me!" she observed.

Just then an old gentleman in a fur coat rushed up to the counter, and asked for a half-guinea basket of assorted. There was no half-guinea basket of assorted on show, and the girl opened the door behind, leading to a sort of store-room, and after rummaging, produced the required confection. The old gentleman put down half-a-sovereign and half-a-crown.

"Keep the change," he said to the girl, benevolently, "for Christmas."

And suddenly, despite the two thousand, Mr. Churner felt very poor and low down the ladder of success.

"And I suppose you are going to be married, Mr. Churner?" the girl pursued, elated by this windfall, but not wishing Mr. Churner to think that a couple of shillings was anything to her.

"Well," he said, in a burst of candour, "I am."

"And it will be to that pretty young lady that used to come with you sometimes in the evenings for a cup of tea and a sultana? Miss Murgatroyd you called her at first, and then you began to call her Minnie."

The girl laughed.

Mr. Churner was inclined to resent this familiarity, but really the girl was so good-humoured and good-natured, and really the feeling of Christmas Eve had so got hold of him that instead of frowning he laughed even more loudly than she did.

"Yes," he admitted, "you're quite right. Minnie Muriel her full name is. I've been up at Tarnside this three weeks past arranging affairs. And I came down last night to fetch her and to buy some things. We shall get to my old mother's to-night about twelve. And we're going to be married to-morrow, Christmas Day that is. My old mother wanted us to be married then; it was a fancy of hers, because she was married on Christmas Day herself, you see."

"And Miss Murgatroyd—where is she?"

"She'll be here soon." He glanced at the clock, which indicated thirteen minutes past six. "It's like this. She's engaged in the millinery at Margrove and Swansdown's, in Oxford-street, and she isn't free till to-night. She would work her engagement out; she's very conscientious. They close at six. I've got her luggage and her ticket. She'll be able to leave at 6 5 or 6 10, and all she has to do is to jump into a cab and drive here. I've arranged for the cab. You see, I was obliged to be here early to look after things and secure seats. I reckon she'll turn up between 6 20 and 6 25. We go by the 6 30 express to Manchpool and change there."

"But," said the chocolate girl, "the Manchpool express leaves at 6 20."

"Oh, no," he said. "It leaves at 6 30. I've gone down by it for years now."

"But it was changed this month," she persisted.

"You're joking!" he faltered, pale and agitated.

"Indeed, I'm not, Mr. Churner! Indeed, I'm not! I would not joke on such a subject. No one knows better than me that the Manchpool express leaves now at 6 20."

"It's impossible!" he said. "She'll miss it! She'll miss it! I never thought of looking at a time-table for the 6 30. Why it's always been 6 30!"

"Well," said the chocolate girl, coming out of her lair by the door, which gave on to the platform, and peering up the platform as though in the hope of seeing Miss Murgatroyd approach, "if she isn't here in five minutes, you'll have to go by the 8 10."

"But the 8 10 will be no use to us," he cried. "Tarnside's thirty miles from Manchpool, and there's no train after that one that connects with the 6 30. Are you sure, quite sure?"

She ran her fingers over an adjoining time-table, and showed him the figures.

"Better go and take your things out of the train," she said, "in case—Speak to the guard. I'll speak to him. I'll speak to him myself. I shall see him. Oh, but he'll never wait, he daren't."

Mr. Churner ran up the platform in a terrible state of mind. Despair had ousted Christmas Eve from his heart. He looked for a guard; he looked for anyone who could counsel him in this extremity, but every soul on the platform seemed selfish, callous, and preoccupied.

"What time does this train leave for Manchpool?" he questioned a foreman porter, who at last happened to cross his path.

"Six-twenty," said the foreman briefly.

"C—can't you keep it a minute or two?" he murmured, hesitatingly.

The foreman withered him with a look and passed on.

Mr. Churner, in a terrible state of mind, ran to a foreman porter.
"Can't you keep the train for a miuute or two?" he spluttered.

IV.

It was 6 18—and it is exactly at holiday times, when every other railway in the country becomes disorganised, flustered and inefficient, that the Grand Junction pulls itself together and determines to be more prompt, more supernatural than ever! The discipline at the terminus that Christmas Eve was worthy of the finest traditions of Frederick the Great. The ticket inspectors were mutilating the last tickets and banging the doors, and the drivers of the two Titanic engines leaned expectantly from their cabs.

"Ticket sir," said the inspector to Mr. Churner, who was standing irresolute in front of the door of his compartment. Mr. Churner produced two tickets.

"Take your seats, please," said the inspector, and passed to the next compartment.

Mr. Churner plunged madly into the train, flung out his portmanteau, flung out the portmanteau of Minnie Muriel Murgatroyd, and, seizing his umbrella and hat, flung himself out also.

"Take your seats," said another inspector, and as Mr. Churner did not move, this second inspector shut the carriage door. The eight people within the compartment thought that the young man was a morphinomaniac, or something of that kind, and subject to weird crises of activity.

As he saw door after door banged to, Mr. Churner, standing amid his luggage as amid the ruins of Carthage, abandoned himself to the blackest blackness of pessimism. He saw the future swathed and draped in all that was not roseate. She had missed the train; that was certain! Well, what then? They could not go on to Manchpool by the next, and spend the night at Manchpool, even at different hotels. No, that was impossible. Anything was better than that. Besides, Minnie would never consent to it. Moreover, if she did consent to it, the plan could not help them. Because Christmas Day trains would be the same as Sunday trains, and he knew that there was only one Sunday train from Manchpool to Tarnside, and that it did not reach Tarnside till after three o'clock in the afternoon. Tarnside was truly an awful place, a deadly place, and an utterly out-of-the-world place. They could not therefore be married to-morrow! What? They could not be married to-morrow? But they must.... Everything was arranged—choir, parson, breakfast, carriages. They must. Besides, the ill-luck, the unspeakable discomfort of a postponement! Nevertheless a postponement was inevitable. And just then a postponement of his marriage seemed to Mr. Churner the most dreadful thing that could happen in the wide universe.

And she would have to return ignominiously to those barrack-like dormitories at Margrove and Swansdown's; all the assistants at Margrove and Swansdown's lived in! Imagine her Christmas Eve there! Imagine the next day, Christmas Day! He simply could not imagine it. Christmas seemed a mockery, a horrid practical joke.

"Why couldn't Minnie be in time?"

He asked himself the question angrily—and instinctively. It was just like a man. Then he recollected that the fault was solely and wholly his, and not Minnie's at all. And he cursed himself, and humbled himself, and said to himself that if any other fellow had omitted to look up the time-table for such an important journey, he would have called that fellow a silly and inexcusable ass. He would have predicted no success in life for that other fellow. He would have asserted that that other fellow did not deserve to be engaged to any girl whatsoever, let alone the most sensible and the sweetest girl that ever sold passementerie over a counter.

All these ideas, sensations, and reflections swept through the brain of Mr. Churner in about fifteen seconds.

And then the clock showed 6 20.

V.

At this juncture there happened one of the most singular things that ever did happen at the London terminus of the Grand Junction Railway. Nothing like it was ever known before, and nothing like it has ever been known since.

There are two guards to all the chief expresses of the Grand Junction, one in front and one behind. Before the departure of a train the guard in front performs a fantasia on his whistle, and waves a green flag to symbolise the general joy; the guard behind repeats these rites, and then—and then only—may the engine-drivers give voice and open the throttles of their mechanisms.

Now the clock showed 6 20 and a half. All the doors of all the carriages were shut, the people within the carriages had finished their goodbyes and their exhortations to the people on the platform, the luggage was all in, and the front guard had whistled and waved.

But there was no reply from the guard behind.

The front guard looked round at the driver of the nearest engine.

"Sticks are off, ain't they?" he demanded.

(This is railway language—something akin to Sanskrit. The man merely meant that the signals were down, weren't they.)

"Ay!" replied the driver, "sticks are off right enough."

"Then why in thunder don't he—?" exclaimed the front guard, and paused.

Still there was no answering wave, and no answering whistle.

"Where in thunder is he?" exclaimed the front guard.

"Blessed if I know," the driver laughed. "Perhaps he's gone to 'ave 'alf a pint."

This witticism caused immense laughter on the two engines.

And then it ran all over the platform that the principal guard for the great 6 20 express to Manchpool had mysteriously disappeared. The entire personnel of the terminus was deeply affected by this item of news. Because it was at once so unprecedented, so comic, and so tragic. The staff did not know whether to laugh or to cry. The train was going to be late, the train was late. And it would throw out the 6 30 to Birmingham, and that would throw out the 6 40 to Sheffield. And it was Christmas Eve! And, oh! It was impossible that the guard wasn't somewhere close by! They searched his van; they even looked in the dining car. Well! He had vanished! An inspector hastened to tell the stationmaster, that terrific functionary who ruled the terminus with whips and scorpions. The train couldn't depart with only one guard. The gilded stationmaster descended upon the scene, used some inconvenient language, and—quite frankly—was nonplussed. Even he could not find a competent guard for a great express at a moment's notice. It is to be borne in mind that the chief guard of a Grand Junction flyer is no everyday mediocre individual; he is a specialist of high attainments and complicated responsibilities.

The hand of the big clock fell to nearly 6 25, and then a shaft of hope pierced Mr. Churner's heart, like a delicious stab. A few minutes more of that miraculous delay, and Minnie Muriel would arrive. He gazed ardently up the platform. Was it she, in the distance? No! Yes! No! Yes! He recognised her hat with the red feather. And she was strolling gently and easily towards him. She was always calm. He ground his teeth, as though that operation might serve to hurry her. Gradually she approached. He opened the carriage door, and flung in the portmanteaus for a second time. He beckoned to her.

Behind her came racing the figure of the missing guard.

"I've done it, with five minutes to spare," said Minnie Muriel, sweetly and tranquilly.

"Have you?" replied Mr. Churner. "Well, jump in and look slippy over it, my dear."

The guard waved and whistled, and sprang into his van

without glancing at the stationmaster, or at anyone; and the 6 20 in theory (6 25 and a half in practice) steamed majestically out of the station.

VI.

"So she caught it?" said the chocolate girl, a fortnight later to Mr. Churner. He was finishing his honeymoon, and his wife was taking a solitary bun in the refreshment room, while he went forth to buy "Woman's Life" for her.

"Oh, yes," said Mr. Churner, with the large expansive dignity of a married man. "Oh, yes!"

"I was determined she should," said the girl, "I'm engaged myself, and I felt for you both. Eh, I did feel for you. I come from the north, too."

"You were—er, determined—?"

She leaned over the counter. "Listen," she whispered. "The guard of the 6 20 is my young man, and, let me tell you, he's the youngest express guard in the service. And some time before he starts, he runs up here, just to kiss me and run off again. He goes in there; I keep his can for him in there." She indicated the little store-room behind her. "I locked him in, that night, till I saw Miss Murgatroyd coming down the platform. It was the nearest shave. Not a second longer dared I have kept him. He was furious, was Jim! But afterwards, when I told him, it was all right."

The girl smiled beneficently.

"I can't thank you," Mr. Churner stammered.

And it occurred to him afterwards that he didn't even know her name.

NOTES

1. *The Staffordshire Sentinel Christmas Number*. December 1904, pages 36, 38, 40, 42. Signed Arnold Bennett. Illustrated.
2. Carl von Welsbach (1858-1929) was an Austrian scientist and inventor. His Welsbach gas mantle was a device for generating bright white light heated by a flame.
3. The Aerated Bread Company Ltd., founded in 1862 to mass-produce additive free bread, became well known for its chain of teashops. These tearooms were significant for providing some of the first public spaces where women could eat without a male companion and not risk their reputation.

THE FARLLS AND A WOMAN.[1]

I.

"Your cousin Godfrey seriously ill; think you should come.—Colpus, physician."

When, one afternoon at the office of my paper, I received this telegram, I could not avoid the involuntary suspicion that the famous or infamous Dr Colpus had wormed himself into the affairs of my disunited and quarrelsome family for some nefarious purpose of his own. Colpus was not at that time so renowned as he afterwards became; his plot with the beautiful Mrs Cavalossi to obtain the Peterson millions, for instance, had not even begun;[2] but as a journalist I had indirectly learnt a good deal about him that was in no wise to his credit, and, despite his almost unrivalled skill in his profession (and out of it), I had classed him in my own mind as one of the two chief scoundrels—Rocco, the great *chef* of the Grand Babylon Hotel[3] was the other—of his generation. I knew that for some years he had been my cousin Godfrey's medical advisor. Had Godfrey been any friend, I should have felt sorry for Godfrey, but as Godfrey had openly declared himself my enemy, I kept my sorrow for more sympathetic and deserving objects.

As for the telegram, of course I felt bound to obey its behest, and after dinner on that same evening I went to Cannon-street to see my cousin; we had not spoken to each other for several years. You may, perhaps, think it strange that a sick man should be residing in Cannon-street, E.C. That merely shows either that you have never heard before of Godfrey Farll, or that you have forgotten his eccentric reputation. Godfrey was a financier of the shrewdest sort to be found in the City. His palatial suite of offices in Cannon-street was regarded with nearly as much awe as those of N.M. Rothschild and Sons not many hundred yards away. My cousin had a genius for finance—all the Farlls had a genius for some one thing[4] (of course, I exclude myself); he gave himself up entirely to finance—all the Farlls gave themselves up entirely to one thing. Lord Farll, for example, my own and Godfrey's uncle, had given a lifetime to the chemistry of the manufacture of steel and had thereby earned an immense fortune and a peerage. I myself, for another and less important example, had given my life to the pursuit of journalism, and had earned—well, very little! To the practice of high finance Godfrey Farll apparently sacrificed all else. He was so devoted to it that he insisted on living in a flat over his offices. For weeks together, so I have heard, he never left Cannon-street. He scorned physical exercise—said it was a fad. When people expressed surprise that he could exist in so noisy a thoroughfare as Cannon-street he would sometimes invite them upstairs for a glass of sherry and a biscuit, and would display to them a few of the wonders of his flat. Not a sound from outside could penetrate those rooms, for there were double windows everywhere, and the system of ventilation by means of shafts and fans was more perfect than anything to be found in Belgravia or Mayfair. The flat, in short, was a marvel of ingenious luxury; it was said to be the most comfortable and quietest flat in London, and I believe it was.

Eight o'clock was striking as I arrived; the season was autumn, dark, depressing; but there was no sign of this in the flat; warmed air, delicately-shaded lights, thick carpets, rich curtains, noiseless menservants—all contributed to a sort of illusion that Godfrey's little world revolved quite independently of the seasons. Nevertheless, there was an atmosphere of dreadful expectation in the place that proved that not even this self-contained microcosm, with its double windows, could keep out the fear of death.

Dr Colpus met me in the ante-room. He appeared to have taken charge.

"I am glad you have come, Mr Frank, if I may use your

Christian name—it saves confusion," he said, suavely, as we shook hands.

I bowed. "Of course. I had no hesitation whatever in coming," I replied.

"There was no one else to whom I could send," he continued.

"Lord Farll is in London, is he not?" I suggested.

"Your uncle is in London: but I regret to say that he also is very ill."

"I had not heard of it," I said. "Are you sure?"

"I have had private information," he answered. "A sudden seizure. Even journalists do not get wind of everything," he smiled. "But doubtless you will have news when you return to your office. The illness of a man of Lord Farll's reputation is bound to become public property without much delay."

"And what is the matter with my cousin? Is it really serious?"

"It is very serious," said Dr Colpus, with much calmness. "Mr Farll only sent for me three days ago. He should have sent sooner. It is a case of brain failure, not insanity, you understand. Brain failure, highly curious, and with a development alarmingly rapid. Your cousin is now suffering from Cheyne-Stokes[5] breathing."

"What is that?" I inquired.

"It is a symptom which is infallibly fatal," said the doctor. "Pray come with me."

I followed him into the principal bedroom—almost a state apartment—of the flat. My cousin, it seemed, was old fashioned, and slept in a four-poster, and this bed was situated between the two large windows of the room. A single electric light burned to the left of the bed, shaded so as to leave the bed in gloom, and under this light sat a man who held fast my cousin's hand.

"You know your cousin's peculiarity," whispered the

doctor. "Of course, I was obliged to get male nurses. He wouldn't have a woman in the place."

It was a fact, as I knew, that no woman had ever been allowed to enter Godfrey's flat. He was reputed to hate the sex. This was his chief eccentricity, and personally I believed it to be nothing but a pose.

We approached the bed. Godfrey lay perfectly quiet. He looked his age, forty-five, fifteen years more than mine: he looked careworn, frightfully apprehensive, and his face was flushed as if with exertion. He caught sight of me and his dim eye brightened.

"The vultures are gathering," he murmured thickly, with a bitter smile.

"Not in the least, Godfrey," I said, and, turning to Dr Colpus, I added, in an undertone, "He certainly looks ill, but his breathing is like a child's."

"Wait," said Colpus, shortly. There was a slight catch in Godfrey's throat; the doctor took out his watch; then gradually the patient's breathing became difficult and more and more difficult, until he fought for it in a paroxysm of despair. The nurse by the bed kept firm hold of his hand, and tried to soothe him. But Godfrey could neither be soothed nor held still. He sprang up in bed in the effort to fetch his breath.

"Frank!" he cried out, in the accents of an excruciating appeal.

I seized his left hand. "I am here," I said; "it's all right."

Then slowly the difficulty of respiration passed away. In a brief space Godfrey was once more breathing like a child, and the nurse persuaded his grey lips to take a little brandy and milk. Then again there was the catch in his breath, and the same awful struggle, and the same awful cry, and then calmness again.

"That crisis recurs every fifty seconds," the doctor murmured in my ear. "This morning it was every seventy seconds. To-morrow—" He stopped and looked at me.

"And that is Cheyne-Stokes breathing?" I said.

"Yes. It is usually the final stage of cerebral softening. I have never known a recovery. I need not tell you that the mental torture to the patient is unspeakable. It is worse than being hung every minute."

I could say nothing. Pity for my cousin swamped all other feelings in my heart. So this was the end of financial greatness! And Lord Farll, that other magnate, ill, too! While I, the third and last member of the family, the despised one, the mad idealist, the pauper, enjoyed health and bodily vigour, and the universal beauty of the world.

"May I trouble you to come into the drawing-room," said Dr Colpus. "I wish to speak with you." His tone had subtly changed. From the omniscient, calm physician, he had swiftly become the creature of intrigue whom I knew by repute. In leaving the room he gave a few brief instructions to the nurse.

The drawing-room was at the other end of the corridor. As we entered, it was lighted only by the glow of the fire, but Dr Colpus turned on the switches by the door-jamb, and I saw in a sudden revelation the superb magnificence of the apartment. It had everything that a drawing-room in Park-lane might have had, and in addition there was a tape-machine inclosed in a marvellously carved oaken case. My cousin could not bear to be out of sight of a tape-machine. Dr Colpus shut the door carefully, and there stood with his back to the fire. I took an easy chair.

"Mr Frank," said he, "your cousin is dying."

"You say that professionally?"

"I say it professionally."

The tape-machine began to click; and Dr Colpus walked over to it. "Pooh!" he exclaimed. "False alarm of fire at a music-hall: two women hurt." He returned to the hearth. "You have not been on good terms with your cousin for some years, I believe?"

"No," I said, briefly.

"Nor with Lord Farll?"

"No."

I scanned the slight, upright form in front of me, the thin, pale, lined face with its long grizzled moustache, the fine white hands. I wanted to know what these remarks were leading up to. But I found no answer to my unspoken query in that inscrutable figure.

"You quarrelled with your rich relatives about politics," he said, with a subdued sneer, as I thought.

"I did not quarrel," I replied. "My cousin Godfrey stood for a Metropolitan division in Parliament. His politics, and those of Lord Farll, were not mine. I was editing an evening paper at that time. My cousin and my uncle seemed to think that I ought to sink my political opinions out of regard for family considerations. I declined to do so. My paper went on its way as usual, and, chiefly owing to the influence of my paper, Godfrey was handsomely defeated by the rival candidate. Neither Godfrey nor Lord Farll ever forgave me."

"You are mistaken," said the doctor. "Lord Farll forgave you, or, at least, partly forgave you."

"He has given no indication of it," I said.

"Pardon me," said the doctor.

"What indication has he given?"

"He has made a will."

"Indeed!"

"I was one of the witnesses."

"A will in my favour?"

"In this way. Lord Farll leaves the whole of his property —not far short of a million, I fancy—to your cousin Godfrey absolutely, unless— "

"Unless?"

"Unless Godfrey dies before him. If Godfrey pre-deceases Lord Farll the whole of the property comes to you—since there is no one else to leave it to."

"I see," I said.

"Your new paper, *The Liberal*, is going on well, I trust?" remarked the doctor, as if changing the subject.

"Excellently," I said, with enthusiasm. "It will be a great success only—" I hesitated there.

"Only what?"

"Well, I need more capital."

There was an awkward pause.

"Your cousin Godfrey is dying," the doctor resumed, in a voice that seemed to me to be very far off. "And Lord Farll is also dying."

"How do you know that Lord Farll is dying?" I asked, sharply.

The tape-machine clicked. The doctor went over again to inspect it. He read out: "Mr Balfour rose at 8.30 to resume the debate on the Irish Estimates. Lord Farll, the great steel magnate was taken ill this morning. He is reported to be slowly sinking. In reply to Mr Swift McNeills speech before dinner, Mr Balfour[5] said that the Crimes Act—"

"That will do, I think, doctor," I interrupted him.

"It is a question whether your uncle or your cousin will die first," said the doctor.

"Yes," I murmured, mechanically.

"The point is important to you, Mr Frank," he pursued.

It was. It was a question whether I was to be a millionaire, or nearly so, and one of the most powerful influences in Fleet-street, or whether my paper, *'The Liberal,'* was to fail for want of capital.

"I may tell you," the doctor went on, remorselessly, "that your cousin Godfrey made his will a long time ago, and left the whole of his estate to various charities."

"Ah!" I reflected, sarcastically, "he was always charitable, was Godfrey!"

"Therefore," said the doctor, "if Godfrey survives your uncle, not only his estate, but your uncle's also, will go to charities. And you will be left out in the cold."

I tried to assume an attitude of nonchalance.

"How long will Godfrey live?" I questioned.

"That depends. His case is hopeless. He suffers, as you have seen, appalling agony. The sooner he dies the better for him. He may die to-night if nature is left alone. I might be able to keep life in him for a few days longer by injections of strychnine sulphate night and morning. Strychnine regularises the action of the heart, you know."

There was another dreadful pause.

"But to what end?" murmured Dr Colpus. "To what end?"

I stood up swiftly.

"Doctor," I said. "No case is hopeless till the patient is dead. Is it not your professional duty to inject strychnine? Surely it is *de rigueur* that you keep life in your patient as long as possible, at no matter what cost of mental agony to the patient? Is not the withholding of strychnine equivalent to killing Godfrey."

"You are a strange man," was all his reply.

"I have known men more strange," I retorted. "Answer me."

"A professional man must be guided by his own discretion. I may or may not consider the injection of strychnine a discreet proceeding." He spread out his hands.

"Why do you tempt me?" I said.

"Tempt you? I tempt you? My dear Mr Frank, I have merely placed the facts before you. I am a physician, but I am a man of the world. I do not like to see men behaving like fools. There is such a thing as common sense, and is greater than sentimentality."

"Why do you tempt me?" I repeated.

"I do not tempt you," he said, with undiminished calmness. But—some day, if we understand each other, you might be in a position to do me a service."

I walked to and fro in the room. The tape-machine was still clicking foolishly. I turned and faced my companion.

"Dr Colpus, as Godfrey's near relative, I request you to administer strychnine to him at once—to do everything in your power to prolong his life. He may recover. Men have survived the death-sentence of the most skilful physicians."

The doctor sighed. "As you wish," he said. His eyes said, "Ass!"

"Further," I went on, "I will, if you please, see the strychnine administered."

And I saw it administered.

"I shall stay the night here," I said afterwards to Dr Colpus, as he was leaving the flat.

II.

I spent not only that night, but the two following, in my cousin's flat. In the daytime, of course, I was engaged in the necessary conduct of my own affairs, and, in particular, I had to busy myself in the search for the capital which was to carry my paper to final and lasting success but in this search my luck seemed to desert me. I found time to call at my uncle's house. Lord Farll was unconscious, and growing weaker hour by hour; nothing could be done there. Almost the same might have been said of my cousin's case; the injections of strychnine alone enabled the sufferer to maintain any sort of vitality.

On the fourth night I had been dosing [sic] in the drawing-room for an hour or so when I was awakened by the consciousness of a presence in the room. I opened my eyes. A woman stood before me. She was a woman of thirty, tall, well shaped, well dressed; on her left hand was a plain gold ring. Large soft masses of black hair framed her face. Her eyes were black and sparkling, her lips red, her cheeks full and rosy. She made a beautiful vision.

"Who on earth are you?" I exclaimed, without thinking, scarcely yet awake.

"I am his wife," she replied.

"Whose wife?"

"Godfrey's!"

"Impossible!" I jumped up.

"I think I shall be able to convince you that I speak the truth, when the time comes," she said, proudly.

I was abashed. "I beg your pardon," I stammered. "But Godfrey has always been regarded as—as a woman-hater, a misogynist."

"Ah!" she murmured. "I knew that. You are his cousin Frank?"

Then she told me that she had lived all her life in a remote village of Northamptonshire, that Godfrey had found her there, an orphan, that she had loved him, and they were quietly married; that he had always insisted on her remaining where he had found her, and called her his refuge from the world, and that it had pleased her well to obey him; that sometimes she did not see him for a fortnight together, but that the intervals of his absence were never longer; that she knew his health had been failing, but had not suspected anything serious; lastly, that she had no idea of his illness until she saw it referred to in that morning's *Financial News*, which she read daily, without understanding it, because it often mentioned his name. She said that Godfrey seldom wrote to her.

"You have seen your husband?" I asked.

"I have been with him this last hour," she said, "and now I come to you for all information. Is he really dying? How long is it since the doctor was here?"

"He is really dying," I replied, and added, "I am glad that there is one soul in the world to regret his loss."

"Why do you say that?" she said, quickly. "Tell me, was he considered a hard man?"

"You are his wife—" I began, and stopped. Godfrey was the hardest man I ever knew.

"You are afraid to tell me," she cried. "Yes, I knew he was

hard. But not to me! Not to me!"

"You have loved him?"

"I have liked him very much." A silence fell. She was a strange and fascinating woman.

The tape-machine broke out into its clicking chatter, but I took no heed.

"And now he is dying!" she said, staring at the fire. Tears stood in her eyes.

"Yes," I sighed. "And all his wealth and all yours cannot save him."

"Wealth!" she said, turning her face away from the fire." A fortnight ago my husband told me he was ruined, unless the shares of a certain company rose to a certain point. They have fallen instead of rising. For months he has kept a brave front, but when he is dead," her voice broke, "the world will know that the great Godfrey Farll was not such a financier as people thought him."

She spoke boldly. To hide my astounded face, I walked across to the tape-machine, and read: "Lord Farll died at his residence in Lowndes-square at nine o'clock to-night."

"You are wrong, Mrs Farll," I said. "Your husband will die rich." And I told her that Lord Farll was dead, and had left a will in Godfrey's favour. I made no mention of myself.

"I must return to my husband," she remarked, quietly and was gone. Her entrance and her exit were equally so sudden and mysterious, and her news had been so startling, that for a few moments I thought I must have been dreaming. But a tiny lace handkerchief lay in a chair. It was hers, and quite sufficient evidence that I had not dreamed. I picked it up and put it in my pocket.

That night, before dawn, my cousin Godfrey died. He had won his right to Lord Farll's fortune, and I had lost the same fortune by exactly six hours. The next morning Godfrey's wife had vanished.

III.

The two male nurses who had been watching my cousin left the flat at once. The blinds were drawn down. The vast offices on the ground floor were not opened. Death reigned where gold had once reigned. As the last surviving member of the family, I stayed to arrange the personal affairs of the financier who had passed away, and I telegraphed to my late uncle's house in Lowndes-square that I should arrive there in the afternoon. The pauper relative of these two plutocrats had indeed enough to do that day.

During the morning Dr Colpus called in again.

"You have lost all," he said, "and it is your own fault."

"I have not lost my self-respect," I said.

"There is still time," he went on, as though I had not spoken.

"What do you mean, doctor?" I said, roughly.

"Your cousin died at three o'clock this morning, but it will be quite simple to say that he died at eight o'clock last night, an hour before your uncle. Merely a matter of form. Nobody will be the worse off, save a few absurd charities. The nurses know me, and can be trusted."

I laughed, and wondered whether it was worth while to report the fellow to the Medical Council.

"There was another witness besides your precious nurses," I said, "to the fact that my cousin was alive after nine o'clock last night."

I was about to tell him of the mysterious feminine visitor, when a servant entered the room. I expected the man to announce "Mrs Farll," but it was only Godfrey's solicitor that he ushered in. Colpus had taken upon himself to send for the lawyer.

This latter produced a will, executed five years before, which he read to us. The doctor had told the truth, the entire estate went to charities. It was Godfrey's last revenge against me. The solicitor also produced a codicil, which left a legacy of a hundred guineas to Dr Colpus, with the request that Dr Colpus would therewith buy himself a chronometer as a memento of the testator.

"I think that is all," said the lawyer, blandly.

"I think it is not all," I said, with equal blandness. "I very much doubt if that will is valid. Marriage invalidates a will, does it not?" I asked.

"Certainly marriage invalidates a will," the lawyer replied. "But—"

The door opened on these words, and my cousin's widow entered; she was in mourning.

I had the melancholy pleasure of explaining the situation. My cousin's widow made good her promise to prove the fact of her marriage.

"Were you my husband's solicitor?" she asked the lawyer, coldly.

"I had that honour, madam; but I fear I was not in his full confidence."

"Perhaps not. But you can inform me whether this document is in order?"

She took a paper from her reticule. It was a will made by my cousin Godfrey three years ago, and a year after his marriage. It left half his property to his wife and half to his cousin Frank Farll.

"It is in order," said the solicitor.

* * * * * * * *

"What induced your husband to relent towards me?" I asked Mrs Farll afterwards.

"I induced him," she answered.

"But why? You had never seen me. You had no interest in me."

"I had an interest in my husband's honour. I admired you for sticking to your politics. I wished my husband to be a just man."

She looked proudly in my face.

"You were fit to be a king's wife!" I exclaimed.

"Did I not say that my poor Godfrey was not a hard man?" she smiled sadly. And then, strangely enough, she began to cry.

So it came to pass that I inherited half of Lord Farll's fortune. Two years later I found myself under the necessity of managing not only my own half, but the other half. I leave your shrewdness to guess by what means this occurred. The codicil bequeathing a hundred guineas to Dr Colpus was executed before Godfrey's marriage, and was therefore invalid. However, I bought a chronometer out of my own purse, had it engraved, and presented it to him. The back of the watch bore this legend: "Cheating never prospers."

"Oh, yes, it does," said the imperturbable Colpus when I gave him the watch.

NOTES

1. *The Queen, The Lady's Newspaper*. 17th October 1908, pages 620-621. Signed Arnold Bennett. Author of "The Grand Babylon Hotel", "Love and Life", "Anna of the Five Towns", "Gates of Wrath", &c. *The Queen* was an illustrated Journal and Review, first published in September 1861. James Hepburn's *Letters of Arnold Bennett I. Letters to J.B. Pinker* (1966) mistakenly dates the publication as 17th October 1903 (p. 36). Anita Miller's 1977 *Arnold Bennett. An Annotated Bibliography 1887-1932* perpetuates the error. (p. 235)

2. Dr. Colpus, Mrs. Cavalossi and the plot to "obtain the Peterson millions" is an intertextual reference to Bennett's *The Gates of Wrath,* published in four consecutive monthly instalments in *Myra's Journal* (1st October 1899 1st January 1900) and revised for novel publication in 1903.

3. Rocco is the villain in Bennett's *Grand Babylon Hotel,* published in serial form in *The Golden Penny* (2nd February 1901-15th June 1901) and as a novel on 9th January 1902.

4. Priam Farll is the painter hero of genius in Bennett's novel *Buried Alive*. (4th July 1908)

5. Darius Clayhanger dies a painful death suffering from Cheyne-Stokes in Bennett's *Clayhanger (1910)*.

6. A.J. Balfour (1848-1930), Conservative politician, and Prime Minister from 1902 to 1905. J.G. Swift MacNeill (1849-1926), Irish Protestant nationalist politician, and M.P. for South Donegal from1887 to 1918.

PART V
WAR-TIME

Walter J. Enright's illustration for the American magazine *Collier's* publication of Bennett's "The White Feather".

THE WHITE FEATHER.[1]

This is a true story, for the essential facts of which I vouch. The final spectacular incident has not yet actually happened, but it may happen at any moment on a fine day.

On a recent afternoon Cedric Rollinson, looking excited and triumphant, entered the great olive-green, white-lettered gates of the establishment of the Imperial Blank Manufacturing Company, Limited. He was twenty-nine years of age, and seemed younger. A conscientious young man, with a considerable sense of responsibility! Also, a successful young man, for he added to conscientiousness much industry, and he had been well-educated, and scientifically trained for his job. His job was an expert job in the establishment of the Imperial Blank Manufacturing Company, and it combined applied science with the handling of human workmen. His salary was, of course, inadequate (the Company always insisting on his extreme youth), but it enabled him to live agreeably in a suburban house and garden with his wife and child ... Yes, the fool—criminally blind to the chances of a European war—had married and become a father.

Soon after the war broke out, the Imperial Blank Manufacturing Company, Limited, also broke out with notices to their employees, which notices were posted all over the walls of the immense manufactory. Copies of the notices were sent to the daily papers, and were duly printed therein, with an editorial headline eulogistic of the firm. The notices ran thus:

FOR KING AND COUNTRY.

IMPERIAL BLANK MANUFACTURING COMPANY, LIMITED.

The Directors wish it to be known that in the event of any employee joining the colours they will, so far as practicable, keep his place open for him, and in addition will pay to the family of the employee (should such family be dependent upon him for support) the difference between his salary from the Company and his pay as a soldier, this arrangement to hold good as long as the war lasts. The Directors hope for an excellent response to the above offer.

GOD SAVE THE KING. By Order.

The thing was not very elegantly worded, but its meaning was clear. Everybody who entered the gates saw the notice. Everybody who passed down the street saw it.

At first Cedric Rollinson could not imaginatively grasp that the notice was a notice to him. But his conscience happened to be a persevering organism, and after a day or two it had got the better of him. He had observed in the intellectual periodicals which he read an urgent advertisement to the effect that 2,000 junior officers were immediately needed by the British Army.

He said to himself: "I have a lot of expert knowledge that might be useful, and, moreover, I am accustomed to handling men. Indeed, I am thought to be rather good at handling men. Perhaps I ought to go."

On the second night he remarked rather timidly to his wife:

"I was wondering whether I oughtn't to offer myself—as an officer, you know." Then he laughed, as if he had only been joking after all.

But his wife startled him by answering seriously:

"I've been wondering about it too, dearest."

In a moment they both knew that the matter was decided. He must go. On all the hoardings he had read: "Your country needs you."[2] With simplicity and single-mindedness he took the call to himself—he did not ram it into the ears of the man sitting next to him in the Tube, he took it to himself. His wife cried, and started to prepare things for him.

At the same time he began to offer himself; and his difficulties began. The attitude of the War Office officials was such as to engender the belief that they did not want officers at all, that in particular they did not want him, and that it was like his infernal impudence to fancy that he could get a commission in the British Army. Nevertheless, having had for years an intelligent notion of what the average mentality of the War Office was, he persisted in his efforts to make a present of himself to the nation, and did at length beat down the first defences of the official mind. Then he made still further progress, and in the end he was "given to understand" that if he could obtain a recommendation from a person of consequence he might conceivably get his commission.

Now he knew a very well-known artist, and this artist knew a sporting peer (through having painted the peer's daughters), and it was borne in upon Cedric Rollinson that the recommendation of the sporting peer would be more valuable at the War Office than the recommendation of ten thousand artists, professors, or philanthropists. So through the artist he arrived at the sporting peer, who was entirely amiable; the recommendation was promised; and the wheels had the air of going round in a satisfactory manner.

It was at this point that Cedric Rollinson, looking excited and triumphant, entered the great olive-green gates of his employers. He was excited and triumphant because he had now almost succeeded in forcing his services on his country, and almost reconciled himself to leaving his wife, his child, and home. The remuneration named by the War Office was not excessive; it was, indeed, quite inadequate for the support of that suburban home and its inmates. But as the Company had guaranteed the difference between his present salary and his future pay, he did not mind. Certainly he was risking life and limb and the whole future of his family; but he would not be risking the immediate welfare of his family; and this contented him.

In the yard in front of the counting-house staircase, he met Mr. Hawker Maffick, a director of the Imperial Blank Manufacturing Company, Limited, and the only director then in London. Mr. Hawker Maffick was a member of the august family of Maffick, some of whose characteristics have already been set forth by H.G. Wells.[3] A bachelor of fifty-eight, he was, perhaps (though Wells may disagree with me), the greatest of all the Mafficks. He was the Maffick who preferred to remain in the Background. Other Mafficks had accepted (or rather bought) titles. But not Hawker Maffick. Hawker was above titles; he was above all inessentials. He never boasted of anything, except that he had the best man-servant in the Empire; he was never ostentatious. But there was not another Maffick—no matter how spectacular and well-advertised he might be—who did not deeply respect and fear Hawker Maffick, and speak with awe of his genius for picking up the right investments, and of the probable amount of the death-duties on his estate. Hawker Maffick's social and political sentiments were apparently correct to the least detail. On no public topic did he ever express views that were inferior to the very best. And he never Overdid It. He was a stoutish man, unsusceptible to flattery save at one point; he liked to be thought "strong-lipped."

"Good afternoon, Mr. Maffick," said Cedric Rollinson deferentially, raising his hat. "I was hoping to catch you before you left. May I have one word?"

"What is it?" asked Hawker Maffick, with a blandness which somehow very firmly indicated to Rollinson that directors must not be kept past a certain hour from their clubs. Hawker Maffick and a few friends had amused themselves immensely of late at the Club by concocting messages to "shirkers" and advertising them in the Agony columns of the *Times* and the *Morning Post*. Hawker's own contribution to the solemn patriotic gaiety had been as follows: "Cotton wool and a glass case will be provided free on demand to any young man who does not feel equal to joining the Army."

"I shall in all probability get my commission, sir," said Rollinson.

"On what?" asked Hawker Maffick—it must be admitted without sufficient reflection. But the mind of even the greatest Maffick runs in a groove.

"In the Army, sir. I'd mentioned it to Mr. Spation."

Mr Spation was the Assistant Manager.

Said Mr. Maffick:

"Come and see me in the morning at ten thirty."

And in the morning a refreshed Maffick, seated in his grandiose, Empire-furnished private office, said to his expert young employee:

"So you're thinking of going into the Army?"

Rollinson did not stick out his chest and reply: "Sir, my country has need of me, and I feel that I must respond to her call!" No, he just said:

"Yes, sir."

"Well," said Hawker Maffick, raising his eyebrows and gently smiling and touching his discreetly-perfect cravat, "of course you know your own business best. I have no doubt that I can find someone to take your place, but you will admit that you put us in an awkward position. However—"

"But surely temporarily, sir—" Rollinson began, already feeling like a criminal in spite of his conscience.

"Temporarily?" Mr. Maffick failed to understand.

"Won't you keep my place for me, sir?"

"You ought to know that we cannot."

"But your printed notice, sir?"

"Ah! Mr. Rollinson. That applies to—er—the hands, naturally—but for those in the higher ranks, such as yourself, the problem is different. Moreover, the notice says 'so far as practicable.' Duty to your country, certainly! Certainly! But *where* is your duty to your country? What about your wife, your family? Are they not part of your country? Are you sure that a youthful itching for military glory, as you imagine it, is not clouding your better judgment?"

Cedric Rollinson asked quietly:

"If I go shall you make up my salary to my wife?"

"I fear we cannot."

"Will you make up half of my salary?" Rollinson demanded with a sort of desperation.

Hawker Maffick gazed at his hands and shook his head.

"In these times," he said, "it would be impossible for us

—having regard to the interests or our shareholders."

He picked up a document and frowned at it. Utterly unconscious of danger, he had not the slightest idea that Cedric Rollinson was on the point of slipping round the desk and punching him violently in the eye. But Cedric, having a wife and family, and having also some remains of prudence, controlled himself. He had to choose between his country and his wife and family, and he chose.

"Very well, sir," he said. "I must stay here."

That evening, as he was walking to the station on his way home, three smartly dressed girls, approaching, barred the pavement. He stopped.

"How young he is, the poor darling!" murmured fondly the central maiden, and, suddenly producing a large white feather,[4] she jabbed it into his waistcoat. And in another tone, fierce and scornful, she added: "That's all you're short of, you Koward! [sic]—Why don't you enlist?"

And off the trio went, laughing. This was the latest sport of bright and pretty creatures in London.

NOTES

1. *The Saturday Westminster Gazette*. 19th September 1914, pages 13-14. Signed Arnold Bennett. *The Westminster Gazette* was founded by George Newnes in January 1893, later acquiring the *Saturday Westminster,* then merging with the *Daily News*.

The story appeared three weeks later in *Collier's,* a New York based American weekly magazine. The American version had minor differences, such as sectional sub-headings and some sentences omitted. It also carried the sub-title "A Sketch of English Recruiting" together with a sizeable illustration by Walter J. Enright.

2. The War Minister Lord Kitchener (1850-1916), having warned that the war would be decided by Britain's last one million men, launched a campaign for volunteers in the summer of 1914, based around the slogan "Your Country Needs You". Alfred Leete's (1882-1933) iconic poster first appeared on the cover of the penny weekly magazine *London Weekly* in 1914.

3. The significance of the name "Maffick" is explored in the Introduction.

4. A.E. Mason's (1865-1948) novel *The Four Feathers* (1902) is the story of an army officer's successful refutation of cowardice after his fellow officers presented him with a white feather. Bennett was familiar with, and reviewed, Mason's work. The Order of the White Feather was founded in August 1914 by Admiral Charles Fitzgerald (1841-1921), supported by such writers as Mrs. Humphry Ward (1851-1924) and Baroness Orczy (1865-1947), author of *The Scarlet Pimpernel (1905).*

THE LIFE OF NASH NICKLIN.[1]

I.

When Miss Mordey smiled at Nash Nicklin in Trafalgar Road, Bursley,[2] and hesitated in her walk as he came towards her, and finally stopped and engaged him in conversation, one of the chief characteristics of Nash Nicklin's individuality at once grew active.

Even at that period Nash Nicklin was already for ever settled down in life. He had reached the age of thirty, and he was the secretary of the Toft End[3] Brickworks and Colliery Company, Limited, a solid and respected enterprise paying 20 per cent. to its shareholders, who were few in number and much envied by all other investors in the Five Towns.

Mr. Nicklin lived in a cottage near the top of Brougham Street,[4] alone, for, though settled down, he was not married.

He walked every morning along the bottom of St. Luke's Square,[5] down Church Street,[6] through a little slum alley without a name, across the foot of Woodisun Bank,[7] and so at length into the straight amplitude of Trafalgar Road—the "great" thoroughfare, always providing comedy and tragedy, which had about seventy years earlier replaced Woodisun Bank and its continuations as the highroad between Bursley and Hanbridge. He then, having crossed Trafalgar Road, walked up its slope for a space until he came to the "Queen Caroline" Inn, where he turned off into Caroline Street, which brought him to the gates of the vast smutty territory owned by the Toft End Brickworks and Colliery Company, Limited. He retraced the route before dinner, and again a third time after dinner, and lastly a fourth time when the day's work was over.

Hence every day four times (but only twice on Saturday) Mr. Nicklin was a noticeable phenomenon in the regular spectacle of Trafalgar Road. He was a rather short man, fair, sturdy, with a very long stride, and he moved in such a way that his knees seemed to be always bent and always preceding the rest of his body. He dressed with care, as befitted the secretary of a successful limited company with rich possessions on the earth and under the earth. And his expression was somewhat challenging, as though the watchful blue eyes were continually saying to the world: "I am somebody in the town. I know my value. Do not be misled by my unassumingness. You are likely to underestimate me. Let me warn you seriously against doing so."

Many excellent persons in the Five Towns go about with a similar expression which is compounded of undue diffidence and undue self-esteem.

Thus the affability of Miss Mordey roused two different feelings in Mr. Nicklin. He considered that her behaviour to him was no more than his right; and at the same time he was staggered by it and could not help receiving it as a condescension towards himself from a superior being. His notion of Miss Mordey as a superior being had been mainly engendered by the fact that she was a stranger to the district. The natural instinct of the Five Towns native was, then, to prostrate himself before strangers, with a simultaneous sneer to save his vanity, and to defend and apologise for his district in one breath.

Miss Mordey had entered the district (on a visit) with a certain prestige, for she was a friend of Miss Overhouse, and was staying with Miss Overhouse; and Miss Overhouse was head mistress of the recently established Bursley High School for Girls.

Bursley was then in the first ecstasies of pride over its High School for Girls. The Endowed School for Boys had given up its quarters in the Wedgwood Institution[8] as being cramped and unhygienic, and had established itself palatially at Shawport Hall.[9] The said quarters in the Wedgwood Institution being therefore empty, it had occurred to some energetic person that they were the very quarters for a Girls' High School, and the High School had come into existence, and a small corps of learned, bright, and critical women had come into the town out of the great world.

These women were inquisitive; they had the inquisitiveness of true knowledge. They wanted to see everything in the district—both pot-works and coal- mines. Miss Mordey had been one of a party that had inspected the wonders of the Toft End Brickworks and Colliery Company, Limited, and Mr. Nash Nicklin, fussy and fluttering, had superintended the exhibiting of the wonders. But he had never hoped nor expected to speak to Miss Mordey again, and especially in the street as a mere private man. On the Toft End property he was more than a man—he was a power; but in the street he was simply Nash Nicklin, and Miss Mordey a mysterious roseate creature from upper circles, higher spheres—in short from Leamington.

II.

She was like a bright splash on the sombre September afternoon in Trafalgar Road. She wore a wide-spreading, lavender-tinted dress with an extensive tunic; over this a short red paletot of Indian cashmere with vast hanging sleeves from out of which peeped elfin hands in yellow gloves; in her ears pendant earrings; on her head a heavy coiffure topped by a very small brown hat whose trimmings hung low behind. She had no visible waist; her hat was the apex of a cone whose sides slanted evenly downward until they ended in the huge circumference of her skirt's hem. Her face was pale and small, and the design of the costume made it seem even smaller than it was, so that she had the effect of a fragile, tiny, tiny living creature sheltering somewhere within the protection of an enormous system of apparel.

Nash Nicklin took one of the elfin hands nervously. His delusion was that the whole town was looking at him as he dallied there with Miss Mordey. The fashionable audacity of her clothes intimidated him. But he said to himself, "And yet, why shouldn't a woman be fashionable? It's fine, and it livens things up." Never before had he sympathized with fashion, but rather scorned it. What pleased him in Miss Mordey more than her fashionableness was her fragility, her slightness, her appealing air of a woman (she had a wondrous way of putting her head on one side and smiling wistfully). Her demeanour combined respect and envy with a realization of her own mysterious force.

She might have been saying: "How I wish I were a great, strong, wise man! Still, it takes women as well as men to make a world; and after all, I can twist you round my little finger—and I will—within reason." Nash Nicklin enjoyed such demeanour in a woman. It caused him to think that most Five Towns women were not women but females. And he was doubly charmed to perceive that learning and cleverness could go with intense femininity. The sole flaw in his pleasure was due to his own inability to behave with the ease and grace of a man of the world. Still, she evidently did not notice this shortcoming in him.

"I suppose you'll be at the Conversazione to-morrow night, like the rest of us?" she said, gathering him at once into the fold of the elect.

He asked incautiously: "What Conversazione?"

Then he remembered having seen small posters here and there announcing that the newly-formed local branch of the Education Society would hold a Conversazione at the Town Hall, and that the recent marvellous invention of science—the phonograph (which repeated what you said better than a parrot)—would kindly be exhibited thereat by Mr. Clayton-Vernon.

"Ah, yes!" he corrected himself quickly. "Yes, I had some idea of going." Though he had had no idea whatever of going. "I'm sure it will be frightfully interesting," said Miss Mordey. Never before had Nash Nicklin heard the word "frightfully" used in such a sense, and quite probably Miss Mordey was the first person so to use it in the Five Towns. Mr. Nicklin was impressed by the delicious originality of her vocabulary. She added, "And of course one ought to support the Society."

It appeared to Mr. Nicklin that "one" meant himself and herself.

"I shall certainly go," said he.

At this point, just when he ought to have developed into social brilliancy, he quite lost his nerve, and could hit on naught to say. There he stood, an uncomfortable boor, tongue-tied, while apparently she waited for wisdom and wit to issue from his mouth.

The predicament was appalling. But almost at the same moment a lorry came rattling down the road behind a trotting giant of a horse; on the lorry was an immense gate and two prodigious posts.

"Now what is that, Mr. Nicklin?" Miss Mordey demanded, amid the din of the lorry.

"Why, God bless me!" answered Nash Nicklin, "If it isn't th' old turnpike gate from up Bleakridge! You know they've done away with the Turnpike Trust at last. I heard yesterday as they'd got th' gate off its hinges. The toll-house is for sale."

The din subsided, while both Miss Mordey and Nash Nicklin stared at the retreating gate prone on the lorry. Nash Nicklin had been among those who were opposed to the abolition of the turnpike. He would have retained the gate (which had to be opened for every vehicle passing between Hanbridge and Bursley) partly from sentiment, partly because he feared that the modern spirit was moving too fast in the land, partly because he could not easily imagine roads without turnpikes, and partly because he regarded the transfer of roads from private to public control as a dangerous socialistic experiment. But now, under the darting eye of Miss Mordey, he seemed to comprehend that a turnpike-gate between two big contiguous towns was a dreadful anachronism that ought to have been abolished ages ago instead of yesterday. He admitted this to Miss Mordey.

Miss Mordey murmured, "Only yesterday! How amusing!"

He said, "I suppose you find us very old-fashioned down here?"

"Not at all!" cried Miss Mordey in accents of sincerity. "Quite the contrary. I think the district is most alert."

"Do ye now!" said Nash Nicklin, very surprised. But if she had replied "Yes" to his question he would have been very hurt. He saw that in causing the turnpike to disappear the district was in truth alert and tremendously up-to-date.

"I love the district!" said Miss Mordey. "I simply love it!"

Nash Nicklin looked up and down the black muddy road, and gazed at the little brown houses, the little shops, the occasional soiled crimson-lake façade of a manufactory, the occasional badly-fenced empty plots of ground, the familiar slatternly-aproned figures and dirty scowling faces that passed to and fro, and the pair-horse tram rolling slowly up the other side of the street. And somehow he imagined that he saw in the scene something lovable and fine that he had never detected till then.

"Rather smoky, eh?" he suggested, enchanted by her appreciation.

"Well, the smoke can't be *helped*," said she, with seriousness. "Business is business."

He smiled, proud and pleased. Like many others, he was at bottom rather complacent about the excessive dirt of the district due to inordinate smoking of countless factory chimneys.

And Miss Mordey, following the train of her own thought, continued:

"There's something about you all—something down-*right*. Nobody could help trusting you ... Oh! I've never been in any district quite like this, and Miss Overhouse says the same." She bowed to a man who had saluted her from the opposite pavement.

"Can you tell me if that is Mr. Sworn?" she asked. "One is

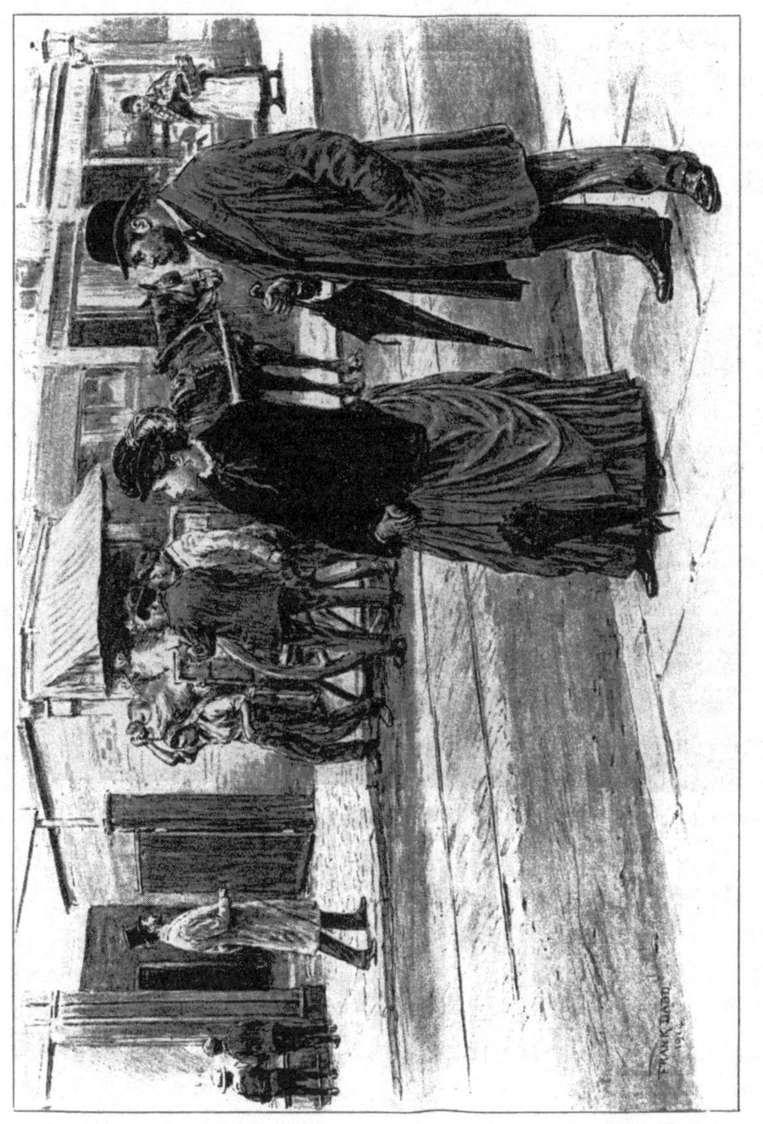

"Can you tell me if that is Mr. Sworn?"

introduced to so many people."

"It's Mr. Sworn going home," said Nash Nicklin.

"D'you know him?"

"Only by sight," said Nicklin shortly. The truth was that he considered Mr. Sworn to be the most conceited ass in the town. He saw Mr. Sworn two or three times every day, but always on the opposite pavement, and the mere sight of the vain coxcomb afflicted Nash Nicklin with nausea. He desired to kick him.

He desired at any rate to cross the road, stand in front of him, and say to him: "Look here! You're a fool."

"I thought it must be Mr. Sworn," said Miss Mordey. "But I wasn't sure about his beard ... Most men seem to wear beards in this district." She spoke the last words with a peculiar air.

"Don't ye like beards?" Nash Nicklin inquired broadly, feeling that he had already grown intimate with the exquisite creature.

She put her head on one side, and smiled a little mischievously, and yet appealing too, and held out her hand.

"Ah!" she archly murmured. "Seeing that you wear one you mustn't ask me that."

She was gone, up the road.

Nash Nicklin thought angrily: "That chap Sworn worms his way everywhere."

In all other respects the state of his mind was entirely beatific. He was happy even to his beard, for a scheme concerning it had come into his head. He smiled to himself all down the road.

III.

That evening he retired to bed an hour earlier than usual, for the reason that he had something unusual to do, and he wished, nevertheless, to be asleep at the usual time. He was a man of habits. In a competition he might well have taken first prize for prosiness, as being the least romantic male in Bursley. He was supposed not to have an idea outside the Toft End Brickworks and Colliery Company, Limited; he was supposed to be incapable of tender emotion. And yet he had carried a pair of scissors up with him to his mean little bedroom, and he was sharpening an old forgotten razor in front of his small dressing-table mirror, in which he could see the reflection of an austere and narrow bedstead.

In saying that Nash Nicklin had a beard, Miss Mordey did not exaggerate. He had a magnificent brown beard—not long, but thick, wavy, and glossy. No beard of its kind could have been finer. He had worn it for some years; his barber never failed to admire it. Well, he was about to remove it—his pride.

He had only spoken to her twice in his life, but she had implied—not asserted—that a beard in a gentleman was objectionable; her opinion as to beards was obvious. Therefore his beard should vanish, and he would appear in front of her at the Conversazione beardless.

He would say nothing to her about beards; he would await her remarks. The sacrifice, far from hurting him, gave him profound pleasure—perhaps the profoundest pleasure he had ever experienced. He was agreeably excited. His thoughts dwelt continuously upon Miss Mordey, and upon her disturbing dissimilarity from other women, and upon her rightness in everything. Come to think of it, beards were vulgar. Smart cavalry officers never wore beards, nor did the men in fashion-plates at his tailor's. Beards smacked too much of the Five Towns. It must not be assumed that he was consciously in love with Miss Mordey. In love with her he no doubt was, but not consciously. He had no aspiration to win her. He did not dream of winning her. He wanted to please her simply because to please her pleased him. His feelings were the purest a man can have.

He was bathed deep in exquisite romance as he began to snip away at his fine beard. He went about the dread task savouringly and slowly, for at that time of night he was alone in the cottage and insured against all interruption. After he had snipped half a dozen times he glanced at the floor, and then went downstairs and returned with a copy of the *Staffordshire Advertiser*, a roomy sheet even in those days. He opened the newspaper wide, laid it on the floor in front of the dressing-table, and stood in the exact middle of it in his shirt and trousers. In ten minutes the scissors had done their task, in twenty he was bleeding but clean-shaven; in thirty he had burned the beard, filling the house and part of Church Street with a very sinister odour.

His neighbour, Mrs. Machin, a widow, locking her back gate, saw the early light in his bedroom, and smelt the strange smell, and mumbled to herself: "What's *he* up to?" She could not guess that she was within seven yards of a unique romance.

IV.

Beardless, Nash Nicklin slept ill, because of the very odd, unaccustomed feeling around his chin, which was like a lamb in an inclement climate. At about 3 a.m. he saw clearly that it would have been better to remove the beard in the morning, so that he might have grown used to its absence during the day. He saw also that in future it would be necessary for him to shave daily. Now he was already, at the age of thirty, the slave of his daily programme, and to change it seemed an enormous undertaking. Still, there could be no doubt that he would have to rise at 6.50 instead of 7.5 in order to breakfast at 7.45. This would mean going to bed earlier, which might mean a complete revolution in his evenings. Further, he would need to spend money on razors. However, all such dark anticipations were lightened by brilliant flashes of bliss in the mere existence of Miss Mordey.

He got to sleep toward 4 o'clock and woke at 6.45. At any rate (he said to himself) he would not be compelled to rise at 6.50 that first morning, as he was already shaved. But when he delicately felt his chin, lo! there was a scrub on it! Tirelessly, inevitably, ruthlessly, the beard during the night had been growing, growing!

"The charwoman looked up and gave a gasp"

And naught that he could do would stop it. He was almost frightened. He arose, and went out on to the landing and called to his charwoman, newly arrived by the back-door, for some hot water in a jug. In the evening he had shaved with cold water, and he was determined not to repeat that folly. The charwoman, startled by the strange demand, came to the foot of the stairs. Mr. Nicklin fled from her sight, not because his night attire was not presentable, but because his chin was self-conscious (though he would not admit it). And when he was shaved again and dressed he had serious difficulty in coming downstairs and entering the parlour, where was the charwoman. It was as if an invisible barrier prevented him from entering the parlour. He painfully forced the barrier. The charwoman looked up and gave a natural gasp, which Nash Nicklin unmercifully throttled by asking in a voice of fury why the tea was not on the table.

The difficulty of getting into the street was more than serious—it was acute. He had to push himself into the street; the street might have been raked from end to end by a murderous infantry fire, and the house might have been bullet-proof. Nevertheless his programme was sacred, and at length he timidly faced the fire and stepped forth ... There was Mrs. Machin cleaning her step! He knew Mrs. Machin, and feared her and liked her; and the redoubtable taciturn widow liked him.

"Had a clean shave," he said as he passed her, with a foolish smile. There was no reason why he should have thus drawn fire, but extreme self-consciousness is a queer thing.

"So it seems," said Mrs. Machin, glancing up.

He stopped.

"My throat was getting very delicate," said he, "so I thought I'd better harden it, you know. Beards always make delicate throats."

"I never heard o' that," said Mrs. Machin.

She gathered together her gear and went into her cottage. Her son Denry,[10] quite a small boy, was richly breakfasting to fortify himself for school. Being eight years of age, he was entirely unfit for confidences as to the sentimental behaviour of adults.

But Mrs. Machin had a way of throwing remarks at him which she did not expect him to comprehend. (As he grew up she dropped the habit.)

On this occasion she murmured, jerking her shoulder in

the direction of Mr. Nicklin's path to business: "*He's* got mixed up with some woman now! Who next, I wonder!"

Denry Machin, unmoved, went on with his meal, and Mrs. Machin said no more.

V.

That evening, in his long and full frock-coat, Nash Nicklin went up to the Town Hall, but by a roundabout way. He told himself that he traversed the whole length of Wedgwood Street and climbed Duck Bank[11] because he did not want to arrive at the Conversazione too soon. But perhaps the true reason was that he wanted to put off the arrival as long as possible. There was a fine distinction between the two motives.

It was a coldish night, according to his chin. Throughout the day he had had difficulty in protecting his chin from worse things than a chill atmosphere. In his imagination his chin had seemed to be the business of the entire town. He would not have been surprised to see his chin in the late edition of the *Signal*. Even the junior messenger who had an errand to the bank in the afternoon had stared at Nash Nicklin's chin with strange effrontery when ordered to call in at the Town Hall and buy a two-shilling ticket for the Conversazione. Mr. Nicklin considered that he had a just grievance, for after all it was his own chin that he had shaved. Had he shaved somebody else's chin, he could have understood the fuss, both uttered and tacit; but he had not.

As he got to the top of Duck Bank the car overtook him, its horses steaming. He heard the brake applied and saw the car gradually stop at its appointed place between the Conservative Club and the Shambles.[12] The dim vehicle was crowded, and with no common throng. Ladies enveloped in cloaks descended from it delicately, with the aid of strong and chivalrous men in high hats. Mr. Sworn descended from it. (Of course, Sworn would worm himself into the Conversazione!) Then a smaller figure, extremely muffled, descended from it. The figure resembled, and was, Miss Mordey. Mr. Nicklin trembled between apprehension and hope that she should see him. She at least would treat his chin with respect, and with reserve; she was not one of these thrice-cursed and clumsy Five Towns provincials.

She did not see him; but she saw Mr. Sworn, and Nash Nicklin was astonished and hurt to witness that (after travelling down from Bleakridge, probably at the opposite end of the car from Mr. Sworn) she greeted Mr. Sworn in exactly the same specially affable manner as she had used to himself. He did not like this at all. Mr. Sworn and she fell into step side by side and marched off together towards the Town Hall, in the wake of Miss Overhouse and two other ladies. Nash Nicklin had a glimpse of her tiny, exciting face, and he heard her shrill laugh. And when he heard that laugh his confidential assumption about her attitude to his chin was disturbed. He had meant to display his chin to her with pride. But now he feared the ordeal. He had parted with his beard for her sake, and now, when the climax was reached, he was afraid to show the symbol of his devotion! Singular situation!

The travellers dispersed, most of them in the direction of the Town Hall. Nash Nicklin stood still in the shadow. He saw the fat old car-driver, made cylindrical by his huge mackintosh driving-apron, take the pin out of the pole, and, lifting the end of the pole in one hand and holding the reins in the other, coax and chirrup the horses round to the rear of the car, making it the front. He saw and heard the driver ring the great bell, and then saw the car start off afresh for Hanbridge, nearly empty. At length he strolled toward the Town Hall. The great windows on the first floor were yellow with bright light in the darkness. The Conversazione was proceeding; the intellect, the wit, the aristocracy of Bursley were therein engaged in elegant and cultivated small talk, and Mr. Clayton Vernon was displaying the latest marvel of science. Miss Mordey had certainly thrown off her dark cloak and was shining graciously in all fair colours. And perhaps she was amiably chatting with the ass Sworn.

Mr. Nicklin felt himself in every way to be out in the cold. He walked off; and he walked off because he simply dared not enter the select precincts. Romance was shattered. He felt weary, discouraged and shamed. He muttered anathema. Then he walked all the way to Turnhill and back, trying to prove to himself that he had not been a fool. But he could not ignore the fatal truth that he had thrown away the finest beard in Bursley, in order to draw attention to a chin of the most feeble and mediocre description. An absurd act!

VI.

A few days later he underwent a great shock, to some extent agreeable, but to a much larger extent disagreeable. As he entered his cottage for dinner he saw Miss Mordey, and then Miss Overhouse, emerging from Mrs. Machin's cottage two doors away. Had he stopped for two seconds on his doorstep they could not have failed to see him, and wondrous matters might have ensued. It was violently agreeable to witness the bright enchanting figure of Miss Mordey in his own dull street and close to his own dull abode, but it was exasperating in a very high degree to discover that, beardless, he still had not the pluck to meet her. He slunk rapidly into his dark cottage, and spied upon them from the gloom as they walked up the street. His secret heart, then, was a horrible disorder of wicked and base thoughts, and shame.

Yes, he was even ashamed of his own cottage, and hoped miserably that Miss Mordey would never know that he lived in a cottage in Brougham Street; yet how often had he said that a cottage was good enough for him, and that it didn't matter where people lived so long as they remained decent, and that the tendency to display and luxury was an evil symptom of the times?

He guessed why Miss Mordey and Miss Overhouse had been to Mrs. Machin's. Lace was the explanation of that. Mrs. Machin, who was a sempstress, usually "by the day," had a unique reputation for dealing with lace, both as to washing and as to mending it. All ladies who were interested in lace on that account treated Mrs. Machin with respect. Some came to her, instead of sending for her to go to them. The Girls' School was only just round the corner in Wedgwood Street, and it was no doubt convenient enough for Miss Overhouse to "pop in" at Mrs. Machin's during the dinner-hour.

Nash Nicklin, though he happened to have speech with Mrs. Machin on several occasions during the next week, said no word as to Miss Mordey. He said no word to anybody as to Miss Mordey. Here was the sole comfortable aspect of the affair—no one knew anything whatever about it. He was safe on that side. He grew more secretive, and his expression grew more challenging as he walked regularly up and down Trafalgar Road; and he was less inclined to stop and chat with acquaintances encountered on the pavement.

His consuming contempt for Mr. Sworn was greatly intensified. Every day when he turned into Trafalgar Road from Woodisun Bank or from Caroline Street he wondered whether his eyes would be afflicted by the sight of that ass. And his eyes very often were so afflicted. He hated to see Mr. Sworn, had always hated to see him; but now he was curiously disappointed if he did not see him. There was something in the mere way that Mr. Sworn walked—something pompous, fatuous, disgustingly self-complacent, that positively enraged Nash Nicklin. But at the same time he liked to watch that gait, in order to despise the man. He enjoyed his own disgust.

Mr. Sworn was encased in conceit. He had probably never suspected that he could be an object of derision. "Ah," thought Nash Nicklin luxuriously, "it would be a bit of a startler for the fool if I crossed over the road and told him to his face he was a preposterous ass. And I will, too, one day. See if I don't!" He longed to cross over the road and communicate his views to Mr. Sworn. But he did not do so. He continued rigorously on his own side of the street, and shot murderous glances at Mr. Sworn, and that was all.

One Saturday afternoon—about three months later—he was on the roof of the lean-to shed in his little back yard, mending it. (He was a great mender, and would mend in the open air even when Christmas was near; but then, like many English people, he seemed to enjoy feeling cold.) And Mrs. Machin was sitting on the sill of her first-floor back window, cleaning it, and offering her grim chignon to the world of back-yards.

"Good day to ye, Mr. Nicklin," said she, as she rubbed the panes.

"Good day, Mrs. Machin."

Mrs. Machin went on cleaning, and then, without looking at Nash, she threw the following words across the intervening backyard:

"So that Miss Mordey's done it!"

Yet Mrs. Machin was very far from being a talkative woman.

"So that Miss Mordey's done it"

"Done what?" asked Nash Nicklin in a voice suddenly husky.

"What she came for. She's hooked a man."

"Indeed," said Nash Nicklin, controlling himself rather well. "I thought she'd left the district."

"So she had. But not permanently like. She'll be Mrs. Sworn before she's a couple o' months older, and then poor old Bursley will have to look out for itself—my word!"

It seemed clear that Mrs. Machin's regard for Miss Mordey had limits.

She added:

"Mr. Sworn or another—it 'ud ha' been all one to her, I lay."

Then she slipped under the window-sash into her cottage. At the same moment, young Denry appeared at the window.

"Oh, Mother," cried he, excited. "Mr. Nicklin's beard's begun to grow again."

Mrs. Machin caught the observant child a sound box on the ear.

VII.

During that week-end Nash Nicklin bit the lips and clenched the hands of his soul, and became more Nash Nicklin than ever. He told himself that he was glad that Mr. Sworn had been hooked, by a poor adventuress. He told himself that, after all, school-mistresses were nothing very particular. They only worked for their living because they thundering well had to; and were they not notoriously ill paid? He could quite understand a young woman like Miss Mordey—who was just a school-mistress out of a job—coming to the Five Towns and looking upon it as a virgin forest full of game—full of fine, solid, dependable, well-to-do prospective husbands. He knew that Leamington was a "cock-eyed" sort of place where retired officers struggled ridiculously to cut a genteel figure on half-pay. As for Sworn, his fate was just what the ass deserved.

On the Sunday evening he ran across Mrs. Machin in the street, and that strange woman began once more to talk about

Miss Mordey, and imparted the information that Miss Mordey would never see thirty again. The fact was that Mrs. Machin had suspected a relation of cause and effect between Miss Mordey and the disappearance of Mr. Nicklin's beard. Mrs. Machin heard a lot of news in the various houses where she sewed; she knew, for example, that Mr. Nicklin had been seen talking to Miss Mordey in the street, that he had promised to go to the Conversazione, and had not gone, and that Miss Mordey did not admire beards—though, indeed, she was now about to marry one. And Mrs. Machin desired to confirm her suspicion. Hence her uncustomary talkativeness to Mr. Nicklin. She failed, however. No sign that she could interpret escaped from Mr. Nicklin. This was a great triumph for him, as anybody who knew Mrs. Machin would admit.

On the Monday morning he set out for the works with his most sardonic and mysterious smile. He was making a magnificent pretence. He nearly deceived even Mr. Nash Nicklin. But far away down at the bottom of his soul the worm was gnawing. True, he despised and stamped upon Mr. Sworn, but he also envied him.

He tried to believe all that he had heard against Miss Mordey, but he could not quite, for to believe meant that he himself had been a ninny, and worse than a ninny. In the matter of Miss Mordey's age he felt that Mrs. Machin must be either mistaken or malicious; he, for his part, had estimated Miss Mordey's age at twenty-four.

At the works he was excessively secretarial. His zeal for the welfare of the Toft End Brickworks and Colliery Company, Limited, grew offensive to those under him, and irritated even the directors, though they were the largest shareholders.

He made two appearances in Trafalgar Road that day without seeing Mr. Sworn, and he feigned to himself that he was disappointed. But on the third and penultimate appearance, after dinner, he saw Mr. Sworn coming down the road, and Miss Mordey was by his side, and the spectacle of them together hurt Nash Nicklin considerably. Oh! he loathed to see them together. As they got nearer Nash Nicklin blushed—he could feel the blush extending to the back of his neck. Now the cause of the blush was his perception that Mr. Sworn no longer wore a beard. The effect upon him of Mr. Sworn's naked chin was very sinister. He felt like Mr. Sworn's twin brother, and hated Mr. Sworn with a still more violent hatred.

As he passed the couple, with the width of the street between, he gazed straight in front of him. He knew that Miss Mordey had "moved" to him, but he would not respond to the salutation; he was proud of his boorishness, and exhibited it as a proof of character in himself.

Early in the New Year he missed Mr. Sworn for a fortnight. It was the honeymoon! Then Mr. Sworn reappeared, and Mrs. Sworn appeared. But Nash Nicklin never again acknowledged her existence. After a time he got quite used to cutting her, and was indeed almost persuaded that he had never spoken to her. He would look at her furtively, and soon managed to see that she was at least the age that Mrs. Machin had accused her of being.

VIII.

Time passed, and Nash Nicklin still walked up and down Trafalgar Road. In the course of years everybody except himself had forgotten that once, for a brief period, his splendid beard had been suppressed. It was now grander than ever; but he always kept it carefully trimmed.

And he also, like his beard, had increased in grandeur. He had become a figure on the landscape and in the life of the town. He stood for the Toft End Brickworks and Colliery Company, Limited, and the Company, with its monotonous 20 per cent. dividend, stood as a symbol of the sterling solidity of the district. And he was looked upon as a man of iron, mysterious, secretive, ruthless, who lived only for the Company. The well-informed knew that he saved money and

"People would say, 'There's Nash Nicklin!'"

bought cottages. People repeated his name with satisfaction; it came well off the tongue. "Nash Nicklin!" "Nash Nicklin!" People would say, "There's Nash Nicklin," as they might have said, "There's Alfred Tennyson," or "There's John Bright."[13] And they would be very circumspect in talking to Nash Nicklin, because, though "he was one of your quiet ones, he had a mighty good opinion of himself." And they would remark facetiously to ladies who were postponing the act of marriage rather dangerously late: "Well, Miss—, Nash Nicklin's still waiting for ye to give him a smile."

It was not quite true that Nash Nicklin lived only for the Company. He lived also for Mr. Sworn. After economy and the creation of dividends, his chief interest in life was Mr. Sworn, whom he still saw several times every day, but to whom he had never spoken. His contempt for Mr. Sworn grew to epical proportions. The wonder was that, when Nash

Nicklin shot a murderous glance at him across the street, Mr. Sworn did not drop down dead. Perhaps only Mr. Sworn's truly admirable conceit saved him. The whole town agreed that Mr. Sworn was a conceited fool, but nevertheless was content to smile at him. Whereas the swing of Mr. Sworn's cane, and the fatuity of his mild, vain glance made Nash Nicklin grind his teeth with fury. Nash Nicklin longed with terrible ardour for some misfortune to overtake Mr. Sworn. But no misfortune overtook the fool. He had once in early life had an idea for a patent plate, and he had found a world-market for his patent plate, and manufactured year in, year out, his patent plate, and nothing else. He had never had another idea, save that of permitting Miss Mordey to marry him. His marriage appeared to run smoothly. Now and then his wife would walk up the road with him, or down the road with him, and they seemed to be on quite amicable terms. And moreover, at intervals, Nash Nicklin, when he saw Mrs. Sworn, could not deny that she was after all a very feminine little thing, even if two-faced; and he loathed Mr. Sworn with a double loathing.

And then, after six years, a misfortune did overtake Mr. Sworn. It is needless, and it would be indelicate, to particularise. Mrs. Machin gave the first news of it to Nash Nicklin. "I'm not surprised, and it's no use pretending I am," said Mrs. Machin. "Women like her, they come into a respectable district for what they can catch, but a good catch doesn't satisfy 'em! No, they must needs bring scandal into the district." It was a painful affair. The *Signal* described it as a very painful affair, and gave two columns to the ultimate legal proceedings.

The affair might have been slightly less painful if a young local curate had not been involved. Fortunately, he also was foreign to the district, and spoke with what Bursley considered to be an affected accent. It was monstrous, in the opinion of Bursley, that strangers should foist themselves on a town which was among the most moral in the world, a town whose abhorrence of any laxity was unusually profound, and then outrage its just susceptibilities! ... Both the strangers were driven out. Miss Overhouse kept a dignified and formidable silence throughout the episode. Mr. Sworn received sympathy and sneers.

Shortly afterwards Mr. Sworn's beard began to grow again. Nash Nicklin could see it growing day by day across the street. And his scorn became terrific.

"Ass!" he muttered to himself. "Ass! You can do nothing that does not prove you to be the biggest ass ever born. And some day I'll come over and tell you so! Why, to be forced to look at you every morning and evening would alone drive any woman into the divorce court! You wait!—I'll come over to you one day, and give you a bit of my mind—in two words."

But Mr. Sworn's exasperating bland and fatuous expression of self-complacency was in no way modified either by his misfortune or by Nash Nicklin's darting glances.

IX.

Another ten years elapsed, and Nash Nicklin, still secretary of a company that was still flourishing, still passed along Trafalgar Road four times a day.

Natives like myself who, having left the district, returned to it at long intervals, observed Nash Nicklin with interest, and remarked, astonished, that he had not altered the least bit in the world. But people who knew him well and saw him constantly said that he was, on the contrary, much changed; these latter noticed the details of his appearance. And certainly, though his hair and beard were yet brown, he had changed. He was nearing fifty, and was considerably older than his years. And he was getting more and more convinced that England's doom was approaching. He spoke of "these modern ideas" and referred to "his young days." The abolition of turnpikes represented for him the last limit of legitimate change. When the horse-cars were abolished and steam-traction substituted, he had sneered. But when steam yielded to electricity and the sky was darkened with wires, he said naught—he was too disgusted. When Miss Overhouse married in the town, and to the stupefaction of thirty-eight thousand people safely became a mother, he thought it was not quite nice. And when the High School for Girls declined and at last died, he thought that was the proper end for such newfangled notions. Occasionally he remembered Miss Mordey, but Miss Mordey ("as was") was dead to the town. Not a soul knew what had happened to her. Mr. Sworn himself did not know.

And then a very strange thing occurred. Nash Nicklin inherited some property, including a nice house up at Sneyd, from his brother-in-law, relict of his sister who had been dead a quarter of a century. The nice house was well situated on the hill-side, halfway between the suburb of Sneyd and the Toft End Company's estate.

It would suit a bachelor. Brougham Street was "going down." There had been talk of demolishing the row of cottages in which lived Mrs. Machin and Nash Nicklin. Mrs. Machin and he had discussed the matter at the time when she had confided to him some of her misgivings as to the astounding enterprises of her now grown-up son. Mrs. Machin did not want to leave the cottages. She feared, when she heard of the inheritance, that Mr. Nicklin would desert her. But she was mistaken.

This was the very strange thing—Nash Nicklin sold the house disadvantageously, rather than live in it. He flouted public opinion by remaining in the Brougham Street cottage. People were united in asserting that a man of his position ought to live elsewhere. But live elsewhere he would not. Whereupon people laughed shortly, and said that after all Nash Nicklin was Nash Nicklin. He gave all sorts of reasons for not taking to his brother-in-law's house. But he did not give them the true one. The true strange reason was that if he had gone to live up Sneyd way he could no longer have marched to and fro in Trafalgar Road. He and Trafalgar Road were indissolubly mated; he felt that he could not do without Trafalgar Road, and that Trafalgar Road without him would not be Trafalgar Road. Moreover, he could not deprive himself of the daily spectacle of the ass Sworn, now an ageing ass, but as exquisitely fatuous as ever. The desire to tell Mr. Sworn what he thought of him still burned red in Nash Nicklin's heart. "And I'll tell him one day, as sure as my name's Nash Nicklin," said he, grimly, lying in bed.

X.

The boast of Nash Nicklin was that he had never had a day's illness in his life. It was not a strictly accurate boast, for he had once suffered from lumbago for five days, and he had been the victim of indigestion for weeks at a time. Nevertheless it was truer than most such statements are. Hence when, at the age of fifty-eight, he was struck down by a vicious form of influenza that was no respecter of secretaries, he became alarmed, because he had to stay in bed, and because he was seriously convinced that the operations of the Toft End Brickworks and Colliery Company, Limited, would come to a stop during his absence. On the third day of the attack, when the doctor came to see him twice in twelve hours, and the height of his temperature was concealed from Nash Nicklin, he really did begin to fear that his earthly career was over. But he recovered—slowly, very slowly. And as he grew convalescent he learned that an epidemic of his malady was ravaging the town, and how near he himself had been to destruction.

After three weeks, he got out into the open air, and he was profoundly changed. He now, even to a careless observer, looked old. His hair, which had been grizzled, was grey, and his stride was a feeble imitation of its former self. He returned to the office, and employees and directors alike bowed afresh to the yoke. Four times during the first day of resumption his eye ranged Trafalgar Road in vain for Mr. Sworn. And he was disturbed. He said to himself: "If I'd kicked the bucket without telling old Sworn what I thought of him, I should never have forgiven myself, and it would ha' served me right."

A strange reflection, possibly; but Nash Nicklin was Nash Nicklin. He took oath privately to cross the road the very next time he saw Mr. Sworn and have a few words with Mr. Sworn. Then he was told, by chance, that Mr. Sworn in his turn was down with influenza. The sincerity with which he expressed the hope that Mr. Sworn would get over it surprised his informant, who was aware of Nash Nicklin's attitude toward Mr. Sworn. Nash Nicklin, getting stronger daily, waited for a week; he waited impatiently for a fortnight. And at last, one afternoon—spring was afoot in the Five Towns—he descried Mr. Sworn strolling up the road—jauntily, conceitedly, fatuously, with an ineffable and an odious self-complacency, just as though he had never had influenza at all.

Nash Nicklin set his lips and crossed the road. It was the supreme action of his whole life. And he deliberately accosted the white-haired Mr. Sworn—looking up at him, for Mr. Sworn was not only older but taller than he.

"Good day to ye," said he.

Mr. Sworn grunted; he was somewhat startled, and not a ready speaker in his old age.

"I hear ye've had influenza," said Nash Nicklin. "And I'm glad ye've got over it, because there's something as I wanted to tell ye."

"Ay?" responded Mr. Sworn, with an imbecile, asinine condescension that almost made Nash Nicklin cry out.

"Yes", said Nash Nicklin. "It's been on my mind for thirty year and more. Thirty year and more I've stood yer walking up and down this road, without telling ye, and I can't stand it any longer. I'm bound to tell ye."

"Ay!" said Nash Nicklin, "You're an ass"

"Ay?" Mr. Sworn encouraged him unsuspectingly.

"Ay!" said Nash Nicklin, rather ecstatically happy in his increasing excitement: "You're an ass. And you aren't only an ass, but a silly ass and a preposterous ass. You're a fool, and a chump, and a blighted coxcomb. Everybody in th' town knew it but you, and now you know it ... Thirty year I've stood your blithering conceit ..."

He stopped. Mr. Sworn was trembling, swaying.

"Look out for yeself!" said Nash Nicklin, and supported him by the arm. The man was very infirm. "Here! I'd better see ye home, I fancy."

Mr. Sworn only mumbled. Clearly there was no stamina left beneath his hide of self-complacency. Nash Nicklin hailed the next ascending electric car, and pushed Mr. Sworn on to it, and helped to lift him off at Bleakridge, and guided him into his home. In three days Mr. Sworn was dead. The doctor said it was a relapse after influenza. Nash Nicklin, to the astonishment of the town, went to his funeral.

And as he came away from the churchyard Nash Nicklin said aloud to himself, crossing Woodisun Bank to get into Trafalgar Road: "And so he was! And so he was!"

And resumed the regularity of his daily peregrinations.

NOTES

1. *Pears' Christmas Annual*. 1914, pages 10, 15-19. Signed Arnold Bennett. Illustrations by Frank Dadd. *Pears' Christmas Annual* was first published in London in 1891. "The Life of Nash Nicklin" also appeared in the American magazine *Metropolitan* in September 1915, with illustrations by Thomas Fogarty.
2. Waterloo Road, Burslem.
3. Sneyd Green.
4. Navigation Road.
5. St. John's Square.
6. William Clowes Street.
7. Bourne's Bank.
8. The Wedgwood Institute, Queen Street, Burslem; built by public subscription and opened in 1869. At one time an Endowed School attended by Bennett.
9. Longport Hall, now demolished. Home of the potter John Davenport.
10. Denry Machin, the hero of Bennett's comic novel *The Card* (1911).
11. Swan Bank.
12. Burslem Meat Market, built in 1836 on a site adjacent to the Old Town Hall, demolished in 1959.
13. John Bright (1811-1889) elected M.P. for Stockport in 1841; founder with Richard Cobden and five others of the Anti-Corn Law League.

THE MUSCOVY DUCKS.[1]

Ingestre, the sole true owner of Chamfreys Hall, stood in the fine gardens there-of. It was a hazy, blue-veiled morning in December. At intervals a pale flicker of flame pierced the veil of the horizon—fire from the mouths of the blast furnaces that marked the southern boundary of the Five Towns. A few incorrigible blackbirds and starlings were hopping about the great tennis-lawn, which had room for two courts. From a thin pipe that stuck out from the crystal side of the vinery steam was issuing. A carpenter was repairing the roof of the adjacent greenhouse. Through a gap in the high trimmed hedge that separated the tennis-lawn from the croquet-lawn could be seen, now and then, the whiteness of swans and the flashing tints of ornamental ducks on the pond. And in the distant hollows of the sloped field beyond the gardens a few cattle were industriously grazing. Close by Ingestre worked two stooping gardeners, who, under his direction, were levelling some turf beneath the new pergola. And in the nostrils of all three men the mild, sharp tickling of winter and the acrid smell from freshly dressed earth mingled with a tonic effect. Ingestre in his shabby suit regarded the scene, and took it in more through his pores than through his eyes and nose. He was happy, and did not consciously realize it, being convinced that his lot was anxious and unrequited.

Behind the vinery and the greenhouse rose the upper branches of a superb copper beech, and behind those the reddish walls and white windows of the hall, surmounted by chimneys, and smoke as fine as cigar smoke. At one of the windows, Ingestre was aware of a man's chin covered with soap, and a hand and razor cautiously moving. This chin and this hand and razor belonged to the being who imagined that he owned Chamfreys Hall and gardens. His name was Stephen Cheswardine,[2] a manufacturer who had made a deal of money out of earthenware, and was now making still more out of iron. Stephen had purchased the property less than twelve months earlier; but no money could make him the true owner in the sense that Ingestre was the true owner. Ingestre had been the head gardener of Chamfreys for eighteen years. He owned the place because he loved it, comprehended it, and gave his life to it. Indeed, he had bought it with his whole existence, and nothing except an injustice could deprive him of his ownership.

For Ingestre, Chamfreys was a garden with a tiresome, necessary, uninteresting house in the middle of it. And the house was naught but a building where he had to keep plants flowering amid adverse and absurd conditions. For Ingestre, the only habitation proper to a flowering plant in winter was the greenhouse. He entered the Hall every morning and saw not its luxury. He saw only the lamentable effect on cut flowers of steam-heating. He knew that after buying the place Stephen Cheswardine had spent four thousand pounds on the house alone; and he reflected that with half four thousand pounds he might have had a garden that would be the wonder of the ages. Still, he was friendly toward Stephen, who had enlarged the garden and endowed him with an extra gardener, making four. But scorn entered into his friendliness—partly for the reason that Stephen was utterly ignorant of all worthy knowledge and partly for the reason that Stephen was evidently a bit of a Socialist. So far as he deigned to consider politics at all, Ingestre, too, was a bit of a Socialist, but he cared not to see such opinions in an employer—they were unnatural there.

Stephen had said to him: "What's the matter with you, Ingestre, is that you don't earn enough. I can't possibly have a head gardener of your experience working for twenty-five shillings a week and a cottage. I shouldn't be able to sleep at nights." And consequently he had raised him to thirty; and had raised the under-gardeners in proportion.

The money was extremely welcome to Ingestre, but it did not in the least influence his verdict upon Stephen as "a green one." Further, when in the autumn Chamfreys Hall had taken the silver medal for the best bloom in the annual show of the Axe[3] and Moorlands Horticultural Society, Stephen had given the medal (which was inscribed with Stephen's own name) to Ingestre, saying, "This is yours, not mine." Another instance of disconcerting queerness, which Ingestre obscurely resented.

Ingestre was not a pleasant man

It may be argued that Ingestre was not a pleasant man. He was not. He was difficult, touchy, harsh, taciturn, censorious, and opinionated. He had no social charm. He was not liked. Only a dog could have loved him, and he had an intense objection to dogs. And why should he be agreeable, and why should he have social charm? He despised such qualities. He possessed greater. He was not vain; he was not conceited; but he had a calm and just appreciation of his great qualities. He was absolutely honest, absolutely industrious, absolutely reliable, and he knew his job absolutely. Morally he was thus invulnerable. Everything outside his job he ignored and despised. A garden was scope for gardening, and for him it was nothing else. A lawn was a field for the display of perfect turf. Fruit, vegetables and flowers were to be grown, not to be eaten, worn or smelt. He did not care for asparagus and had only tasted it once; but he grew the finest, and when asparagus was grown the end of asparagus had been achieved. Gardeners from all around came to consult Ingestre. He acted as judge at cottage flower-shows. The greatest nurserymen approached him with the respect due to one who seldom found it necessary to buy from them, and who could teach them a thing or two.

Ingestre saw himself in an unjust and a topsy-turvy world, in which the supreme importance of gardening was never grasped, in which the most ridiculous importance was given to matters of an ignoble pettiness, and in which the consciousness of perfect ability was the only genuine reward that perfect ability would wisely expect. Well, after all, the reward was rich, had Ingestre known it. To be great, and to be everlastingly aware that you are great—what human experience can equal this?

An aged man came leisurely and not quite in a straight line across the tennis-lawn toward the unfinished pergola. His face was handsome and even distinguished, but spoiled of it full effect by the absence of many teeth and the untidiness of the rest. He was sixty-six years old, and he had never earned regularly more than sixteen shillings a week, and sixteen shillings only since the advent of Stephen Cheswardine; he was, in fact, the fourth and least helpful gardener; yet if he had never had to work in the rain, and had therefore never suffered from twisting rheumatism, and if he had been taught to talk and to walk properly and clothed in expensive raiment, he might easily have passed for a venerable county magnate. The ancestry of peasants is often obscure and sensational.

Ingestre said to him impatiently, but not unkindly:

"Now, old gentleman, bring them turves there a bit nearer here, so as we shan't be running to and fro all morning."

The old gentleman stood still, a faint artful smile—habitual with him—on his fine features. He was a worthy old gentleman, but his pleasure in life was to prove that something ordered to be done could not be done.

He replied: "Missis wants them two green ducks ready in a basket at eleven o'clock. Her's going out in the motor, and her wants 'em ready agen her goes."

"Them muscovy ducks?"

"Ay!"

"Both on 'em?"

"Ay!"

Ingestre's tone suggested that the caprices of the ruling classes were incomprehensible and idiotic. The old gentleman's slightly stupid and slightly malicious smile answered that it was none of his business to prevent in any way a member of the ruling classes from acting like a lunatic, and that, on the contrary, it was rather a good thing to encourage him or her in foolishness. All the secretive cunning developed in the serf by half a century of contact with the tyrant caste shone in the old gentleman's eyes.

"Better go and catch 'em now," said Ingestre, regretfully and spitefully. "It may take ye half an hour to cop 'em."

The old gentleman departed through a gap in the hedge to the pond, and as he passed the pile of turves he smiled again his recondite smile.

Ingestre grumbled to himself rather savagely. At that

moment his face was not a pleasing sight. Mrs. Cheswardine was his enemy—his arch-enemy, bold, powerful, unscrupulous. He knew that she hated him, and that he was not in love with her.

"Hi!" he yelled out to the old gentleman, who with imperturbable deliberation looked round and then came back.

"Who gave ye the order?"

"Frenchie."

This was the French maid, Henriette.

"Hm!" Ingestre grunted. "All right. Get it done."

He loathed Henriette, who had the right to pick flowers for her mistress. Henriette fully confirmed him in his long-held low opinion of the French race. He knew by instinct that the French had the most silly French notions of gardening. He could name forty roses better, in his opinion, than the Gloire de Dijon, or even La France. He believed in English roses. He had once had a fearful shindy and altercation with Henriette on the subject of flower-picking, and, Henriette obtaining the support of madam, he had been beaten to a finish. He had been obliged to grow greenstuff in the greenhouse (imagine it!), because Henriette wanted salad at all seasons of the year and had infected madam with her own preposterous continental taste. And he had been obliged by madam to pick certain vegetables—French beans, for instance—before they were, in the true gardening sense, ripe, because madam averred that unripe they were tenderer to eat. An outrage!

But his chief grievance against the mistress was that she was continually robbing him of his staff, for ends of her own. Her menagerie of aquatic birds took a couple of hours of the old gentleman's time every day. Whenever Mrs. Cheswardine wanted anything done in a moment (and it was always in a moment), she would lop off one of the gardeners. Her argument was monotonously the same, namely, that there were four men in the garden doing nothing and that one could obviously be spared to serve her. The grounds comprised twelve acres. This argument infuriated Ingestre. To try to answer it would have been folly.

Another grievance, second only to the chief grievance, was that the mistress *would* leave his greenhouse and vinery doors open. That she demanded particular blossoms and vegetables at impossible seasons was relatively a trifle compared to the doors grievance.

And Ingestre, conscious of perfect rectitude, feared her as much as she hated him. She could undo him utterly. She held an unfair advantage and knew it. He surmised that he had Cheswardine on his side, but he surmised also that, if Mrs. Cheswardine chose and circumstances were favorable, she could twist Cheswardine round her little finger. He could not count on Cheswardine. The one sufficient secret ally would have been Henriette. But Ingestre had no fancy for French maids and no conception how to win them. The immense influence of Henriette was added to the forces against him.

He heard a few minutes later the protesting quacks and the beating of wings as the old gentleman captured first one duck and then the other. In due time the old gentleman amiably ambled into sight again and began to work delicately on the turves. And the new pergola proceeded toward perfection without further incident until, shortly after eleven o'clock, Ingestre's ear caught a fearful and unusual sound—a scream—and then appalling shrieks, from the front lawn. He dropped a tool and ran, for everything that happened in his garden concerned him.

Vera Cheswardine, clothed from head to foot in the skins of various animals untimely dead, stood at a distance of about five feet from the cheval-glass in the boudoir, and regarded herself, so small and slight, in the enlarging furs. She was an attractive creature, without an idea in her head save for her own advancement. Some serious persons said that she was not attractive; that, indeed, she was insufferable. But other persons still more serious found pleasure in her company.

She had no culture, no spirituality, no artistic taste (liking the very worst drawing-room songs and musical comedies that could be bought, seen or heard in Hanbridge);[4] and assuredly her facts were almost always wrong. She was not charitable. Her sparkling eyes did not sparkle with angelic benevolence. She did not even practise works of charity, which is a different thing from being charitable, and an easier. She never thought of her immortal soul. She was a snob. One of her highest ambitions had been to have a French maid; she got one. This sole item estimates the woman for you. Many said that she was an empty-headed little fool, and would be so to her dying day. Possibly! And yet she was profoundly wise and clever—as an animal is profoundly wise and clever. She knew what she wanted and she ruthlessly obtained it. She always encouraged Stephen to make money, and she never chid him because he failed to do things which a man busy in making money cannot do. (In this she was rare.) She knew that money, and plenty of it, was essential to her felicity. She knew further that the love of Stephen was essential to her felicity. And she most carefully conserved his love. She did more—she kept her affection for him, bald

Vera thought herself a very clever woman

and rather gross as he was. These were achievements in life.

Vera thought herself a very clever woman, full of character. And who, in face of such achievements, will deny it? Who will deny that to be able sincerely to despise what one cannot get, and to be convinced that what one has or hopes to get is superior to aught else, is high, deep wisdom? Vera had this wisdom. Moving now in the indefinitely fashionable country-house world between the entity of the district and the entity of the county, she was quite sure that those ladies who did not and never would call on her were inferior in all desirable details to those who did call on her.

And, after all, no man that was truly masculine would or could dispute that she emanated a peculiar piquant charm, with her twitterings and her gestures, and her puttings of the little head on one side. To meet her was a tonic to any man truly masculine.

In brief, Vera was not a disappointed woman. She had reached success. She had everything to make her happy (even a hopeless faithful adorer or two) except one thing. And the absence of this one thing might have spoiled the remainder of her existence had she not continually—again with instinctive wisdom and cleverness!—taken steps to prevent it from doing so.

What Vera lacked was merely the secret of eternal youth. She was not old. Oh, no! But she was at that age when people will say of a woman, "She is still a pretty woman." People had begun to say it of Vera. She was thirteen years younger than Stephen, and Stephen was little past fifty. She was bidding good-by—a protracted ceremony of adieu—to youth and a fine complexion, and to the tyrannic powers which youth and a fine complexion enjoy. It is a tremendous ordeal for any woman of physical attractiveness, and especially for a woman such as Vera, without intellectual resources or heavenly loving-kindness.

But Vera was coming through it very well. She was

preparing other powers for herself, powers springing from social prestige and from habits carefully imposed on companions. Thus she had rendered her house so agreeable an organism that the mistress of the house was a factor with which neighbors had to reckon. And she had so insinuated her personality into Stephen's intimate existence, so hypnotised him into the belief that she was unchangeably the bride of sixteen years earlier, that he could never escape from his prison of illusion. She was sure of Stephen.

And up to the time of their removal to Chamfreys she had been sure also of Charlie Woodruff, a lifelong friend of Stephen and a lifelong adorer of Vera. Vera considered that it was a good plan for a wife to have a harmless faithful adorer, because the adorer acted unconsciously as a sort of pace-maker to the husband, and proved to the husband that he was, indeed, a lucky man to possess what others vainly sighed for. In a word, it flattered the husband, and confirmed him in his taste. But for certain reasons Charlie Woodruff could scarcely ever come on a visit to Chamfreys. In default of Charlie, Vera had discovered Mr. Maccles, a prosperous bachelor (personally much more impressive than Charlie), who lived all alone in a picturesque house with a garden of twenty-three acres.

Vera had keenly enjoyed their first lunch at Mr. Maccles'. In the first place, Mr. Maccles had an admirable cook. In the second place, he was obviously delighted to have Vera in his abode. In the third place, he cultivated his twenty-three acres with the labor of only three gardeners, whereas Stephen had to employ four gardeners for less than half the acreage. This enabled her to support her contention that Ingestre was an idle wastrel who got the better of the simpleton Stephen all the time. She had wandered over the entire twenty-three acres with Mr. Maccles and Stephen, and at every turn had compared the marvelous variety and excellence of Mr. Maccles' gardens with the general poorness of their own. In the fourth place, she had admired Mr. Maccles' white doves, and the next day Mr. Maccles had sent over a couple of doves with his homage and full instructions for making them feel at home in a strange dove-cot.

"Oh! Steve," she said, on returning home, "I *do* like visiting at a house where there are no other women about!"

It was true.

Then Mr. Maccles had come to lunch at Chamfreys and admired Vera's green muscovy ducks, and Vera had promised him the couple for the lake at the end of his garden. He had begged her to bring them herself, together with Stephen, one day soon and stay for lunch, and to come early and remain for tea. She had accepted. She fancied she saw in Mr. Maccles the makings of a first-class harmless faithful adorer (but she had not then perceived that he was a man of vast experience).

And now she was going to the lunch.

She continued to regard herself for a few minutes in the cheval-glass at a distance of five feet or so, and then suddenly she went close to the glass and put her face against it and courageously inspected every tiny wrinkle and seam. She had pluck. Being optimistic that morning, she decided that she was still richly good enough to dazzle Mr. Maccles, and would be for years to come. She liked Mr. Maccles and hoped that Stephen would have the sense to like him, too.

The automobile was waiting for her at the garden entrance; but Stephen was not waiting for her, although it was Saturday and he had nothing else to do. Nor were the ducks waiting for her in their basket as ordered. She reproached Stephen in her heart, and had an extraordinary and delightful feeling of righteousness because, for once, she was not late and somebody else was. She spoke with friendly sharpness to both the chauffeur and the parlor-maid about the importance of the ducks. The parlor-maid murmured "Oh!" and jumped and the chauffeur also jumped. The parlor-maid produced a small basket that had lain in readiness behind the front door, and the

Vera caught her breath and then gave a scream

chauffeur assiduously received it from her. Vera was standing on the edge of the lawn, glancing up with frowns at Stephen's front window. She glanced down at the basket.

"What's that?" she demanded.

The chauffeur replied with his usual dignified deference:

"The ducks, madam."

And he looked at the parlor-maid as if to say, "Is it not the ducks?"

"But surely those gardeners can't have been so silly as to cram them into a little basket like that, poor things! Let me see them."

The chauffeur approached and as he did so he opened the basket.

Vera caught her breath and then gave a scream. The ducks were dead. They lay side by side in the basket as in a coffin. A flush spread over Vera's cheeks and then she turned white; and then she tried to speak and was stopped by a sob. The sight of the beautiful iridescent birds, exquisitely formed and tinted, which that very morning had eaten out of the pocket of her garden cloak, and which in fancy she had already seen elegantly voyaging on Mr. Maccles' lake—the sight of these lovely innocent animals in death, murdered, assassinated beyond recovery, inspired her with horror and rebellion. She was outraged. She was utterly overcome. True that frequently she ordered the death of a common white duck, and would help to eat it at night with no qualms. But common white ducks did not swim on the pond, and she did not feed them herself, and they could never serve as a lien between herself and Mr. Maccles. The muscovies were petted, ornamental, and full of grace—except when they toddled across the lawn. It was a soulless and malicious infamy to kill them.

"Who—who—?"

No! She could not speak. She stamped on the lawn with her little feet. She wrung her hands. She screamed afresh. Her features were startlingly transformed. The chauffeur blushed, but the parlor-maid, more rigorously trained, showed by no sign that in her opinion something unusual had happened.

"Who gave the order about these ducks?" Vera at length found a passage for the words.

"Henriette, madam," said the parlor-maid.

"Who did she give the order to?"

"Friskin, madam."

Friskin was the old gentleman.

"Where is Henriette?"

"She said you were sending her into Knype,[5] madam. She's caught the eleven-fifteen train, I believe."

Vera stamped the lawn and wept anew, wiping her eyes openly, without the slightest regard for the servants. She was now no longer a mistress—she was a woman desolated and infuriated, and foiled to the point of helplessness. She would have liked to kill both the parlor-maid and the chauffeur merely because they stood so stock still; also Stephen, because he was not present. Then she heard a stealthy step and saw Ingestre before her.

The first thing that Ingestre noticed, really, was that Mrs. Cheswardine was digging her high, pointed heels into his best turf. The next thing that impressed him was the enormity, the ferocity and the crass injustice of her anger. He knew that the accident to her thrice-cursed ducks was due to no mistake in his department. Without any hesitation he attributed it to some error, some characteristic imbecility, in the female department of the Chamfreys' organism. Then he wished that he had not so precipitately dashed out into the open to meet the foe. And further, he wished that the laconic and impartial Mr. Cheswardine had been present.

Vera exclaimed madly:

"Ingestre, what do you mean by having those poor ducks killed, when you knew perfectly well I wanted to give them to Mr. Maccles for his lake?"

"I knew nothin' about 'em, ma'am," said he, sullenly.

"Henriette told Friskin perfectly plainly that I did *not* wish them killed. How anyone in their senses could imagine such a thing I cannot imagine!" said Vera, not listening to Ingestre.

Ingestre walked away and called out:

"Friskin!"

Presently the old gentleman appeared, wearing his faint, cunning smile.

"Did the maid tell ye to kill them ducks?" Ingestre questioned.

"Yes, her tow'd me to kill 'em," said the old gentleman, calmly.

Ingestre glanced at his mistress. Vera gave no attention whatever to the old gentleman. (Among the gardeners she cared for Friskin alone, because of his face, and she would find a way to spare him.) Ingestre was to be her victim. He was deeply aware of it.

Controlling herself somewhat, Vera said bitterly to Ingestre:

"Henriette gave no such order. This is too much. And I shall stand no more." She repeated, momentarily august, "I shall stand no more."

"I'm very sorry, ma'am," murmured Ingestre. "But— "

"No you aren't," Vera stopped him. "And I don't want any imp–imp–impertinence."

More tears.

Stephen Cheswardine, very tall and big and phlegmatic, came out of the house. And immediately Vera ceased to be a mere woman, and rose again sublimely, save for an occasional whimper, to the height of the mistress. She told Stephen of the horrid misfortune, and according to her account there was no excuse for Ingestre. Ingestre, without waiting for Stephen to pontificate, reasserted the innocence of himself and his staff and tacitly reproached the absent Henriette.

Vera cross-examined:

"Did you or didn't you tell Friskin to kill the ducks?"

"He told me his orders were to kill 'em," Ingestre replied, gloomily.

"That's no answer. Did you tell him to kill them yourself? You know you made a great fuss not long since about your authority, as you call it, over the other gardeners, and it was arranged they should do nothing except through you. Did he kill the ducks on your orders or not?"

"He said Henriette had told him particular—"

"Did you authorise him to kill the ducks or didn't you?" Vera implacably pursued.

"Yes, ma'am. But Henriette—"

"Of course!"

"Where is Henriette?" Stephen demanded.

"Of course Henriette isn't here," said Vera, with a peculiar accent; as if to imply, "If she had been here no accusation would have been made against her."

"Then we will go into it this afternoon when we come back," said Stephen stoically. "In the meantime the ducks are dead. We might take one at any rate to Maccles. He could have it cooked tomorrow. Pity to waste them."

"And I have promised them to him!" whimpered Vera, still agitated. "And—and—don't ask me to eat the other one. Oh!"

If Ingestre could have seen into Vera's heart, and comprehended that for her the tragic demise of the ducks symbolised the destruction of her most charming incipient friendship with Mr. Maccles, he would have been even more intimidated than he was.

As the motor drove hooting out into the high-road, and the parlor-maid, bird in hand, stood staring at him with a vague amused pout, and Friskin stood staring at him with his eternal recondite smile, the head gardener guessed that they both gazed upon him as upon a victim irrevocably condemned. And he departed stiffly and sullenly to the pergola. They well knew, and everyone in the establishment well knew, the state of relations between him and the mistress.

And their eyes proved that in their opinion the mistress had at last got her chance and would use it to his ruin.

Ingestre thought so. He remembered all the passages between himself and Vera in which he had won, and each of them seemed now to be a nail for his coffin. He ought never to have won. It was in a high degree impolitic to have won. He was innocent, righteous, insulted, faultless; to dismiss him would be the absurdest, most monstrous injustice. Nevertheless he would be dismissed. In a week he might still be the finest gardener in the district, but he would be a gardener out of a place—and out of a cottage. Where could he get another place? A day laborer could get a place any day, but jobs suitable to the finest gardener in the district were not to be picked up like mushrooms. In his glory and his pride he had heard people say, and he had believed, that any owner of a good garden would jump at him. But he felt differently now. Would anyone jump at him? He doubted it.

He saw his home disintegrated, his wife shamed and broken, the schemes for his two sons' education blasted forever ....

But was it conceivable that Stephen would allow the wicked injustice to be done? Well, it was. Ingestre could conceive it, because he had noticed Vera snuggling up to Stephen in the car with a plaintive smile and caress. She meant to cajole him, and the purpose of the cajolery was Ingestre's destruction. Husbands with a sense of justice have sometimes to choose between domestic peace and their consciences, and consciences are sometimes more easily pacified than wives. Ingestre had lived. He knew what marriage was. He had no illusions about marriage ....

He satisfied himself that the old gentleman had spoken the truth. And then, as an honest employee, he went back to the pergola. He did not hang about the kitchen entrance to wait for the return of Henriette. He had no illusions about Henriette either. Henriette's blunder was obvious, but never would she admit the blunder! She would swear that she had very particularly told Friskin that the ducks were to be put in a basket alive, and her mistress would triumphantly exclaim, "Of course!" And the mistress's hypercritical assumption, at once incredible and fatuous, that he, Ingestre, had maliciously caused the death of the ducks in order to annoy her, would harden and crystallize in her mind until it became an axiom, a religious dogma, an article of faith.

A little after three o'clock, when the dusk was already beginning to gather itself together in the hollows of the meadow and under the big trees, Ingestre saw the black-and-white figure of the parlor-maid hurrying toward him.

"Master wants you at the front, Mr. Ingestre."

He had already heard the return of the car. He dropped a tool which he was using, and it seemed to him that with it he relinquished his stern authority over the three men working by his side. As, with set face, he strode in his shabby clothes in the direction of the front door, following the girl, he made no attempt to prepare for the scene awaiting him. He could not. He had been home to dinner and could not even say a word to his wife of the affair, though he had had plenty of tongue to be extremely disagreeable to her. He merely contemplated with bitter calm the prospect of ruin and the coming triumph of injustice. He knew in his heart that he might soon meet the hideous fate of being an under-gardener again.

Mr. Cheswardine was tapping one of the front tyres with his toe and talking to the chauffeur, who leaned over respectfully to the right from his wheel. Then the car buzzed and slowly disappeared behind the house. Mrs. Cheswardine was not visible.

"Yes, sir."

"Oh!" said Stephen. "I forgot to give you the wages this morning. Let me have the change later on, will you?"

And he handed Ingestre the customary five-pound note,

out of which Ingcstre paid himself and his staff.

He was saved for the moment. But he knew it was only a reprieve. He could tell from the self-consciousness in Mr. Cheswardine's voice that Mr. Cheswardine had been influenced, intimidated, wheedled, inveigled, seduced. He was profoundly aware that, if not next Saturday, then some other Saturday not far off, he would be informed of the sentence against him.

Then Henriette came mincing in at the gate. She was carrying a small parcel. She looked like a lady, but not like an English lady. She could not walk like an English girl. Her feet flirted and fussed with the ground. With demure downcast eyes she kept in a straight line for the path leading to the back of the house.

Stephen called out: "Henriette."

Ingestre's pulse quickened. Henriette glanced up, startled, and, as if her head and limbs were articulated with delicate springs, she swerved and minced toward the husband of her mistress.

Stephen, in his heavy male voice, questioned her with a sudden frown:

"Henriette, why didn't you tell Friskin that those ducks were to be killed this morning?"

Henriette burst out hotly:

"I did, monsieur. I did say to Friskin that he must keel the ducks first. He ask me must he keel the ducks, and I said yes. If you ask him before me—"

"All right! That'll do!" said Stephen. Henriette, dangling her parcel, turned away obsessed by her own righteousness and by the wickedness of servants. (She was not a servant, but a lady's-maid.)

Ingestre comprehended perhaps for the first time that his employer was a very clever and astute man. Also that Stephen had been fighting his own battle as well as Ingestre's, and had won it. Ingestre perceived in a flash the relative unimportance of a knowledge of gardening when compared with a knowledge of living.

Almost at the same moment Mrs. Cheswardine came from the hall into the garden coaxing her Pekingese.

"I say, Vera. Henriette says she did tell Friskin to kill those ducks." Stephen spoke carelessly.

"Who says she says so?"

"She's just told me so herself."

Vera bent to the flaccid and lovely animal.

"Then she must have misunderstood me," said she.

An instant later she added, looking at Ingestre:

"It's a very good thing for you Henriette is so honest."

She seemed to imply that Ingestre, a criminal, had been saved from wrath by the angelic kindness of Henriette.

"Get me that change, Ingestre," said Stephen, gruffly and impatiently.

Ingestre departed. He felt by no means absolutely secure for the future, but he felt less insecure than for a long time past.

From the distance he heard Mrs. Cheswardine ordering the parlor-maid:

"Tell cook we'll have that duck tomorrow night. That will be your night out. Be sure and tell Evelyn not to offer any to me. But I dare say I shall go to bed before dinner."

NOTES

1. *Metropolitan*. July 1915, pages 23-25, 50, 53. Signed Arnold Bennett. Illustrations by Everett Shinn. The *Metropolitan* was a monthly magazine published in New York.
2. Stephen and Vera Cheswardine were a Five Towns couple featured in four of the stories collected in Bennett's *The Grim Smile of the Five Towns* (1907).
3. Axe: Bennett's fictional Staffordshire Moorlands market town of Leek.
4. Hanbridge: Bennett's fictional town of Hanley, one of the six towns of Stoke-on-Trent.
5. Knype: Bennett's fictional town of Stoke, one of the six towns of Stoke-on-Trent.

PART VI
POST-WAR

By the late 1920s more than 7000 different cosmetic products were on sale in America, funding an advertising boom for the magazine industry. This Rubinstein advertisement accompanied Bennett's story "The Flight".

THE GREAT HUNTRESS.[1]

The Smiles and Soft Words of Women of Fashion Are the Weapons with Which They Make War Upon Each Other. This Is A Short Story of Conflict, Fought Bitterly Where You Would Least Expect It to Be Fought, in the Drawing Rooms and Over the Dinner Tables of London's Fashionables

When the telephone bell rang that afternoon Mrs. Walbash and her brother, Charles, were sitting in the lesser drawing room of their house in Cadogan Square, London.[2] They were twins; Mrs. Walbash was the widow of the illustrious Walbash, who had made a certain amount of money by the lavish use of the knife, and still more by his skill in running a nursing home, where the subjects of his keen scalpels were kept chill and hungry and enslaved in return for a weekly payment of from twelve to twenty guineas.

Nevertheless, Mrs. Walbash was a nice woman and had some good friends, though her black eyes showed a hard glint, and her voice was a little harsh and her elocution too precise. She was forty-two, with a tendency to plumpness which she vainly tried to counteract by missing the soup, the meat, and the savory of her own excellent dinners and other people's.

Charles (commonly called "Carlo") resembled his sister, save in the glint and the voice; he had what the French call a "white voice." They adored each other, helped each other in this difficult world, seldom bickered. Carlo had never loved anybody except his sister and himself, but he liked some scores of persons.

The economic basis of their existence was just safe, and no more. Mrs. Walbash, after paying all taxes, had about two thousand a year clear; Carlo somewhat over a thousand. They lived in a large house of many stories; indeed, one hundred stairs (so good for strengthening the leg muscles of domestics) separated the basement from the attic floor.

The rent was low, but large houses full of furniture and

bric-a-brac need service; moreover, Mrs. Walbash's profession was that of an ambitious hostess who always offered 1911 champagne. So they had to "manage." Thus there was a butler but no motor car—and very few taxis. Mrs. Walbash prided herself on her skill in using omnibuses and was well known on the lines Nos. 19, 19a, 22, and 46. She would hop out into Sloane Street and stop the great scarlet juggernauts with the authority of long habit.

The ground floor of the house was given to reception and eating. Of the two drawing rooms on the first floor the smaller one served as Mrs. Walbash's bookish boudoir. The second floor had Carlo's bedroom, study, and bathroom. The third floor was Mrs. Walbash's inviolable lair. The fourth belonged to the servants, except the butler, who slept in the basement between the silver and the wines.

Mrs. Walbash said to the telephone:

"How perfectly sweet of you, Clara darling! Commander De Bure, did you say? Ah! We should have loved to come, but I've got some tiresome people for dinner on that very night. So sorry. Most sweet of you. See you soon. I loved your shawl the other night. No! Yes! No! Of course not!" (A laugh, silvery.) "Au revoir." Down went the receiver. Click!

"That the Slipcombs?" Carlo asked.

He had guessed right. The name "Clara" was enough. But the tones and terms of endearment also would have been enough, for Mrs. Walbash treated no two of her friends alike. Further, the principal occupation of the telephone was the arranging of hospitalities. The weekly engagement cards were kept near the instrument.

The twins lived chiefly for dinners, either given or received. They—or, rather, Mrs. Walbash—had always to be looking ahead, scheming, fitting in, avoiding the clash of dates. No sooner was one dinner over than the next had to be created—morally and materially. Whom should they ask? Whom had they recently not asked? Who had recently asked *them*? Would

So-and-so suit So-and-so?

Yes, it was a vast and an intricate business. In fact, a highly curious business—since it was all for eating, drinking, and chatter, and nothing whatever resulted from it! And it involved hard work, constant attention. To judge the always changing relative importance of personages in the governing world and the world of culture you had to be abreast of all the news in the political, commercial, legal, literary, musical, and artistic movements. (The scientific, teaching, and theological movements you only glanced at.) You had to read the latest books, go to the latest plays, concerts, and picture shows; study the parliamentary reports and the law reports, study the stock markets, and heaven knows what besides.

And all in order to be able to talk well at dinners! No other purpose! Slim Carlo was a very fine talker, if somewhat too apt to dwell on the careers of the Brontë sisters, upon which he was the leading authority on earth and upon which he had written books. He ran the Brontë cult against the Jane Austen cult, and a hard struggle it was.

"Commander De Bure will never get the defense ministry," observed Mrs. Walbash. "Not a ghost of a chance. He's lost all his ground this last week."

"Yes."

Here was an example of their knowledge of current affairs, and of their need of it.

A few minutes later the butler brought in *The Evening Standard.*

"Good heavens!" exclaimed Mrs. Walbash, looking at the paper. "He *has* got the defense ministry, after all!"

At this point, standing near the telephone and the fire, in her loose, roseate tea frock, she became suddenly heroical and magnificent; and Carlo, lounging at ease in his neat blue suit and playing with his grayish hair (whose arrangement displayed a touch of fantasy, to indicate that he was an artistic intellectual, something more than a mere man of the world)—

Carlo recognized the superior force of her individuality.

Mrs. Walbash's master passion, her demon, her tyrant, had taken possession of her. Her master passion was to know everybody who was Somebody and, if possible, to call him by his Christian name. She preferred the Somebodies to be interesting, but, interesting or not, she must know them.

Within a day or so of her first introduction to them she would invite them to Cadogan Square. They often declined, for often they had heard of her in advance. But it was useless to refuse. She would try again. She would write, "Will you come for dinner on the twenty-fourth, twenty-fifth, twenty-sixth, twenty-eighth, or twenty-ninth, or for tea on the twenty-fifth, twenty-sixth, twenty-seventh, or thirtieth? Or for lunch—" etc., etc. Such tactics were bound to beat you unless you wrote simply, "I will not come for any meal on any date." But no one could ever be so brave and so cruel as to pen a refusal in such terms.

Commander De Bure had been nobody, and was now very definitely somebody. High cabinet rank! Mrs. Walbash did not know him, and she had just lost an admirable opportunity of meeting him in ideal circumstances—at the Slipcomb's! Obviously the opportunity must be recovered at once. Obviously the end would justify the means, whatever the means might be. It was inconceivable that a mere ordinary prior engagement should prevent her from meeting Commander De Bure at dinner on Tuesday next week.

Commander De Bure was the personage of the moment. Not to know him, not to have him well on the way to Cadogan Square, would be monstrous, absurd, tragic. To know him was the highest good. She was like a cocaine taker, and Commander De Bure was the cocaine.[3] No price was too costly for him; he was incomparable.

She might have been a prime minister who had to secure the welfare of a great nation and who realized that in so immense a crisis such notions as right and wrong could not exist. Her whole career as a collector of Somebodies seemed to be in the balance.

Mrs. Walbash was about to take up the receiver when the butler showed in two separate callers who had arrived simultaneously. The tea tarried. The callers tarried, though Mrs. Walbash tried every inducement to shift them—short of throwing them out. The instant they had gone Mrs. Walbash did take up the receiver. Number engaged! In half an hour she made another attempt. Mrs. Slipcomb not at home—gone out! Mrs. Walbash was nearly beside herself. Just before dinner she got the direct connection.

"Clara darling. Such a funny thing has happened. Carlo has to go up to Oxford on Tuesday for a meeting of the Oxford Brontë Society. He's only told me this moment. Says he absolutely must go. So I have to countermand the invitations for *my* dinner. If you *could* find a little corner for me somewhere at *your* dinner, I should be simply frightfully pleased. Of course, I don't want to inconvenience you in any way. But *if* ... O, Clara, that's most sweet of you! Sure I shan't be in the way? Thanks awfully!"

"But the Oxford Brontë Society has been dissolved," said Carlo, who was still sitting near her. He spoke quite calmly and ordinarily, made no protest, showed no surprise at her maneuver. He knew and respected the tyrannic power of her master passion.

"O, well, dear! Some other place then. I'll say you told me wrong... That's nothing," Mrs. Walbash replied, with a calmness equaling his own.

She had got the cocaine and was in heaven.

On the following afternoon Mr. Slipcomb and his wife, Clara, sat in a lesser drawing room of their house on the other side of Cadogan Square, partaking of tea; and Clara at any rate was wondering how she could most pleasantly pass the time until she had to dress for dinner. She had risen at eleven, been out late to lunch, and was now a little exhausted and a little animated by a dispute with a British workman on the premises whom she had charged with the capital sin of sloth.

A slim young woman, of almost perfect figure, lithe, very dark, very vivacious and restless, with roguish eyes! In order to marry she had abandoned an adventurous career as a solo violinist whose emoluments consisted chiefly of flowers and flattery. Nevertheless, she was a nice girl, bristling with good qualities, and had many genuine and honest admirers.

As for Sam Slipcomb, he was large, jolly, middle aged (save in energy and mind), and exceedingly rich. Out of nothing at all he had developed into a financier, with various mysterious interests and influences. He had shares in oil and newspapers and fashionable dressmakers; and from an office in the city he gorgeously directed the affairs of the Consolidated Equivalent Securities Corporation, Limited. The C. E. S. C., L. was merely another name for himself.

He did not much care in what style he lived, nor did his wife care—their house was markedly inferior to that of the Walbashes. All he wanted and all Clara wanted was heaps of money at call. They had it. They would spend as much on a single entertainment at a dance club as would have kept the entire Walbash establishment on its feet for a week. Nobody quite knew how many motor cars were theirs, but they certainly employed two chauffeurs.

On the other hand, they had no habits. The nature of their performances on Monday gave no clue to the nature of their performances on Tuesday. They were always high spirited—especially when they quarreled—and they would tolerate anything except boredom. Clara had a wonderful series of smiles; but Sam was a laugher, and when he laughed he opened his mouth wide and laughed with all his might.

The parlor maid entered. Clara abhorred butlers.

"Are you at home, madam?" A momentary pause. "Lady Cammer."

"Your mistress is at home," said Mr. Slipcomb quickly.

The parlor maid bowed and retired.

"How do you know I'm at home, Sam?" asked Clara, putting her head archly on one side and smiling with an attractive frown.

"Private information," said Sam.

Then Lady Cammer appeared, blonde, slim, very elegant, and sweetly odorous, and there was such a fine fond clasping and kissing between the pair of married girls (sixty years between them) as would have quickened the heart of even a Methusaleh. The thing had scarcely finished before the parlor maid came in again with an extra cup and saucer.

"I was passing," said Lady Cammer, "and I thought if you happened to be in and willing, and Sam didn't mind, we might do a little music."

Lady Cammer played the piano very well, indeed, for an amateur, and this was the bond between herself and Clara.

"I should love it," said Clara eagerly, though in secret her attitude as a professional toward Lady Cammer's powers over the piano was somewhat condescending.

Clara poured out tea, and Lady Cammer leaned back fluently in an easy chair and drew off spotless white gloves. Then she dropped her diamond-studded gold cigarette case tinklingly and warningly on to the tea table, as if saying, "Be it known that I am about to smoke much."

"How's your husband getting on with the strikes business, Katie?" Mr. Slipcomb inquired in a rather grave tone.

Sir Cedric Cammer was chairman of one of the biggest railway groups.

"O, I don't know, Sam," Lady Cammer replied negligently. "At least all I know is that he says he will fight for a further all around reduction, and this is the very best time for a fight because the union's losing members—hundreds a week."

"So that's what he says, is it?"

"He says if we fight now we can put the union out of action

for five years certain. He says he's about sick of unions."

"O! So he's sick of unions, is he? Well, you tell him he'd better have a talk with me. I'm a member of the public, tell him." And Sam laughed, but it was the mirth of a man who knew that his views were sought for and respected by the chiefs of every department of commercial activity.

Lady Cammer paused before speaking.

"I'm sure Rick would like that. I'll tell him. I'll tell him to telephone tonight," she said, in a new, impressed tone; and then turning suddenly to Clara, she lightly laughed: "I say, Clara, have you heard Cynthia's latest?"

Cynthia was Mrs. Walbash, who, by reason of always being the subject of the "latest," was an ever joyous subject of conversation in the houses of her friends and acquaintances.

"No," said Clara, leaning forward in anticipation of some gleeful anecdote.

"No, of course you couldn't have. It only happened today. Do you know of anybody of great importance staying at Oxford just now?"

"No. Why?"

"Do you, Sam?"

Mr. Slipcomb shook his head.

"Because Carlo's going up there next Tuesday on one of his Brontë stunts and Cynthia's going with him. And you know she *never* goes with him. So she must have scented some new prey."

"Is that cat under the sofa?" Mr. Slipcomb asked quickly, turning his head.

Instinctively Lady Cammer turned her head also, and in that instant, sure of not being seen by the lively guest, Mr. Slipcomb winked at his wife. The wink meant that he had a jolly idea and that she was to go warily in the talk and leave the initiative to him.

"O!" said Clara vaguely. "How did you get hold of this pleasing information?"

"Quite simply," said Lady Cammer. "She told me herself

this morning on the telephone. I must say she was very frank. She had to tell me because she'd invited Rick and me for dinner on Tuesday, and she had to cancel the invitation first. Cool, eh?"

"Are you sure," Mr. Slipcomb suggested to Clara, and his eyes gleamed at his wife. "Are you sure she isn't merely throwing you over so that she can accept some invitation or other for herself?"

Mr. Slipcomb's eyes gleamed because he was indulging his master passion, the passion for chicane. He loved a plot, and still more he loved a counterplot. Plots and counterplots had been the foundation of his wealth and his prestige in a world where neither wealth nor prestige is easy to acquire. Clara perceived, from customary symptoms, that the passion was rousing in him, and she waited eagerly, admiring and puzzled, for striking developments.

"O, it couldn't be that, surely!" Lady Cammer protested. She had often said that Mrs. Walbash would stick at absolutely nothing to satisfy her craving for intercourse with the illustrious, but she could not believe that so illustrious a pair as Sir Cedric and Lady Cammer might be regarded by Mrs. Walbash as second to anybody whatsoever in any circumstances whatsoever. Indeed, she was shocked.

"Well, if I were you I shouldn't be too sure, Katie," said Mr. Slipcomb, and he laughed loudly and Clara smiled with a delicious malice. "We all have our weaknesses, and sometime or other all our friends without exception have to suffer for them. Cynthia's only got this one fault, and there are worse faults."

"I think it's horrid of her, and if you're right I'll never go into her house again."

"I'm right," said Mr. Slipcomb. "But you *will* go into her house again. You'll have to, because she's far more obstinate than you are. She's a great woman, Cynthia is. She's carried the national vice so high that she's made it a virtue, like Don

Juanism or desperate gambling. She's a great heroine, Cynthia is, and I admire her. I admire anybody who does anything really thoroughly and lives for it night and day."

"What's the national vice?"

"Snobbery, my innocent."

"Well," Katie insisted. "You'll see if I'll enter her house again! You'll see!"

"Now for Tuesday, Katie," said Mr. Slipcomb, with hearty benevolence. "You're out of a job for Tuesday, aren't you? You and Cedric come and dine here with us, will you?"

"O, do!" Mrs. Slipcomb urged brightly. "That would be lovely." Of course she saw in a flash the mischievous naughtiness of her husband's scheme; she pictured the marvelous scene which he was aiming at. Of course, it might spoil the dinner party, but no price could be too high for such a spectacle as the evening promised.

Lady Cammer accepted.

"And that'll give Cedric and me a chance to talk about the forthcoming railway strike."[4] Mr. Slipcomb thus clinched the matter.

"Sam," said Clara in her bedroom after Lady Cammer had departed, "Sam, you are simply awful."

Roaring out his hilarity, he picked up his feather-wife and kissed her. And she giggled happily.

When Cynthia Walbash walked across the square on the Tuesday night to the house of the Slipcombs, she walked across with her brother, Carlo. It was a fine night in the square and in her heart. She had obtained in the morning a very interesting piece of information about Commander De Bure, which news had decided her to tell Carlo that he must not go to Oxford, nor even pretend to go. She had then telephoned to Clara Slipcomb and said frankly that Carlo's visit to Oxford had been put off by the Oxford people themselves, and poor Carlo would be all alone at home, and of course it was absurd to suggest that Clara could find a little place for Carlo at her lovely dinner, but *if* by *any* chance Clara *could* ... Clara had cut her short, with enthusiasm. Of *course* Carlo must come, of *course* there should be a place for him, Carlo was always such an addition to any dinner party! And so on. Cynthia Walbash had been quite startled by the darling's eager warmth, for as a rule there was a dim background of a chill or sardonic quality to Clara's cordiality.

Commander De Bure, as became a naval man, had arrived early, ignoring the great London conventions that a quarter past eight really means half past eight, and that punctuality amounts to bad form. He was a man of fifty, obviously shy, carelessly dressed, with a bald head and the most heavenly nervous smile.

Upon being introduced, Mrs. Walbash, the early bird, had him to herself. She seemed to surround him like an atmosphere. She produced in him the illusion that he had made an instant "conquest," that he was completing her life at last, and that nothing else mattered now. She performed this feat so well because her attitude was perfectly sincere.

Every celebrity conquered her and completed her life—until the next one came along; and in the presence of every new celebrity she was as if charged afresh with marvelous, irresistible charm and vitality.

Other guests entered, and they all either openly or surreptitiously watched, almost spellbound, the terrific spectacle of Mrs. Walbash acquiring the latest celebrity. The spectacle was indeed among the major sights of the West End.

"Evening, Cynthia."

Mrs. Walbash glanced round sharply from her duologue with the commander. It was Lady Cammer's voice in her ear; it was Lady Cammer's light, pressing touch on her arm. And both the voice and the hand seemed to have trembled slightly.

Mrs. Walbash was thunderstruck. Here, to her amazement and horror, was the woman whom she had invited to her own house for dinner on that very night and whom she had put off on the plea that she and Carlo were compelled to go to Oxford! And the glorious assemblage of handsomely dressed persons round about her in the glowing reception hall seemed every one of them to be regarding the encounter with fascinated and cruel gaze.

Katie's eyes, too, had a strange light of emotional agitation in them. As well they might have, for Katie was bearing two separate shocks; the shock of meeting both Mrs. Walbash and Carlo, and the shock of realizing that Mr. and Mrs. Slipcomb, her dear, mischievous friends, must have deliberately contrived the awful quandary. The life of the room was magically arrested in this moment so frightful for Mrs. Walbash and so exasperating for Lady Cammer.

However, Mrs. Walbash gave not a sign of being stricken. True, she could not speak to Lady Cammer, because her tongue was absolutely paralyzed, but she managed to nod and smile brightly at her bosom friend. Then she turned back to Commander De Bure, who had not perceived that he was assisting at a formidable battle. The world of the drawing room admired the matchless sangfroid of Mrs. Walbash, far surpassing that of Lady Cammer.

"Ai! Ai!" exclaimed the hostess under her breath. Lady Cammer had viciously pinched her.

"You ought at least to have warned me," Lady Cammer whispered resentfully.

"Sam wouldn't let me," whispered Mrs. Slipcomb. " But isn't it fun?"

Then up spake Sam, the host, clearing his great throat as if for a speech:

"We have an extra guest at the last minute. That will make thirteen of us. I'm sure none of you is superstitious, but Clara thinks I ought to warn you. Anybody object?"

A few laughed uneasily, half-heartedly; but nobody spoke. Not a soul protested his defiance of the grand, immortal superstition.

"Amos," said the host to the butler, who had entered to announce dinner.

"Sir?"

"What's the day of the month?"

"The ninth, sir."

"So it is. And what's the century? I can generally remember the day of the month, but not the century."

"The twentieth, sir."

"You're sure it isn't the twelfth?"

"Yes, sir," said the butler imperturbably, for he was accustomed to his employer's verbal caprices.

"Well, lay a little table for two, please."

"Yes, sir." Amos vanished.

"It will never do to let one person sit by himself, so there must be two," Sam continued to the company. "We'll draw lots who are to be the two, and we'll all stand in equally. That's the only fair method. Wife, got any visiting cards handy?"

By a strange chance Clara had a whole packet of her visiting cards lying on the table! Mr. Slipcomb counted thirteen cards and drew forth his gold pencil case and scribbled a number on each of them with surprising speed.

"Now," said he, holding the cards with the numbers downward and shuffling them earnestly. "Two of these cards have the same number, six, on them. The two of you who draw sixes will please sit together at the same table."

And he distributed the cards. (But it was a different set of cards, a set which he had been concealing in his large hand.)

"Six," said Mrs. Walbash, trying to convince herself that Commander De Bure had drawn the other six.

"Six," breathed Lady Cammer faintly.

"Two intimate friends," said Sam with calmness. "Pity it's two of the same sex—I certainly ought to have thought of that —Clara, why didn't *you* think of it?—but what does it matter, after all? Anyhow, it would be very unlucky to interfere with the draw, wouldn't it?"

Shortly afterward they went in to dinner, not in pairs, but quite higgledy-piggledy; the Slipcombs had little use for conventional formalities. And Mrs. Walbash and Lady Cammer sat down together at the small table by the fireplace.

"Sam's capable of anything," reflected Lady Cammer. "Fancy ruining a dinner party for the sake of a joke on Mrs. Walbash!"

But the dinner party did not appear to be ruined; at any rate the big table at once became vivacious and noisy.

"It's all so simple," reflected Mrs. Walbash. "Why shouldn't I have had to go to Oxford with Carlo, and then the visit be unavoidably postponed and me be invited here? Nothing extraordinary in that! But she'll never believe me! Never!"

The small table was silent for a space. Nevertheless, after this space of desolated silence the mighty force of the social obligation to converse at any cost prevailed also at the small table.

"I wonder why they're so fearfully animated tonight," said Mrs. Walbash brightly, referring to the extraordinary jollity of the main table.

"My dear," said Katie Cammer, with a dangerous sweetness, "can't you guess?" (And her words conveyed: "Why keep up the pretense? You know perfectly well that I can see through you.")

"No," said Mrs. Walbash. "Why?" (And her words conveyed: "Don't take me for a simpleton.")

"It's because you've been fairly caught out for once, my dear, in your lion hunting. Everybody knows, because Sam's told everybody. And so everybody's gloating over you in your predicament. That's why they're so hilarious. And I have to suffer so that you may suffer! You may depend on it Sam faked those visiting cards. He had it all planned in advance. But I must say I don't know another house in London where the host would *dare* to do such a thing. It's outrageous. However, they're super-rich. The new Huns, I call them."

"I should think it *was* outrageous, dear," Mrs. Walbash agreed. "But what do you mean about *my* predicament?"

"Well, darling, didn't you feel yourself in a bit of a predicament when you found that Cedric and I were invited here tonight?"

"Dearest, you don't mean to say you don't believe ... about Oxford!"

"O, of course I believe it, darling!" (And Katie's words conveyed: "I do not believe it, and you know I don't believe it.")

"I'm so glad. And, after all, I don't see that you've got anything to complain of, dearest. You're much better off here than if you'd been dining at my house. You were dying to know Commander De Bure, and now you know him, and you wouldn't have known him if you'd been at my house."

At this point Mrs. Walbash suddenly turned toward the main table.

"O, Commander," she cried, firmly and boldly. "I do hope you're going to stick up for the Brontës!"

"O, I am, my dear lady," said the Commander, blushing slightly.

"You are an angel," said Mrs. Walbash.

The long table wondered at and admired the presence of mind and the courage of the great huntress. She was not in the least abashed by her situation or by the public knowledge of it; and the gap between two tables had not availed to keep her from her quarry. What the long table did not know was that, having heard that Commander De Bure was a passionate admirer of the works of the sisters Brontë, she had specially brought Carlo, the supreme Brontëist, to the dinner and given him secret instructions to inaugurate, in his own inimitably subtle way, a conversation on the respective merits of the sisters Brontë and Jane Austen. The discussion was fairly in train, and Carlo Walbash, with the almost mute but still powerful moral support of the Commander, was routing the Jane Austenites, for there was none among them who did not wish to be agreeable to the new and charming and unaffected cabinet minister.

As for Cynthia Walbash, who never ate roast meat at dinner, she totally ignored the joint, twisted her chair round a little, and appropriated more than a fair share of the conversation of the table from which she had been so ingeniously excluded. Lady Cammer ate meat, and on this occasion she ate it in melancholy silence. The long table wondered at and admired still more the prowess of the huntress who had declined to be hunted. Sam Slipcomb lost all interest in his plot. And Jane Austen suffered a calamitous defeat.

In the drawing room after dinner the women sat thoughtful and nearly speechless while the men tarried unconscionably below. When the reluctant men appeared Sam Slipcomb went into a corner with Sir Cedric Cammer and these two remained in earnest converse about the labor situation for the rest of the evening. Sam, because he was so very rich and autocratic, could thus safely ignore the ordinary obligations of a host. People criticized him (not to his face), but they said:

"Well, he's very rich."

Commander De Bure was the center of a court of ladies who liked his high office and positively adored his smile and his nervous simplicity. But in due course the experienced and wily Mrs. Walbash extricated him from the court and monopolized him.

"Will you dine on the fourteenth, Commander?" she was heard to say, consulting the little book she always carried in her bag.

"No? Engaged? So sorry. Well, then, the sixteenth, seventeenth, nineteenth, twentieth, or twenty-second. Will you choose?" The well known shock tactics of Cynthia! How could so simple a man as the commander hope to withstand them?

And later, when the dinner party of the long and the little tables (which from the morrow onward was to be the talk of the town)—when this party broke up, Mrs. Walbash said to Commander De Bure:

"My brother and I live just across the square, Commander. Do come over, now—if it's only for a minute or two—and let Carlo show you his Brontë first editions and his corrected proofs of Wuthering Heights. You'd make him so happy. He loves to show them to enthusiasts like you. We can walk round. It's a lovely night. Tell your chauffeur to follow us."

"Commander," murmured Lady Cammer, stopping the captive on the front steps, "will you dine with us on the nineteenth? We should be so delighted."

"I should have been very glad, thank you so much, dear lady. But I'm engaged for the nineteenth to Mrs. Walbash."

"My dear," said Mrs. Walbash cheerfully to Lady Cammer. "I hope you and Cedric will come to me on the nineteenth to meet the Commander."

Well, Lady Cammer accepted. Yes, she accepted.

And Mrs. Walbash triumphantly carried off her noble prey, with Carlo behind for a rear guard. She might have known the Commander for four years instead of for four hours. But what Commander De Bure really thought of the unique Mrs. Walbash was only known to his crony, Colonel Josh Fallip, with whom he consorted at a still later hour at the ancient services club known as the Rag.

NOTES

1. *Liberty*. 20th September 1924, pages 46-51. Signed Arnold Bennett. Illustrated by Nancy Fay. *Liberty* was a Chicago weekly paper. "The Great Huntress" was the first of its seven Bennett contributions published between 1924 and 1930.
2. Bennett took a lease on 75 Cadogan Square, once the home of a Viceroy of India, in December 1923.
3. A socially period-specific simile. For those with wealth and a position in society the early 1920s was a liberating and permissive period. Drugs - cocaine, opium, morphine - were acceptable, and used by respectable society ladies such as Mrs. Walbash, without either social opprobrium or legal prosecution.
4. 1924 was a year of railway disputes. At the start of the year The Associated Society of Locomotive Engineers and Firemen went on strike because of a unilaterally imposed pay cut, brought in by the National Wages Board. Mr. Slipcomb may have been more immediately exercised by the Cabinet meeting in June 1924 to discuss, as a matter of urgency, the disruption caused by a sudden strike on the Underground and Great Western Railways.

LEADING TO MARRIAGE.[1]

This is the story of the episode which led to Mr Capstain's second marriage.

The illustrious Mr Capstain sat down at his desk in his vast house, Belgrave Square, London. He was a man of business, a director of the biggest manufactory of its kind in the world. No manufactory could have been directed with less friction. Never a strike there! The delegates of trade unions never troubled there! Mr Capstain was not only the director, but the working staff, the everything of the manufactory. He happened to be a novelist, playwright, and journalist. He knew that he was not a genius, but he also knew that he was the most popular, the most efficient, and the most prolific literary performer of his time. He made more money and spent more than any other author on earth.

The hour was midnight.

At midnight his day's labour began. He toiled till 7 a.m., with an interval at 4 a.m. for light refreshment. He breakfasted at 7 a.m., went to bed, slept six hours, arose at 1 p.m., lunched at 2 p.m., and had then a glorious stretch of ten hours in which to see the world. This wonderful plan of existence he had taken from the life Balzac.[2] Herein was his sole resemblance to Balzac.

In the blaze of the electric light he passed his hand over some notebooks. He looked at his fingers. Dust. He rang the bell.

A butler entered.

Mr Capstain was reputed to be the only man in London who employed two butlers. This one was the night-butler, necessary because of Mr Capstain's nocturnal refreshment and early breakfast.

'Crowther,' he asked blandly, 'who dusts this room nowadays?'

'The new head-housemaid, sir.'

'What's her name?'

'Maisie, sir.'

'Her surname?'

'I don't know, sir. She's only been here ten days.'

'Has she gone to bed yet?'

'Oh no, sir.'

'Send her to me.'

Mr Capstain had spoken blandly, for the reason that he never allowed himself to be other than bland. He believed in harmony, as the best aid to industry. He never had the slightest dissension even with his two widowed sisters, who lived with him and on him. They adored him, though he was a plump fellow of forty-five, with a bald head, a manner exasperatingly imperturbable, and an ironic tongue.

The new head-housemaid came in. A young lady of pleasant but serious features, very neat.

'Yes, sir.' A rather cultivated voice for a housemaid, even for a head-housemaid.

'Maisie,' said Mr Capstain at his blandest. 'By the way, what is your surname?'

'Dyton, sir.'

'Well, Maisie, I told Crowther yesterday about the inefficient dusting of this room. Did you get the message?'

'Yes, sir.'

'See here, then.' Mr Capstain passed his hand again over the notebooks, and showed dusty fingers.

'I'm sorry, sir.'

'You possibly don't realise that this room is the most important in the whole house. Everything comes out of it, including your wages.'

'I'm sorry, sir. I had to go out. I was detained, and there wasn't time....'

'Excuse me, Maisie,' Mr Capstain blandly stopped her. 'Your affairs are not mine. You've been here ten days. You and I are at liberty to cease business relations at the end of the first fortnight.' Mr Capstain knew this interesting fact about the conditions of British domestic service because part of his equipment as a novelist was to know everything. He continued: 'At the end of your fortnight you will have the goodness to leave. One of my rules here is never to give an order twice.'

'Yes, sir.'

Maisie turned to leave. Mr Capstain scribbled, 'New Housemaid' on a note-pad. At the door Maisie turned back and remarked:

'I suppose you wouldn't like me to suggest a plot to you, sir?'

'A plot?' repeated Mr Capstain, alert.

'Yes, sir.'

'If it suits me, I'll pay you five pounds for it,' said Mr Capstain, unperturbed.

'Well, sir. There was a girl who had to earn her living, or part of it. She had literary leanings, and tried to be an author. She wrote two novels. One she couldn't sell. The other was published, but it failed completely. She had a son, a young boy. She couldn't be a secretary, because that wouldn't have suited her temperament. So she decided ...'

At this point Crowther re-entered, apologetic.

'Crowther,' said his master, 'you well know that you have no right to come in unless I ring.'

'The house is on fire, sir.'

Mr Capstain showed no emotion; neither did Maisie.

'Oh, is it?' said the master. 'Which floor?'

'Above this, sir. Back.'

'Serious?'

'Maybe, sir.'

'Then telephone for the fire-brigade.'

'I have, sir.'

'That's good. Get all the servants downstairs before the staircase is alight. Are your mistresses in?'

'Not yet, sir.'

'Very fortunate. Thank you. That will do... for the moment.'

Exit Crowther.

'Fires always burn upwards, not downwards. So we're in no danger,' observed Mr Capstain. 'You're not afraid, Maisie?'

'Oh no, sir.'

'But your things upstairs?'

'I sleep in the basement, sir.'

'Good. Now to continue that plot.'

'So as she understood and really liked housework,' Maisie continued calmly, 'she decided to enter domestic service, and she became a housemaid. Her little boy was ill, and she went out one evening to see him—at her sister-in-law's. And that got her into trouble about some dusting. She had to leave. And to find just the right sort of situation was not very easy. Is that a good beginning of a plot, sir?'

'Very,' said Mr Capstain. 'Are you a widow?'

'Yes, sir.'

'What is called a lady?'

'I suppose so, sir.'

'Will you sit down, Mrs Dyton.'

'Thanks.' Mrs Dyton sat.

They talked for some time—indeed until they heard the beating thud-thud-thud of a fire-engine.

'Perhaps we ought to be going,' said Mr Capstain. 'Everything's insured, except my manuscripts. I'd better take them.'

He opened a drawer and pulled out a pile of manuscript. Maisie rose to go.

'One moment,' said Mr Capstain. 'Forgive me, but you're rather a wonderful young woman. I should like to ask you one question. Do you intend ever again to write?'

'Nothing would induce me to.'

'Then you're also a very wise young woman, and I'm relieved,' said Mr Capstain.

They went forth through the double-doors to the landing, smelt smoke, discerned the romantic figures of firemen above.

Notes

1. *Colliers*. 26th April 1930, page 16 and reprinted in the *New Statesman*, 10th May 1930, pages 147-148. Signed Arnold Bennett. The *New Statesman* started publication in April 1913. Bennett became a shareholder in 1915 and later a director. He wrote a regular column from 1916-1919 as well as contributing stories and articles until 1930. The story was reprinted in *New Statemanship: An Anthology* (London: Longmans, 1963) - this is the version reproduced here.
2. Honoré de Balzac (1799-1850), French novelist whose Eugénie Grandet serves as a model for Bennett's *Anna of the Five Towns*. He was much admired by Bennett, as much for his life-style as for his writing: "I am constantly disgusted that I can't work like Balzac, who literally wore out four chairs, and died exhausted at 52, despite a superb constitution. This is how I want to work - to pour it out in vast quantities, pell-mell, vast, immense, various. But I can't, for the ridiculous reason that I get tired." (*Letters II*, p.151)

THE FLIGHT.[1]

Mr. Saxton Seaforth was paying an afternoon call. He went up the bare oak stairs that flanked the Italian restaurant, and up the next flight that flanked the offices of a firm of button manufacturers, and then faced an old oak door on which was a small brass plate bearing the words: "Miss Moina Larchant." He rang the bell and waited.

He was a plain man, apparently simple, well but not smartly dressed, and too plump for his years, which were less than forty. His vocation on earth was that of detective novelist. His name was familiar to the readers of the lighter monthly magazines and of three-and-six-penny books in startling covers; but it was not very familiar to the smart world because, being a plain man, he did not attend first nights at the theater and similar solemnities, and therefore his photograph rarely appeared in the back-chat illustrated weeklies. Nevertheless he made a steady four thousand a year and was as content as any human being ought to be.

The door labeled "Larchant" opened.

"Miss Larchant in?" Seaforth asked with a twinkling eye of the exceeding smart young maid who stood on the stairs which began immediately behind the door.

He passed in front of her up the narrow steep stairs. She closed the door. The greater universe was excluded and he was in the secret universe of Moina Larchant. Thick carpet. A woman's room. All divans and cushions and tender tints. Plenty of upholstery and little visible woodwork. In the midst a low tea table, laden; among its cargo a steaming kettle. Seaforth glanced to see whether his favorite sandwiches were also among the cargo. They were. He had the least odious of moral infirmities: greed. Those exquisite thin sandwiches were a sensual magnet which helped to draw him again and again to the abode of Moina Larchant.

She entered, from what Seaforth rightly assumed to be her bedroom; he knew absolutely nothing of Moina's secret universe except her drawing-room. Moina welcomed him with the utmost sweetness. She was a brunette, tall, elegant, jeweled, deep-voiced, lithe, thirtyish. She flattered, not in words, but with gestures, tones, facial expressions. She was Seaforth's sole link with the smart world. She knew everyone and addressed nearly everyone as "darling." Her name and her photograph were continually in the smarter pages of the popular press. She might be rich, but Seaforth had convinced himself that she was poor, that when she did not smartly dine or lunch out, or munch an egg and a sardine at home, she ate in the Italian restaurant below for about one-and-six, and that the dressy maid was engaged by the hour like a charwoman and wore her piquant frock and apron and cap only for callers.

Withal, Moina was a remarkably agreeable companion, full of odd anecdotes which served Seaforth most usefully in his trade, and she scarcely ever said a word about her own troubles. Further, she was never distant and never too intimate.

After the customary social preliminaries Miss Larchant said:

"I'm so glad you rang me up today."

"Why? Anything interesting?" Seaforth demanded eagerly,

for there was perturbation in her voice.

"Of course you know Jack Wren."

Seaforth shook his head.

"Haven't you seen he's been appointed general manager of the Eastern Electric Company? He's only thirty-five, and it's ten thousand a year. Terrific post."

"Oh! What about him?"

"He's disappeared," answered Miss Larchant. "He came for tea here two days ago, stayed quite a long time, and so far as I know he's not been seen since. He was to have taken charge at the Eastern Electric yesterday morning. I telephoned him yesterday at lunch time. He simply hadn't arrived there at all. And no message. Nothing. They were upset, naturally. I telephoned to his rooms. No news there either. Except that he hadn't slept there. And the same thing today. No news of any sort. He must have had some dreadful accident."

Seaforth gave a negative sign. "I doubt it. People don't have accidents. And if they do they're taken to hospital, and if they're well-to-do they always have some evidence of identity on them, and the hospital communicates at once with the address. And if they've been killed the police are told, and the police tell the relatives or friends in two jiffs. No. He must have just vanished, for reasons of his own. Lots of men do it and women too."

"But he couldn't have had a reason!" Miss Larchant protested. "He was in splendid health. And he was at the height of his career. Everything was going perfectly for him—and he'd deserved it all. No family. Not married. Nothing to trouble him."

Miss Larchant appeared to be pleading a case. Less and less did she hide her anxiety.

"Have you said anything to the police?" he inquired with a casual air. The sandwiches no longer excited him.

"I? No! How could I? I've got no—er—standing for that."

"But he was a friend of yours—a great friend, seeing that he came for tea and stayed a long time, and yesterday you were trying to get him on the telephone."

"Well, *I* couldn't start the police. It would have been too serious a step."

Seaforth saw tears in Miss Larchant's eyes. She was more human to him than she had ever been. The sight of her, stricken, touched him; and in a moment he was entirely carried away by an idea.

"How should you like me to look into the affair?" he suggested rather timidly.

"I wish you would," said Miss Larchant. "The fact is I meant to ask you to."

He rose and walked feverishly about the room, a new Saxton Seaforth. As he walked he put many questions, the replies to which, frank enough, gave him no help whatever in the formation of a theory.

"What's his address?"

Miss Larchant stated the address.

"And have you a photograph?"

Miss Larchant had a photograph and produced it.

"*Au revoir*," he said. "I'll run round there now. You shall hear from me."

Miss Larchant's soft gaze thanked him.

At the door he turned back—and blushed.

"I say—you'll excuse me. But I suppose you aren't engaged to him?"

"N-no," said Miss Larchant hesitatingly and then added with positiveness: "No. I certainly am not engaged to him."

"But you would have been, inside a week," thought Seaforth, saying aloud: "Forgive me. I had to ask."

"Of course, darling," murmured Miss Larchant.

Outside, standing vaguely in front of the Italian restaurant, was another plump man, somewhat older than Seaforth.

"Hello, Saxton!"

"Hello, Jim!" Seaforth responded, shaking hands. "What are you doing here, wasting your time in Soho?"

Jim was Detective Inspector Brown of the Criminal Investigation Department, Scotland Yard, a reliable friend of Seaforth's and the original of at least one of Seaforth's fictional portraits of detectives possessing genius.

"Well," said the inspector, "I saw you go up, so I thought I'd better wait till you came down. I might have been in the way."

"Do you mean at Miss Larchant's?"

"Yes."

"And what are you after with her?"

"This Wren disappearance."

"But who put you folks onto it?"

"Eastern Electric," said the terse Brown. "She's told you about it?"

Seaforth nodded. "Yes; but she doesn't know the Yard's been told."

"Hear anything interesting?"

"Not a word," Seaforth cautiously replied. Although the inspector was a friend, the novelist on this occasion instinctively regarded him as a rival who ought not to be helped.

"Got a theory?" The inspector smiled a little quizzically.

Seaforth gave a negative sign. "Only a theory of exclusion. It isn't a crime. The man's slung his hook. Are you having the ports watched?"

"No. He'd never take a Channel boat. Too well known. Always on the Continent, to and fro—so I was informed at his rooms. All the same his car's still in the garage."

"Curiouser and curiouser," observed Seaforth, also quizzically. "But there are trains."

"Too well known at all the terminals," said the inspector.

"Well, Jim, I may see you later. I'm in a hurry now."

The two parted.

Seaforth said to himself: "I hope she won't tell him I'm on the job too."

At the far end of the street he saw a garage with the sign: "Motors for hire." He strolled toward it and went in.

He had very suddenly been visited by a theory. He knew from Moina Larchant that the vanished Wren had stayed with her until after half-past six two days earlier, and also that he had not returned to his rooms on that evening. Therefore either he must have made arrangements for flight previous to his call on her; or, something having occurred at the interview to induce or to precipitate his departure, he had decided, on leaving her, to disappear immediately and had planned the flight at once. Supposing that, as he emerged into the street, he had caught sight of the garage sign and impulsively gone in and hired a car.

A clerkly young man was sitting in a little glazed cubicle or office just inside the open gates.

"Do you recognize this photograph?" Seaforth asked him in a firm brusque tone without any kind of preliminary and he slapped down Wren's photograph on the soiled desk. The clerk looked intently at the photograph and then at Seaforth.

"May I ask who you are?" the clerk demanded.

"I'm a detective," Seaforth murmured confidentially.

And he spoke the truth, for he was a detective, though merely an amateur and temporary detective. He proceeded blandly:

"This man probably came in here the day before yesterday in the early evening, to hire a car."

"You've got it," said the clerk. "He did. I remember him now. But he wasn't dressed like this."

"How was he dressed?"

"Oh! Shabbyish blue suit. And a cap."

"What time did he call?"

"I should say about seven-fifteen or a bit later."

"And what name did he give?"

"Here! Give me a chance while I look at the order-book," cried the clerk. "Said he was chauffeur to Lord Porlock and had instructions to meet his master with a car at Exeter before six next morning."

"Had he any luggage?"

"Yes, a rotten old suitcase. I explained to him that he ought to pay in advance and he did so. I happened to have a car and a driver free, and as soon as they'd filled up with petrol they started."

"Has the car returned?"

The clerk, hearing a familiar voice, looked forth.

"Yes," he answered. "Here it is."

An old car drove into the garage and the driver thereof stepped from the wheel. In a few minutes Seaforth learned that the fare had not engaged the driver in conversation throughout the journey, that on arriving in the vicinity of Exeter cathedral, the fare had left the car and returned after a short delay, and had then requested the driver to take him on to St. Erth, which place the car had reached at eleven in the morning, breakfast being eaten en route at an inn. At St. Erth railway station the fare had duly paid the driver for the distance between Exeter and St. Erth and walked into the railway station, which was deserted.

To all this the amateur detective ejaculated simply, "Hm!" and quitted the garage. In his enchanted mind he easily reconstructed the events of the previous evening but one. Between Wren's departure from Miss Larchant's flat and his entry into the garage some forty or forty-five minutes had elapsed. In that period of time Wren had visited a second-hand shop and bought a suit of clothes and a cap, and a suitcase, and—somewhere—had changed from the stylish to the shabby blue suit, had packed the stylish suit into the suitcase and then had attacked the garage which he had previously noticed.

The amateur detective had possessed himself of a truly important, perhaps a decisive clue; and he would rest on his laurels. Still, he was dashed.

Next morning Saxton Seaforth was in Penzance. More, he was on the steamer quay in Penzance Harbor. He had arrived in Penzance by the distinguished and smooth sleeper from Paddington, pursuant to a process of logical reasoning. Why had Wren motored to St. Erth? What was the interest of St. Erth? Seaforth had never before heard of St. Erth. A serious study of the Great Western Railway Guide had given him what he decided must be the correct answer to these questions. St. Erth was the junction for St. Ives and Penzance. Wren had finished his journey by train, probably in order to produce a "fault" in his tracks. He had gone either to St. Ives or Penzance. No regular passenger steamers sailed from St. Ives. Hence doubtless he had gone to Penzance. Only one line of passenger steamers sailed from Penzance—the service to the Scilly Isles. Hence Wren had gone, or was going, to the Scilly Isles: which Seaforth deemed to be an ideal archipelago for a fugitive from the world. What detective, save Seaforth, would dream of ransacking the Scilly Isles for such a fugitive? Seaforth was once again feeling rather proud of his gifts as a sleuth.

He had now stationed himself on the quay to watch the passengers—chiefly holiday-makers—board the *Scillonian Princess*. He scrutinized them one by one as they passed along the gangway to the deck of the ship. He had seen several Wrens as they walked down the quay, but when he saw them close none of them proved to be Wren or anything like Wren. His excitement grew as the hour of departure came nearer. Three minutes. Two minutes. Steam-whistling. One minute. Passengers hurrying. Should he go on board or should he wait? Of course Wren might have sailed on the previous day.

But Seaforth's process of reasoning was against this probability. Still Wren might, just might, be at that moment safe on some Scilly island.

The withdrawal of the gangway decided the point for Seaforth. He was left behind. And no sooner had the *Scillonian Princess* begun to steal away from the quay than Seaforth began to address himself as an ass for not being in her. He deposited his overcoat and bag at the quay office and then strolled about in the gentle sunshine, thinking, thinking. Soon the *Scillonian Princess* was diminished to a curl of smoke in the offing. On the opposite side of the harbor Seaforth descried a yacht, a ketch of some hundred tons, as he was able to guess, being himself addicted to yachting.

"I seem to recognize that yacht," he reflected. He did recognize the yacht, which was the *Sea Blossom*, property of his friend Charlie Mitcham, a retired merchant, a bachelor, who loved to sail the seas alone. Seaforth had once been aboard her for a few hours at Cowes during a regatta.

He walked round the harbor and saw Charlie Mitcham seated in a Bombay chair on the deck of the yacht reading the Times. He cried a greeting. Mitcham was a tall fellow of fifty or so, with a big nose and the sort of facial ugliness which women call masculine beauty. In a few minutes he was seated in another Bombay chair opposite Mitcham, who despite his habit of solitude was unmistakably delighted to get a little relief from solitude.

"What about some beer?" Mitcham suggested in his deep voice.

"Well, what about it?"

The beer was promptly served by a very smart steward in a white jacket which had shrunk somewhat in the wash.

In answer to questions, Seaforth said that he was on a short holiday, gathering material for a book, and had no particular program.

Life was perfect—save that Seaforth felt himself to be sartorially unworthy of the scene

"Come with me for a few days," said Mitcham. "I had a notion of going to Scilly."

"This ship of yours has a motor, I think?"

"You bet. Seven knots, my lad."

The thing was settled.

"I must get my bag from the steamer office."

"I'll send a man for it."

"And I must send a wire."

"I'll have it sent off for you."

"No, Charlie, I must send it myself. It isn't for the general eye."

He winked. Charlie winked. The pair went off into Penzance town together.

Seaforth, for the second time that morning—but now in a much greater degree—was excited, extraordinarily and agreeably excited. He thought: "The hand of destiny is in this business. How clever I was after all!"

"Not so bad, is it?" said Charlie Mitcham with an owner's pride.

"It is not," Seaforth agreed heartily but quietly.

The owner and his guest, on the poop, were taking coffee after lunch. The captain, close by them, had the wheel and there was one deckhand forward of the main-mast. The rest of the crew was below. The *Sea Blossom*, ten miles from Penzance, under full sail and not using her engine, was doing a good six knots on the starboard tack in the fresh northerly wind. The sea rippled and the ripples glinted in the sunshine. The deck and all its paraphernalia had the final touch of smartness in polished brass, coiled ropes and taut sheets. The burgee of the Royal Thames Yacht Club stood stiffly out from the main-peak and the blue ensign waved aft. And the owner's white-topped cap and blue suit with the buttons of the Royal Thames Yacht Club were as smart as the yacht herself. Life was perfect—save that Seaforth, in shore togs and overcoat and wearing borrowed white shoes too large for his feet, felt himself to be sartorially unworthy of the general scene. Withal, he was highly content with the present and confident as to the immediate future. Less than twenty-four hours ago Miss Larchant had not begun to tell him of the Wren mystery, and now he had the sensation of having lived in the Wren mystery for weeks. The steward came to remove coffee cups from the poop.

"Spry sort of chap, that!" said Seaforth casually.

"Used to be a steward on the Cunard Line," Charles Mitcham explained. "I could wish that his fingernails were in not quite such heavy mourning."

"I say," Seaforth proceeded with a short laugh. "Scilly's all right of course; but I wish we were bound for Guernsey. I haven't been to St. Peter Port for years."

"Nothing to prevent us from being bound for Guernsey," said Charlie Mitcham gayly. "A couple of squints at the chart and Molton can lay the course, can't you, skipper?"

"Yes, sir." The wizened middle-aged captain's tone was zealous, eager, very obliging, for long experience had accustomed him to the caprices and vagaries of yacht-owners.

That night after his host had gone to bed, Seaforth, in pajamas and overcoat, climbed on deck to enjoy the night before retiring. The night was lovely. The wind had held, but not freshened. The yacht was on the port tack, heeling slightly, with sails well filled. The mate had the wheel and the steering was so easy that he scarcely took the trouble to glance at the binnacle. No sound except the swish of water along the sides of the ship. No illumination except the distant Eddystone and the faint red and green reflections of the navigating lights on rigging, and the gleam of the twin electric lamps on the white face of the binnacle.

But as he moved aft from the deckhouse doors Seaforth's ear caught the rumor of voices in violent altercation at the other end of the yacht. He recognized one voice, that of the captain. The sounds ceased abruptly. He was thrilled by delicious premonitions of adventure and he wondered whether, when the right moment came, he would be daring enough to do the right thing.

Charlie Mitcham, being a man of the world, began the day with coffee and a cigar, which he consumed in the deckhouse while inspecting the weather and the deck-scrubbing. Seaforth, being a mere author of detective novels, began the day with tea and a cigarette, which he consumed as he lay in bed in his cabin. He had rung the bell; the steward entered with a tray. As the steward was making ready to deposit the tray on Seaforth's knees, Seaforth, who had already greeted the man, said to him:

"I always like to know people's names. What's yours? I haven't heard it."

"Roper, sir," the steward replied.

"Oh!" said Seaforth. "That's odd. I had a wild notion it was Wren."

"No, sir."

"Then what's the meaning of this?" Seaforth snatched at his dark mustache and pulled it off.

Nothing happened that Seaforth expected to happen. The steward just laughed, rather loudly and with excellent good humor. When he had finished laughing he observed:

"Now I understand why your books are so interesting, Mr. Seaforth. You're a born detective yourself." And having safely relinquished the tray he sat down on the bed at Seaforth's feet.

"I believe I am," Seaforth agreed. "Still, I've had a bit of luck."

There was a silence in which the noise of scrubbing overhead became very plainly audible.

"And when were you a Cunard steward?"

"I wasn't ever."

"But you're a fine steward, Mr. Wren. Where did you learn your duties?"

"I learnt them by teaching stewards on my little yacht years ago. Now, Mr. Seaforth, I don't mind telling you that what was good luck for you is bad luck for me. I was wandering about Penzance Harbor the day before yesterday and it was vouchsafed to me in the way of gossip that the former steward of this ship had eloped with a girl and left the yacht in the lurch. I applied for the post and I think I'm filling it. I told Mr. Mitcham I hadn't my papers with me as I wasn't hoping for a job. And as he wanted a steward more than I wanted a job, he took me on without papers."

"And the yacht was going to Scilly."

"What's that got to do with it?"

"Oh! Nothing."

"And may I inquire how you twigged me, Mr. Seaforth?"

"My trade compels me to keep my eyes open, you know. I noticed your mustache was a shade crooked this morning. But your hands are very stewardish, Mr. Wren."

"Ah!" said the steward. "That's art, not nature. I attended to my hands in the train."

"Not in the car?"

"Here!" the steward exclaimed, "you seem to know quite a lot."

"No," said Seaforth blandly. "I've told you I only had a bit of luck. I'm frightfully clever, but not so clever as you might imagine from my—er—success." It was no part of his plan to give to Mr. Wren the slightest hint of the circumstances which had tempted him to assume the role of detective. "Why did you get Mr. Mitcham to change his destination?" the steward asked as he carefully restored his mustache to its place.

"That's simple. We should have reached the Scillies last evening. And you might have deserted. And I wanted to have a nice long chat with you such as I am having. There's another thing. Are you aware that the police are after you?"

"Who told you that?"

"A Scotland Yard detective. You see I'm very friendly with Scotland Yard. I have to be, for my trade. And by mere chance I met the detective who has your affair in hand."

"But why in heaven's name are the police after me? I've done nothing."

"No. I don't think you have done anything. But you've vanished. And when the new manager of the Eastern Electric vanishes on the very morning when he ought to be taking up his duties, naturally the world is a bit curious. You'd be curious yourself. You say you've done nothing, and I absolutely believe you. But if you haven't done anything somebody might have done something to you."

"Nobody's done anything to me."

"Queerer and queerer," said Seaforth almost in a whisper. "You've been appointed to one of the highest posts in England. You must have had ambition. You've realized it. And you choose that moment to disappear."

"Yes," returned the steward. "I did choose that moment. Listen, Mr. Seaforth. I've been pretty open with you. You won't give me away?"

"Why shouldn't I?" Seaforth parried, and paused. "Nevertheless I won't—on one condition. Tell me quite candidly why you did disappear. It's a psychological mystery that interests me tremendously—in my professional capacity as a novelist. I shall respect your secrets. I shall even forget them. You can trust me."

"Well," said the steward at length, with an air of having reflected and come to a decision. "I'll keep on being open with you, and I'll trust you. I disappeared because I wasn't sure that my future would satisfy me. I wanted to think things out for a few months. I've worked awfully hard and I was beginning to suspect that the brilliant results might not bring in a lot of happiness. I'm not a worldly man and I've no desire for worldly success. I was earning five thousand a year before I accepted the ten-thousand-a-year post. And I can live well on three thousand a year and keep a thirty-ton yacht too."

"But engineering success isn't worldly success, Mr. Wren."

"No. But it involves worldly success."

"Why? How's that?"

"Well, I feel it would. And I couldn't do with too much worldly success. I hate snobs, and luxury for the sake of luxury, and being in the swim. And all that. Now I'm being straight with you. And I shall rely on you not to give me away."

"Shall I tell you what I think?" said Seaforth boldly. "There's a lady in the case. Excuse my bluntness."

"I'll excuse it. But I'm not really entangled with any woman. And that's a fact. I was afraid you wouldn't accept my reasons." The sound of the bell was heard. "That's the deckhouse bell. Mr. Mitcham ringing for me. I must go."

Within half an hour of *Sea Blossom's* arrival and anchoring in the harbor of St. Peter Port Mr. Jack Wren, general manager of the Eastern Electric Company, found himself with a large two-handled bass bag on his arm, being rowed ashore in the yacht's dinghy. The member of the crew called the caterer had caught his foot in one of the anchor chains as it ran out and was lying on his back in the forecastle, smoking. Someone had to do the catering. The cook was ready enough to do it. But an order had come from the poop that steward Roper must do it.

Jack Wren stepped onto the quay; the dinghy returned to the yacht. Wren knew almost nothing of the town and quite nothing about provisioning; nevertheless he had to go and buy some fifteen different matters for the cook and a few for the captain. He felt rather lonely and inefficient on the quay. Indeed he almost wished that instead of being on the quay he were in the general manager's office of the Eastern Electric, autocratically functioning.

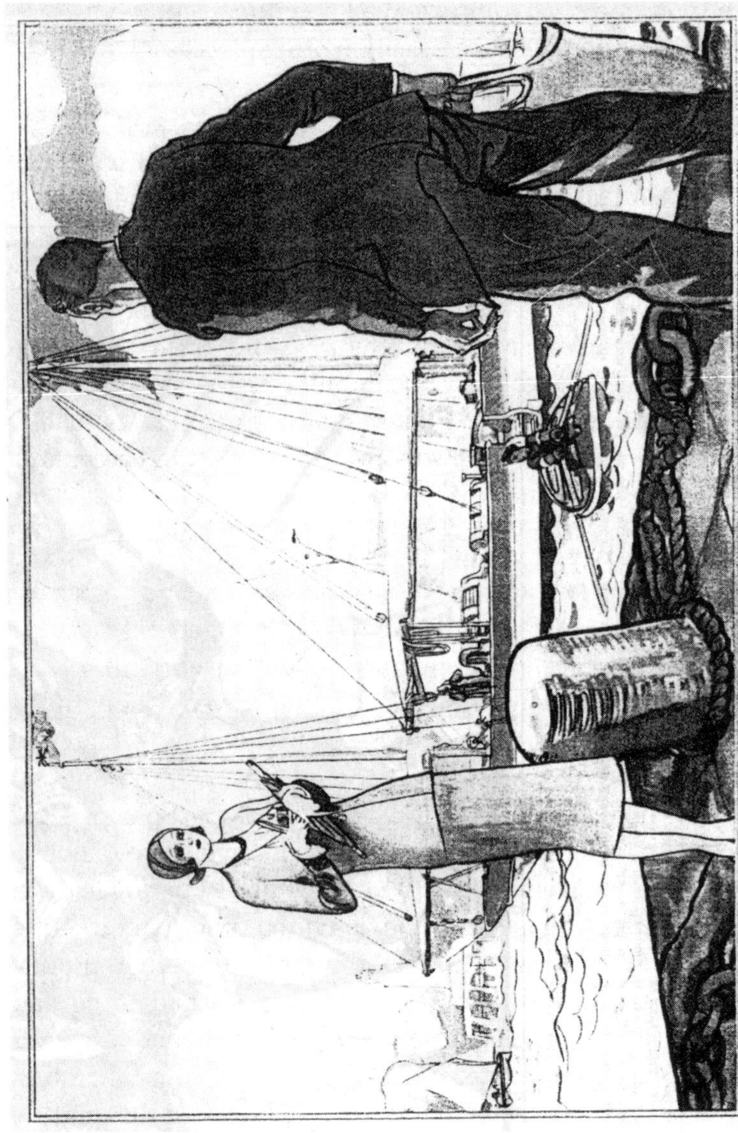

She might be a too chic creature and an in-the-swim creature, but she was irresistible

But the next moment he would have given a large sum of money to continue being lonely, whether inefficient or not. And he was ashamed of his shabby blue suit and his big white shoes and especially of the bag. He saw a tall youngish woman in a very smart traveling costume strolling along the quay. Moina Larchant. He glanced at the yacht as at an unattainable refuge from trouble and perceived in the distance the figure of Saxton Seaforth with marine glasses fixed upon himself. And then in the tenth of a second he became furious, like a lion in a net, and he strode furiously up to Miss Larchant.

"Good morning," said he with cold false calm, though his heart was beating fast. "What are you doing here?"

"Oh!" ejaculated Miss Larchant. "I just came here for a change."

She was very agitated and the sight of her agitation gave a wonderful reality to Wren's calm.

"Well," he said brutally, "you shall have a change. I'm steward on a yacht and I've got to do a lot of shopping. You're a woman and therefore a shopper. The least you can do is to come and help me."

He ceased to be ashamed of his attire. He turned with decision in the direction of the town and Moina Larchant turned also.

"How did you know I'd be here?"

"I didn't know," said Moina. "But I thought you might."

"You're unnaturally clever. But someone told you. The detective-novelist fellow, no doubt. He must have telegraphed to you."

"Jack," said Moina in a soft voice, "why did you run away?"

"I didn't. I walked and drove. And why shouldn't I? I'm a free man I suppose?" He didn't really suppose anything of the sort and he knew that he was not behaving well, but he gloried in wrong-doing. "Still, I'll tell you, and I'll tell you straight. I didn't like the look of my prospects. I've been my own master for years, and on reflection I didn't fancy myself as the servant of a board of directors. So I merely went. I can always make a living. And that's all. I know if I earn a lot of money I shall have to spend it. And I'm not a spender."

"But you needn't spend your money."

"I should be forced to."

"Who'd force you?"

"You would. You're an in-the-swim woman."

Upon these shocking heartless words followed a silence, during which the pair walked. Somehow they arrived at the open space in front of the Parliament House of the States-General of Guernsey, and there they stood.

"Where's the shopping street in this vast city?" Wren grimly murmured. But he did not feel grim. A sensation of happiness permeated his being. He was naturally flattered because Moina had so astoundingly hurried after him to Guernsey. She might be a too chic creature and an in-the-swim creature, but she was a magnificent creature.

"How could I force you? What am I to you?" Moina questioned gently.

"You're this to me: If I'd stayed five minutes longer with you the other afternoon I should have asked you to marry me. And you would have accepted. And you know it. Only I didn't stay five minutes longer—because I've got to have a quiet life."

All the while as the words issued from his mouth he well knew that they were extraordinary inexcusable impossible words to utter to a woman with whom one was, or had been, undeniably in love.

"Jack," said Moina Larchant, still gently, "you are terribly wrong about me. I'm not a bit an 'in-the-swim' woman. I'm just a hard-up woman. I have a lot of smart friends, but I can't help that; I was brought up among them. (It's true I like some of them.) But I have to live. And I live as I do because there's no other way. I get a lot of free meals and free presents and free visits and holidays; and without them I should probably go under. To come here I used up some of my last pounds, my very last. I don't want to be in the swim. I'm the most economical woman you ever met. I've had to be. All I want is to be happy with a man who tells me he can't be happy without me."

Her attire was the attire of a woman in the swim, but her eyes were irresistible; so much so that Jack Wren began nervously to swing his sack to and fro. Then startlingly her face changed into a reproach and a fearless resentment and she went on:

"And I think you didn't behave at all nicely to me in running off. You say you didn't ask me to marry you. Well, you didn't—not in words, but all your tones and your looks were asking me every minute of the time. Well, I shan't bother you any more. Good-by. I was wrong to come down. I'm going back at once. Good-by." She raised her head proudly and defiantly and moved away.

"Wait a moment, please," Jack Wren stopped her. "You won't refuse to help me with my shopping, will you? I'm the lowest mortal on earth, but I need your help and you won't refuse it."

"Wh-a-at is it you have to buy?" Moina asked, still resentful.

But the question amounted to a surrender; and he knew it was a surrender.

"You're a darling," he said.

"If I am, it's more than you are," Moina retorted bitterly.

No matter! He loved her bitterness and her sudden anger. He was perfectly aware that he had been absurdly hasty in his flight, that he had misjudged her, and that he ought to have found out for himself the real explanation for her apparent craze for being in the swim. And what satisfied and reassured him in the demeanor of the too chic creature was the natural ease with which she accepted the experience of being seen in public on intimate terms with a man in a shabby blue suit, a cap, unclean fingernails and a bass bag. But the supreme achievement of the too chic creature was her sublime affectation of not noticing the false mustache.

She seemed pathetic to him, and he keenly desired to embrace her in front of the Parliament House. Their first kiss, however, did not occur till a fortnight later, at the end of the yachting season.

"I don't want to go back to the *Sea Blossom,*" he remarked.

"But you must," she answered firmly. "You've shirked one job. You can't shirk another."

How she became the means of restoring smooth relations between her young man and the Eastern Electric is another story.

Jack Wren returned to the yacht with a heavy bag. Moina Larchant remained on shore. For the rest of the cruise he insisted on being strictly Roper the steward to Saxton Seaforth. But Seaforth had a sure conviction that everything was all right, and indeed he received on the yacht a telegram in this sense. And although destiny had come to his aid, his good opinion of himself as a sleuth was very considerable.

NOTES

1. *Woman's Home Companion.* April 1932, pages 24-26, 120, 122, 135. Signed Arnold Bennett. Illustrated by Steven Spurrier. The monthly magazine began life as the *Ladies Home Companion* and was published in Springfield, Ohio, from 1873 to 1957. Bennett contributed several articles to the magazine but "The Flight" was his only story. Published posthumously in America it was the last of his stories to appear in a periodical either side of the Atlantic.